The Factory

Alan Butters

Also by Alan Butters

The Telford Redemption

ISBN: 978-0-9922675-1-3

PROLOGUE

A True Story – Huntsville Texas

"His head and shoulders jerked, he coughed six times, and at 12:31am, he was pronounced dead"

So read the final entry in the Huntsville Penitentiary record for convicted killer Joseph Paul Jernigan. Jernigan had been a death row prisoner for 12 years after being convicted in 1981 for burglary and murder. He broke into the home of Edward Hale and while trying to steal a microwave oven, was surprised by the homeowner. Jernigan shot Hale dead. A lethal injection ended Jernigan's life on August 5 1993.

While in prison, Jernigan was persuaded by the local prison chaplain to sign his body over for scientific research or medical transplant. Ordinarily, Jernigan's form of death would rule out his organs for transplant use. Instead, Jernigan's body was destined for a more macabre, more public fate. Jernigan's ordinary life was about to be catapulted into the public eye.

Jernigan's corpse was selected from over two thousand potentials by a team of researches working on the Visible Human Project. The project is based at the National Library of Medicine (NLM) in Bethesda Maryland. In 1991 a research grant of US$1.4 million was given to researchers at the University of Colorado to select, prepare, and digitally image a cadaver for the Visible Human Project database. Joseph Paul Jernigan had won first prize. Because he was an average Joe.

The grisly process involved encapsulating Jernigan's body in vivid blue gelatin and then freezing it to minus seventy degrees Centigrade. The body was sawed into four blocks with cuts at the nipple line, the upper thighs, and just below the knees. Jernigan's body joined about thirty others in a similar state in the freezer while the team of specialists debated which cadaver would be the most suitable.

The team's objective was to find a body free of infectious disease, cancer, bone deformation, trauma of any kind, and without any artificial hips or other prosthetics. The only thing the team knew of Jernigan's background was a death certificate showing he died from a barbiturate overdose. Several months later, a committee of specialists decided that Jernigan was their man. At 95kg and 177cm tall, he fitted the profile ideally.

Starting with the block containing his legs, each block was attached to a machine called a Cryomacrotome in which a laser guided planer essentially shaved one millimetre slices from Jernigan's body. After each new sliver had been removed, the end of the block was photographed and a digital image generated. By the time the process was complete, 1,871 images had been made.

The images were loaded into a powerful graphics animation processor where Jernigan's body was digitally recompiled into a complete three dimensional image.

As bizarre as this all sounds, the applications for the data and images gathered are numerous. All manner of simulations using the virtual body can be undertaken in the name of medical science. The trajectory of bullets through the body can be calculated, complex surgery may be simulated, and even replacement joints could be tested before use. All things considered, it was a very noble end for a body that achieved little in its 39 years among the living.

Following this ground breaking if not gruesome experiment, the medical press was awash with discussion regarding both the potential uses as well as the ethics of what had been done. Much was made of the public nature of the experiment. A massive database of images available to anyone who could demonstrate a credible use.

A good deal of the media's interest in the subject came from the fact that a convicted killer's last resting place was in cyberspace where he served as a representation of the average man. A sort of digital afterlife, if you like. Naturally, there were detractors who claimed that somehow our disposition toward crime and violence is hardwired into our individual body structure and therefore Jernigan's selection was inappropriate. Eventually, as most things do, the fuss died down.

***

What didn't die down was the interest of another group entirely. A military group. This group wasn't at all concerned with virtual bodies but they were fascinated by the idea of a virtual *mind.* Jernigan's reanimation into the digital world had them hooked. Perhaps there was a way to go further. To capture the *thought* process of a human being and reanimate it in cyberspace. Possibly then a weapon of an entirely new class could be constructed. Invisible, remorseless, calculating. Lurking around inside the networks of the world where conventional operatives could never go. Disabling the enemy's infrastructure. Spreading fear and misinformation, turning citizens against each other. Sent in before ever a real soldier had to set foot on enemy soil. Completely dispensable and utterly ruthless.

It was frightening to think that it could be done.

It was terrifying to discover that they went ahead and did it.

PART ONE

"Information-warfare (IW) … actions taken to degrade or manipulate an adversary's information systems while actively defending one's own. Over the next two decades, the threat to U.S. information systems will increase as a number of foreign states and sub-national entities emphasize offensive and defensive information-warfare strategies, doctrine, and capabilities."

Lieutenant-General Patrick M. Hughes, US Army, Director, Defence Intelligence Agency, Washington D.C., February 2, 1999

ANN ARBOR CHRONICAL

Local News

Keen observers will notice the completion of the latest edition to the Ann Arbor Technology Precinct on East William St. The attractive building has been something of a local curiosity during the last twelve months as its construction unfolded. Sources close to this writer have suggested that the building will be used as a secure repository for classified Government defence documents. The Department of Defence today would neither confirm or deny the story. Regardless, the City welcomes its latest neighbours.

CHAPTER 1

A man could develop serious leg muscles living in this town. This had been Charlie Ganderton's first thought as he began his weekends pedalling around Ann Arbor getting to know his new home. Leg muscles that would burn from the punishment given them by the two ridges that run along the east and west sides of the city. The ridges were pushed up by twenty glaciers that had blanketed the area over the last two million years. The glaciers also left boulders. Lots of boulders. Many of the early settlers had built the foundations of their homes using boulders. Charlie had cycled past the largest of them, on downtown Washtenaw Avenue near Hill Street, a mammoth chunk of Canadian limestone serving as a memorial to George Washington.

Charlie hadn't even owned a bike before moving to Ann Arbor but he figured it would be a good way to see the place. Since his wife had moved on, he'd starting doing lots of new things. *Can a person really change?* he wondered, or is this just another phase in life. Hell, maybe it's the same thing. Who can know. Charlie had come here wanting a break. Wanting to do something different and to try achieving things on his own. After the split a good friend told him that his ex-wife had been a control freak and, in hindsight, Charlie felt that she'd managed more of his career than he had. She'd almost convinced him that the success he'd enjoyed so far was down to her guidance and support. Although the thoughts weren't fully formed in his mind even now, at some level Charlie knew that one of the reasons he came here was to prove her wrong.

These days when Charlie thought of this place, the word *Unlikely* often came into his head. Unlikely that this unpretentious place would have a thriving IT precinct and one of the best universities in the country. Unlikely that he would ever have moved from California to a town of just over 100,000 people. Unlikely that he would have grown to love its trendy and quirky ways. Even more unlikely that Ann Arbor would be home to one of the most secure military research facilities on the planet.

I guess that's the idea, Charlie figured.

Folks sometimes thought Charlie Ganderton a little odd. Not weird-odd, not the kind of odd you might expect from an on-the-run acid bath murderer if you happened to meet at the gas station. No, more the slightly-eccentric-academic type of odd that can appear either unsociable or remote. Not entirely surprising considering that Charlie spends most of his working life studying and developing Artificial Intelligence systems. He is occasionally liable to tune out in the middle of a conversation. Or to sometimes interrupt mid sentence and ask what appears to be an out of context question - usually in an attempt to understand the thought process that led to what was generally an innocuous comment by the bewildered other party. Charlie was enthralled by the concept of a system that could create ideas of its own the way we do, without really knowing how we do it.

"Definitely too nice to drive" Charlie said out loud to no one in particular. In his open neck shirt and sports coat, briefcase in hand, Charlie feels light on his feet as he strides purposefully down leafy East William Street on a spectacular summer morning. The August sun energises Charlie. *Great* to be alive. He dodges around tables that spill out onto the sidewalk from a tiny café, the smell of freshly roasted coffee teasing him. As he crosses Maynard Street he catches a glimpse of his destination through the sun dappled leaves and smiles at the thought of the AIWR building's pyramid-like mystery.

The Academy for Information-Warfare Research on the corner of East William and Harold Streets is an unusual building. Outwardly it appears like many of the other medium sized office buildings in the upmarket, well-watered technology precinct. It's the realisation that most people don't give the light green building a second glance that amuses Charlie.

One of the Department of Defence guys who works for Charlie let slip that the building's external design was contracted out to the respected Chicago firm of Architects, Granwell & Fischer. Charlie wished he could have been a fly on the wall in that first briefing between the firm's senior partners and the DoD staffers. It wouldn't have taken long before Mr Granwell and Mr Fischer were wondering what the hell they had gotten themselves into on this particular project. Still, all in all, Charlie thought, they had done a pretty good job with concrete, metal tubing and glass and it was actually quite amazing that nobody seemed to give the place a second glance. Even the perimeter fence with its bluestone pillars and heavy steel fencing looked sufficiently decorative and stylish that its true nature was concealed.

It was Granwell & Fischer that had first called the place The Factory. Like many project names it stuck and to most who worked within, the AIWR building would always be The Factory. That The Factory had no windows was just the beginning of its unusual nature. The locals would have been stunned to realise that the building had six floors with five of them underground including two parking levels. Also, the locals appeared not to notice that there were no signs on the building. No company name, no "deliveries at rear," nothing. There weren't any doors in the building above ground either, just a ramp descending through a steel grille into the lower levels. No antennas were visible on the roof; no overhead lines of any sort connected the building with the street.

Had someone taken the time to observe the solid brick guardhouse at the entrance to the facility they would have seen two more curious things. Firstly, the usual middle-aged pot-bellied security guard, the mainstay of guardhouses all over the nation, didn't work here. Instead, drivers were greeted by young and athletic looking men who could pass as off-duty soldiers. Actually they were soldiers but very much on duty.

The second curious item was the guardhouse itself. It was only slightly larger than the traditional one man booth, but a variety of guards appeared at the window over the course of the week and yet our astute observer would have noticed that none of them ever left the guardhouse. The solution to this little mystery was simple. Inside the guardhouse, a trapdoor led down to a compact but comfortable room in which two guards worked at high resolution consoles allowing them to monitor the entire facility. This underground bunker connected to the main building via a security corridor. Great for getting back to your car in the winter when your shift was over.

"If people knew what they were actually looking at they'd freak" mused Charlie as he approached the guardhouse.

"How's it hangin' Dr G.?" called Joe, one of the regulars on duty as he slid the fingerprint verifier out for Charlie to check in.

"Pretty damn good actually Joe" replied Charlie, pressing his right thumb to the gold square of the verifier, anticipating the green light.

"Decided to leave the GT-3 at home?"

Charlie was always amazed at how many times people reminded him that he drove an expensive car. Although he didn't try to pretend that the car meant nothing to him, the reality was that while he enjoyed driving the Porsche, he no longer had a photograph of it on his desk. It's surprising what becomes normal after a while.

"Yep, figured I could use the exercise this morning for a change."

Joe shook his head and said, "Man, if they were my fuckin' wheels I'd be *sleepin'* in that damn car."

Charlie, watching for the green light on the verifier, smiled. As the biometric system blinked and confirmed Charlie's identity, something substantial stirred in the concrete under his feet and The Factory's main gate began to slide open.

"Have a good one," called Joe.

As Charlie walked down the dazzling concrete driveway toward the underground entrance he was aware that he was being recorded by multiple cameras and probably also being scoped by twin automatic vehicle-tracking .50 calibre machine-guns concealed within the decorative steel structure comprising the roof of The Factory. Despite having made this walk many times during the four years he'd worked on the project, he never quite got used to it. Today, a pang of anxiety momentarily fluttered in Charlie's stomach.

For as long as Charlie could remember, he had been cursed with an intensely inquiring mind. He would look at numbers on a page and see associations and patterns. As he walked, Charlie thought back to a conversation he'd had with a previous security guard about the thumb print verifier. Charlie had been new to The Factory. The fact was that the guard didn't open the gate, the computer connected to the verifier did. The guard's job was to make sure that the verifier was only used by people whose faces matched their ID badges. So, Charlie had asked, what if someone chops off my thumb, takes you guys out, and then uses the verifier? Doesn't the gate open?

The look that the guard gave Charlie that day felt like a punch in the chest, causing Charlie to rack his brains in case he'd somehow said the wrong thing. After an uncomfortable pause the guard coldly explained that unless Charlie's *perpetrator* could figure out how to keep a pulse going in the thumb and maintain it at body temperature, the verifier wouldn't give a shit. It sounded obvious when you knew and Charlie had felt his face burn at asking what the guard obviously considered to be a pretty dumb question for a guy who drove a Porsche. *Perpetrator*, the guy had said. The word lodged in his mind following that conversation. Charlie thought only cops in movies used those sorts of expressions. Welcome to a military project, Charlie boy.

This little encounter illustrated one of the difficulties Charlie had faced as head of the software team. How to get civilians and military personnel who sometimes saw the world entirely differently, working together as a real team. When the new DoD Information Corps had been formed five years ago by pulling in the best that the DoD, the IT industry, and the medical and biometric fields had to offer, its detractors said it would never achieve anything. Still, Charlie felt he was doing a pretty good job under the circumstances. The military people didn't all live down to his grim stereotype and he'd been allowed to choose the best people he could find. Sure, he had a few problem staffers, but "if it was easy, anybody could do it" he often reminded himself.

Ahead of him the second gate inside the entrance to the ramp began to move. Charlie could feel a low rumble through the warm concrete of the driveway as the massive gate slid to one side. The gate with its vertical steel bars in front of a black cavernous entrance made Charlie think that he was walking into a huge mouth. As if The

Factory was alive and he was entering its stomach like Jonah and the whale. Had Charlie known that the day was rapidly approaching when he would feel the full menace of The Factory, leaving him fighting for his life, he might have simply turned on his heel right then and there.

Charlie's bright mood was already beginning to slide. As he left the warmth of the morning sun and descended into The Factory he felt its hidden bulk begin to close around him. "I don't know what it is about this damn building" Charlie muttered as he took off his sunglasses in response to the interior gloom. As was happening more and more often these days, the best part of Charlie's day was about to be left behind.

CHAPTER 2

Dr Elizabeth Van Dorf had been in her office on the ground floor of The Factory for two hours already. An important project meeting had been called for 0930 and she had been awake half the night agonising over her presentation. The project had a new DoD liaison officer and his first action was to demand a full project briefing. As the senior neurologist, it was up to her to explain what the medical team had achieved so far in trying to capture the essence of the human mind.

She felt a pang of resentment towards her boss, Christopher Witherspoon, (actually Christopher R. Witherspoon, more often than not), who was happy to take the credit for the medical team's work but who always managed to wriggle out of the presentations. He'd constructed a role for himself at The Factory, which seemed to require his presence for only a couple of days a week. God only knows what the man's doing the rest of the time, Elizabeth thought.

"I've heard he's a real prick" Elizabeth said as her assistant Ric Montez flopped into her visitors chair.

"Heard who's a prick?" Montez asked.

"Jack Lantini, who else." snapped Elizabeth, and then immediately,

"Sorry, Ric, I'm just a bit wound up this morning. Sometimes I think that ten years of med school and twelve years of research count for zip in this place."

"Sounds like someone got out the bed on the wrong side this morning."

"Maybe, but if this guy is anything like the others, I'll have to work twice as hard as any of the men in the briefing and I'll still get stuck with the tough questions. It just pisses me off that these people sweep in and demand the world with no idea of the challenges we face."

"Yeah, it's tough" said Montez, rising to his feet. "I better get on with those slides you asked for."

"Jesus Ric!" said Elizabeth, her head snapping up from her computer screen. "You promised you would have them for me first thing! Now I'll be racing around trying to fit them into my presentation at the last minute."

Montez knew better than to make excuses to Elizabeth and decided this might be a good time to make his exit.

"Hey, no problem, I'll get them to you with a half-hour to spare. Trust me."

Elizabeth wanted to scream. Why does no one else around here seem to take this stuff seriously she thought. I've had it with him needing to be micro-managed every minute of the day. It's about time I pulled him into line again. That thought made Elizabeth feel slightly better the way formulating a plan always seemed to do. It wasn't that Ric was dumb, actually he was one of the smartest assistants Elizabeth ever had. She'd spoken to him once about going back to school to further his career but he didn't seem too keen. Smart but lazy, she thought, a frustrating combination.

Elizabeth was acutely aware of being a woman in this particular man's world. When she was offered this role many of her friends tried to talk her out of it. They told her horror stories about military projects and the misogynists that ran them. The message was that she'd be perfect for the job if only she was male instead of female. Perversely, this negative pressure only increased her resolve. Elizabeth's mother knew her daughter well and wasn't at all surprised.

"You've never been one to take the easy road." Her mother had told her before she left, hugging Elizabeth tightly. "And I reckon you're not about to change now. Give them hell, kiddo." Elizabeth's mother was one of the strongest women she knew. Surely some of that must have rubbed off on me, she often thought. It didn't always stop the loneliness though. Sometimes at night in bed by herself, or when she'd cooked a nice meal and sat down in her apartment to eat it alone. Not a sad desperate loneliness, but even so, a hollow feeling that she didn't like. Nevertheless, things were starting to look up.

Elizabeth paused, stretched her graceful neck through 90 degrees and took a couple of deep breaths. It was Friday, almost the weekend. She thought of her date tonight with Charlie and the weight seemed to slide from her shoulders. She had been seeing Charlie for three months now and she was starting to think that he might be the one. She was always tough on relationships with work demanding so much of her time but Charlie seemed to understand this and didn't expect anything of her. It wasn't that she had any trouble hooking up with men, her willowy figure and delicate features made sure there were always admirers. No, it was just that she seemed to intimidate most men. They would either become stupidly competitive or get frightened off. Not Charlie though. He wasn't the least perturbed about her intellect or ambition; in fact he encouraged and celebrated it.

She was actually amazed that he hadn't suggested yet that she stay the night. Previous men in her life seemed to want to pass GO! and collect their two hundred bucks after the first date. That was one of the things she liked about Charlie. He was a bit shy. Still, she thought, better not move too fast. Charlie's divorce had come through only two years ago and he was still a bit cautious about getting involved again. That was ok by her; she wasn't one to hurry into things either.

They had talked once about Charlie's ex wife. One day she just up and left. There were no kids but Charlie took it hard. He couldn't understand how he didn't see it coming, thought that said something ugly about him. All she would ever say was that she wanted more spark in her life. Charlie never really knew why she left. As Elizabeth got to know Charlie she had wondered the same thing. When it's all boiled down, Elizabeth thought, couples are like clothes. Some work together and some don't. That's just the way it works.

Through her office window Elizabeth could see Ric bent over his PC with his back to her and she felt a stab of guilt for her outburst.

Particularly that unprofessional crack about women in a man's world. I must have sounded like a shrew. I'll make it up to him this afternoon she thought as she reluctantly pushed Charlie out of her mind and went back to rehearsing her presentation.

* * *

The ground floor of The Factory was, like any regular building, situated above the surface. Unlike most buildings, the floor numbering then went backward so that level one was the first level under the ground floor and level five was the lower parking lot. It all seemed to make sense when you were inside. The medical team was located on the ground floor, at the top of the building. They liked to think that this was in deference to their level of education or their value to the project as a whole. A bit like having the corner office with the view of the bay. Except of course that no one in The Factory had a view. Still, being the only ones above ground made some of them feel special.

In true military tradition, the real reason was more pragmatic. It was much easier to secure the floors below ground than above. While the research conducted by the medical team was vital to the project, the defence specialists, the programmers and the computers running the simulations had to take priority where security was concerned. That meant they had to be below the surface. While it was well known that conversations inside buildings could be detected from outside by bouncing a specialised laser off a glass window, bricks and concrete were thought to be safe from this method. Even so, at The Factory, no chances were taken.

The conference room for the briefing was located on level two. This secure space could comfortably seat thirty people at the long granite table dominating the room. The table was dark grey, almost black, with spidery white lines running through it that resembled lightning. An additional twenty black leather chairs were placed around the walls. No one at The Factory could ever remember the table being full. Need-to-know principles operated and briefings were only as large as they had to be.

Elizabeth's name was on the computerised list of attendees and when the verifier outside the door sampled her thumb the computerised access system allowed her to push the door open. Stepping inside, she immediately saw Charlie chatting with the audio-visual technician who would stay until everyone got their presentations set up. In conventional business meetings most folks casually stroll up to the lectern with their laptops and simply plug in the overhead projector. The Factory is different. Laptops are forbidden. Removable media such as USB drives or CD-ROMS is also forbidden. Nothing left The Factory, either by intent or by accident. Instead, the presentations of the individual project members were stored on a centralised server farm and loaded up from the conference room.

Charlie looked across and smiled at Elizabeth who quickly averted her eyes. They had both decided it was probably not a good idea that their growing relationship be common knowledge at work. It was just easier that way. Neither felt that there was any professional conflict of interest that arose from their seeing each other. They just didn't want to have to explain themselves. Or have folks looking out of the corner of their eyes, wondering if they were sleeping together, cracking double entendres in their presence. Life was too short for that. Elizabeth didn't trust herself to smile back at Charlie without blushing and that would be a give-away. Instead she waited for Charlie to finish with the audio-visual tech and then made sure her own presentation was ready to go.

In ones and twos, the rest of the senior staff arrived and there was a buzz of good natured banter around the big table. Whenever someone new attended a briefing, you could count on them to ask how on earth they got the damn table in the room to start with. You could also count on one of the engineering guys to have an answer. Elizabeth's train of thought was interrupted by the entrance of Jack Lantini, a severe looking man, and his assistant, a slight fellow with a harried look who reminded her of a basset hound, and Leonard Darville, the head of the project.

Darville was the man they all thought of as the boss. He was old school military, a bit grizzled and spiky but he had a good mind and was even-handed most of the time. Elizabeth was very fond of him and saw through his crusty protective shell. The man cared for his people and they responded well to him. This would probably be his last project before retirement and Elizabeth knew he'd be sadly missed.

"Listen up folks," Darville said when everyone had taken their places.

"I'd like to introduce you all to Major Jack Lantini. Major Lantini will be our new DoD liaison following Colonel Nash's redeployment and I would like you all to make him feel welcome. Major…"

"Thank you, Leonard," said Lantini, looking around the room, his face impassive. "I've heard that you have a fine bunch of people here."

"My role," Lantini continued, "is to ensure that the funding from the DoD, which is considerable, gets used wisely within this project." Leonard Darville shifted a little uncomfortably in his seat. It was obvious that he didn't think this was Lantini's role at all.

"What I want from you people, and I thank you for being ready at short notice, is to help me understand the status of this project. I've been briefed as to the overall goal but I need to know where we are at right now. The first decision that I have to make is whether we want to continue funding it."

Around the room, people's hearts skipped a beat. The loudest noise in the conference room was the clock ticking on the back wall. This was the first anybody had heard that the project might be in trouble. Sure, it had been chugging along for four years, but they were getting very close. Elizabeth looked over at Darville but was unable to read his expression. My God, they've sent this prick to close us down, she thought.

"I understand that this may come as a shock to you," Lantini continued, "but funding is tough right now with all the new drone and robotics initiatives the DoD is pursuing. This project fights with other excellent programmes and has to survive on its own merits. One of the main reasons that I've been given this assignment is because the department feels that there are simply too many open projects on the books. There are active research projects that have been continuing for ten years but are no closer to producing a result now than when they started. Frankly, that's just not good enough, and sure as shit, it's not going to continue, pardon my French. The Department is embarking on a new scheme. One we call T.P.I, Targeted Process Improvement."

Oh God. Elizabeth thought. Not another department initiative. They had seen reorganisations before. Cluster groups, cross discipline teambuilding, top down – bottom up. At the end of the day she remained unconvinced that any of them improved the situation. You can mix it up and call it anything you please, she thought, at the end of the day you either have talented people and passionate, capable leaders or you don't. The old adage associated with pig's ears and ladies accessories skittered across her mind.

"What this means is that we want to get to the bottom of whether a project has any merit much earlier in the process and then bring along those that we're sure are worth doing, at a much faster rate. Right now we're starting way to many half-assed programs that should have been killed at birth and the good ones are getting lost and never damn well finished. Money is tough to come by right now. The focus is shifting toward results. Projects and programs that deliver. That's where it begins and ends. My initial target is to review our top fifty R & D programs which constitute the bulk of the department spend and reduce them to twenty. Whether this project is part of the twenty that survive round one will depend largely on you folks. I have to warn you, I will be ruthless in expecting results from long running programs such as this."

"To be really frank," Lantini continued, "I have to tell you that I'll need to see something special here today if I'm to be convinced that you people are on to something."

Lantini sat down and for a few seconds nobody breathed. Clearing his throat, Darville rose and broke the silence.

"Well, people, you heard the major. I think we do indeed have something pretty special to talk about so let's get on with it. Charlie, you're up first."

With a growing sense of dread, Charlie collected his papers and moved to the lectern. Charlie could actually hear his own heart beating and he allowed himself an extra few seconds by making a show of arranging his paperwork. When he looked up, half of the project team sitting around the table had their eyes down. Lantini, leaning back cross-legged in his chair, was staring directly at him with a slight smirk on his face. Okay tough guy, Charlie thought, let's get this show on the road.

"You have been briefed, major, so you will understand that one of our difficulties has been modelling the aggression characteristics required for the VIWAP to be eff..."

"Define VIWAP." Lantini spat the words across the table like a projectile.

Charlie bit back his first reply and continued.

"The project objective is to create a virtual covert operative. VIWAP is an acronym for Virtual Information-Warfare Assault Probe. The VIWAP would be unleashed on an enemy command and control network as a first strike..."

"An automated hacker," Lantini again interrupted.

"Yes and no. Certainly it's in our interest to shut down an enemy network and thus degrade, for example, their capacity to detect strike aircraft or to communicate with ground forces, but that's only the half of it. Imagine a scenario where the VIWAP could actually take control of an enemy state's infrastructure and use it against them. Fool their systems into thinking that they themselves are the enemy."

"Is that feasible?" Lantini said, showing, Charlie hoped, the first glimmer of interest.

"We believe it is. In developed nations, almost every system today, from the utility companies to the traffic network is computerised and part of a network of some sort. These networks are almost always connected together in various ways, a fact that is exploited regularly by hackers. The VIWAP would be able to get inside these networks and move between them, potentially seizing control as it went along."

"What would be the point of controlling the damn power plants and traffic lights?" snapped Lantini.

You're not so smart after all, thought Charlie

"One of the basic tenets of Information-warfare Technology is to apply psychological pressure to the enemy. To return to the examples I cited, imagine the chaos caused in a city if every traffic signal was unpredictable. Would you drive? Imagine continuous and random blackouts across the city. Picture the crime and violence that would flow from it. You're on your way to breaking the spirit of the citizens of that city. I would have thought that was obvious."

Darville shot Charlie a look that said don't push it, don't push it. If Lantini had noticed the barb, he didn't show it.

"And of course it's not limited to civil infrastructure." Charlie continued, warming to his topic. "We are talking about potentially taking hold of military infrastructure as well. Controlling weapons and delivery systems. Changing targeting coordinates, initiating firing sequences, activating self-destructs, and so on."

"You mean using their own hardware against them," Lantini said.

"Exactly. And at the same time perhaps paralysing their decision-making capacity by injecting misinformation into all levels of government. Just as the Denial of Service attack is a common weapon used by hackers to swamp a server or network by bombarding it with traffic to render it unusable by any legitimate users, misinformation can have a similar effect. Perhaps it can be even more effective than disabling the target systems."

"How so?"

"A sufficient quantity of high quality misinformation can paralyse a command chain or government into inaction. While they're trying to sort out the truth and deal with in-house issues, they're not doing what they're supposed to. What we aim to accomplish is to essentially cripple their command structure through mistrust and fear. Pitting them against each other. Diverting their energy and attention toward internal security issues, dividing their loyalties, and so on."

Lantini's gaze continued to be locked onto Charlie's face as if he were trying to gauge the amount of credibility to afford to the ideas being laid out.

"So what's the hold-up?" he asked after a moment's silence.

"I'm sorry?" Charlie replied, catching that look again from Darville.

Lantini continued as if spelling it out to a small child.

"We are having this discussion because while we all agree that this VIWAP thing is a great idea, you people haven't built one yet. We're still talking about how good it *will* be, capabilities it *might* have. So, I'm asking you why not. Why haven't you done it yet? Is that clear enough, *Dr* Ganderton?" Lantini's words betrayed his contempt.

"This is a non-trivial exercise, major," began Charlie but before he could finish Lantini just exploded with anger.

"Damn-it man, I don't want to hear how hard it is! That's why we have the best people working on it for Christ's sake. I want to know why, after spending seven hundred and fifty five million dollars of fucking DoD money, all we're doing is *talking* about this thing. Where in hell are we at? What's the damn hold-up here?"

It suddenly occurred to Charlie that the only person in the room that was at that instant not looking down uncomfortably at his notes was Alex Fox, one of his team leaders. Odd. Before Charlie could respond, Leonard stood up.

"Perhaps it would be better if I gave the helicopter view" Darville offered, moving toward the podium.

"Just the facts, and straight," Lantini said in a low voice.

"Okay thanks, Charlie," Darville began. "The hold-up, as you call it, major, is that we're trying to develop something that stretches to the limit all of the technologies involved. We are trying to synthesise the human thought process, and it's never been done before. We have ideas and we test them. Every night we run simulations and every day we refine the code and do it again the next night. We have achieved outstanding results and have built some amazing capabilities into the VIWAP but we're not confident of releasing anything yet. We figure another twelve months with a focus on the neural net algorithms and an improvement in our synapse function capture tools. The upside is that at the end of this period we'll have a revolutionary new weapon, one that will entirely change the landscape of modern warfare forever."

"Right. So you want another year to fiddle and tweak, and then you might have something useable." Lantini said without looking up.

"Well, I might not use exactly those terms but essentially, on current indications, that's my assessment."

"Okay, here's the deal. You have six months. I'll return in three and we'll have this little chat again. On that occasion I want you to show me something concrete or I'll pull the pin on this whole show right there and then. Thankyou for your time, ladies and gentlemen."

With that, Lantini and basset hound rose, and without another word simply walked out of the conference room. No one spoke for fifteen seconds and then the room erupted with emotion. After a couple of minutes when sufficient steam had been relieved, Charlie spoke.

"Can he do this, Leonard?"

Darville took a deep breath. "I'm afraid he can." Howls of protest around the room again.

"All we can do is try to accelerate our program. Somehow we need a breakthrough to keep that SOB from crapping all over everything we've worked on for the past four years. We just have to find a way."

"Do you think he's bluffing?" asked Ed Furneaux, the senior network security specialist.

"Perhaps so, but I'm not prepared to take a chance. I've spent enough years in the military to know crap like this just happens. Lantini, as the new guy, gets a pat on the back for saving money and we get shafted. Let's regroup at 0900 on Monday after we've had time to calm down and do some thinking. Then let's start planning on how we'll blow this bastard's socks off come November. That's it, folks. Let's get back to work."

There seemed nothing more to say and the group filed out of the conference room. It had apparently escaped their attention that one of their number, Alex Fox, had quietly slipped out of the room a few minutes earlier while they were all venting their anger at the injustice of Lantini's ultimatum.

Alex Fox had his own ideas about this project and the people who were currently running it and he didn't want Lantini leaving without an opportunity to whisper in his ear. For Alex, who considered himself the smartest guy in any room, Lantini's tirade had been music to his ears.

CHAPTER 3

There were only three this evening. The Usual Suspects, Alex called them. They tended to be the first to arrive and the last to leave. It had become something of a tradition for some of the single members of the project team to get together for a beer after work on Friday at Applebees on West Eisenhower Parkway. They had a corner table reserved at the back of the restaurant under the Budweiser neon. This particular Friday at The Factory was strained. While little was said to their staff by those who experienced Lantini's outburst, everyone knew the briefing was important and had figured that it didn't go too well.

"I guess it's not surprising that most people didn't show tonight" said Ric Montez, gazing into his beer at a fine stream of bubbles rising toward the surface.

"I know you can't say much, Alex," Mary Peters whispered, "but is the project really in trouble?"

Mary had joined the project a year ago. She'd worked hard to integrate herself into the team, but as the only military programmer in Alex's group, she always felt like an outsider. It didn't help either that this was her first serious project since college. For the first six months Alex had hardly spoken to her and even now, he seemed only to tolerate her. The only reason she persevered with these Friday night get-togethers was to stay in Alex's good books. Alex was her first real boss. One day she would need him to give her a job reference.

"Well, G.I.," Alex said, "What I *can* say is, if the whole thing goes off the rails, you can thank that dumb-fuck Ganderton for flushing us all down the tubes."

Mary had long since become used to Alex's "Potty Mouth" as her mother would have called it but she still hated it when he called her G.I., which was all of the time.

Mary pushed a rogue lock of hair behind her ear.

"I dunno Alex, I think Charlie's no dummy. He's got a PhD in Elliptical Curve Cryptography and they don't exactly hand them out for free with a tank of gas you know."

"Well, you would think that G.I., you being a Crypto yourself an' all."

Mary swallowed down her irritation. She was used to being needled by Alex about her training, which centred on codes and code-breaking. She also knew that Alex wanted her on the team specifically because of this area of expertise so she didn't take it too seriously. Before she could think of a suitable riposte, Alex continued:

"Anyway, I'm not talking about smarts here."

"What then?" Ric, looking up from his beer.

"I'm talking about balls. The man hasn't the fucking stones for the job. I think it's about time someone lit a rocket under this project's sorry ass and I think that someone will have to be me."

Mary and Ric just stared, Ric with his beer halfway to his lips.

"Don't tell me your thinking of running COGNOS-2 on the simulator. Tell me you're not thinking that" Ric said, putting his beer back down without taking a sip.

COGNOS had been the breakthrough that the project needed in the first couple of years. Alex's team had come up with it but everyone knew that Alex himself was the architect. COGNOS was an acronym for COGnitive Neural Operating System. The engine that drove the VIWAP. It was the heart of the entire project and one of the most brilliant pieces of work Charlie had ever seen in his 20 years in the software industry. If this had been a commercial project Charlie had said they'd all be at least millionaires by now.

Alex however, wasn't entirely happy with COGNOS. For the last eighteen months he had been working on COGNOS-2 while his group laboured at optimising version one. Charlie, of course, didn't know the extent of this moonlighting and in his mind, COGNOS-2 was just a collection of ideas they had up their sleeve. Charlie was reluctant to move away from the original system that had given them so many good results thus far.

The Usual Suspects knew about Alex's private project. They also knew that Charlie wouldn't be happy if he discovered Alex spending serious time on it at The Factory. Charlie was quite firm that it would take too much time to qualify the code before running it on the simulator and he felt that they were close with the original COGNOS engine. Alex had threatened in the past to just go ahead and run it but they always figured it for so much hot air. This time they weren't so sure.

"Why not run it on the simulator?" Alex asked innocently.

"Charlie would go apeshit for one," Ric replied, shaking his head in disbelief.

"You could get yourself fired. You and Charlie are not exactly bosom buddies at the moment."

"Somehow I don't think Jack Lantini would like to see me fired after the conversation we had this morning," Alex said.

"What did you say?" gasped Mary. "I can't believe you spoke with him."

"I merely said that Charlie might just be suppressing the breakthrough that we all need if our pay cheque is to keep turning up each month."

"Shit," said Ric, "you certainly don't mind rolling the dice. What he say?"

Alex paused. "He said *find a way.* And he gave me his card and said I could call him anytime if I hit roadblocks."

Ric rubbed his eyes, wishing he hadn't had that last beer so he could think straight.

"But how would you capture a brain scan using the new COGNOS-2 ruleset without Elizabeth knowing?" Ric asked. "No way she'll go for it. Not with her having the hots for Charlie an' all."

Mary sprang to attention "Are Charlie and Elizabeth…."

Alex cut right across her "Shut up for a minute will ya, G.I."

"We don't need Elizabeth to run the scan, we only need someone who knows the protocol."

Ric shook his head. "You don't mean me? No way, man, I'm not losing my job over this, no way."

"What fuckin' job?" Alex yelled, prompting a couple on the next table to turn their heads. "If we don't come up with something in the next twelve weeks we have no fuckin' jobs, None of us. Not me, not you, not G.I. here. The whole damn team will be fucked. Do you want to trust everything to Mr Steady-as-she-goes, by-the-fuckin'-book nice guy? Because I for one will *not* wait around while that gutless asshole flushes my career down the toilet at age thirty-two."

"It might not come to that," said Mary in a small voice, frightened by Alex's anger.

"No, Mary," said Alex, gently now, using her name for the first time she could remember. "It might not. But I can tell you this. There is nothing new in the medical or software pipeline. What we've been doing for six months is optimising what we've got. Lantini wants a breakthrough. With Charlie pulling the levers, we don't have one. A successful trial of COGNOS-2 is our only hope."

Mary pushed up her glasses from where they had slid down her nose. "So why don't we go talk to Charlie?" she said. "Convince him."

"You know I've been talking to him for six months," Alex replied holding his palms skyward in supplication. "He won't go for it."

"He might since Lantini's visit," Offered Ric.

"Okay," continued Alex, "how about this. We have our cake and eat it too. We do a scan tomorrow, when Elizabeth works on the weekend it's almost always on a Sunday so we should be sweet. While we're capturing the scan data, we boot up COGNOS-2 on the redundant system. When we have the scan, we load it, run the simulation and check it Sunday night. If it works like we figure, we go see Charlie and suggest we give it a try without telling him it's already been done. If he says yes, we pretend to do it all again the next week. If he says no, well, I call Major Lantini and Charlie's out on his ass."

Ric nodded his head.

"Either way, we don't end up looking like chumps."

Alex made a gun out of his fingers and pointed it at Ric's head.

"And we give Charlie a chance." He said looking directly at Mary.

Mary was shaking her head. "I don't know, Alex. What if you get caught?"

"Caught doing what? My job? Trying to save the fuckin' project? We can always play the Lantini card. You shoulda seen how he tore Charlie a new asshole. Whaddya say, Ric?"

Ric didn't glance up from the beer he'd been nursing. He just simply said in a low voice:

"Fuck it. Let's do it."

"What about me?" whispered Mary.

"All you have to do, GI" replied Alex, "is enjoy your weekend and keep that mouth of yours shut. Can you do that for us?"

Mary took a deep breath and said the words she would later have given anything to take back:

"I guess I can do that."

* * *

It is not unusual for someone to be working in The Factory on the weekend. It would have been more unusual to find it empty. There always seemed to be a few cars in the fifth level lot at any time of the day or night. Of course, the security systems in place ensured that every access was logged but there was nothing unusual about Alex's presence after hours. Ric was another matter. He seldom came in on a weekend and certainly not without Elizabeth. The automatic security log analysis that ran continually as part of The Factory's INFOSEC strategy would be sure to pick up such an anomaly and report it to the security staff. On the walk back to their cars Ric had said as much to Alex.

"No problem," Alex had responded. And he was right.

The systems in The Factory operated on the basis of a descending level of trust from the senior staff down. One of the first rules drilled into everyone as part of their induction training was not to use their ID to allow anyone else into the building. This is exactly what Alex did. The only difficulty was getting Ric past the security on the main gate. Alex simply stopped a couple of blocks before the gate and had Ric get into the cargo space of his Explorer. He tossed a blanket over Ric's prone form together with his sports bag and golf clubs and, as he suspected, the guard on the gate didn't look in the back or ask to look under the blanket. Once into the parking lot they simply entered through each security point together.

"But aren't we being filmed?" asked Ric.

"Of course we are." Alex replied. "But there are hundreds of hours of security video generated each day. Unless the auto scanner throws up any unusual logins, nobody ever checks the damn stuff."

Once into the medical lab, the pair needed about two hours undisturbed. Ric activated the NMR-Imaging-In-Process indicator above the external doors to keep out any casual visitors looking for a chat. Ric then loaded the new Synapse Capture Algorithms that Alex had prepared into the custom-built hardware after verifying that he had a copy of the original code so they could set everything back before they left.

Alex fitted the ear buds of his game console, ensuring the wires snaked behind his ears before settling back in the surgical chair that had been specially adapted for the scanning process. Ric carefully placed the Neural Net Capture Headset around Alex's head ensuring that each of the fine needle points had good contact with the skin. The Headset looked like something from a 1960s science fiction movie and incorporated a nest of blue wires that came together into a loom, which was clipped into the chair's headrest. Chair of the Demon Dentist Elizabeth had called it. Once positioned the subject had very little movement. Ric had done this many times before. What he did next was unusual.

As Alex lay back, Ric injected a 25cc solution of gamma-amino butyric acid (GABA) into a vein in Alex's hand. The effect of this neurotransmitter was to increase the aggression levels that Alex experienced during the scan. Standing by was also a vial of a chemical known to block GABA activity for when the scan was done. Alex knew that these solutions were in the lab because of what Ric told him about Elizabeth's research on antisocial personality disorder. Alex had read the literature on the topic and was prepared to take a risk in using himself as a subject. Besides, as an online computer game addict, he was intensely curious to see how it affected his playing ability. Ric just shook his head at Alex's machismo.

If Ric had been honest with himself he would have also admitted that he was a little frightened of Alex Fox at times. Sometimes he was hard to read. An enigma. People said that he had infinite patience with the local kids he coached in martial arts each week in his spare time but he could snap in an instant if crossed by an adult. Not only was Alex the smartest guy Ric had ever met, he was also the toughest. Alex held a third degree black belt in Aikido and Ric had once gone along to watch him compete in a local tournament. Alex had been victorious and his speed and agility had been awesome. What shocked Ric, however, was the look in Alex's eyes as he dealt the winning blow to his opponent. That look was one of pure distilled hatred. The image always replayed in his mind whenever Ric thought about the tournament.

Alex flipped open the laptop he had hidden along with Ric in the back of the Explorer and woke it up from standby. His game of choice was Quake, a classic violent first person shoot-em-up, highly modified for increased difficulty. Alex selected the level he would play.

"Start the fucker up," he called as he began slaying the first bot.

* * *

A few miles away on South Main Street, Charlie and Elizabeth were seated at Gratzi, a stylish Italian restaurant that had become one of their favourite eating spots. The ambience was lush with large subtletly lit frescos around the walls. The main lighting was conveniently dim and the prices sufficiently expensive to keep away most of the people with whom they both worked.

Charlie had suggested moving their Friday night date to Saturday. He figured that after Lantini's little performance they both needed some time to cool down. He didn't want their mood destroyed by what was happening at The Factory, nor did he want work to dominate the conversation. As it turned out, they both did feel a little better but work stuff kept creeping into their conversations anyway. Elizabeth had ordered the roasted duck with fettuccini, radicchio, fennel, and onions. After the waiter collected the menus and left with their orders, Charlie proposed a toast to happier times.

"Well," said Elizabeth, putting down her wine glass, "I thought you were just wonderful. I don't know how you kept your temper with that shit-of-a man."

"Thanks" said Charlie. "I'm not sure how much good I did. Maybe I provoked him in some way."

Elizabeth took a sip of her wine. "No way, partner. I think he came with the specific agenda of putting us all on notice. I'm not sure what we could have done to avoid his outburst, short of giving him the VIWAP gift-wrapped in a box. I was very proud of the way you handled it." Charlie felt the heat rise to his face. "Thanks, Elizabeth."

"Do you really think we can come up with a breakthrough in three months?"

"I just don't know. Alex has been badgering me about a new version of COGNOS that he feels is an improvement but I'm not sure whether switching horses mid-stream is such a good idea. Particularly at this stage."

"You don't think Alex might be on to something?"

"I don't know. I really don't. Sometimes I actually wonder whether Alex still works for us at all."

"What do you mean, Charlie?" asked Elizabeth taking his hand in hers.

"Well, he seems to go out of his way to contradict, stall, and embarrass me. He's the most brilliant programmer I've ever known but without a doubt the most frustrating person I've ever had to manage. Just lately I've been wondering if he's been working on something else. He's so distant all of the time. I think it's been months since we even had a game of chess over lunch."

"From what I hear, you shouldn't be complaining too much about that!" Elizabeth replied in an attempt to lighten Charlie's mood.

"I certainly never beat him, that's for sure" said Charlie with a sheepish grin.

"Maybe you should ask him out for lunch and just put the cards on the table. Tell him straight out about the way you feel. Maybe take another look at his ideas. See if there's anything new."

"As usual, I think you're right," said Charlie, shaking his head. "You're so very level-headed and incisive. I'll set something up on Monday. Thanks."

"You might not be thanking me when I send you my bill. Smart consultants like me don't come cheap, you know." Elizabeth said.

"No, but I'm sure you're worth it." Charlie replied, feeling the heat rise into his face again.

Elizabeth giggled. "You better believe it. Anyway, enough work talk, let's change the subject before we spoil our evening together."

"I'll drink to that," said Charlie raising his glass…

* * *

By Sunday morning it was done. The capture had been completed and COGNOS 2 was loaded on the redundant system in the computer lab. Alex had finished loading the scan data into the simulator and had the whole thing running. The simulator would prove whether or not the experiment had been a success by testing the VIWAP's abilities in a controlled environment and with a quarantined target network.

Alex was heading back to his apartment where he intended to have a solid sleep. He wasn't one hundred per cent sure if it was the culprit, but the GABA appeared to have given him a pounding headache and he figured he would just crash for a while. One thing was for sure, Alex thought with a grin, he couldn't wait to show his gaming buddies the score he achieved during the sixty minute scan. It would piss them off big-time.

As Alex turned into Clark Road his cell phone went off.

"High Alex, Ric. How'd it go."

"No problemo, my man. I'll check in tonight but I'm guessing we'll have a winner."

"Great!" enthused Ric, "You'll let me know tonight?"

"You'll be the first to know, bud. Catch ya!"

Alex flipped his phone closed and tossed it onto the vacant seat next to him.

"Get ready to eat yourself some humble pie Dr fuckin' G." he said out loud as he pulled into his lot.

Ric had just been the last person from The Factory to ever speak with Alex Fox.

CHAPTER 4

On Sunday Charlie had left a message on Alex's home answering machine suggesting they get together early before the Monday meeting Darville had called and perhaps go over the ideas that Alex had been talking about on COGNOS.

Charlie was surprised, and a little annoyed when he arrived at The Factory at 7:30 on Monday morning to find Alex absent. Charlie had guessed Alex would be busting a gut to get his ideas on the table. He also didn't put it past Alex to bring up some new ideas in the meeting in front of Darville and leave Charlie on the back foot looking like a fool. Charlie wanted to get in first to ensure that they had some consensus about what they would reveal before getting themselves in too deep. Managing expectations is what Charlie called it.

Maybe Alex had car trouble Charlie thought absently as he dumped his briefcase under his desk and went to log on to his computer. His hand froze halfway to the keyboard as he caught sight of a note stuck to his monitor. It was from Dan Foster, the head of IT security and it simply said:

Charlie.

Call me the minute you get in.

Dan F.

When someone left a paper note at The Factory, it usually meant that they didn't want anything recorded on the internal messaging systems. Charlie felt a twinge of unease at the note and its urgent tone. He picked up the phone and dialled Dan's extension. Charlie listened for several minutes with a deepening frown on his face. "I'll be right down" is all he said.

It appeared, for the first time ever, a hacker had managed to break into The Factory.

***

Ric Montez was in a panic. He had waited for Alex to call on Sunday night. When he didn't, Ric called his apartment and his cell phone but with no success. After a restless night he'd come into work early in case Alex turned up. When he realised Alex wasn't at work he tried his cell phone again.

"Shit," Ric said under his breath "Shit, shit, shit." He couldn't understand why Alex hadn't called or why he wasn't answering his phone. A thought leaped into his mind that almost stopped his heart. What if Alex had some sort of reaction to the solutions he had injected? What if he was so sick that he couldn't get to the phone? God, Ric thought, I could be screwed if anything goes wrong. I injected the damn stuff into the stupid bastard. Suddenly, the whole exercise looked more dangerous and reckless than it had on Saturday.

Why the hell did I allow myself to get suckered into this damn mess, he scolded himself. Ric possessed a keen sense of self-preservation. He knew he didn't have the ambition to rise to dizzying heights in his profession but he'd pretty much figured out how to do just fine without working too hard. He had a good job, one that wasn't too demanding on his time and there was an inexhaustible supply of female grad students to be pursued over at the U. Ric had a thought that made him groan inwardly. What am I going to tell Elizabeth. God, she's such a stickler for protocol, she'll have my job for this, no mistake. Shit Ric, you're such a dickhead.

Ric frantically thought back to see if there was anything to tie him to the injection that had been administered. I think I'm Okay he thought with relief. The syringes had been disposed of outside The Factory and there was no record of him coming to work on Saturday anyway. He might just get away with this after all. Ric felt himself relaxing and then experienced a small pang of guilt for his selfishness. I have to go and check on Alex he thought, grabbing his keys from the desk drawer.

"Elizabeth, this is Ric. It's 7:45am on Monday and I've just realised I've left something at home. I should be back within the hour."

With the voicemail message left, Ric was in his car on the way to Alex's apartment inside five minutes.

***

Dan Foster's office is on the third level but he wasn't in his office, he was in the main computer room down the hallway. All of The Factory's main systems were in this area and someone had once told Charlie that the cost of the hardware in this room alone equalled the cost of the entire building. Charlie made his way past the bank of massively parallel computers that had made the large Cray T3E Supercomputer sitting in the middle of the room with its distinctive red stripe largely redundant. Contrary to most people's expectations, modern computer rooms usually don't have walls of flashing lights and exposed wires with nutty bespectacled types running around with clipboards. In fact the entire room has a false floor under which most of the cable mess is hidden. The equipment itself generally looks a bit like the whitegoods department in a discount store. Rows and rows of cabinets resembling large washers and dryers. All humming the same droning song generated by their cooling fans and power supplies. Charlie spotted Dan sitting with Ed Furneaux at a bank of computer screens.

Charlie had no need to come down here very often but whenever he did he felt a real buzz from the sights and sounds of serious computer muscle. He could stand mesmerised in front of the automatic digital backup system as its robotic arm plucked solid state cartridges from their storage hoppers and inserted them adeptly into a rack containing a dozen drives. Although not a mechanical engineer, Charlie had a soft spot for beautiful and complex machines. Today, however, none of this registered with him.

Dan and Ed were staring at a large flat panel display in the centre of the console.

"Charlie, thanks for coming down." Dan said, moving his chair to one side allowing Charlie to see the screen.

"What do we have, guys?" Charlie asked.

Without speaking, Dan handed Charlie a printout with a section of text highlighted in fluoro yellow. It said:

Your system has been fatally penetrated by a superior force

Any resistance that you offer will be met with overwhelming violence

Before you die you will learn some lessons about The Science

Kensei

"Where did this come from, Dan?" asked Charlie, continuing to study the printout.

"That's why I asked you down here, Charlie. It was on the main console of Sullivan. I thought you'd want to know straight away."

"Oh, God." Said Charlie. "This is all we need."

It's the habit of network engineers all over the world to assign names to their computer servers. Charlie's team had a pair of custom built massively-parallel systems which ran the simulator each night. Gilbert was the main system with Sullivan serving as the backup.

Charlie looked confused "I thought our simulators were isolated from anything outside."

"They are." Ed replied.

"And so how did this Kensei guy manage to hack in?"

"Well," Ed continued, "all the systems in The Factory are tied together in various ways. There are some outside lines but those are only used for transferring data out of the building to other secure DoD networks and only then during small windows of time. No one has any access the other way. It's theoretically possible that someone in another secure DoD network could gain access but they'd have to get through our firewalls and those things are locked down just as tight as you can get. What's got me beat is that the simulators are connected to nothing else. Even if you get into the main systems, there are just no connections to the simulators for you to exploit."

"Well, somebody *did* get in." Dan added. "And our first job is find what they got up to while they were here. I'm going to have to ask you not to use your systems for a while until we can figure out what's going on. Our INFOSEC protocol dictates that I'll have to inform Leonard and he'll probably be required to let Lantini know."

"That's just great," said Charlie. "Do we have to do that? Another nail in our coffin."

"I'm afraid so. Look on the positive side, Charlie, we find the hole, plug the leak, back in business. Hell, it could even be one of Lantini's people trying us out.

"What do you make of these specific threats?" Asked Charlie rereading the printout.

"Just some Darth Vader crap," Ed replied. "Take no notice, these bozos think they rule the universe."

"Give us a few hours to go through the logs. I'll call you around lunchtime and let you know what we find," said Dan, returning to his screen.

Charlie started toward the door, deep in thought. "Thanks, guys."

* * *

As Ric rounded the bend in Clark Road he caught site of Alex's apartment building. There were police cruisers, fire trucks and an ambulance parked across the driveway and on either side of the street. Ric had to pull over and walk the last fifty yards. Police tape had been tied across the entrance and Ric had no chance of getting into the building.

With a sinking feeling he spoke to the first cop he came across.

"What happened here?"

"May I ask what your business is here, sir?" the cop replied, his steady gaze suddenly making Ric feel uncomfortable.

"My buddy didn't show for work this morning and he lives in this block. I'm just checking up that he's okay."

"Do you have any reason to think he might not be okay? How do you know that he's not simply running late?"

Suddenly Ric realised that it was only 8:00am. Of course the cop would be suspicious.

"Well, I don't, but we had an appointment this morning early and when I last saw him he wasn't feeling too good so I thought I would check on the way to the office."

"I thought you said he didn't show up for work? How do you know that if you haven't been in yourself?"

Ric just stared and after a couple of seconds realised his mouth was still open. "Well, I guess."

"What's the name of your friend" The cop interrupted.

"Alex. Alex Fox."

"I think you better come with me and have a talk to the detective."

* * *

Charlie walked back to his office with a deepening sense of dread. If Lantini hears about this, Charlie thought, he'll have us for breakfast. We'll look like complete incompetents. He flopped into his chair and logged on to his computer. As the system was coming up he bent to pull his encrypted electronic diary from his briefcase. When he glanced back at the screen his chest tightened as though someone had just sat on it.

There are four walks of life:

The ways of the knight

The ways of the farmer

The ways of the artisan

The ways of the merchant

What is your way, Charlie? This, too, we will discover.

Kensei

Charlie picked up the phone and pressed redial. "Dan, I think you better come up here."

* * *

Get a grip on yourself, Ric thought as he followed the uniformed cop into the apartment building, you can't bullshit these guys. The detective, a tall man with a weathered face that suggested he'd seem most things at least once, was in the small courtyard next to the building's side entrance speaking with a man who could have been in maintenance considering his greasy coveralls and red steel toolbox. As Ric approached he caught the tail-end of the maintenance man's conversation.

"…almost like it sorta went up and down a coupla times on the poor bastard. He's a mash. Man's just a mash. Jesus H. Christ, what a mess…" The maintenance man looked like he was having trouble staying on his feet.

"Excuse me, John," said the uniform, "This man is a friend of Mr Fox and he swung by on his way to work to check on his buddy. I thought you might like a word with him."

Ric thought he saw a look pass between them but he couldn't be sure. He also couldn't ever remember hearing Alex referred to as Mr Fox. It sounded weird. He was trying to make sense of what he'd overheard but his senses felt like they were being overloaded.

"What's going on here," demanded Ric, trying to gain some control. "Is Alex okay?"

"My name is Detective John Lord," said the cop, completely ignoring Ric's question and leading him by the elbow toward a quiet corner. Ric found himself staring at a red and yellow fish in an ornamental pond. To Ric the fish appeared to be appraising him. As if trying to make up its mind as to his fitness to be here.

Glancing around the courtyard and satisfying himself that they had some privacy, the detective continued. "What's your name, sir, and exactly what is the nature of your relationship with Mr Fox?"

The cop's voice broke the spell that the fish seemed to cast over Ric. After asking for the question to be repeated, Ric told the detective his name and related his previous story being careful this time not to fall into any traps.

The detective looked up from his notebook. "Unfortunately Mr Fox has been involved in what seems to be a freak accident. It would appear that the elevator in the apartment building malfunctioned causing Mr Fox to step into an empty shaft. He fell three floors."

Powerful emotions washed over Ric in rapid succession. Relief that it wasn't the injection, surprise at the nature of the accident and then horror at the thought of his friend's last moments. All this in what seemed like one or two seconds.

"But how could it happen?" Ric stammered. "I thought these things had safety systems and stuff."

"Yes, Mr Montez, that's what we thought. We have the engineer here from the elevator company trying to figure out the same thing. Do you feel up to making a statement about your whereabouts over the last forty-eight hours? It might help us figure out Mr Fox's movements."

"Yeah, sure." Said Ric, his mind miles away.

The detective spotted someone out of the corner of his eye.

"If you wouldn't mind waiting here a moment, Mr Montez, I'll have one of the uniformed officers take down a few notes. We may need you to come down to the station later to complete a formal statement."

Ric sat down on the concrete edge of the pond with his head in his hands and waited. He hoped he didn't get the first cop back again.

The detective had seen a pathologist from the Medical Examiners Office over in Wayne County stepping out of his white coveralls and wanted to have a quick word with him before he left. The two men shook hands and traded banter about the fact that they only ever saw each other when the shit hit the fan.

"So what do you think?" asked Lord.

"Well, you'll need to wait for my report for the official word but it looks like some sort of an accident. The elevator guy is not sure how it happened yet but it's pretty obvious that the victim attempted to take the elevator down to the parking lot. We found his briefcase so it appears he was on his way to work. Maybe he was distracted, but when the doors opened he apparently started walking. Elevator must have stopped on the floor above."

Lord shuddered. "I'll never step into a damn elevator again without looking first. Christ."

"You and me both. Anyway, he fell three levels down and landed at the base of the shaft. There is a well under the base of the elevator deep enough to take a man but our guy must have been unconscious after the fall. His lower body was in the well but his torso was resting up against the side wall. As the car came back down it essentially crushed the victim's upper body. His right arm was sheared off at the scapula, and the head was separated just below the chin. What's left was forced into the elevator well. Lucky for us he had ID in his pants pocket, the mechanism destroyed the mandible and tore off most of the face. It'll take some time to clean up the mess."

Lord grimaced as his imagination recreated the scene. "Poor bastard. So you've ruled out foul play?"

"Again, you'll have to wait for my report but these modern elevators are all computer-controlled, John. It's unlikely that someone could mess with them to cause something like this."

"Okay," replied Lord, glancing over at Ric in the corner, still with his head in his hands. "Anyway, thanks for the heads up, Bud. I better let you keep moving."

* * *

"What's your take on this?" Charlie and Dan were staring at the latest message that had appeared from the hacker.

"It's got me beat, Charlie. Your workstation is on a completely different network to the simulators. It's connected to the outside, sure, but with some serious firewall systems between them, and we're talking the best the DoD has. I'm afraid we might be in real shit here. I'm thinking I might just leave your systems down until we can do a sweep and see where this creep got in. I might come back tonight and shut everything down. Do the damn thing properly."

"But won't that mean that the security systems will shut down too?" Asked Charlie.

"Sure some of them will, but I'll only need an hour to do the sweep and it's the only way to do it comprehensively. I'll sweep the essential systems first and then bring them back up. After that I'll do the rest. In the meantime I'm inclined to try some new software we just received from Washington. I'll set it running and it will scour every audit trail and log entry, cross-checking the login files and looking for anything unusual. It's supposed to be state-of-the-art so this is as good as any time to give it a spin."

Dan sighed and stretched his back. "I guess I better go face the music with Leonard as soon as he's through with this morning's meeting."

"This message seems to have you more concerned than the one we got on the simulator system."

"Well sure, Charlie. This is *different.* This guy knows your name, for Christ's sake. He's sent a message to *you.*"

CHAPTER 5

The senior team had been waiting in the conference room for about fifteen minutes by the time Leonard Darville arrived. To Elizabeth he looked ten years older than he had yesterday and she felt a momentary pang of concern.

"I'm afraid I have some bad news and I wish I knew a better way to deliver it," said Leonard, sitting down heavily in his usual chair. "I just got off the phone to the police and it seems that Alex Fox has been involved in an accident. I'm afraid he's been killed."

Around the table the news was greeted with the silence of disbelief. Elizabeth looked directly at Charlie who seemed to be frozen. Eventually, he was the first to speak.

"Accident? You mean a car wreck? What?"

"Well, the details are still sketchy but I'm told it was a freak accident involving a malfunctioning elevator in his apartment building."

Elizabeth gasped, putting her hand over her mouth as if she didn't trust herself to speak.

"The police contacted me for his next of kin details and I had to tell them that Alex had none. As you may know, Alex came to this country when he was a child. He had no brothers or sisters and his parents both died in an auto accident when he was thirteen. Looks like the department will claim the body and take care of the funeral. I'll be attending to these details as soon as the Medical Examiner has completed his work."

Charlie thought that Leonard looked every one of his sixty-three years and then some this morning. What is it about tragedy, he thought, that can add ten years to a man's age overnight? Almost like God just hit the fast-forward button on their internal clock. Leonard rubbed his eyes with the tips of his fingers.

"I don't know about you people, but I'm not sure I want to plough through project updates today. Why don't we reschedule for later in the week. Sorry, folks."

Several thoughts whirled across Charlie's mind. I never had that last chance to speak with Alex, maybe iron out a few things between us. Set things straight. I didn't ever make enough effort to get to know the guy, can't even remember when was the last time I had a beer with him. God, how am I going to replace him? And then, guiltily, we've lost whatever ideas it was he'd been thinking about.

Leonard rose stiffly and left the room with his head bowed. Elizabeth went after him to give him some support. Charlie glanced around the room and thought God, what a way to start the week. He took a deep breath and steeled himself for the task of telling his people. What, with their computers down and now Alex's death he was inclined to tell them all to take the rest of the day off. Lantini could go to hell.

* * *

"I know you were his friend, and I'm so sorry, Ric." said Elizabeth when she returned from lunch only to find him gazing at the wall with a vacant expression on his face.

"There isn't anything that anyone can really say at these times to make you feel better. I just want you to know that I understand the shock that this must have been to you. Maybe it would be better if you took a couple of days off. There's not much we can do until our computers are fixed anyway."

Ric's eyes snapped back into focus.

"What? What did you say about our computers?"

Elizabeth was startled by his response. "Sorry, I guess you've been too shocked to try logging in. It's confidential still but it looks like someone has hacked into our main simulator system. Dan Foster and his guys are trying to get to the bottom of it but until they're done, our systems are off the air."

"Are you okay Ric?" Elizabeth thought he looked as if he was in shock. She crossed the room and placed a hand on his arm. He didn't appear to register the touch. His skin felt clammy, his arms broke out in goose bumps. Elizabeth's medical training took over and she spun his chair around on its wheels so that she could look him in the eyes, afraid he was about to faint.

"Ric, are you okay?" She asked again, looking directly into his vacant stare.

It took him a few seconds to resurface from wherever he'd gone.

"Yeah, sure…look, if it's all the same to you, I might just head for home. I'm not sure if I could concentrate today."

"No problem, Ric. Would you like me to give you something to help you relax and sleep? You look awfully peaky right now."

"Thanks, no. I'll be okay. I just need some air."

"Sure, Ric. Let me call a cab for you, you don't look like you should be driving."

Ric simply waved away her offer of transport as he rose to his feet.

"At least let me know how you're doing or if there is anything I can do to help out."

Ric nodded and turned to leave but before he reached the door Elizabeth remembered something.

"Ric, I almost forgot. Mary Peters from Level Two called a couple of time this morning looking for you. You probably don't want to think about it now but she said it was urgent."

"Thanks." Ric replied without enthusiasm. "I'll give her a call later." Without looking back, Ric stepped through the doorway and headed for the elevator.

He would never set foot in Elizabeth's office again.

* * *

Charlie sat across from Elizabeth with the empty take-out containers and screwed up napkins that formed the remains of their dinner on the table between them. Elizabeth had suggested that Charlie come over to her apartment after work and collect some food on the way. Neither of them felt like cooking and Elizabeth figured Charlie could use some company after the events of the day.

"So what's happening with the hacker thing?" asked Elizabeth. Charlie fiddled with his chopsticks.

"Well, Dan's stumped, I think. He couldn't find a trace of this Kensei guy's access in any of the logs. He's going in tonight to shut the systems down and do a sweep. It looks like Alex worked on the weekend and loaded some files into the backup simulator but there's nothing unusual in that. You know how these software guys are…"

Charlie's voice wavered as the events of the day threatened to overwhelm him. Elizabeth came around the table, crouched by his chair and hugged him.

"It's not your fault you know." She whispered. "It was an accident. It could have happened to anyone." She kissed the side of his face. "You put more energy into your people than most managers I know. You can't beat up on yourself just because there were things between you that went unresolved."

"I know," replied Charlie, dabbing his napkin at the corner of one eye. "But thanks, anyway for saying it."

"It's hard when someone you know dies, whatever the circumstances. You wouldn't be human if you didn't feel upset, Charlie." Elizabeth kissed his neck tenderly.

"Thank you," was all Charlie could manage.

Elizabeth stood up and stretched. "Let's clean up this mess and I'll make us a pot of coffee."

The distraction proved useful and the pair chatted about the weekend and their plans for Charlie to meet Lily Robillard, Elizabeth's friend since college. Lily did her PhD in East Asian Languages and Civilisations at Harvard before taking up a teaching role at the University of Michigan. One of the attractions for Elizabeth in accepting her job at The Factory was the opportunity to be near her old friend.

"Three doctors in one room, people will think we're elitist," said Charlie with a smile as they settled back into Elizabeth's old, but supremely comfortable, sofa.

"Nah, every second person in Ann Arbour has a PhD. I think you'll really like Lily, she's a lot of fun."

Charlie had a distant look on his face. "Why don't you mention the name this creep is using to Lily. You know, Kensei. It sounds Japanese. She might be able to shed some light on some of the weird stuff he said. Maybe he's given something away that might help track him down. It can't hurt. You don't have to tell her we have a hacker."

"How do you know it's a *him*," Elizabeth teased.

"Well most hackers are males, but, point taken."

"Sure." Replied Elizabeth, giving Charlie a squeeze. "I promised to call her and confirm this weekend so I'll ask her then. If anyone knows anything she will."

***

Dan Foster pulled into his reserved lot on the upper parking level of The Factory. He'd spent a few minutes with the soldiers in the guardhouse explaining what would happen while he ran the sweep. As the verifier system would be down, nobody could enter The Factory until the job was done. Dan would call the guardhouse when the systems came back online and together they would run some tests to ensure everything was okay.

Dan worked his way to the main computer room and flopped into the chair. He hated coming out again after dinner but he didn't want to give the job to anyone else. He had a bad feeling about this and wanted to be on top in case it got worse. Paging back through the screens of data generated by the SecureSys software that he'd left running confirmed what he'd been dreading all afternoon.

He ran his fingers through his rapidly diminishing hair. "Shit." Dan fired off an email to Charlie and copied Leonard Darville. We're in for a witch-hunt now, he thought, returning to the main console. For a moment, Dan considered not even running the sweep based on what he'd just discovered. God knows there's plenty of other things I'd rather be doing right now. An image of himself and his wife sitting back watching an old black-and-white movie on their new wide-screen TV popped into his head. "No Dan, do the damned job properly." He scolded himself out loud.

Dan turned his attention to the task at hand and the checklist he'd taped to the desk. Shutting down large, complex computer systems is not just a case of throwing a switch. Dan would need fifteen minutes at least to take everything off line. As he began typing he heard a hiss, which appeared to come from the far corner of the computer room. Dan turned, slid his chair to the right and looked between the rows of cabinets but there was nothing to see. Must be the robotic backup system, he thought. Can't normally hear it when you get a few people in here. He was tempted to get up and check it out but then decided not to bother.

Dan stretched his shoulders as he waited for the system to return control to him. Right now it was sending an automatic message to every user giving them a minute's notice to log off. Most of those users were at home watching their TVs Dan figured. God, I feel tired, he thought. Then he became aware of a strange odour. Sort of sweet but unnatural somehow. Not unlike the smell of burning sugar on the stove but with another, more delicate metallic tinge. It was rapidly getting stronger. His own olfactory thesaurus tried to place the smell, to link it to an object, or a place, or a situation. Something started pinging at him urgently from a primitive part of his brain. A part of his brain to which he had almost forgotten to listen. Warning him of immediate danger. Dan lingered for a few seconds before deciding something was really wrong.

He tried to stand and move to the door but suddenly realised he was on the floor. He didn't know how he got there. There seemed to be a gap in his consciousness. Like a missing piece of film causing the movie to jump to a new scene. His glasses were gone and his face seemed to be bleeding. Although it made no sense, he realised that the smell must be some sort of gas leak. When he lifted his head he could see the blurry outline of the exit only fifteen feet away. It was as if he was watching himself from above. Detached somehow. He saw himself claw his way to the door. His arms worked but his legs felt like dead weights. His hands slipped in the blood running from his nose and lips. His entire body felt like it was getting heavier by the second.

With his heart desperately hammering in his chest and his mind starting to hallucinate, he was almost certain that someone was sitting on his back, riding him like a horse. He couldn't figure out why anyone would do that while he was so obviously in trouble.

"Get off me, you fucker!" He yelled, spitting blood across the floor, but the weight remained. Through tears of anger he could see the blurred outline of the exit sign and he kept clawing his way forward. With a bump to his head he realised he was at the door. With all of his fading strength he groped for and found the door handle directly above where he lay.

It was locked. Dan fell back. His resolve was gone. His energy, his anger, his desire, had ebbed away. His heart stopped beating. His chest became still. He could still see the ceiling of the computer room although, strangely, everything now was silent. He could even see the red handle of the fire axe. He couldn't see the bastard that had been riding him. Odd. Then he saw nothing.

CHAPTER 6

In the guardhouse, Joe's shift ended in another hour and he was growing uneasy. It had been over fifty minutes since Dan Foster went into The Factory. He didn't want to get stuck at the end of his shift, midway through some dumb system tests.

Joe called out to the two men on duty in the room below.

"Either of you wanna check on the computer guy? We shoulda heard something by now."

In the bunker was Jim Warburton, a Vietnam Vet and former military policeman who started his career in the crazy days before the fall of Saigon and who was now very happy to end it by pulling the sort of duty that didn't get you killed. Ten feet to his left was his much younger partner Steve Gonza. For some reason that Steve had never understood, his buddies all called him Gonads. He liked to think it was because of his outsized frame and macho vigour.

Jim made a show of flexing his bad leg with tiny metal fragments still embedded, a legacy from harder times. "How about you go for a walk, Gonads." He said. "I'll keep an eye on things here."

"Where'd he go?" Steve called back, pulling a notepad from his shirt pocket.

"Room 304. You know, the big computer room."

"Give me a minute. Let me check the video."

Joe smiled and thought how quickly these new guys caught on. Why waste time walking when you can simply patch in to the security cameras. Then an odd thought crossed his mind. The cameras shouldn't be working. Either Foster should have called and said the system was coming up, or the system never went down in the first place. Weird.

"See anything" he called.

"Well, we don't cover the entire room but I'd say our man ain't there. I better go take a look I s'pose."

"That'd be great." Joe replied. "Dan Foster, ID DM009945, room 304, entered at…" He checked his computer screen. "1955 hours."

Steve stood, stretching his well-developed shoulders and collecting his aluminium flashlight from the rack where its batteries remained on permanent charge.

"Gotcha."

As Steve walked down the well-lit security corridor, which entered The Factory at Level 1, he passed the first overhead security camera. He was pretty sure his partner back in the surveillance room would be watching and so as he passed the camera he put his arm behind his back and flipped it the bird. Two seconds later a single click of acknowledgment sounded on his radio causing Steve to laugh out loud. Always watchin' he thought. Steve loved his job at The Factory. He enjoyed the town, the feeling of belonging that seems to come more easily in a small place, the interesting folk that worked at The Factory, and the pay wasn't bad either. The gym down the road was pretty good and, for most of the year, the place was packed with girls. Some days he felt he'd died and gone to heaven.

Five minutes later, Steve approached the windowed double doors of the computer room. Already he could see that one of the chairs where the computer operators normally sat had overturned. His training started to kick in as he instinctively slipped the safety strap from his sidearm. Slowly he revolved on the spot taking in every office and cubicle, his eyes not merely flitting over what they saw but sweeping, and analysing. He listened intently for sixty seconds and heard nothing unusual beyond the hum of the ventilation and the low drone that always seemed to emanate from the other side of the glass.

He started to approach the door but then froze as he caught sight of a streak of bright red on the white tiled floor near the overturned chair. Like a giant bleeding snail-trail. He slid his nine millimetre pistol from its nylon holster and felt reassurance in its weight. Safety off, finger outside the trigger guard, thumb on the hammer. His actions instinctive.

As he drew close to the windowed doors, he had his first glimpse of Foster's body. A foot with a slip-on shoe. A leg inside blue denim. A black belt and the beginning of a blue checked shirt. Steve was standing outside the doors now and he saw that Foster was slumped against the other side. He stood on his toes and pressed his face up to the glass to increase his already considerable height advantage. What he saw made his skin crawl and for a moment he thought he might vomit as a wave of nausea washed over him.

He stepped back, took a couple of deep breaths, rotated his shoulders and went to the glass again. He could see Foster's chest and he studied it intently for a while. Not moving. He forced his eyes back to that terrible face. He could only see part of the head as it was lying almost at his feet but on the other side of the door. The eye was wide open as if surprised and many of the capillaries had burst putting red where the white should have been. Foster's teeth were drawn back in a snarl and his tongue was dark blue, almost black. Steve thought it looked like the poor bastard had an oversize squash ball in his mouth. Satisfied that Foster had to be dead, Steve stepped away from the glass, put his back to the wall and pulled what could have easily been mistaken for a cell phone from his belt.

Steve's radio operated using a custom CDMA hybrid technology, which the DoD called HAPCOM. The bottom line was that the security staff had excellent reception both inside and outside of The Factory but it was impossible for anyone to eavesdrop. The other advantage of the system was that it was completely independent. The Factory could lose all power, have all of its systems crippled, be cut off from everything, and HAPCOM would keep on working.

Steve waited until his heart rate began to subside, until he had himself under control again and then called in what he had found. As he waited for backup to arrive before entering the computer room, he weighed the coincidence of two people from The Factory dying in one day.

* * *

Elizabeth's head snuggled into Charlie's shoulder, one arm and one leg draped languidly over his naked body. A single sheet covered them both against the cooling evening air.

Later, neither would be quite sure why it happened that night. A certain level of ease in each other's presence maybe. Desire unlocked through a little too much wine perhaps. Their mutual need for comfort even. Maybe all of the above. The why didn't seem to be so important.

Lying on his back, Charlie couldn't remember feeling more relaxed. The cares of the day seemed far away as his finger gently traced the curve of Elizabeth's back. The smell of her hair, the warmth of her body. Her breath on his neck. It had been a long time since he'd felt so close to another human being.

"I could die now," Charlie whispered.

Elizabeth kissed the side of his face. "Oh, I think you have a few good years left in you yet."

"I think I'd like to spend them with you." Said Charlie, drifting off to sleep.

* * *

Steve's call triggered a chain of events. There is some confusion initially as to jurisdiction. No one ever died in The Factory before. The Factory is a military establishment but the deceased is a civilian. Eventually the decision about who to call first is made in favour of the police.

It's after midnight and any idea that Joe might have entertained about finishing his shift on time has been torpedoed. The computer room is now a hive of activity as photographs are taken, measurements recorded and samples bagged. Leonard Darville looks on while security guards Joe and Steve give animated statements to a uniformed officer. Away from the main activity, John Lord stands with his heavyset partner Louis Armstrong, his hands firmly in his pockets, his eyes taking in the room. Naturally, the local police know about The Factory. It would have been politically stupid and simply discourteous not to tell them that they had a special facility on their patch. However, this is the first time anyone from the City of Ann Arbor Police Department has been inside the building.

"Quite a place they got here. That thumbprint gadget's pretty slick, whaddya say?"

"That's a fact, Lou, our taxes at work, I guess."

"What's your take on this, JL?"

"I dunno, Lou. My instinct tells me that something's not right."

"You mean two guys in one day?"

"Sure, that. But even this guy. They're saying maybe he had a heart attack."

"Could happen. Guy's got to be fifty. These computer execs get pretty stressed." Louis offered.

"Sure. But imagine it's you. The pain hits. So bad you take a nose dive into the tiles. Then you manage to crawl fifteen feet, slipping in your own blood towards the door."

Louis shrugged his shoulders "So? Guy makes the door, heart busts. Game over."

Lord shook his head in irritation. "Think about it, Lou. This guy crawls fifteen feet when he has a phone on his damn belt and another on the desk! Christ! Where the hell's he going? Wouldn't he try to call someone? There's three guys out in that damn concrete bunker, coulda been here inside two minutes. I'm telling you, Lou, it makes no sense."

"Maybe our guy just panicked."

"Yeah, maybe. And maybe if my aunt had balls she'd be my uncle. I've had it. Let's get out of here. We'll see what the autopsy turns up."

Two hours later, everyone is done. The body is on the way to the

Wayne County Medical Examiners Office and Joe finally gets to go home. Secretly he's thrilled to be in the middle of what's sure to be a huge story at The Factory. He won't sleep tonight though. The frozen scream on Foster's dead face will be with him long after the excitement of the last few hours fades.

* * *

When news of Foster's death broke at The Factory next morning, Mary Peters left early mumbling to her new supervisor she was sick. Actually she's terrified. She hasn't slept for forty-eight hours and her vision is blurring. Her hand shakes as she unlocks the apartment she shares with a female U of M student. She tries calling Ric's home phone again and this time she connects. As she blurts out the latest tragic news Ric slides down the wall until he's sitting on the floor at the other end of the phone line.

"Oh, God, Ric, what are we going to do?" she wails. "We have to tell Charlie what Alex did before something else awful happens."

"For God's sake calm down, Mary." Ric interrupts regaining some of his composure. "Let me get this straight. You're saying they think he had a heart attack, yes?"

"They don't know yet but it looks like it."

"Then it could be just coincidence. It's not like they've both been murdered or anything. We tell Charlie and this turns out to be nothing more than coincidence, then what."

"You think so?"

"You've seen Foster. The man was driven. It's no surprise to me that his heart gave out. No, I think we sit tight for a while. Nothing to be gained by running off at the mouth. Okay?"

"I don't like it, Ric, I'd never forgive myself if something else happened."

"It won't. Calm down. We don't know that Alex had anything to do with this. Take a sleeping pill and get some rest. Let's talk tomorrow. See how you feel then."

Mary sighed, "okay. I guess you're right. I'm so damned tired I can hardly think..."

Ric hung up the phone. God, this whole shitfest just goes from bad to worse, he thought. He felt his entire world starting to slide out of control. One day everything's going gang-busters and then the whole thing starts unravelling. He felt a whole lot less confident than he'd pretended to be but if Mary is right and these deaths are related to Alex's software, they were in some serious shit already. He figured waiting couldn't make it much worse.

* * *

First thing Tuesday morning Charlie and Leonard sit in Charlie's office with the door closed. After he had logged in this morning Charlie saw the email sent to him the previous night. When he saw who it was from it was as if Foster had reached out to Charlie from the grave. Unconsciously, he took a sharp intake of breath and then held it. Then he read the message and his world tilted to one side.

Hi Charlie,

I'm afraid my fears of this afternoon seemed to be confirmed. The SecureSys software I told you about has finished running and it's come back with nothing. It shows no outside access on any port on any system in the last 30 days. Trust me, this package is the best. It checked everything.

Unfortunately that means our hacker is inside this building. It's going to be a bitch but we will have to report this. I'll need to hand it over to the external DoD INFOSEC people and they'll turn us inside out. That means all of your staff too. Maybe especially your people. Sorry.

I'm about to run the sweep now I'm here but I'm sure it will be a waste of time. Sorry for the bad news, buddy. Talk to you tomorrow.

Dan

"I just can't believe it, Charlie. Two of our best people. Taken from us in one day. What are the odds of that happening? I've never been a religious man but I believe. This sort of thing sure makes it hard to understand what's going on up there."

"What do the police think?" asked Charlie.

"You know what they're like, Charlie, those sons of bitches down on Fifth Avenue think there's a skeleton in every closet. That Detective Lord is convinced that someone bumped Dan off."

"How?"

"Oh, I don't know, poison or something I suppose. Who can know what those suspicious bastards will come up with. I would have been much happier to see our own MPs on the job."

"Did you see the security footage?"

"Sure I saw it. Dan sits and types. Suddenly he pitches up like he's seen a ghost and then crashes face first into the floor. Starts crawling toward the door until he's out of the picture. I tell you, Charlie, as long as I live I'll never forget the sight of that poor bastard dragging himself along those tiles."

Charlie studied his hands. "Why do you think he went for the door, Leonard?"

Darville shrugged. "That's what Lord asked. We'll never know. Your heart is ripping itself apart, how straight is your mind? I've seen action in the military, Charlie, and I've seen wounded and dying men do some pretty bizarre things. You can't make too much out of that."

"Yeah, I guess you're right."

"How're you getting along with that favourite doctor of mine?" Darville asked changing the subject. "Don't think I haven't seen you two making eyes at each other. You could do a whole lot worse you know."

"Well, Elizabeth and I…," Charlie stammered, colour rising to his face.

"Oh, come on, Charlie, it's me you're talking to, not the girl's damn father!"

"She is pretty special," Charlie replied with a sheepish grin.

"Damn straight she is. Don't you let her get away by beating around the bush, you hear me?" Charlie thought back to last night and figured that when it came to the seriousness of their relationship, the days of beating around the bush were well and truly over.

"Anyway, enough of that. We better get down to work," Darville went on, suddenly businesslike again. "Unfortunately, Charlie, we are going to have your buddy Major Lantini all over us like a rash tomorrow morning and that's the thing we have to focus on as of now. Firstly, do you have any idea at all who this asshole is that's sending these stupid damn messages?"

Charlie shook his head. "No. In fact I can't believe that *any* of my people would be so stupid."

"That's pretty much what Dan said to Ed Furneaux yesterday afternoon about his staff. But we have to face the facts, Charlie. If it didn't come from outside it must have come from inside. Not too many other options left."

"What will you do?"

What Darville decided to do first was to call a staff meeting that afternoon with everyone who worked in software development, analysis, internal IT and so on. In short, anyone whose training and experience meant that they could possibly be the hacker they now reluctantly admitted was in their midst.

The mood in the conference room was sombre. The room was full and even with the seats around the edges of the wall occupied, some staff had to stand. Leonard Darville addressed them.

"The reason I have called you people here at short notice is not for a chit-chat, as you may have guessed. What I'm about to say must not leave this room. It pains me to have to say it. As you know, our Head of IT Security, Dan Foster, died last night in this building. He was investigating what appeared to be a hacker attack on our simulator system. Certain threatening messages were left. Dan had come to the conclusion after much investigation that the hacker had to be in this building."

A murmur of dissent rippled around the room.

"I know, I know," continued Darville. "None of us likes to think one of our own is responsible for this foolishness. The fact of the matter is that we have a protocol to follow and in this case we have to turn the whole thing over to external INFOSEC."

Now a collective groan filed the room.

"That's right. Someone has made life difficult for everyone here. As things stand all of you will need to be interviewed. All of your email will be scrutinised. Your work for the last six months will be audited and everyone will be under a cloud of suspicion until this thing is over. Some of you may know that we're not exactly in the good books with our new DoD liaison Major Lantini. He will be here tomorrow to get the ball rolling."

Expressions of anger now started to erupt around the room.

"Okay people, here's the deal. I'll be in my office until 1900 hours this evening. If one of you feels like clearing this up before we all endure a witch-hunt, I'll be waiting. I can't guarantee what the outcome will be but I can tell you this. If we have to endure this thing and *then* we find the chump who did it, the SOB's feet won't even touch the ground before he's out on his ass. No negotiation and definitely prosecution. Do I make myself clear?"

"Okay people. Do the right thing. 1900 hours. Questions?"

There were none. Everyone filed out of the room muttering about who would be dumb enough to pull this stunt and what they'd do if they got their hands on the bastard.

CHAPTER 7

The Wayne County Medical Examiners Office in Detroit is a hectic place with 2,500 autopsies involving 500,000 tests carried out each year. John Lord had to call in a favour to get Foster's body bumped up the queue. He figured his case was way more important than the usual intake of homeless bums that made up much the pathologists' work. He was smart enough not to put it in those terms. Lord didn't buy into the heart attack theory and he hoped the autopsy would give him some leverage to start turning the screws. The pathologist had promised to call him when it was done. Mid-morning she said.

At the investigative division of the Ann Arbor Police Department, Detective John Lord grumbles about the growing pile of paperwork on his desk as his long time partner Louis arrives with a box of Krispy Kremes.

"Those things'll kill you dead Lou," quipped Lord

"Lotsa things tryin' to kill my ass, JL. None successful so far." Replied Louis, flipping open the cardboard box and making his selection before placing the box on Lord's desk.

Lord just laughed and helped himself to the largest one he could find. "I'm doin' this for your sake buddy." He said through a mouthful of crème, "one less to clog up your arteries."

"Well it makes me feel a whole lot better havin' you lookin' out for me."

Their repartee was interrupted by the phone.

"That'll be Sue down at the morgue." Said Lord, swinging his feet off the pile of phone books next to his desk. He picked up the phone and listened intently for a few minutes, then carefully replaced it in the cradle.

"Well, Well. You'll never guess what the Medical Examiner found." Lord said folding his arms across his chest.

"Don't tell me. Guy died from a radioactive probe up his ass."

"Nope. But it wasn't a heart attack. They've sent blood samples off but his heart was good for another fifty thousand miles. Poor bastard's arteries were as clean as a twenty-year-old's."

"So what's their guess" Louis asked wiping his mouth demurely.

"Not sure. Maybe poison. Too early to tell I guess."

"That could put a new spin on it. You wanna pay 'em another visit out at Fort Knox?"

"No, let's just sit on it until we get the results of the blood work. Should have it in the morning."

* * *

Charlie walks to where his car is parked in the upper lot. Out of the corner of his eye he spots Darville putting his briefcase in the trunk of his Mercedes. As Charlie changes direction to catch him before he leaves he reflects again on how a few bad days can age a man. How long has it been? Two days? To Charlie it felt like a month. Leonard slammed the trunk shut and looked up at the sound of Charlie's footsteps echoing across the almost empty lot.

"Hell of a day Charlie." He called, leaning against the side of the immaculately kept vehicle. The Mercedes is Leonard's Retirement Car. He's told everyone at The Factory that he intends going out in style. Charlie feels a twinge of sadness for the man as he remembers this. He can't imagine the old soldier pottering around the garden and taking naps in the afternoon. Suddenly an image flashes into Charlie's mind. Darville, a rope around his neck, dangling under a large shade tree. A suicide note placed carefully on a drink tray next to the overturned chair. He banishes the awful picture from his mind with a shrug of annoyance.

"I don't suppose you had any takers tonight?" Charlie asks, quickly recovering his composure.

"I'm afraid not, Charlie. Looks like we'll be doing this the hard way. God, I hate it when one of our own damn people doesn't have the guts to come forward and take it on the chin. Probably would've gotten away with a slap on the wrist."

"I don't want to make the whole situation worse than it is but we may never find out who did this you know."

"What do you mean, Charlie?"

"We already have the best of the INFOSEC guys working *here,* Leonard. Together with the best we could find out of the industry. I mean, you know how good Ed Furneaux is, and he said that these messages seemed to come from the damned operating system itself."

"Hell, Charlie, we'll be crucified if we can't find this bastard. There has to be something we can do. This thing needs to be put to bed, and soon."

"Our best shot is if he keeps sending the messages. But my guess is whoever did this will clam right up and we'll never know."

"I hope you're wrong, Charlie, I really do." Leonard ran his hand over the grey bristles of his military-style crew cut.

"Anyway, I've had as much of this business as I can take for one day. I'm getting too old for this shit. So long, son."

"Drive safely, Leonard." Charlie said as he turned and headed for his car.

* * *

The next morning Ann Arbor is once again bathed in sunshine, the cloudless sky promising a delightful day. As Charlie drives toward work, the weather, and the opportunity for exercise it might have afforded him, is the last thing on his mind. How a few bad days can change a man.

At the same time and thirty miles away at The Medical Examiners Office, Susan Arbroath, the pathologist assigned to the Foster case is sitting in her undersized office studying a fax, her sizeable body serving to shrink even further the area surrounding her. Around the walls of the compact space are kids' drawings done in the vivid coloured crayons and paints that small children find irresistible. As if by wallpapering the room with them, she can somehow compensate for the death and mayhem so often discussed inside. There is just enough space for a small desk, a bank of filing cabinets and an overflowing bookshelf. A pile of medical journals in the corner threatens to overbalance if a another copy is added.

She looks up and smiles as she hears a tap on the window next to the open door.

"Hi John, I was just thinking about you."

"Yeah, I get that a lot. I figure it must be my big gun."

Susan let go a raucous belly laugh and poked her tongue at him.

"So Doc, you have anything for me yet? I know you said you'd ring but I was on the way to the station and figured I'd stop by just in case."

Susan feigned shock. "John Lord you are such a liar. I know you live over in Barton Hills, there's no way you just called in on your way to work. When are you going to face the fact that you just can't live without me?"

"You got me there Doc. Can't hide anything from you. I'm just fixin' to bump off that bum of a husband of yours and then claim you as mine."

"Just let me check on his insurance policy first." She said, smiling.

Lord had lost count of the number of cases they had worked together and there was an ease between them built on mutual respect for the other's skills. Lord knew of several cases that would have remained unsolved had it not been for Susan's dogged determination to bring closure for *her people*, as she called them.

"In fact." Susan continued. "The reason I was thinking of you was this fax that just came from the lab. Foster's blood work. Why don't you fix both of us a coffee while I finish reading it."

"Sounds good to me Doc. Don't move a muscle."

When Lord returned with two steaming mugs and cleared a place on Susan's desk to put them down, she tilted her chair back, the springs protesting at her ample frame. Removing her reading glasses, she tossed the report on top of the several inches of paperwork that already covered her desk. Lord liked her style. In his view a tidy desk was definitely the sign of a sick mind.

"Interesting John." She said, reaching for her mug.

"How so?"

"It appears that our guy was gassed."

"You're kidding me."

"No I'm not. His blood shows lethal levels of Chlorofluorocarbons and Bromine. It was also detected in the lung samples I took. There were no puncture marks on his body and gas would be consistent with the indications of asphyxia."

Lord was puzzled "You mean the chloro-whatever stuff as in the ozone layer?"

""Pretty much. The most common CFS / Bromine combination I'm familiar with is Halon."

"How would've Foster come into contact with this stuff?"

"Like all CFC's Halon has been phased out in most places. Its main use was in the plastics industry and as a fire suppressant chemical in computer rooms, telecommunications centres and the like"

Lord sat forward "Computer rooms?"

"Yes, it's just about the best stuff for suppressing electrical fires. There was a huge stink when the government legislated to have it removed. Nothing else works as well."

"Well I'll be damned." Said Lord shaking his head. "Two freak accidents in one day?"

"You mean the body they brought in from the elevator accident."

"Yeah. Both guys worked at the same facility and Foster died in the computer room."

"That's pretty tough."

"Too tough for my cynical mind. I think I better take a ride over there and have me a little chat with those good folks."

Lord drained his coffee. "Thanks Sue, as usual I leave a happier and better informed detective."

"You look after yourself John. You know how I feel about accidents happening to my friends."

"Sure, say hi to Bill and little Heidi for me." With that, Lord headed down the corridor to his vehicle, deep in thought. We either have one very smart bastard or something really weird is going on in that damned place.

* * *

Charlie looks around and thinks that he's starting to hate the sight of the conference room. Lantini, accompanied by his canine assistant is sitting at the end of the big table in the same chair from which he delivered his ultimatum last week. Was it really only last Friday? Charlie asks himself. The meeting is about to start but Darville is on the phone in the corner of the room. He sounds flustered. Ed Furneaux sits patiently to Charlie's right, giving his hands some occupation by cleaning his glasses thoroughly. I wonder if Lantini really is the asshole that everyone thinks he is, Charlie speculates. Maybe it's just because we're only seeing him in the context of crisis. Maybe he's a nice guy when you get to know him. His ex-wife would tell him he's just being soft but Charlie's experience is that people generally are not simply one dimensional. There are often surprises in store when you get to know them better, when you scratch below the surface a little. Charlie likes to think that he gives people a chance before he forms an opinion of them. He tries to imagine Lantini at home with kids or maybe laughing at a barbecue with a beer in his hand. It doesn't work. Probably just an asshole, Charlie decides.

Finally, Darville puts down the phone and sits heavily. "We have two detectives being escorted here as we speak. They have a number of questions regarding Dan's death. I tried to put them off but they wouldn't have it. It might be good for you to meet them Jack." Lantini shrugged.

"Let's give them what they want and piss them off."

Another period of uncomfortable silence ensues. Nobody appears to be interested in small talk. Lantini looks perfectly relaxed. A security guard ushers the pair of detectives into the room and Darville makes the introductions. Lantini smirks as Louis is introduced.

"Did you bring your trumpet with you, detective?" He asks.

"No, I don't like to mix business and pleasure." Louis replies with an easy smile, unaffected by Lantini's little joke. Lord inclines his head questioningly toward Charlie and Ed as he catches Darville's eye.

"As I indicated to you on the phone detective, we are in the process of having a very important meeting. One that the Major here has travelled some distance to attend. These other gentlemen," he gestured toward Ed and Charlie, "are senior members of staff. You can speak openly in their presence."

Lord took a seat leaving Lou standing with his back to the wall. Charlie noticed the cop ploy. "So gentlemen. What's more important than a death on the premises that your meeting couldn't wait a few minutes?"

Darville looked at Lantini who spoke first, "I can't see how Department of Defence business is pertinent in a case involving someone dying of natural causes."

"Let's clear that one up right now." Replied Lord. "Dan Foster did not die of natural causes."

"What are you talking about?" Lantini shot back.

Lord ignored the question. "Can someone tell me whether or not the computer room in which Mr Foster died is fitted with a Halon fire system?"

Darville looked across at Ed "Do you know Ed?"

"Excuse me, detective," interrupted Lantini, "how exactly is this information germane to your line of inquiry? The details of this facility are classified."

Lord nodded as if he considered this to be a fair question.

"The results of the autopsy give us reason to suspect that Mr Foster was gassed."

Lantini's anger began to show through the thin veneer of civility that he was managing to maintain with some effort.

"Gassed! What the hell are you talking about? How does a man get gassed in a computer facility? This is absurd!"

"Actually it isn't as absurd as it might sound." Ed offered. "Many DoD computer installations are fitted with fire suppression systems that still use Halon gas to kill the fire quickly. Regular sprinklers could cause millions of dollars worth of damage if they flooded the equipment. Naturally there are systems in place to ensure that any staff have time to exit the computer room before the doors are locked."

"Are you telling me that the Goddamn system locks the doors and then pumps the room full of poison gas?" Asked Lantini, shaking his head.

"Sure." Replied Ed. "But the systems give plenty of warning and the gas is completely pumped out afterwards before people are allowed back in. It sounds spooky but it's the best thing there is for controlling fires. Anyway, there's a fire axe on the wall by the door in case anyone is trapped inside."

"Shit, you wouldn't get me working inside a gas chamber like that." Lantini said.

"So." Lord continued. "To return to my original question, now that we have established that it *is* germane to the inquiry, does the computer room in which Dan Foster died contain such a system? Ed?"

"Yes it does, the DoD is exempt from the new restrictions. But the suppression system didn't activate when Dan died."

"How can you be so sure?" Lord demanded.

"Because there was no fire. All of this stuff is logged by the computer. If the fire suppressors activate there are lights and alarms and log entries recording the whole thing. Even the video footage would have showed it."

"Okay. Humour me for a minute. Let's say the system *did* activate. Let's assume that's why Foster was trying to get to the door. Let's also say that either this happened because of a malfunction or..."

"But it can't malfunction without a..." Ed started to interrupt.

Lord cut him off "Go with me on this. Let's say it *was* on the fritz. Is there any way, other than the computer system, for us to tell if it activated?"

Ed thought for a moment. "Yes. Quite easily in fact. The Halon cylinders will need recharging."

"Excellent! And we can check that quickly?"

"Sure, the cylinders have gauges."

Lord rose to his feet "What are we waiting for gentlemen?"

"You better not be wasting our Goddamn time detective." Lantini grumbled as they filed out of the conference room.

The Halon cylinders are contained in a cage against the wall in the upper parking level. Ed retrieved the key and led them out into the parking lot.

"I guess the computer room is directly above us?" Asked Lord, looking up at the concrete ceiling with its mess of pipes and cables.

"That's right detective." Ed replied. "The gas cylinders are located here for all of the labs so that if we have a leak it vents into the car park space."

Ed unlocked the cage doors revealing about two dozen large steel cylinders.

"Christ! I didn't expect this many" Lord exclaimed.

As Ed consulted the sheet located on the inside of the cage door he explained it to Lord. "These are not all Halon of course. The labs use several different gasses, some of them highly inflammable. We keep them all in one place. Ah here it is, tank 14, Fire suppression –

main computer room" Ed craned his neck to see the dial.

"What do you see?" Demanded Lantini

When Ed turned back to them his face was impassive. "All the tanks are full."

In the parking lot, Lord just glared at the small group clustered around the cage. This made no sense at all.

"Could these tanks have been changed this morning?" He asked.

"I guess it's possible" said Ed, "but only if it they had been ordered forty-eight hours ago, but how could anyone know they would be needed?"

"How can we check?" asked Lord.

"Oh, come on! I think we're clutching at straws here detective." Lantini said

"How can we check?" insisted Lord, his eyes never leaving Ed's face, impatient now.

Ed rubbed his chin. "I know! When the tanks are replaced, an entry is made in the log book kept in the cage."

Ed grabbed the book from where it was attached to the inside of the door and flicked to the last entry. He froze. When he looked up, his face was ashen.

"What's it say?" Demanded Lord. Ed just turned the book around so they could see.

Written in neat blue printing was today's date and a time of 0830.

* * *

They are all seated again at the long table in the conference room. Lantini speaks first. "Somebody better tell me what's going on here. First we have a hacker and then our equipment kills one of our own people. What kind of operation are you running here Leonard? Christ!"

Lord's head snaps up from his notebook. "Hacker? Nobody told me about a hacker. Would someone like to tell me why?"

Darville cleared his throat. "This is a high security military facility detective. That is not information we would normally disclose. We didn't see any connection with the unfortunate death and so didn't raise it." Darville stood and began to pace restlessly. "However, I have to tell you detective Lord, that we now have an increased understanding of the source of the incidents."

"Which means exactly what sir?"

"We are now almost certain that hacker is one of the staff at this facility."

Lantini stood so quickly that his chair almost overturned. "Jesus Christ Darville! You're telling me this asshole works for you? Our own people are hacking into our most secure systems. My God man! This is getting worse by the minute."

Lord raised his arms. "Let's just all calm down here. Like you Major, it would appear that my partner and I have heard only part of the story. Let's all sit down again and have Mr Darville here explain to us slowly and precisely what is going on."

Darville ran his fingers over his grey brush, his frustration simmering dangerously close to the surface. "Please call me Leonard, detective. Otherwise it's *Captain* Darville if you please." Lord merely nodded, unruffled by the rebuke. Darville then explained in detail what had occurred, including their first thought that the hacker came from outside and how Dan had realised only last night that the culprit had to be internal. Lantini listened silently as his aide-de-camp scribbled copious notes.

"So let me summarise what we have here." Said Lord, tossing his notebook onto the table and counting on his fingers as he checked off each point. "We have an internal hacker, and a very smart one at that, who goes by the moniker of Kensei. Sending hostile messages, including threats of violence and death toward anyone who gets in his way. We then find the head of IT attempting to locate this guy. The poor bastard dies in a freak accident that our expert friend Ed here didn't think was possible, and someone knows in advance to trigger an order for replacement cylinders before they're even used. And my guess is the fire people will find zip when they look at that system. Just like the elevator people couldn't find a problem with a flaky elevator that mashed Alex Fox into the next world."

Lantini shook his head. "Surely detective, you're not saying that the two deaths are related in some way?"

"I'm not saying anything. Just relating the facts as we know them. One bad egg inside, two freak accidents, two dead men. One day. After twenty years as a detective, I trust my hunches and I can tell you, something stinks. Until I'm persuaded otherwise, I'm treating at least the death of Dan Foster as suspicious."

Darville took a deep breath. "Okay detective, how can we help you?"

"Starting first thing in the morning, Louis here and myself will need a pair of rooms set up where we can conduct interviews. We'll start with the computer people and then broaden out if we need to. I'd like a list of everyone's job title and function as well as their movements within this building over the last thirty days. You can give me that Leonard?"

"Certainly. Ed can organise a computer printout from the access control system and I'll have a couple of spare offices cleaned out on the ground floor."

"Excellent. I suggest that you get started and we'll see you at eight tomorrow morning."

When they were back in the cruiser, Louis spoke for the first time. "What you think we'll find talkin' to these propeller heads?"

"Don't know Lou. I'm hoping someone knows something. We shake the tree a little. See if anyone falls out. Okay by you?"

"Sounds like a plan."

***

Ric returned to his apartment on Tuesday afternoon after running for forty-five minutes. Usually after a run his head is clear by the time he takes the steps back up to his apartment, but not today. He can't shake the awful feeling of being trapped. The sensation of the world closing in on him. As he pulls off his sweat-soaked T-shirt and tosses it onto the pile of dirty clothes in the corner, the winking light of his answering machine beckons him over.

He presses the play button and fills a glass with water from the refrigerator, expecting to hear Mary's voice. Instead he hears Darville's assistant asking him to come to work tomorrow for an appointment with the police. They need to interview him as it appears he was one of the last people to speak to Alex. Oh shit, he thinks, I just don't know if I can go through this. I'm no good with these suspicious bastards. I can't play that game the way they can, listening and remembering every word and glance and gesture. They'll trap me some way for sure and then I'll be fucked. I'll lose everything, my job, this place, Christ! I'll be lucky not to go down for somehow killing the damn fool. At least manslaughter or negligence or some other legal crap. God no.

The glass slips from his grasp and falls onto the tiles and shatters, splashing his bare ankles with icy water. Without warning, his legs are unable to support him. The room begins to turn grey. Ignoring the broken glass, Ric drops to his knees and begins to sob.

CHAPTER 8

Ric steps from the shower and begins to vigorously towel himself dry. The cold water of the shower has refreshed him and he's angry now that he let himself be overwhelmed by events at The Factory. Of course the police would be suspicious, he figures. After all two deaths in a single day among people who work in the same organization has to be unusual. As he casts his mind back over the weekend, he's almost sure there is no way to connect him to what he and Alex did, although something keeps tugging at the back of his mind, making him feel uneasy. No way those cops are going to wade through countless hours of video looking for nothing in particular he reassures himself.

As he walks to the bedroom and reaches for the closet door to find a clean shirt, his hand freezes an inch from the knob. The disk! "Shit!" Ric yells at the empty room. "Fuck!" The DVD with Alex's private version of capture software is lying on the bench next to the equipment. His fingerprints will be all over it. For an instant, he feels real, paralysing fear. He slowly lets go of the breath locked in his chest and forces his mind to contemplate the possibilities. Could Elizabeth have found it? With relief he realises that it's unlikely as their data capture work together is all but finished for the time being and she has no reason to use the equipment.

Ric sits heavily on the bed. He doesn't believe that Alex or Dan's death is in any way connected with their weekend work but he's already made a statement to the police stating that he hadn't seen

Alex since the Friday night drinks at Applebees. Did the disk have a date on it? Ric can't remember. If Alex burnt the disk that morning and dated it before giving it to Ric, it might be a problem. Ric hadn't been anywhere near the medical lab since Saturday. Bad enough to bring storage media into The Factory, even without Alex's software. I have to get that disk and I have to do it before tomorrow, Ric decides. As he stands and reaches for the closet door again the phone rings.

This time it's Mary. She too has received a message calling her into The Factory to be interviewed by the police and she is almost incoherent on the phone. Ric tries his best to calm her down and then tells her to sit tight until he arrives. The realisation now dawns on Ric that there are two problems to be dealt with. The disk, and Mary.

* * *

Charlie and Elizabeth are back in Elizabeth's apartment but on this occasion there is no take-out food. Elizabeth has decided to cook for them both and as she slices the vegetables, Charlie leans back in a kitchen chair, a glass of red wine in his hand.

"We'll be lucky to come through this mess without being closed down." He said to Elizabeth, shaking his head. Elizabeth isn't quite sure whether Charlie is simply being a pessimist or whether he's right. There's something inside her head that won't allow her to assume the game's over. She wishes sometimes that Charlie had a bit more fight in him. Her anger flares up momentarily as she thinks about what Charlie has told her about his ex-wife. She's amazed how a person's self-confidence can be worn down by many years of negative comments by a spouse. Silently she renews her determination to help Charlie get it back again.

"I'm not so sure." She replies, scraping onions from the cutting board into a large wok on the stove. "My guess is that Lantini's bark is worse than his bite. I figure that when he understands the progress we've made he'll cut us some slack."

"You think?"

"Sure. Look, he's been sent around because the department feels that too many projects are never going to lead to anything. They've been going on for years and are no closer to producing any useable research. That's not true for our research. Even if we didn't ever achieve our core objective, there have been so many ground-breaking developments in both the medical and software domains that the whole thing would have been worth the effort. There are probably multiple projects that could be spun off of our research already."

"Maybe. Poor old Leonard isn't going to come out of this smelling so sweet though. They'll probably be looking for a scapegoat and he's close enough to retirement to be the fall guy without too making too many waves."

Elizabeth puts the knife down and looked over at Charlie. "He's a good man and it would be really shitty if his career ended like that. I feel bad for him, I really do."

"Yeah, me too. He doesn't deserve this."

"Do you have *any* idea who this hacker might be?"

"I honestly don't. I've spoken to most of my people and they all seemed surprised, angry, amazed. I can't see it being any of them but Ed Furneaux tells me the same thing about his staff so I don't know what to think."

"The police don't believe that Dan's death was an accident do they?"

"Well, the detective in charge is pretty suspicious about the circumstances, particularly when you put the hacker's messages into the mix. And he's right, there are a few things that don't add up right now. But, for my money, thinking it was murder is even harder to swallow. I mean, who would want to kill Dan? What's to gain? It doesn't make sense. The man was well liked and respected by everyone. How would anyone at The Factory profit by killing the poor guy?"

The meal began to sizzle and Elizabeth's face was momentarily lost in a cloud of steam as she stirred. "I just hope this can be over quickly and we can all get back to our routine."

Charlie came up behind Elizabeth and put his arms around her waist. He loved her slender figure and the way that she seemed to fit perfectly against him as if they were made for each other. She leant her head back against his chest.

"Perhaps *this* could become our routine." He whispered, kissing her behind the ear.

* * *

Ric sat across from Mary in the kitchen of her shared apartment. Mary looked like she had the flu and hadn't slept for a week. Her eyes were puffy and bruised and she couldn't stop her hands from trembling. Ric filled a glass of water and set it down on the table in front of her as he outlined his plan.

He would book a flight for Mary this evening to Minneapolis where her mother lived and she would stay there for a week or two until the whole thing settled down. Ric figured that the cops wouldn't bother trying to interview her there, Mary's CV didn't exactly make her out to look like a killer and she certainly didn't have the required experience to be a hacker. Ric guessed that being a young woman and new to the team would cause the police to lose interest in her very quickly.

Ric would cover by telling Charlie that Mary had gone to her mother's the day before and had some sort of breakdown after Alex's death. She needed some time.

Mary blew her nose and tossed the tissue onto the growing pile by her elbow.

"Are you sure this will work Ric?" She said.

"Absolutely. You're in no state to be badgered by these guys and the rest at your Mom's will do you good. Charlie will understand, he knows we were all friends with Alex. It'll all be over in a few days. Trust me."

"I guess so." Mary said, wiping her eyes.

"Okay then. You pack, I'll call the airline. After I've dropped you I'll call into The Factory and pick up the disk. No problem."

* * *

It's eight pm and Ric has left Mary at the Northwest terminal after walking her to the gate and ensuring that she has her ticket. As he turned to leave, Mary hugged him forcefully and thanked him through her tears for taking care of her. Ric was touched and thought that maybe when this was all over he might just ask Mary out for a drink one night. Just the two of them. She didn't feel too bad in his arms. Not bad at all.

At The Factory Ric joked with the guard on the gate and made sure that he gave a good reason for his late arrival, using as an excuse the fact that he's had two days off and needs some paperwork to help prepare for a meeting he has next morning. He wanted the visit to seem casual and he concentrated hard on trying to appear relaxed. He plans to be in and out in a few minutes.

Ric parks in the upper lot and moves quickly to the medical lab, not bothering to turn on too many lights as he goes, the emergency lighting throwing long angular shadows into the corridors. Surveillance cameras pan through wide overlapping arcs. Ric knows this part of the building well. The Factory has state-of-the art equipment and laboratories and the medical lab where Ric works is large by commercial standards and has benches running around three sides. Specialist computer controlled analytical instruments sit under their cream dust covers lending the lab an air of purpose and capability. One wall is covered by racks of glassware over a gleaming stainless steel trough. Above the bench on the opposite wall, a row of glass cabinets contains hundreds of bottles, vials, and packets of chemicals and medications. The entire room is clean, white and unsympathetically sterile.

When Ric arrives at the lab he opens the door with his gaze locked on the equipment across the room where he knows the disk to be. As the door closes silently behind him Ric tenses. That smell. At first he's unsure of what it means. It's a foreign smell but somehow he knows it. As his brain identifies the odour, familiar but much stronger now, he acts instinctively and runs for the emergency shut off valves in the gas supply lines, the disk momentarily forgotten. Large red levers on the wall at the back of the lab. He lurches over the bench and grabs for the valves, knocking over and breaking several glass beakers that are drying upside down in a rack near the wall. By now his mind has identified the smell to be acetylene.

He gets one valve shut down when he hears a metallic clicking sound. Ric has heard this sound many times before. He recognises it. It's the sound of the automatic piezoelectric ignition system in the lab's atomisation chamber. His head rotates toward the sound of the noise, the Atomic Absorption Spectrophotometer, still covered and standing against the wall at the far end of the lab. His hands fly from the levers thinking he must be touching something that's causing the machine to start up. His brain doesn't even have time to register how unlikely this would be, his senses becoming dulled by the gas. Then his world turns a blinding white.

The windows of the medical lab are hardened against explosions due to the nature of the tasks performed there. The force of the explosion is so massive that this fact becomes irrelevant. Ric's body is hurled brutally toward the glass as the intensely hot air expands outwards. The windows are ripped from their frames and laboratory equipment is propelled into the offices across the corridor. Ric's flailing body is torn apart as it explodes through a confusion of furniture, medical apparatus, steel framing, electrical wires and glass.

As the sound of falling debris fades away, sirens can be heard all over the building. Fires begin in multiple locations on the ground floor of The Factory as burning pieces of equipment come to rest against carpet and scattered paperwork. The office area has a high capacity water mist suppression system and immediately a dense fog starts to fill the area. In the upper level car park, automatic systems turn off the gas, now flowing freely like a flamethrower from the wall.

The small fires soon subside, the sirens continue. The disk with Ric's fingerprints will never be found. Hundreds of parts of Ric's body will be discovered and bagged over the next few days, intermingled with thousands of pieces of wreckage and debris, the most poignant being the tip of a single finger found wedged inside the outer glass barrel of a hypodermic syringe.

***

As the police forensic team pick their way through the devastation at The Factory, Northwest flight 803 from Detroit to Minneapolis, due to arrive at 2230 is about to touch down four minutes late. The warm day has come to an abrupt end with a summer storm and the cloud is low to the ground. Cleared to land into the north on runway R21, the pilots struggle with the turbulence caused by the storm. Both men peer intently through the rain streaked windshield for the runway lights..

Right about the time that the pilots expect to get their first glimpse of the airport on their direct approach, they break through the low cloud ceiling.

"Tower this is Northwest 803 inbound from Detroit, we are on final approach and have visual on runway R21."

The two pilots continue to prepare the aircraft for landing, working their way through the checklist as they've done hundreds, maybe thousands of times before.

In the cockpit the captain takes over from the automatic guidance system, which has placed them exactly where they expected to be.

"I have control." He says automatically to the co-pilot.

"Captain has control." Echoes the equally automatic response.

Although the pilots have received permission to land, there has been no acknowledgment of their last transmission from the tower. On the ground they can see several aircraft queued, awaiting departure. The captain is troubled but not overly so. This isn't the first difficult landing he's made and he's sure it won't be the last.

"Must be the damn storm." The captain says, fighting the crosswind and the disturbed air of the weather front. "Or maybe the ACARS computers are down. Better repeat that last call. Sam."

"Repeating, tower this is Northwest 803 inbound from Detroit, we are on final approach and have runway R21 on visual."

At this stage the aircraft has washed off much of its speed and is trimmed and committed to the landing. Factories and storage sheds whip underneath as the plane crosses that familiar no-man's-land that seems to be found on the perimeter of every large airport

As the aircraft descends rapidly toward the runway, a swirl of mist scuds over the rain-lashed tarmac. The captain's eyes flick automatically between his instruments and the windshield as he keeps the aircraft level and controls its rate of descent. As the mist clears, the captain realises to his horror that a United 767 is taxiing directly across the runway on which they're about to land. Immediately he calls "Abort! Abort!" Both pilots' hands jump to the throttles and push them to maximum. The huge jet engines spool up to full power as the captain yells "Pull up!" The pilots heave back on their control columns with the strength of desperate men as the fully loaded aircraft claws at the air, struggling to gain sufficient airspeed to arrest its deadly descent.

The United flight continues into runway R21, seemingly oblivious to the menace hurtling toward it at over 200mph. For a moment the captain thinks the two planes will miss each other. A second after his hand reaches to retract the undercarriage his main wheels smash into the top of the United's fuselage and explode out the other side, tearing a twenty-foot section of the upper fuselage away and killing everyone on the flight deck and all of the business class passengers instantly.

The effect on the Northwest aircraft is catastrophic. The 737 pitches violently forward as the two massive sets of wheels are torn away. The nose of the aircraft smashes into the ground with the engines still at full throttle.

The aircraft appears to disintegrate as it spins and tumbles along the runway with fires breaking out and flaming wreckage hurled into the night sky like some sort of ghastly pinwheel. By the time it comes to a halt within fifty-feet of the runway's end, the entire tangled mass of wreckage is an inferno.

Mary Peters and the other 122 passengers and crew aboard flight 803 are dead before the wreckage comes to a stop.

CHAPTER 9

The Factory is closed to everyone for three days following the blast. DoD engineering teams swarmed over the building checking its structural integrity, verifying major systems and performing any critical works needed to render the building safe. The finding was that half of the ground floor would be unusable for a couple of months as repairs are made and new equipment installed. Elizabeth and her team squeezed into the remaining space and some of the unused room on Level One where a small group of electronics engineers worked alongside the Administration staff.

The external walls of the building proved to be sound as interior walls and partitions absorbed most of the explosion's force. Some damage has been done to the ventilation system but it can be easily repaired. The general consensus among the staff is that this will be the end of the project but everyone is surprised and relieved to see the haste at which the DoD teams set about repairing the building so that they could get back to work.

During the closure, the interviews that had been scheduled by John Lord proceeded, following a few changes of plans, at the Ann Arbor police building on Fifth Avenue. At the end of two gruelling days, Detective Lord has nothing new. The initial investigation into the explosion has established the gasses involved and a conclusion of faulty laboratory equipment is drawn. Once again Lord is amazed to learn about what is considered to be the norm inside The Factory. At first he was incredulous when it was explained to him that the medical laboratory contained an Atomic Absorption Spectrophotometer, and that this machine atomised samples using a high temperature furnace supplied by explosive gases. He simply shook his head when he further discovered that these high-tech computer-controlled machines are routinely used in laboratories all over the world.

It was surmised that Ric triggered some sort of spark as he grabbed for the valves, perhaps a static discharge, and this was sufficient to ignite the explosive mix with catastrophic consequences.

Needless to say, Lord didn't believe a word of it. With access to The Factory available on Saturday morning, Lord has scheduled another meeting with the same team as before and is determined to move things forward. On the day before, the news arrived that Mary Peters had been killed in the plane crash that had dominated the national news during the second half of the week. An investigation had been launched into how the accident happened but the results weren't expected for several months. Lord heard whispers that the computers were at fault and he was beginning to wonder if there was anything left in the world that wasn't controlled by the damn things.

In the conference room, the scene looked just as it had done a few days earlier with the exception that two INFOSEC officers were now present. Keep this up and we'll have more uniforms around this table than we have at the precinct, Lord thought. The INFOSEC men sat on one side of the long table next to Lantini and his aide-de-camp, with Darville on the end. Charlie and Ed sat on the opposite side next to the detective. Louis maintained his watching brief by the door. Before this meeting could be held, the two detectives had to submit to an extensive background check so they could be privy to specific details of the project. Lord had ranted and table-thumped his way in here and so he could hardly complain about submitting to the clearance. It didn't improve his mood however.

"Thank you for coming together again gentlemen," Lord said to the group sitting around the giant table. "We've had ourselves one hell of a week so far and I know that it's been distressing for all of you. However, we need to revisit our discussions of last Tuesday while events are still clear in our minds."

Lord looked around the room at each man in turn before

continuing.

"Firstly, is there anyone in this room who still believes that what happened here is a coincidence? Putting Miss Peter's death on one side for a moment, we have three apparent accidents inside a week. Two of which occurred in this very building and all of which were incredible to say the least."

Charlie, who hadn't slept in several days, was the first to speak.

"I think there can be only one explanation detective. I've been racking my brain trying to invalidate it but there's only one scenario that makes sense. Leonard and I have spent several hours going over it this morning and I think I'm confident in saying that we're both on the same page." Lord glanced over at Darville who simply nodded his head.

"And what would that explanation be?" Asked Lord.

"Well," Charlie continued, in a voice almost completely drained of emotion.

"You may remember when Dan Foster scrutinised the logs looking for a trail that the hacker might have left behind, the only anomaly he could find was that Alex Fox loaded some very large files into our backup simulator. I believe he loaded a highly modified version of COGNOS and set it running."

"Whoa. Slow down," said Lord. "Can someone explain to me what the hell COGNOS is and how it relates to our problem here?"

Charlie looked over the INFOSEC guys who nodded for him to continue, no expression betraying their state of mind. Lantini, on the other hand, resembled a trembling volcano. Charlie walked Lord through an overview of the project and what he thought Alex had done and why he had done it.

"So you're telling me that we've released a sort of rogue computer program and it's backfired on us?" Asked Lord, struggling to take it all in.

Charlie rubbed his eyes. "Unfortunately it's much more serious than that but essentially correct. I think that Ric was involved in helping Alex gather the data he needed and possibly Mary was drawn in also."

"Now just hang on a minute." Lord said. "I thought I was the sceptic here! Are you saying that this VIWAP thing crashed the plane and killed all of those people because it wanted Mary Peters dead?"

"I think so, yes." Said Charlie, looking down.

Unable to contain himself any longer, Lantini jumped to his feet

"Holy mother of God! If this gets out we'll be crucified! How the hell could this happen?"

Darville spoke for the first time.

"Jack, sit down for Christ's sake. We've been working on this thing for four damn years. It looks like one of our people had the breakthrough we'd hoped for. Hell, that you demanded. He unfortunately didn't appear to have followed procedure and it's just possible that we're seeing the consequences."

Lord held up a hand to Lantini and the two INFOSEC men who suddenly looked like they were in danger of having a stroke simultaneously. Obviously this was going way beyond what they were comfortable releasing. A thought flew across Charlie's mind, my God, they hadn't even made that connection yet. Lord was staring intently at Charlie.

"Let's suppose you're right. Just how bad is this thing" he said in a quiet voice. Charlie appeared to be wrestling with himself just to stay on his feet.

"If my theory is correct, it's potentially the most dangerous weapon the United States has ever created. It's out of our hands, it's primed, and it's pointed directly back at us."

CHAPTER 10

Revelation that the project may have spiralled out of control triggered a chain of events. The INFOSEC officers made their report and within twelve hours a response team arrived. The brief sounded simple: Ensure that the premises are safe for staff and that integrity is restored to all systems. Achieving this target would prove to be slightly more complex: Evacuate the building. Physically separate all external network connections. Ensure the safety of key staff while every system is shut down and cleansed. All data storage to be reinitialised. Each computer to be reloaded with its appropriate operating system and then brought back on line. Work files are then to be reloaded, following which the system in question is to be shut down again. When every system has been cleansed in this way, the entire network is restarted.

The response team is ruthlessly efficient. The process will take ten days, the last three devoted to testing and verification. Alex Fox's workstation and all of his files will be removed. These will be examined separately. The building will be swept for hidden listening devices and most of the offices are scheduled to be repainted while they are empty. The carpets will even be replaced during the closure. When it's over, The Factory will be pronounced fit for duty and, except for a section of the ground floor that is being refitted, will be ready for business as usual. Perhaps even more importantly, to those who work here, the building will give every indication of having been swept clean by the time they return. With its new colour scheme and carpets it will look uncontaminated and fresh. The department psychologists understand the power behind these visual indicators, so much more significant than anything that can be said.

Two DoD psychologists are brought in and installed in a small vacant office downtown. While the response team carries out its mission, most staff are given two weeks paid leave and all will have at least one session with a psychologist during that time. Some will truly benefit from the sessions; most will simply see the attendance requirement as a small price to pay for an unexpected vacation.

* * *

Detective John Lord sits at his usual place in the Ann Arbor Police Department, his feet resting on top of the battered phone books next to his desk. He slams onto the desktop the official DoD letter that arrived in the post this morning, "I tell you Lou, this whole thing is gonna get swept right under the Godamn carpet."

"How you figure?"

"The place is crawling with DoD guys over there. They've been going at it for three days straight so far, twenty-four hours a day. By the time they're finished, that place will be cleaner than a Baptist revival. Yes, sir, nothing to see here. A few system malfunctions in the past but just-as-good-as-new now. Shit! It makes me boil."

Louis picked at a piece of lint on his sleeve. "We've still got three dead guys and a plane crash."

"We've got Jack Shit Lou." Lord responded, kicking the phone books and starting to pace around the small room that serves as their second home. "What we've got are accidents, industrial accidents. Happens all the time. Nobody's fault! Machine on the fritz, game over. Sorry, pal. And a plane crash! Shit! We'll be lucky to get the report on that one inside two years! Christ, it'll take 'em the first year just to put all the bits back together."

"What about Ganderton's idea about this VIPER thing?"

"VIWAP." Corrected Lord. "You saw the state of that guy, Lou. The poor bastard could hardly stand from anxiety and lack of sleep.

They've put him out on stress leave for Christ's sake. By the time they've finished fumigating that damn building, whatever the truth *was* will be cleaned away with the VIWAP and the rest of the crap in the place. And the thing that pisses me off? Even if Ganderton's right, where's the damn crime? We can't prosecute a piece of flaky software! At best we could have Alex Fox for negligence or whatever, but the guy's one of the victims for God's sake."

"So where's that leave us?"

"Pissing into the wind 'ol buddy. Just where they want us. One thing's for sure, if we breathe a word of this to anyone else, our careers are finished. They made that pretty damn clear to the Old Man. Put the fear of God into the old guy with all their bullshit about National Security."

"Look on the bright side, JL," Louis responded, trying to lighten the mood. "Case closed on three deaths inside of a week. Won't do our figures no harm."

"The department might have it closed but I sure as hell don't add it up that way." Lord walked to the window and watched the leisurely traffic flow three floors below. "No, we just keep our eyes and ears open, Lou. See what happens. My gut tells me that we're not out of the damned woods yet."

* * *

Elizabeth and her old friend Lily sit opposite each other across the small table in Elizabeth's kitchen. The meal over, Charlie has just stepped out of the room to make a pit stop and Elizabeth seizes on her chance to speak to Lily alone.

"So what do you think?" She whispers.

There's a mischievous twinkle in Lily's eye as she leans conspiratorially across the table. "What about? The weather, the price of gas? What?"

"Don't be a pain! You know what I mean!"

"He's a peach. If you get tired of him you just point him in my direction."

"Don't even think about it, girlfriend! I've already put my stake in the ground here."

"Oooh" Lily teases. "Sounds like he's been the one putting the stake in."

Elizabeth's face colours but she can't help laughing at her old friend. She slaps Lily on the arm.

"You're disgusting! Trust you to say that."

"So what's the plan?"

"Well, we're taking it one step at a time. We both have some time off work and we're planning to go up to my folks' house on the lake for a few days. God knows, Charlie needs a break."

"You mean that great little love-nest on Thunder Bay?"

"The very one."

Lily begins to laugh. "Step into my parlour said the spider to the fly."

At that point Charlie walks back into the kitchen. "You two sound like a couple of school girls. I'm not sure if I'm safe alone here when you get together."

"Lily was just asking me when I was going to meet a nice man and settle down. I told her there was nothing on the radar just yet but I'm still looking."

Charlie stared at them both for a second, unsure of whether he was being set up. Before he could answer they burst out laughing and Charlie realised he was no match for the duo.

"Just wait until I get you home." He said. "But I *am* home." Elizabeth replied with a pout. Lily pretended to rise.

"Perhaps I should just slink away and let you two get on with it," she said. Now it was Charlie's turn to laugh.

"No, Lily, I think I can restrain myself for a few minutes longer. Besides, I want to pick your brains."

Lily rolled her eyes. "Story of my life. Men only ever want me for my brains. Why can't they just treat me like an object for once?"

"There's a line in there somewhere but I'm not brave enough to deliver it!" Charlie replied. Then, becoming a little more serious. "Actually I was hoping to talk to you about a problem we had at work. Someone has sent threatening messages and I was hoping you might be able to shed some light on them."

"What makes you think I might be able to help Charlie?" Lily asked.

"Well, Elizabeth has told me that your specialty is Asian culture and languages. The person sending the messages signs them as Kensei. The wording is also peculiar as if modern English is not his first language."

Lily leaned forward in her chair, her bright green eyes boring into Charlie's face.

"Can you show these messages to me?"

"Unfortunately I don't have them anymore. We're having something of a spring clean and they've been whisked away."

"Can you remember any of the details?"

"One of the messages spoke about four professions, you know, warrior, farmer, artist. I can't remember the last one."

Lily sat back and stared at the floor for a second. "I'd have to look it up but what you say rings a bell. I certainly know the name but after a few glasses of wine I'd be lucky to dredge up all the important bits. Let me do some research next week and see what I can come up with."

"That would be great. Don't spend too much time on it but if you can easily put your finger on something I'd be curious to know."

"Sure, it would be my pleasure." Lily looked at her watch.

"I might call it a night, guys, I have to get up in the morning to keep the wolf from the door. No rest for the wicked and all that."

As Lily gathers her things, Elizabeth calls for a cab and together they walk her to the street. Outside the sky is clear and the air crisp. The run of warm, clear, weather looks like continuing a while longer.

It's after midnight and the cab has left with Lily in the back seat, mildly drunk but happy. As they step back inside the apartment, Elizabeth puts her arms around Charlie's neck.

"So, do I need to call another cab for you? You don't look like you're in a fit state to drive."

"I guess I could just hunker down on the couch, now I'm a man of leisure an' all."

Elizabeth, looking up, kisses him on the neck. "Oh, I think we can find a more accommodating scenario for you than that." She leads him by the hand toward the bedroom door.

* * *

Next morning Charlie wakes and is momentarily unsure of where he is. As memories of the previous evening return, he reaches across the bed for Elizabeth before realising she is up already. The smell of bacon is a sudden reminder that he's famished. Slipping into Elizabeth's robe he ventures into the kitchen. Elizabeth turns as she hears him enter.

"Good morning, cutie. You look very sexy in that pink robe."

It strikes Charlie that it's been a long time since anyone spoke to him like this. It feels nice. He could get used to it. He walks to the stove and puts his arms around her, inhaling the smell of her hair.

"Ah, domestic bliss," he teases.

"I expect nothing less in return." She says, stepping out of his embrace and putting the eggs and bacon onto wholemeal toast. Charlie sits at the table, pulling the robe closed as it threatens to reveal his nakedness underneath. Elizabeth smiles as she notices this small display of modesty out of the corner of her eye.

"I am just starving this morning. That smells so good."

Elizabeth puts the plates on the table and they eat together contentedly without feeling the need to make small talk. Eventually Elizabeth breaks the silence with the subject that she's been waiting for the right moment to raise.

"How do you feel about being put on stress leave at The Factory, Charlie."

Charlie puts down his fork. "You know, I'm not really sure. There's part of me that resents the implication that I've cracked up in some way. There's another part of me that just wants a rest from it all. I guess the part that wants the rest wins."

"You don't think they're trying to sideline you in some way?"

"Oh, I think that's part of it. The speech I made about the rogue VIWAP nearly caused the INFOSEC guys to have a coronary. They'll probably never forgive me for saying that stuff in front of the detectives. I guess I was at the end of my rope that day. Anyway, the only way they can sort of sweep it under the carpet is to say that I'd momentarily taken leave of my senses I suppose."

"That's bullshit and they know it!" snapped Elizabeth.

"Maybe they're right. I was pretty whacked by the time we had that meeting. Who knows. It all sounds a bit imaginary now, even to me."

Elizabeth gave Charlie a prolonged stare.

"Don't tell me that you're starting to have doubts Charlie. Leonard believed you, I believe you. It's the only explanation that makes any sense."

"That's true but there are still so many unanswered questions, even if we allow my theory to be true."

"Maybe so but don't let them get to you, Charlie. You've got a superb mind, you just need to have more confidence in your intuition. You may have been tired but your brain was still putting two and two together and getting the right answer. Please don't let them convince you of anything else, otherwise they win. Your mind is what makes you so special, Charlie, it's your greatest asset. Christ, it's what they pay you for. *You* have to believe that. They can only mess with your head if you allow them to. You can't let that happen, Charlie. You just can't."

Charlie ran his fingers through his hair, which was still dishevelled from sleep. "I know you're right. Thanks for the pep talk. I just hope that the VIWAP code is erased with what they're doing out at work now."

"You think there's a chance it won't be?" asked Elizabeth in alarm.

"I'm not sure. I still don't know how it got out of the simulator and into the main networks. To allow that possibility is to attribute a level of ingenuity and intelligence way beyond what we ever hoped for. And the plane crash that killed Mary? To manipulate the systems involved requires a comprehensive understanding of air traffic control protocols and the airport's system architecture. We basically designed the VIWAP to break things. Its capability to manipulate systems is relatively primitive. In the cold light of day, even I'm struggling to believe this could be any more than an incredible coincidence."

Elizabeth was quiet for a moment. "You don't know what Alex did. You said yourself that the two of you were having trouble communicating. Who knows what he might have developed."

"I guess we might never find out. Maybe we'll know more after the briefing in Washington."

"That's so typical. They put you on three weeks stress leave and then two weeks later expect you to fly to Washington and take part in a high level analysis. Christ! Talk about wanting your cake and eating it too."

"Could be worse. I thought they might fire me at first. Someone has to take the blame, that's how it works."

"If they fire you, they're even more stupid than I imagined."

Charlie smiled. "Not that anyone could accuse you of being biased or anything."

Charlie looked at his watch only to realise that he's not wearing it. Catching his glance, Elizabeth offers the time.

"Gotta run. I have an appointment for lunch." Charlie said, rising from his chair.

"I hope she can't make breakfast as well as me" Elizabeth teased.

"*Nobody* makes breakfast as well as you." Charlie called over his shoulder as he headed for the shower.

* * *

John Lord and his partner are working in silence at their desks. Every few minutes one of them grumbles about the mountain of paperwork that plagues their lives as police officers. Lord finds it especially irritating as he works on the files for the deaths of Dan Foster and Ric Montez. While there will still be a military inquiry into the incidents, it's pretty clear to Lord that the finding in both cases will be accidental death with no contributing person or persons. Leonard runs a tight ship, thinks Lord. All of the records are in order regarding scheduled system maintenance inspections etc. As far as Lord is concerned, this makes the whole thing stink even worse. Eventually Lord can stand it no longer. He tosses down his pen and props his feet up on his makeshift footstool.

"You know what really drives me nuts about this whole fiasco?"

"Ah, let me guess. You don't get the girl in the end?" Louis replies.

"Nope. What drives me nuts is the fact that whichever way you look it doesn't add up."

Louis sighs and caps his own pen, any thoughts of concluding the arduous paperwork tussle banished.

"How you figure?"

"Let's just go with the nutty doctor's theory for a minute."

"You mean the VIPER did it?"

"Yes, let's suppose the VIPER did it. If it was Alex Fox's brain scan that provided the canvas for the VIWAP, how come Alex was the first guy killed? And after topping *himself*, if you get my drift, why then Montez? I mean, I can understand Foster, he was pretty much the enemy. You know, trying to flush the VIWAP out of the computer an' all. But why go to all the trouble of organising a plane crash to kill Mary Peters? It doesn't add up I tell you."

"Maybe these folks were a threat to the VIPER."

"Maybe. Good theory, Lou. But how so? That's what I want to know. I just want one damned angle that adds up here. You know what this reminds me of Lou."

"No, but I be thinkin' you're gonna tell me."

"When I was kid my old man gave me one of those Hungarian puzzles. You know, the ones that you twist and they have little coloured squares on 'em."

"A Rufus Cube or something."

"That's it, a Rubiks cube. Anyway, when I take it out of the wrapper it's all perfect, every colour on every side correct. The old man grabs it off me and twists the bejesus out of it then gives it back and tells me that I'll *never* get it right again. Then he just laughs and walks away. Jesus, I was pissed at him. Not for messing up the puzzle but because he believed I couldn't do it. Anyway, that's not the point. The point is that I nearly busted a gut trying to get that thing right. Tried for weeks. Every time the old bastard went by and saw me struggling he'd laugh. The thing with those stupid puzzles is that just when you think you have it figured, you end up with one or two damned squares wrong and you have to start all over. That's what this case is turning into."

Louis was silent for a moment. "You ever figure it out? The Rubik's Cube?"

"No but I got the old man back. I peeled off the little coloured squares and then stuck them back in the right places, so it looked as though I'd solved it. Then I stuck it in his face."

"You sly bastard! What he say?"

"He just grunted and asked who solved it for me. I was so mad and ashamed that I'd cheated just to show him that I ran out of the room and bawled my eyes out."

"And now you're a cop and get paid for solving puzzles. I reckon there's shrinks would wet themselves over that."

Lord shook his head, as if to clear it. "Just a bit harder to cheat on this puzzle, Lou." he said.

"Maybe not. Perhaps you gotta go talk to the Doc."

"Ganderton?"

"Sure, why not?"

"'Cos the case is closed for one thing, Lou. You saw the letter from the department. Done and dusted"

"I dunno, JL. Man meets another man in a bar. Has a few beers. Get's to talkin.' You know how it goes. Our man gotta unload himself some. Ease the pressure."

Lord looked at his partner thoughtfully for a few moments. "You're one sneaky brother, you know that?" Lord stroked his chin. "Could happen. I wonder where our Doctor Ganderton goes to relax...."

* * *

When Charlie leaves Elizabeth's apartment he heads toward the University of Michigan to meet Ed Furneaux at a small café. Most of the IT staff at The Factory know that the best and cheapest food is to be found on campus.

"Hey, Charlie!"

He spots Ed at a table toward the rear of the crowded café and threads his way through laughing students and waitresses with trays of beer and white wine.

"Good to see you, Ed." he says, taking his seat at the minuscule aluminium table. "How's things at The Factory?"

"Not too bad, Charlie. The first few days went pretty well and they've told me I'm not needed today which is great. I actually had my compulsory session at the shrink this morning so at least that's out of the way. I'm just hoping now that I can get the rest of next week off, but I doubt it."

"I guess you're one of the few people that they need in there."

"Yeah, I'm sure they could do the whole job without me but it would take longer."

The waitress approached and the two men hastily scanned the menu before giving her their order.

"So how was the psychologist?" Charlie asked when the waitress moved out of earshot.

"Actually, Charlie, she was very good. I didn't think there'd be much value in going but when I started talking to her about Dan's death I almost broke down. She was really great and I left feeling a whole lot better. I might even go back for another session."

"That's good to hear. I have an appointment tomorrow morning and I must say I haven't been looking forward to it at all."

"Well, all I can say is that it was good for me."

Their conversation was interrupted by a young woman with a shaved head and a blue badge announcing that she was named Amanda, bringing them two beers. After a toast to the future, Charlie spoke quietly. "Have they made any progress on the VIWAP stuff?"

Ed glanced around the room before answering as if he expected someone could be eavesdropping.

"Actually they think they know how it escaped the simulator, but I'm not supposed to tell anyone so this is between you and me. Right?"

Charlie leaned forward. "Sure Ed, of course."

"Well, when we looked at the auto backup system, some of the cartridges were in the wrong locations, as if they'd been exchanged."

"Someone swapped them?"

"No. The log files would have shown anyone opening the panels to the unit. Nobody touched it."

Charlie opened his mouth to speak but it was a few seconds before the words emerged as his mind grappled with the alternative. "They think the VIWAP seized control of the backup system and used it to copy itself onto another network by manipulating the cartridges?"

"That's exactly what they think."

"But that's impossible. Come on, Ed. Surely?"

"That's what I said but when you think about it, all of the documentation to the backup system is online, including the complete command set and cartridge mapping charts. The backup system is the only thing that links the simulators to any other system. And the cartridges *have* been transposed. They figure that on the next backup cycle the tapes would have been put back and no one would have ever known."

Charlie simply stared at Ed, lost for words. Eventually he spoke. "But Ed, that means two things. Firstly, the DoD guys believe the VIWAP is responsible for what happened at The Factory, and second, they believe that its capacity for learning and environmental adaptation is way beyond anything we could have foreseen."

"That's what it looks like Charlie."

Charlie flopped back in his chair. "Shit."

"Exactly."

Ed checked the room again and lowered his voice to a whisper. "And I'll tell you something else, Charlie, and you better take this to the grave with you. I think they knew that Alex was working on this stuff privately. I think they *expected* this to happen."

PART TWO

"It is clear that while information may be used as a weapon, strategists must use it with caution and common sense. It is not a silver bullet weapon. Rather, the strategist should plan the use of the information weapon in conjunction with more traditional weapons and employ it as a precursor weapon to blind the enemy prior to conventional attacks and operations."

Whitehead, Y. L., (Maj. USAF), "Information as a Weapon: Reality Versus Promise," *Airpower Journal,* Vol. 11, No. 3, Fall 1997.

ANN ARBOR CHRONICLE

Local News

A spokesman for the Government Document Repository on East William Street indicated today that it was now business as usual following two tragic accidents at the facility. The spokesman, who declined to be named, told this reporter that an overhaul of systems and procedures would prevent future occurrence of what he termed "breaches of guidelines" that resulted in the recent tragic deaths of two employees. "I'm confident that our previous exemplary safety record will be restored," he said

CHAPTER 11

Eight thousand miles away on the edge of the East China Sea, the Chinese Datong Class submarine *Yichun* slips almost silently through the frigid darkness. After five years of covert construction in the shipyards of Tianjin, the five hundred-and-twenty foot *Yichun* is on her maiden voyage with Captain and crew proud of her capabilities and restless to test her systems. The brief on this first voyage is simple. Stay on patrol for sixty days and return without being detected. In the case of contact with other vessels, track and evade.

The modern nuclear-powered submarine is among the most complex machines that man has ever assembled. *Yichun* represents the culmination of years of research, espionage, and experimentation. The development cost of this high tech weapons platform is considerably greater than the Gross National Product of many nations. The cost per vessel is greater than the defence budgets of all but the world's largest economies. All of this cost pales against the potential advantage of marine superiority. To be able to slip into and out of any port. To steal within striking distance of any target and retreat without trace. This is the capability that submariners dream of but, to date, could only approximate. Until now.

The secret Datong Class represents the pinnacle of Chinese submarine technology. She is a superb weapons platform carrying 18 Dragon II Sub Surface to Air missiles, 36 Maoxing class torpedoes and other classified weapons systems. The Vertical Launch System aboard *Yichun* is revolutionary. The two-stage Dragon II missiles can be fired from any depth and therefore eliminate the vulnerability that most modern submarines suffer because of the requirement to be at periscope-depth for missile launch.

Captain Tze, along with his masters in Beijing, eagerly await his first contact with US submarines or anti-submarine aircraft. According to their research, handled correctly, *Yichun* should be practically undetectable to the Ohio Class US submarines. Needless to say, the captain is anxious to prove this reckoning as well as his own skill as a submariner. Many are the times he has limped away in frustration after being pinged by the superior technology of the Americans while commanding the obsolete Romeo Class boats. While admiring the technological advances made by the American designers, Captain Tze has longed for a fair fight. At last he has a real chance to pit his skills against the best the world has to offer in this marvel of Chinese ingenuity.

"Not any more my American friends, not any more," he says under his breath.

Although capable of 35 knots plus, the massive steel fish glides unhurriedly in the indigo depths, making only the speed necessary to maintain direction as she enters the Pacific Ocean, the Japanese island of Yaku-Shima slipping away on her port side. Her Pressurised Water Reactor can produce enough water and oxygen to permit a well provisioned crew to exist for six months without surfacing. Her black silicone-like outer skin slips through the water with less friction than two ice cubes sliding over each other. The well-trained crew go about their duties silently, the rubber-coated steel walls and walkways inside deadening any accidental contact. In a submarine this silent, the humans inside represent the greatest threat to the cloak of invisibility.

Yichun has been on patrol now for thirty-three days. Several vessels, mostly commercial, have passed within striking distance. Ten days ago, the Chinese destroyer *Shenzhen* tracked directly overhead, towing an anti-submarine warfare detection array as the crew remained motionless in their sleek killing machine three hundred feet below. Captain Tze took great pleasure in the knowledge that the fate of the potent ship above him rested in his hands. Even though Chinese surface vessels had been placed on alert during this exercise, the warship hadn't detected *Yichun* and he could have sunk the six-thousand ton warship easily had she been an enemy destroyer.

So far, almost everything has gone smoothly during the shakedown voyage. The crew are becoming accustomed to the vessel's systems, and life on board is vastly superior to anything they have experienced in their careers underwater so far. The captain would dearly like to play a little cat-and-mouse with his American counterparts but his orders preclude this and he will not be looking for trouble on this voyage. Inside *Yichun*, the crew at the communications displays sit in comfortable well-lit surroundings, their eyes and ears locked into the vessel's systems. At a depth of five hundred feet, the ocean is always dark.

The tranquil scene is suddenly shattered, the men snapping to attention. The main Active Sonar display spits out a line of text and figures, which immediately begin to flash in orange indicating the signature of a recognised aircraft approaching overhead. The Senior Active Sonar operator informs the captain immediately. Captain Tze has taken to walking around his boat and spending time with his men at the various stations throughout the submarine. Normally his position would be in the Control Room but the captain is keen to get to know the men on this first voyage together with his boat and so uses every opportunity to move around.

Taking up position behind him, the captain whispers to the Sonar operator to provide range and bearing. Under his uniform, a small trickle of sweat runs down the operator's back as he relays the details. American P-3C anti-submarine aircraft flying at fifteen hundred feet. One turboprop engine out of four shut down to conserve fuel. On routine patrol, the Captain thinks to himself. Here we go. The revolutionary thousand-yard sonar array being towed behind the submarine has located the aircraft while it is still fifty miles away. The aircraft will track directly overhead. The captain orders silent running. The submarine is now drifting silently in the negligible current.

At this depth it isn't possible for the crew to hear the aircraft and so their entire sensory focus is on their instruments. At its current speed, the aircraft will pass over them in eight minutes. The general alert goes out to all the crew who slip wordlessly into their stations. As the minutes tick by, the only sound is the gentle hum of the ventilators and the breathing of the men. There is an unspoken but palpable tension inside the Sonar room. The P-3C is purpose-built for detecting submarines and its Magnetic Anomaly Detection systems are capable of revealing any craft that this crew has operated before.

A smile crosses the captain's face as the aircraft passes directly overhead. The game has changed. No longer do the Americans have the upper hand in this undersea ballet. He feels a rush of satisfaction that he could not translate into words. The technical miracle of invisibility. His smile rapidly turns into a frown as the instruments show the aircraft changing direction and losing altitude. Sixty seconds later it's obvious to everyone in the Sonar room that the P-3C has reduced speed, settled into a giant circle above them and has dropped to five hundred feet. Impossible, the Captain thinks. No technology exists that could find us at this depth from an aircraft. After all this time, surely the American technology is not still so superior that they can detect his boat so effortlessly? Surely all of their efforts haven't been in vain? He refuses to accept what seems obvious, that his superb vessel has been spotted. His anger threatens to overwhelm the normally reserved and cautious seaman.

Before he can decide on his next move, multiple alarms sound inside the submarine. He physically jumps at the sound as it carves through the silence and order of his vessel. The hands of the seamen controlling the Active Sonar dance over their consoles. The Americans have dropped three airborne torpedoes into the water. The systems aboard *Yichun* identify the acoustic signatures as MK-48's, torpedoes capable of 30 knots and carrying six-hundred-and-fifty pound high explosive warheads. Two of them have already acquired *Yichun* with their active targeting systems and are closing rapidly.

The captain is completely unprepared for the aggression and haste of the Americans. His brain is struggling to comprehend the fact that they have found him so quickly and are now moving without hesitation to destroy his beautiful vessel. No attempted contact, no warning. Not even the dropping of electronic Sonobuoys which would be the expected procedure for an unknown contact. And he is now in international waters! He gives the order for full speed. No logic in hiding any longer. The giant turbines powered by their nuclear reactor begin to rotate faster and the submarine accelerates swiftly, making a hard turn to starboard as it does. Electronic countermeasures are released into the water, generating immense amounts of electronic noise and bubbles in an attempt to distract the torpedoes. In sixty seconds the entire voyage has been turned into a fight for survival.

The captain pulls himself to his full height. "Flood deck tubes one and two and arm the missiles." The executive officer hesitates for a fraction of a second before relaying the order. He engages the captain's stare. Resolve blazes in the captain's eyes. We are being unlawfully fired upon, we will respond with deadly force. When the weapons are ready and the firing solution has been determined, the captain gives the order to launch. This will be the first time the Dragon IIs have been released from their underwater pens outside of carefully controlled and guarded tests.

As the torpedoes close on *Yichun*, the missiles spiral up toward the surface creating a massive convection trail behind them. The problems associated with launching missiles from this depth, notably the noise generated by their underwater stage which can betray the submarine's position, are the last thing Captain Tze has on his mind as he fights for the very survival of his boat and crew. Fifteen seconds later they break the surface, their rocket engines ignite and the missiles scream into the night sky searching for the enemy with one thought in their cold and merciless electronic brains: Destruction.

Inside the submarine it becomes obvious that the torpedoes will strike within ten seconds. The captain braces himself on the overhead pipe-work as the Sonar operator counts down. Abruptly, the torpedoes and the circling aircraft disappear from the displays and silence returns to the submarine. The stillness following the sirens and warning alarms is strangely disorienting. The seamen frantically adjust and recalibrate their equipment but to no avail. In an instant the aircraft has disappeared and so have the torpedoes. The captain's mind is racing, trying to comprehend what has occurred. The only explanation possible is a malfunction of their new electronic systems. The training module somehow activated itself or was activated inadvertently. There was no aircraft, the entire episode was a simulation, hence the uncharacteristic aggression of the American crew. The pieces rapidly fall into place in the captain's agile mind.

In the night sky the Dragon II missiles race on, searching

unrelentingly for the prey that their internal systems have promised them. Ninety seconds later, with no target in sight and having attained an altitude of twenty-five thousand feet, their automatic self-destruct mechanism activates and both weapons detonate with a blast that lights up the ocean like daytime and that can be seen with the naked eye for three hundred miles in every direction. The explosions are registered by multiple satellites, both commercial and military, by two commercial long-haul 747s, by ships at sea, and by scores of astronomers in Japan.

In the submarine the captain stands with his eyes closed as the echoes of the explosions reverberate through every space in the vessel. Nobody speaks. The enormity of what he has just done begins to settle on him. He orders the vessel back to port and with darkness stealing into his heart, returns to his cabin to try to make sense of what has occurred. Already he knows that his career is over. His family disgraced, his country's national security possibly compromised. And for him, even if he escapes prison he will never escape court-marshal. In that second he makes his decision. He will return his vessel to port and choose the only honourable option left to him as a soldier.

* * *

One second after the rocket engines of the Dragon II missiles ignite, three US satellites record the light burst against the black surface of the ocean. Forty-five seconds later, a DoD computer has determined that the missile's signature has not been recorded previously. Following the missile explosions, military computers are calculating the altitude and payload of the devices even before the debris hits the sea.

Eight minutes later a pair of P-3C Sub Hunters have altered course to begin a search. Four minutes after that a flight of F-14 Tomcat jet fighters is scrambled from the deck of the USS *Carl Vinson* to investigate the source of the disturbance. The carrier battle group on exercises in the Pacific is diverted toward the source of the detonation and is put on full alert.

Thirty minutes later, the president of the United States, Commander-in-Chief of the US armed forces is woken from his sleep and briefed on the developments.

***

Elizabeth and Charlie are relaxing on the front porch of the tiny cabin. The evening is mild and the rough timbers of the porch are thrown into relief as the shadows lengthen. The drive down was pleasant and they chatted comfortably. One of the things that Charlie was beginning to love about spending time with Elizabeth was that she was so easy to be with. He didn't feel any pressure to be anything other than who he was. Also, not once did she mention his Porsche. They had the top down and she obviously enjoyed the feeling of it but she was neither impressed nor cynical. She just accepted it for what it was and simply took pleasure in the experience. This little thing struck Charlie as surprisingly refreshing. He felt like a king with her sitting in the passenger seat, basking in the sunshine like a cat.

The water of Lake Huron laps only a few yards from where they sit and the sun has just dipped below the horizon. The cry of a loon carries to them across the water. Other than the splash of an occasional fish jumping at an insect skimming the surface, they sit in silence. Elizabeth has her head snuggled into Charlie's shoulder and, as he takes a sip of his wine, he wishes the moment could last forever.

"How long have your folks had this place?" he asks.

"Oh, I don't know. As long as I can remember. I used to come here as a little girl. They don't use it that much any more but I can imagine you and I escaping here from time to time."

"I could definitely get used to this," Charlie said.

Elizabeth sighed, her breath warming Charlie's neck. "I think it's good for us to get away together. This place always helps me to forget the pressures of regular life. I don't think it's possible to stay stressed here."

Charlie kissed Elizabeth on the forehead. "It sure seems to be working for me."

"Hungry?" asks Elizabeth, sitting up.

"Famished!"

"Why don't I get started on dinner and you can serenade me."

"Sounds like an equitable division of labour to me," says Charlie, finishing the last of his wine. The two go inside to the small but well-equipped kitchen and Elizabeth starts to unpack the vegetables that she'll turn into a pasta sauce. Charlie flops on the couch opposite after ensuring that they both have full glasses of the great Australian Cabernet that he recently found. It occurs to Charlie that it's been a long time since he's felt so happy. He knows that it's due to Elizabeth and feels incredibly lucky that their orbits aligned. Lucky *is* the word, thinks Charlie. If I hadn't taken this job or if Elizabeth had accepted one of the other offers she had at the time, we would never have met. Many things in our lives balance on a knife edge, he reminded himself.

Elizabeth stops and looks up from her preparations. "Charlie, can I talk about one work thing for a moment?" They have agreed not to dwell on the activities of The Factory while they enjoy these four days together at the lake.

"Sure. I'll grant you a Papal Dispensation for this one time only."

"Thanks. It's just that I had a chat with Lily the other day and I keep forgetting to tell you about it. She did a little research on your Kensei character and found some information."

Charlie wasn't entirely sure he wanted to talk about this right now but he didn't want to inject a negative into their evening by making a stand on it either.

"What did she find out?"

"Well, the most famous Kensei was a warrior, a *Ronin*, I think she called him. I guess like a Samurai. His name was Miyamoto Musashi but he's known in Japan as Kensei, which means The Sword Saint. Not sure why. Anyway, he wrote an instruction book in sixteen hundred and something for Japanese Warriors. The book is called *The Book of Five Rings* although Lily said a more accurate description would be *The Book of Five Spheres*. Anyway, the book was discovered in recent years and has become something of a bible for businessmen. You know how those men in suits are, imagining themselves as warriors engaged in battle and all that crap. Kensei's book is all about the science of warfare and lethal assault."

Charlie put down his glass and sat up on the couch. "The science. Interesting. So what else did she say about this Kensei guy?"

"Lily said that he was a very skilled warrior who eventually became sort of unemployed due to the oppression of the ruling Shogun at the time. Apparently he wasn't alone in this. Seems some of the unemployed Samurai became schoolteachers or priests but our man became a dueller and also a martial arts teacher."

"Was he good?"

"Lily said he was invincible. I think she said he killed almost seventy men starting when he was only thirteen years old. Apparently, towards the end of his career, or whatever you call it in the Samurai world, he started fighting with a stick instead of a sword."

"A stick?"

"Yes, a wooden stick. You know, the sort of thing they might use for practice. And he was so good he still killed everyone he fought even though they had swords. Lily also said he didn't ever comb his hair or wash. He didn't ever settle down anywhere or take a wife. He seemed to be a bit of an ascetic. Probably a stinky one, I'm thinking."

Charlie pondered on what sort of meaning this could have. "So what's a *Ronin*. Did Lily say?"

"She said that was the name for these Samurai who had lost their masters for some reason and became kind of wanderers. Maybe like a gun for hire. Or is that *sword* for hire?" Elizabeth asked, chuckling at her own corny pun. "Anyway, apparently these guys became quite a social problem. Some of them turned to crime and caused a hell of a disturbance. An interesting story, don't you think?"

"Absolutely. I'm not quite sure where it fits in or what to make of it. Thanks for letting me know though."

Later that night, with Elizabeth sleeping soundly by his side, Charlie lay awake listening to the sounds of the lake and thinking about what Lily had said. Something was tugging at the back of his mind but he couldn't seem to form it into a thought. Something that he'd seen. A picture maybe. Something that tied this new information with what he already knew. Some sort of link between things. He struggled for a while but finally gave in to the soothing sounds of the lake and fell asleep.

CHAPTER 12

The Pentagon was never an easy building to enter. Its massive size didn't help, being virtually a city in itself, home to 23,000 employees. Since 9/11, security has been increased with the formation of the Pentagon Force Protection Agency. The new agency effectively absorbed the old Pentagon's police force and doubled its size.

When he saw the size of the sixteen parking lots, Charlie was glad that they had made the decision to take a cab from the airport rather than hire a vehicle. At least this way they started out in the right spot. This place was a world away from where he and Elizabeth had spent their last few days. And not nearly as nice. Back to the real world with a vengeance, Charlie thought.

One of Charlie's DoD colleagues had told him that the building had seventeen-and-a-half miles of corridors. Another fact he'd been told and one that stuck in his mind was that the Pentagon had 284 restrooms. Charlie couldn't help calculating that the average distance between them, given the miles of corridors, (assuming random rest room distribution) was therefore approximately one-hundred and-eight-yards. As the cab threaded its way toward the entrance Charlie wondered mischievously whether this was some sort of magic number. Someone's PhD thesis on maximum distance to micturition perhaps.

The cab eventually pulled up at the Transit building and Charlie, Ed, Leonard and Christopher Witherspoon stepped out into the crisp morning air. The ride over had been uncomfortable in its silence, particularly with the four of them squashed into one cab. The truth was, none of them knew Witherspoon particularly well and what they did know of him didn't exactly endear the man to any of them. Elizabeth had told Charlie that the only reason that Withered-Spoon, as she called him, was going at all was to ensure that no blame could be attached to his department. That and being able to boast to his medical cronies that he had a meeting at the Pentagon. Ass-kisser Elizabeth had called him. That's my girl, Charlie thought with some amusement as he watched Witherspoon preening himself before entering the building.

After going through the required security screening the four men were escorted to a large, austere room housing the ubiquitous conference table and with one wall dominated by a large American flag. With some surprise, Charlie observed that the table appeared to be constructed from laminated particle board. It can't hold its own next to the granite lightning of its Factory counterpart. With the typical reserve of men in a new environment, no one was keen to choose the first seat at the conference table. Darville took the lead and selected a safe seat toward one end but not at the head of the table. The others fitted in around him. Charlie observed this little ritual with amusement.

After a few minutes of small talk, what constituted a small crowd of DoD staffers and secretaries entered the room and immediately took seats. Lantini was not present. This fact struck Charlie as curious, as did the number of people in the room for what is obviously to be a briefing on a highly classified project, but before he had time to draw any conclusions, the conference room door was thrust open. All eyes swivelled toward the sound. A tall straight-backed man with an unmistakably military bearing stepped through the door. Some of the DoD staffers started to rise but the man waved them back and took up a position at the head of the table, his back towards what looked like a massive whiteboard. His weathered face is impassive as his eyes sweep the room. Without preamble he began to address the group from The Factory.

"Good morning. I am Lieutenant-General James Chapman. Please call me Jim. The other folks here are my senior staff and their personal assistants. You can speak freely in their presence. The reason we're here is to understand what seems to be a series of tragic accidents connected with the Ann Arbor technical facility. I am aware that there are some theories circulating as to what might have caused these accidents and I want to explore these so that we can all move forward. I have been briefed to some extent by one of my staff, Major Lantini, whom I believe you have all met. Questions?"

At this stage the four visitors decide that silence is probably the appropriate response. Charlie figures Chapman must be at least six feet six tall. None of them can imagine addressing the Lieutenant-General as Jim.

"So." The three-star general continues, "I believe that Doctor Ganderton has proposed an explanation that has, how shall I put it, cast the cat among the pigeons somewhat within the department. I believe I'd like to explore this theory a little further. Doctor, would you like to recap for the benefit of the others present, and then perhaps answer some questions for us?"

Chapman was looking directly at Charlie as he addressed his remarks, causing Charlie to wonder how Chapman knew his face. He didn't have time to mull over this as all eyes were now fixed on him. Before he spoke, Witherspoon decided to interject.

"Sir, if I may just make a couple of explicatory comments..."

Chapman raised his hand to silence the interruption. "I would prefer, Doctor Witherspoon, if we could explore Doctor Ganderton's views first. If we need amplifying information as we proceed, I'll be sure to ask for it."

This together with a smile that went no farther than Chapman's lips and a steel edge to his voice offered an unmistakable warning to speak only when spoken to.

"Please continue Doctor Ganderton. Perhaps you would like to come to the front of the room so that no one gets a fold in their neck." Charlie would have been perfectly happy to stay right where he was but he obediently collected his papers and moved toward the head of the table.

Charlie gave them the reader's digest version of events without the emotion that coursed through his veins the last time he'd expounded his controversial views. He tried not to leave anything out but also not to draw too many conclusions. Charlie figured that, in this forum, it was safer to just relate the facts as he knew them rather than to postulate any theories for which he had no absolute proof. He had the distinct impression that he wasn't dealing with a friendly audience here. When he'd finished, the room was silent. At length, Chapman spoke.

"So, Doctor Ganderton, do you think that this boisterous software entity might have been subdued by the response team at the facility?"

For the first time, Charlie felt a pang of alarm. They don't take me seriously, he thought.

"I think there is a strong possibility that it may have been deactivated by the purge, assuming that it hadn't exfiltrated by then."

"Exfiltrated?" Chapman asked. "An interesting word choice, doctor. Why would that happen? I thought that one of the beauties of the hacking paradigm was that it could be done from anywhere in the world."

"Well, that's true, sir, but we're not really dealing with a hacker here. One of the VIWAP's major offensive capabilities is its mobility. It has the ability to move to a site favourable to its mission. And to relocate if endangered."

"So you're saying it could have left the facility and be anywhere in the world by now?"

"That is conceivable, sir, yes."

Chapman appeared to ponder over this information.

"Would not the fact that one week has elapsed without incident suggest to you that our roving VIWAP may in fact have been decommissioned?"

"That's certainly a conclusion that could be drawn, sir."

"But you don't think so."

"The VIWAP has state-of-the-art Artificial Intelligence built into its strategy engine. It would not be out of character for it to be active and then lay dormant for a while."

"Character? You speak about it as though it had a mind of its own."

"There comes a point in the development of AI systems where the system gives the *illusion* of being able to think for itself. To make decisions that are not entirely predictable, contra-intuitive even. The problem is, it's just an illusion. On the VIWAP program we were very close to stepping over that line."

"What line is that exactly, doctor?"

"The line that divides simulated intelligence from real intelligence."

"Are you able to define the difference for us?"

"Well, it's complex because every time we come up with a definition someone develops a system to simulate the requirements of that definition. For example, the ability to learn can be simulated. We have computers today inside automobiles that control adaptive transmissions and learn when to shift gears, based on the owner's style of driving. We also have programs that can discover the rules of a game and then become invincible players."

Chapman appeared to be interested in this concept.

"But you would say that these systems are not intelligent. Yes? Because they are following a set of rules that have been programmed into them I assume."

Charlie looked down at his hands for a second as he struggled to find words to put with his thoughts.

"It's correct to say those systems follow rules, but so do people. The rules of our upbringing are very powerful and can control and guide our life. To use the previous analogy, a truly intelligent system would be capable of creating a game of its own and then not only become a master at it but to choose when to play and when not to play, and perhaps who to play with. Creating its own rules, its own morality. Choosing sides, showing loyalty, taking risks. These capabilities become very complex and, in our application, dangerous."

"Dangerous? How so?"

"Because there must be a balance between aggression, ingenuity, stealth, and so on. We expect our weapons to be effective but we don't expect them to turn on us. Or to decide that the other side is more just and to switch allegiance. Or to evolve so much that they become uncontrollable."

"So how do you test this sort of weapon?"

"Well, sir, we design the best cage we can. We essentially build up a mini network system using the best security technologies that we have. Then we let it loose to see if it can get out. Naturally we build layers of protection to ensure that if it's successful we don't lose it all together."

Another voice from the opposite side of the table.

"Are you saying that you test this thing with the most secure technologies we have? Classified technologies?"

"Yes, sir, we have to. It's the entire point of the research, to build something that is able to defeat the best defences we possess, based on the assumption that the US is the leader in this technology. If we can defeat what we know to be the best, we should be in good shape anywhere in the world."

Chapman sat back in his chair, giving the impression that his mind was working the angles.

"So if you check on the cage and the beast has gone, you've succeeded beyond your wildest dreams?"

"That's pretty much it, sir. That's the two-edged sword. We have to test it against the best systems we have and that we know or we suspect our enemies have. It's like designing the ultimate acid. How the hell do you store the stuff if it dissolves everything?"

Chapman smiled at this metaphor and looked around the room.

"I think I've learnt a thing or two today!"

Charlie had the uneasy sense that Chapman actually knew a whole lot more about this project than he implied. He had the feeling that the discussion so far was aimed at bringing the others in the room up to speed on the project rather than extracting information. Before he could ponder the significance of this possibility, the sound of a throat being cleared towards the back of the room snapped him out of his train of thought.

One of the officers that had entered the room immediately

before Chapman spoke up.

"Doctor Ganderton. Could you explain to us how this VIWAP of yours seized control of the elevator that was responsible for the death of Alex Fox? I do assume that you believe this scenario to be correct?"

"I think it's very possible, sir."

"Okay. Perhaps you could explain to us how it might have happened."

"It's difficult to say with any certainty at this stage, sir."

"Can I take it that you don't know?"

"No, not accurately, but a remote maintenance link would be an obvious possibility."

"Are you aware, Doctor Ganderton that the elevator system was not part of any external networking system? In other words, had no access for an outside agent?"

Charlie started to get the feeling that he was on trial.

"The vast majority of these systems have a dial-in line to allow remote maintenance and troubleshooting by the equipment provider and so I had assumed this to be the point of access."

"So you would be unaware that the elevator system in Alex Fox's apartment building had no such dial-in line? That the building owner never had it installed following a dispute about the contract with the equipment vendor?"

For Charlie, the room seemed to contract. "No, I was not aware of that."

"So we must conclude that the death of Alex Fox has no relationship with the research project at the facility where he worked?"

"Without any external connection to the elevator system that would appear to be a logical conclusion, yes."

The officer paused before resuming as he consulted his notes.

"Would you be aware, doctor, of the number of accidents that result from accidental ignition of gas in laboratories worldwide each year?"

"No, I'm unaware of that figure." Charlie replied, an awful dread sitting in his stomach like a lead weight.

"How does the figure of three thousand sound to you."

"That's very surprising, actually."

"And of these three thousand accidents, approximately one hundred result in fatalities. Does that also surprise you, doctor?"

Charlie wished that the earth would open up and swallow him at this point. The agenda of the meeting became crystal-clear. He is to be discredited. His theory dismissed out of hand.

"It does surprise me, yes."

Chapman now took control of the meeting. His tone a little softer.

"Perhaps these accidents, although tragic, are simply just that. Accidents. An unfortunate series of unlinked and highly unusual events. The strain on everyone at the facility would have been enormous. Quite understandable that things get a little out of context."

Heads turn towards a new voice.

"Is it true, doctor, that you are currently on a leave of absence due to stress?"

Here we go, thought Charlie. The knife is twisted.

"Yes, I was asked to take three weeks off work."

"And would you concede that your judgement could have suffered some impairment due to the effects of that stress?"

"I still think my judgement was reliable, sir."

"But you would allow that stress takes its toll on our clear thinking ability?"

"Of course it's possible."

Chapman's body language indicated that he wanted to wrap things up.

"We have given this incident, and the project more broadly,

extensive consideration. Our decision is to terminate the program. All of the documents and working files, together with the pertinent data will be archived, pending a possible future decision to proceed.

Charlie felt winded. While it wasn't entirely unexpected, it was still awful to hear the words. He glanced over at Darville who looked beaten. His shoulders slumped. Darville spoke. "If I may be permitted to speak frankly, sir, there are a lot of highly trained folks in my facility who have put their heart and soul into this project. They will be devastated if the place is closed down."

Chapman smiled again. "Who's saying anything about closing down? Your people have done a superb job. The program has generated significant new understanding and data that we'll use to seed new research. On the contrary, Leonard, we want you to get started immediately on a new assignment."

"A new assignment?" Darville asked, taken aback.

"Yes. Major Lantini will brief you in due course on the detail but it basically involves strengthening our position in self-protecting network technology. I think this will be right up Doctor Ganderton's alley. We're all looking forward to him returning to active duty, as it were."

Witherspoon piped up at last. "And my team? What is…."

"We have something in mind for the medical squad, doctor. Don't worry," Chapman replied.

Charlie felt completely at sea with the way the meeting was panning out. "May I ask a question, sir?"

Chapman gave him his best mouth-only smile. "Certainly doctor."

"What about the VIWAP."

"We consider the probability that the probe escaped the facility to be close to zero. The unfortunate accidents are coincidental. The computer systems and files at the facility have been cleansed and all traces of the research has been removed and stored securely. I don't think we have anything to worry about as we move forward. This is classified information and you will not disclose it. I will be recommending several staff members for a service award, including you Doctor Ganderton. The work your people have done is excellent. The current climate is not one in which we wish to pursue this particular research. This is not negotiable and is my final word on the matter."

As if to punctuate his words, Chapman looked up and clapped his hands together. "That's it, folks. Thank you for attending this morning. Enjoy the rest of your day and have a good weekend." Then, turning to Charlie and his colleagues, "I'll have an officer escort you to the foyer, gentlemen. Major Lantini will be in touch. Thankyou for the briefing." Chapman shook hands with each of them, pivoted on his heel and exited as abruptly as he had entered.

* * *

An hour later, the four men are sitting in a quiet corner near the window in a bar at the Washington National Airport overlooking the Potomac River. Having been lost in their own thoughts during the cab ride to the airport, Charlie, now nursing a cold Michelob, is the first to speak. "What the hell happened in there, Leonard?"

Darville shook his head. "I know what happened, I've seen it before but I'm not sure *why* it happened, Charlie. We seemed to have been given a pat on the back while they blew smoke up our ass."

"It doesn't add up." Ed Furneaux said. "If our work was so good, even good enough to earn us some sort of medal, why are they shutting the project down? And what the hell is *the climate* that he was talking about? I would have thought that the climate now is even more conducive to our research than before. And the hacker. What about the hacker? We expected a witch-hunt but the hacker didn't even get a mention! I figured those INFOSEC guys would have us for breakfast over that one. Shit! I just don't get it."

Charlie looked at Ed and started to speak. "Yes and what you told.." He stopped suddenly. In his frustration Charlie had almost blurted out the confidential information that Ed had given him over lunch last week. He made a show of retracting the comment saying it was nothing and mentally chided himself for almost breaking a confidence. On the other hand, Ed *had* confided in him and the story he told didn't line up with the actions that Chapman had taken to kill the project. Still, not the sort of problem to try and solve with a beer in one hand, Charlie thought.

Witherspoon, with his fingers steepled under his chin, looked thoughtful. "I wonder who else might be on the list for the commendations?"

"Who gives a shit, Christopher!" Leonard said. "I don't trust these bastards and I don't like the way they think they can just sweep four years of work under the carpet without a trace."

"Yes, of course, that." Witherspoon nodded in a way that he must have figured looked sagely but that to Charlie looked theatrical and phoney.

"I guess that was part of their task at The Factory." Charlie said.

"Get rid of all traces. It's going to be tough switching gears after all this time, Leonard."

"That's for sure. Some of our best people are only working with us because of this project. It won't be easy talking them in to staying. Jesus! What a pain in the ass."

"Are we still on track to open again on Monday?" Charlie asked, changing the subject.

"Definitely. These bastards are like clockwork. I might make a few calls over the weekend to some of our key people. Just give them a heads-up and some reassurance so they don't get this news cold on Monday."

"I'm not officially back for another week, Leonard. Do you suppose anyone would mind if I turned up too?"

"Probably better if you didn't, Charlie. They can be sticklers with this stuff. Look, I know you're fine but just humour the SOBs and stay away next week. Have yourself a vacation. It'll be business as usual soon enough."

Ed asked the question that had been foremost in all of their minds during the ride back to the airport following the meeting. "Charlie, do you think their low-probability assessment of the VIWAP threat is credible?"

"You mean, do I think the VIWAP wasn't responsible for what

went on, didn't decide to eliminate the only people who could know of its existence, didn't escape, and has been disabled by the response team?" Ed couldn't look Charlie in the face. "I guess that's what I meant, yes."

"I'm still chewing on that one, Ed. Some days it makes sense and then the next minute I'm doubting myself. The problem is that whichever way you figure it, you come up short. Nothing adds up here and the fact that the program's been swept under the carpet but we get rewarded makes no sense either. Most of my professional years have been spent in commercial businesses so maybe I don't know the military too well but I can tell you, I thought we were all going to be fired."

Darville took a pull on his Corona. "I've spent my whole life in the army, my daddy too, God rest his soul. I can tell *you* Charlie; I figured this to be the last meeting I'd ever attend. Just about got used to that feeling too. Damn!" Darville's tongue-in-cheek comment launched them all into stress-breaking laughter.

"But I agree with Charlie." Darville continued. "I can't figure what these people are up to. But I know one thing. I've spent four years working with Charlie here and that's taught me to listen when he speaks. I for one am not willing to piss away his judgement the way these smarmy bastards seem so quick to do."

Charlie felt strangely touched by Darville's comments. A new thought occurred to him. Everyone around Charlie seemed to have greater confidence in him than he had in himself. Maybe there's a lesson for me in there somewhere, he thought.

"Leonard, when you said that you had seen what they did today before, what did you mean?" Charlie asked.

Darville took a deep breath. "They're obviously trying to cover their tracks. They wanted the project buried but they didn't want any of us worrying that it might affect our careers so they gave us the pat on the back as well as a gong of some sort to keep us happy. That way nobody complains. If one of us did complain, it looks like we have no basis. They made sure that there were a few senior people present and that Charlie's theory was shown to be flawed. It was no accident that Charlie's stress leave was raised."

Witherspoon appeared to be confused. "And so what exactly was the point?"

"To leave a trail, Christopher, to leave a trail. If any of the senior people present are asked about the situation they will dismiss it as a combination of unfortunate accidents and stressed-out workers. If someone digs into the records, you can be sure that the discussion in today's meeting will surface. There must have been half a dozen aides taking notes. Each of those managers will have a record in their files and the records will all agree with the official report. Accidents, unsubstantiated allegations stemming from stress. Project shelved, employees managed appropriately, good work recognised, new project started. All nice and neat. Nothing to raise any suspicion. Nothing worth investigating."

Ed shook his head. "The assholes! I can't believe we've just played a part in their little pantomime. Christ, what a setup!"

Darville shrugged. "Unfortunately, these guys are masters of this game. I'm not sure there's any point in challenging them on this. Best for us to just move on and set about confirming our value to the department on the new project." In answer to their howls of protest, Darville raised his hands and then continued. "Yes. I know, I know. It stinks. But there it is."

Charlie says nothing but he's not sure this will end so neatly. He *is* sure that he doesn't like being taken for a patsy by these bastards. Perhaps I'll just do some of my own snooping on the side, he thinks. Charlie feels a twinge of sadness and some guilty resentment that, despite all of his tough talking, Leonard is so quick to give in to the department. Perhaps that's what happens when you work in the machine for your whole adult life. You become institutionalised, lose the will to fight.

I'll be damned if I'll let that happen to me, Charlie decided.

CHAPTER 13

In the White House, the president and his chiefs of staff are gathered for an emergency meeting. The tensions with North Korea are dominant as they try to put meaning to the events in the Pacific. This is way too close for comfort and the Japanese Government has already communicated with Washington, appealing for information. So far the Chinese are silent and no one in the room knows what to make of the explosions.

"No chance this was one of ours I guess?" the president asks, rubbing his eyes with his knuckles.

"None whatsoever." The negative response is echoed from several positions around the room and is accompanied by a good deal of head shaking.

"So what do we know?"

The secretary of defence clears his throat. "Well, sir, we're still collating the data but it appears that at 2205 hours two missiles were launched from the sea approximately four hundred miles south-east of the Japanese island of Honshu. The missiles appear to have been armed with conventional warheads and our best estimates are for one thousand pound high explosive payloads. The missiles then tracked around in a pattern that suggests they were attempting to acquire an airborne target. Ninety seconds later having achieved an altitude of approximately twenty-five-thousand feet, they both detonated within one second of each other. Our guess is it was a self-destruct."

"Why self destruct?" the president asked without lifting his head.

"Principally because our information so far shows no other airborne target of significance in that area. No aircraft, nothing. The detonation altitude and time since launch would also be consistent with that explanation."

"Could these missiles have been accidentally fired?"

"That's an explanation we favour Mr president. What is interesting is that the missile signature has not been recorded previously. It looks like a new device. Also, by chance we had a couple of P3-Cs on night patrol out of our detachment in Japan and they were in the area within fifteen minutes. We're assuming a submarine launch but there was nothing to see, not even a phosphor trail. Certainly no surface craft that could have been capable of launching a missile of this size.

"Whoa!" the president said. "So we could be looking at a new submarine *and* new ordnance?"

"That is our concern at this time, sir."

"Chinese?"

"It's obviously difficult to be sure at this stage but if we figure a new submarine program, accidental firing, in that part of the world, it's hard to go past a new boat out of the shipyards around Tianjin and the Yellow Sea."

The president shook his head. "Weapons-testing?" he asked.

"We think not. If you have a new boat and new missiles, it wouldn't be smart to launch the missiles from the boat and alert the whole world. Also, it's unlikely that anyone would select this location for secret testing. And you certainly wouldn't fire two missiles simultaneously with no target."

"Yes, yes, I get the point. A simple no would have sufficed."

"I'm sorry, Mr President."

The president massaged his temples. "Sure. I guess we're all a bit on edge tonight. Nothing like being woken out of your damned sleep to the news of bombs going off to rattle a man's cage. One thing's for sure we're going to need to keep a very close eye on this part of the world. I don't want any more surprises. Sounds like there's not a lot more we can accomplish tonight. Let's all try to get some sleep and hit this again in the morning."

* * *

It's Monday morning and The Factory is buzzing. The word has spread down from the supervisors that a new project is to start soon. This news is greeted with a variety of responses but there is one common theme. Everyone's mood has been lifted by the realisation that the building is not to be closed down and that jobs are safe for the foreseeable future. As the DoD spin doctors predicted, the new carpet and paint job have the psychological effect of making things seem new and fresh. The place even seems brighter as if the lighting has been turned up a notch. Despite the fact that almost everyone has attended multiple funerals in the last two weeks, there is an air of optimism that's contagious. The power of self-interest is very strong within the human psyche. Most people spend the day tidying up their workspaces and rehanging pictures following the response team's spring clean. That and lounging around the water coolers catching up with two weeks of gossip.

Elizabeth's office appears almost the same to her as before but not exactly so. It feels like someone has taken a photograph of the room, removed everything and then returned her stuff according to the photo. Things were close but not quite right. Like the angle of a photo frame on the desktop or that space between the wall and the bookshelf where her briefcase used to fit snugly but now is too small. Her colleagues had made similar comments. It was obvious that the building had been turned inside-out.

She is working on a replacement for Ric Montez and has a meeting scheduled with a recruitment agency for later in the week. The workmen are still bustling around on the ground level but things are starting to head toward normal.

Charlie is sitting in his apartment wishing he were back at work. It's funny how you figure that if you had more time you'd do all sorts of things but when you have the time you don't feel like doing any of them. The information from Lily still sits uncomfortably in his mind. It's irritating because at some level he knows it is important but he can't articulate why. He knows the dots need to be joined in a way that is eluding him. Charlie gazes out of his kitchen window at the rain falling steadily and is reminded of what a wonderful run of fine weather they'd been having until now. It also shocks him to realise that this instant is the first time he has even thought about the weather in the last couple of weeks. His mind has been so occupied he's just taken the sunshine for granted.

Charlie stands up abruptly and puts his coffee mug into the dishwasher. "You can't stay at home all day, Charlie boy." He says to the empty room. He decides on a trip to the local bookstore to pick up a couple of escapist novels. Nothing like a distraction when it's raining, he thinks. As he reaches for his jacket hanging on the stand by the door, his arm freezes. Charlie remembers what has been floating at the back of his mind, just out of reach since his conversation with Elizabeth at the cabin.

Alex's jacket.

Alex had been leaving The Factory for the dojo where he taught marshal arts to the local kids a couple of times a week. He stayed late and drove directly to the dojo on these days. Alex was apt to get changed into his training gear before leaving. His Ninja outfit, Elizabeth had called it. Charlie was working late and Alex had poked his head into Charlie's office to tell him he was leaving. As he turned to go, Charlie had noticed that the back of Alex's jacket had a picture on it. In Charlie's memory it was an old drawing of some sort. A Samurai warrior. There was something about that picture, Charlie was sure. Something about that picture and Lily's information. Things he had to connect. Charlie needed to see that jacket again.

* * *

In the White House, an extraordinary security briefing has been organised over lunch. Present is the president, secretary of defence, the joint chiefs of staff as well as the chiefs of staff of the navy and the air force, and the director of the defence intelligence agency.

Once again the secretary of defence is the spokesman.

"We have had several discussions with the Chinese Government, directly and through our ambassador here in Washington. They deny all knowledge of the missiles and claim, in fact, that it was one of our submarines and that we're somehow trying to flex our muscles by a display of force. They are also protesting strongly about the presence of our *Carl Vinson* carrier battle group."

"That's just bullshit." Said the chief of staff of the navy, tossing down his pen.

"Obviously, but that's their position."

The president stands and begins pacing the room. "Do we still figure the Chinese as responsible, Dan?"

"It's still our preferred theory, sir," replied the secretary of defence.

"So what the hell are they up to?"

"We're not sure but it's of great concern and threatens to further destabilise the region."

"No kidding," replied the president with a shrug. "How does the navy see this?"

"We recommend *increasing* our presence in the area and doubling the P-3C patrols out of Japan and immediately looking for that damn sub using as many S-3B Vikings and SH-60 Seahawks from USS *Carl Vinson* as we can keep in the air."

"That's quite an aggressive position to take."

"Maybe. But by the same token, we have an unknown submarine in the area with God only knows what capability launching unidentified anti-aircraft missiles into open airspace with enough punch to bring down a damn fleet of 747s. I don't think we can sit on our thumbs here while these bastards monkey around deciding what to shoot at next."

The president smiled at the old seaman's uncompromising perspective. "Point taken. What's the position of strategic command?"

"We concur with the navy, sir."

"And the intelligence community?"

"We're very concerned that we had no advance indicators of a new submarine program, if that's what we're dealing with here. Based on that assumption, right now we must consider the possibility that there have been multiple boats manufactured and that the intentions of the government behind this, China we assume at this stage, is hostile. We must also play with the scenario that in fact we're seeing a North Korean program developed with Chinese assistance."

The president shook his head, "God, I hope that's not the case. I really do."

* * *

Darville is working in his office on the second level of The Factory. After two weeks away, the constant flood of emails had backed up depressingly. With no access to email outside The Factory the messages just pile up. Darville had been at work since 7:00am and needed a break. He pushed his chair back and rolled his neck in an attempt to ease the tension that he could feel building there. It was at times like these that he wished for a window to give him a glimpse of the world outside. His phone rang.

"Hey, Charlie, how are you, my boy?"

"Pretty good, Leonard. Look, this is important. Can you talk?"

"Sure, Charlie, what's up?"

"I have to get hold of a jacket that belonged to Alex. I figured you would know where all his stuff ended up."

"I think all of the personal things are in storage on Level Three. We're having his furniture stored until we can figure out what to do with the stuff and whether he has any living relatives. No luck so far. What's this about, Charlie?"

"I'm not sure, but I think there's something on that jacket that's important."

"I'm not with you, Charlie. Important in what sense?"

"In connection with the VIWAP program."

"Charlie, Charlie. You know what's going to happen if you start stirring this pot again don't you?"

"Yes, I know. We might have to be careful with this. Can you cover for me Leonard? Keep this one below the radar?"

"Jesus, Charlie, you sure this is worth it to you?"

"I am."

Leonard closed his eyes as he considered the request. Coming quickly to a decision he glanced around his office to ensure no one was standing near his doorway.

"Okay, here's what I'll do. I'll go see the guy in stores and tell him that you loaned Alex the jacket before he died and didn't get it back. I'll have to sign for it but I can't see that causing any problems. You guys worked together after all. How does that sound?"

"Sounds good. Thanks. It's a black leather jacket and has a picture of a Samurai on the back. You better go find it yourself rather than pass that information on."

"Jesus. Okay, I'll collect it today. How will I get it to you?"

"Why don't you give it to Elizabeth. I'll see her tonight."

"Christ, Charlie, I'm not sure I want her involved in any of this shit."

"It's only a jacket, Leonard. Besides she'll know all about it soon enough."

Darville sighed. "Okay, but take it home for Christ's sake. I don't want it discovered at Elizabeth's apartment."

"Sure. Thanks, Leonard, I appreciate it."

"No problem. And Charlie?"

"Yes?"

"For God's sake be careful. Talk to me before you talk to anyone else here. Even Ed. Will you do that for me?"

"Sure, Leonard, of course. Thanks."

Darville replaced the receiver into its cradle with a troubled look on his face. As much as he didn't like the smell of what was going on at the Pentagon, he sure didn't want Charlie getting in over his head with these bastards. Four people dead is more than a big enough price to pay, he thought.

CHAPTER 14

Taiwan is a thorny issue for China and for China–US relations. In 1949, the defeated General Chiang Kai-shek fled to Taiwan with Mao Zedong's Red Army on his tail. At that stage the USA wasn't particularly interested in what happened to Taiwan. This changed, however with the outbreak of the Korean war in 1950. Overnight, Taiwan became a critical part of the US defense chain. During the next twenty years, Taiwan, with help from the US, took off. The US pumped economic aid, training, weapons, and technology into the island. It also gave US security guarantees that allowed the People's Republic of Taiwan to behave as an independent state.

By the early 1970s, things were changing and the US was in the process of trying to extract itself from Indochina. The Soviet Union was becoming the new problem and the US needed to devote resources to containing its growing menace. Taiwan looked as though it might be abandoned to China. The US even began making serious noises about finding a peaceful settlement to the 'Taiwan question.' Eventually the Soviet Union sorted itself out by collapsing wholesale. Meanwhile China was seen to be demonstrating a less-than-spotless record on human rights. Once again, Taiwan would become important. With the Soviet Union out of the picture, China was emerging as the only power capable of challenging US dominance in the Asia-Pacific Region. In 1992, US President George Bush approved a deal worth almost six billion dollars to sell one-hundred-and-fifty F-16 fighter aircraft to Taiwan. The US–China relationship took a nose dive.

Currently, the situation is tense. China grows impatient that the issue of sovereignty has not been settled. No Chinese leader wishes to preside over the loss of Taiwan. Positions are entrenched. If China attempts to take the island by force (a non trivial exercise considering Taiwan's military capacity) The US would be expected to intervene. The result could be two nuclear-capable powers in what may well be an escalating conflict. Japan would likely be drawn into the struggle. Even without armed conflict, the increased tension over the island has the capability of destabilising the region, threatening key regional trade and security building blocks such as APEC, ARF, and CSAP. So, a sort of Mexican standoff exists. China needs good relations with the US, its largest export market, as it builds its internal infrastructure. China also needs Taiwan, an important source of direct foreign investment.

* * *

The carrier battle group protecting the USS *Carl Vinson* lies on-station one hundred miles east of Taiwan. The immense assemblage of state-of-the-art hardware costing tens of billions of dollars with its highly trained personnel is on full alert.

Yesterday, Chinese Soviet-built SU-27 fighter aircraft made low passes across both the Taiwanese island and the US battle group. This is not an unexpected ploy. It's a show by China of its displeasure at the US presence so close to Taiwan and a reminder that Taiwanese independence is not an option from the mainland Chinese perspective. Even though both governments know the rules of the game, the destroyers and guided missile frigates in the carrier group take these fly-overs seriously. After all, when you have a pair of armed and highly capable strike aircraft heading towards your ship at six hundred miles an hour, it's better to be alert than dead.

As the sun rises on a new day, the airborne warning systems aboard the E-2C Hawkeye Tactical Warning and Control System aircraft from the Golden Hawks, Carrier Air Wing Nine keeping a permanent watch over the group detect the return of the SU-27s. The speed and positional information of the Chinese aircraft is transmitted to the carrier battle group. Inside the target computers on the guided missile frigate USS *Ford,* a firing solution is calculated as the aircraft are tracked. The skipper of the USS *Ford* doesn't expect to have to launch against the Chinese troublemakers but the exercise is good for the men and the group will not be caught unprepared should something go wrong.

The aircraft are thirty nautical miles away when something astonishing happens. The weapons displays aboard the USS *Ford* unexpectedly begin screaming that both of the approaching fighters have turned on their target-acquiring radar systems and are locking onto the surface vessels in the group. This presents a clear and present danger to the battle group and is definitely not within the rules of the game. It represents an act of aggression that cannot be ignored. With the aircraft closing at slightly less than the speed of sound, the skipper has less than three minutes to act. He attempts to raise the commander of the battle group but all communications appear to be jammed.

The skipper is on his own. The communications interruption serves to strengthen his concern about the intentions of the aircraft. He cannot take a risk. He has to make the most important decision of his career and he has to do it quickly and alone. He has no choice. With the firing solution already calculated he gives the order to fire four AIM-7 Sea Sparrow missiles. Three seconds later he sees the flash of their launch and with a terrifying shriek they spear into the sky eager to deliver their ninety-pound Annular Blast Fragmentation warheads. The entire company can hear the roar of the rocket engines as the twelve-foot long missiles accelerate toward their two thousand seven hundred mph top speeds.

The reaction from the two Su-27s is almost immediate. Their own systems detect the radar from the Sparrow missiles and they peel away in opposite directions, firing out electronic and mechanical countermeasures in an attempt to distract the missiles. The pilots clearly see the approach of the sleek Sparrows as they turn under maximum power, the afterburners of their twin-engine fighters generating more than fifty-thousand pounds of thrust. Sufficient to catapult the aircraft vertically as if it were a rocket. At low altitude and against four missiles their chance of evasion is slim.

The first two missiles launched have locked on to the Su-27 that banked to port. For a second the pilot thinks he has escaped as the pair of missiles streak under his wing. Unfortunately, the six G turn has cost the Chinese pilot too much speed and the missiles are sweeping around in a wide arc and have acquired his aircraft again. With much of his speed washed off, he knows this zero-sum game is over. He pushes himself back against his seat and reaches up for the ejection handles. With all of his strength he pulls down on the black-and-yellow banded hoops. One second before the first missile flies into the rear of his aircraft, the pilot is blown to safety. Three seconds later his chute deploys and his seat falls away. His vision stabilises just in time to see the tragic demise of his wingman.

The second pilot is not so lucky. His evasive manoeuvres are less effective and he momentarily loses sight of the twin messengers of destruction. His head swivels rapidly within the confines of the cramped cockpit. As the possibility of success flashes across his mind, one of the missiles literally flies into his engine exhaust and the fifty million dollar fighting machine is obliterated in the explosion.

Aboard the ships of the battle group, all eyes watch in horror as the drama in the sky unfolds. As the debris from both aircraft plunge into the Pacific Ocean, the battle group commander orders a boat launched from the nearest vessel to collect the downed airman. His next task is to communicate with the missile frigate. He is in no mood for pleasantries.

"What in God's name happened, Chris!" The commanders voice booms in the deathly silence of the bridge.

The frigate's skipper is taken aback by the ferocity in the commander's tone. "They were painting us, sir!" He replies.

"Stand by!" The commander roars.

It becomes quickly apparent that the only vessel registering the target radar of the aircraft was the USS *Ford.* Every ship in the group was aware of the approach but none of their systems detected the threat. As the commander waits for the Chinese pilot to be brought aboard *Carl Vinson*, he communicates the preliminary assessment to Washington. Something has gone snafu big time and the political instinct of the commander shouts at him that damage control is the most urgent requirement.

When the downed pilot is brought aboard *Carl Vinson*, employing surprisingly fluent English he wastes no time in informing the commander of the injustice of the situation. The crew have to physically restrain the enraged pilot who is hell-bent on making someone pay.

In Washington, all stops have been pulled out in an attempt to defuse the situation. The Chinese don't believe that the missile launch was an accident. They have too much respect for American technology to believe this was anything less then deliberate aggression. While the diplomatic staffs argue and the leaders of the two countries try to stay calm, the Chinese military is placed on maximum alert.

The *Carl Vinson* carrier battle group is now in danger, should the conflict escalate. The US secretary of defense has no choice but to sign the order to deploy two more battle groups to the area. And so the tension builds, neither side daring to stand down. The frigate USS *Ford* is taken off line while naval technical experts crawl over her systems in an attempt to figure our what went wrong. As a show of good faith to the Chinese, the skipper is suspended pending an inquiry. Already it's obvious that he acted appropriately given the circumstances. Everyone on the bridge will testify that the aircraft's target radar had them in its deadly embrace. The computer logs demonstrate that fact clearly, just as clearly as the flight recorders from the Su-27s will demonstrate the exact opposite when they are retrieved from the ocean floor two weeks later.

CHAPTER 15

Charlie has arranged to fix dinner for Elizabeth at his apartment when she finishes work and he's anxious to see the jacket. He grabs his own coat and heads out to collect some ingredients for the risotto he plans to make. The shopping and book-browsing consumes most of his morning. By now it's lunchtime and Charlie's stomach is reminding him of the fact. Not a fan of eating long meals alone, he decides that a burger will be quick and will hit the spot. He knows a decent place over at the university and decides to stop there on the way home.

The burger is as good as he expected and even bigger than he remembered. Charlie feels a brief pang of guilt over the greasy food. Better start watching my diet he thinks. Not getting any younger. Charlie rationalises his weakness away as an issue for another day. He orders a coffee but before it arrives a familiar face swims into his vision.

"Hello doc!" Calls John Lord, making his way over to Charlie's table.

"Hi detective," Charlie responds, "please call me Charlie."

"Right you are, Charlie. Mind if I join you?"

This was a complication that Charlie hadn't counted on but he doesn't want to appear rude.

"Sure, take a seat."

The waitress returned with Charlie's coffee and took Lord's for a hot tea.

"So, Charlie. When do you start back at work?"

"Next Monday, all things going well."

"It's been a rough time for you guys over at the facility. I have to say you look a hell of a lot better than last time I saw you."

"Yes, it was pretty tough there for a while."

"Are you happy with the way the department has handled the whole thing?"

"Well, you know how these things go."

Lord's tea arrives and he squeezes some lemon into his cup before taking a sip.

"No, actually. How do these things go?"

Charlie's confidentiality radar begins to beep and he knows that he must be cautious.

"Everything's getting back to normal and the department's happy that things are under control."

"Maybe. I was sort of wondering what *you* thought."

"I guess you heard what I thought at the briefing."

"Sure I did. You were pretty persuasive too. Had me worried. Those army guys listening, you think?"

"I guess they draw their own conclusions."

"Maybe different from yours though?"

Charlie sighed. "Look, detective, it's hard for me to speak candidly with you. You know how it goes, confidentiality and need-to-know. That sort of stuff."

Lord spread his hands, palms up. "Hey, Charlie, relax. The case is closed. I'm on your side here. I don't want you to say anything that'll get you into trouble. Four people die in one week, that's going to keep my gears turning for a while is all."

Charlie took a deep breath. "Sure. I know. I don't mean to be defensive."

Lord tried a different tack. "It must have been tough when Alex Fox was killed. I hear he and you worked together for a long time."

"Yes we did. Alex was one of the best programmers that I ever met. He wasn't an easy guy to get to know but there are a lot of people who will miss him."

"What made him so good do you think?"

"I guess he was quite brilliant technically but he also had great intuition and creativity. It also didn't hurt that he worked sixty or seventy hours a week." Charlie said with a lopsided grin.

"A terrible way for a guy like that to end up. Killed in a freak accident. The poor guy who discovered him will never trust his elevators again, that's for damn sure."

"Who did find Alex?"

"The guy from the elevator company."

Charlie gave Lord a puzzled look. "How did he get to be the first on the scene?"

"You shoulda been a cop, Charlie. I asked him the same thing. Seems these modern elevators have got lots of bells and whistles. Guy told me the competition is fierce to get the maintenance contracts. The company has to specify how quickly they can get on site if the thing goes on the fritz. Anyway, if the elevator dies, it gives them a call and the maintenance guy can be out before the building supervisor starts taking heat from the tenants 'cos they have to use the stairs. Damn building's only four floors high for Pete's sake."

"Charlie? Is everything okay?" Lord reached out and touched him on the arm.

Charlie's eyes snapped back into focus, all of the colour drained from his face.

"Sure, sure. Look, I'm sorry, detective, but I've got to run, I've just remembered something."

With that Charlie rose unsteadily to his feet and headed for the door leaving Lord staring at Charlie's half-finished coffee, a surprised look on his face.

Lord shook his head in amazement, drained his tea, tossed a few bills on the table to cover both of their drinks and the burger and fries that Charlie had obviously consumed. He walked outside to his vehicle where Lou has been waiting for him since they spotted Charlie entering the café and climbed inside.

"Hey, JL." Louis says. "Our man give anything up?"

Lord rubbed his chin, a thoughtful look on his face. The detective's mind began to replay the conversation, wondering what triggered the panic in Charlie's eyes.

"Yes and no, Lou. He was playing his cards close to his chest but we got to talking about Alex's death and he suddenly looks like he's seen a ghost. Face was whiter than the damn table top. Then he just got up an' left. Just like that. I had to get the check!"

"Smart man our Ganderton." Louis chuckled. "Have to try that trick myself sometime. I saw him come out lookin' like he was gonna puke. I figured it was just your charming company."

"Trust me, Lou. Nothing I could have said to him caused that reaction."

"So what were you talkin' about at the time?"

"He asked me who discovered Fox's body and I was explaining how the maintenance guy gets summoned by the busted elevator. Next thing I know, he's completely spaced out. I almost had to slap his face! You know, like in the movies."

"Maybe we missed something when we talked to that elevator guy. Come to think of it, he sure was keen to get the hell out of there."

"You can hardly blame him, Lou. It's not every day that you find a pair of legs and a hundred pounds of mincemeat in the bottom of your elevator shaft."

"Amen to that."

"Still an' all, maybe I'll give that grease monkey a call when we get back to the station. Just go over things once more now he's cooled down."

* * *

Charlie is on autopilot as he prepares the meal for this evening. He's pulled himself together following his shock in the café but he's far from relaxed. His hands are going through the motions but his mind is elsewhere. His stomach feels sore from tension and he's just taken two Tylenol in an attempt to stay in front of the headache that's building. He tells himself to calm down, step back from it, but his mind keeps bringing him back to the same point. The elevator. His thoughts are broken by a knock on the door. He throws open the door and hugs Elizabeth tightly.

"Wow. Thanks for the welcome!" She says, taking off her coat. "You sure know how to make a girl feel special."

"I'm just glad to see you," Charlie says, blushing at his spontaneous display of affection.

"I have a package for you from Leonard. It's all very mysterious. He told me not to open it and to be sure that I put it directly into your hands. I feel like a spy making a drop off!"

Elizabeth reached into her bag and pulled out a package wrapped in brown paper and secured with what appeared to be miles of tape. Charlie tore open the wrapping and pulled the jacket out. He flipped it over and laid it down on the table, exposing the image on the back.

Elizabeth noticed Charlie's agitation and laid her hand on his arm. "What is it, Charlie?"

Charlie stared at the image. It's just as he remembers it. A reproduction of what looks like an old woodcut showing a warrior with robes swirling around his arms. In his hand is a sword. A brown wooden sword. Underneath the picture are the words *Individual School of Two Skies.*

Elizabeth slipped her arms around Charlie. "What does it mean?" She said. "Whose jacket is this?"

"Alex's." Charlie responded. Elizabeth's hand flew to her mouth.

"This is what Lily told me about. This must be him, Charlie! Kensei. You were right all along! My God! Alex, the hacker, and the VIWAP are somehow connected. Just like you said."

"I can't see how it can be any other way. And there's another thing..."

Elizabeth put a finger on Charlie's lips to silence him then led him to the sofa and made him sit. She then refilled his glass of wine and brought it over to him. She perched on the edge of the sofa. "Now, take a deep breath and tell me about this other thing."

"I met up with Detective Lord today while I was eating lunch and we got to talking. He told me that the elevator guy was on the scene of Alex's death so quickly because the company had been alerted to the malfunction electronically. They monitor a link to the elevator systems."

Elizabeth's hand flew back to her mouth. "No!"

"Apparently so. When Lord told me I almost fainted. I just charged out of the café and left him."

"My God, Charlie. That means those department pricks were lying to you in Washington. And it went on the record. They're screwed."

"I can't believe they would be so stupid but somebody is lying. Either there's a link to the elevator or there isn't. It's as simple as that."

"So did you say anything about it to the detective?"

"No. I was too shocked. I needed time to think."

"I think you did the right thing."

"Thanks. I get such a bad feeling about this. Something big is going on and we're in the middle of it all. I just know it."

"What are you going to do, Charlie?"

"I'm going to talk to Lord again. I think he smells a rat already."

"But didn't you tell me that Leonard ask you to speak to him first? Shouldn't you go to him before involving the police?" Elizabeth looked alarmed at the prospect.

Charlie took both of Elizabeth's hands in his own. "Look. I know you're very fond of the old man. Hell, I am too. I'm just not sure how involved he is in all this."

Elizabeth pulled away. "Charlie! Surely you don't think Leonard had anything to do with our people dying? Please tell me you don't think that!"

"Of course I don't. But I'm starting to think that he knows a little more than he's letting on. He might be trying to protect me but he sure was quick to roll over after the meeting in Washington. That's not like Leonard at all."

A tear welled up in the corner of Elizabeth's eye and Charlie was overwhelmed with his love for her. Elizabeth seized his hands in a grip that surprised him with its strength. She looked directly into his eyes.

"I hope you're wrong, I really do. But if Leonard is somehow mixed up in this, you better be *really* careful Charlie. I don't like the sound of this at all."

* * *

In the Ann Arbor Police Department, Detective Lord places the receiver back into the cradle on his desk with a puzzled look on his face.

"Damned if this don't keep getting curiouser and curiouser."

"How's that, Alice?" Louis said, returning from the men's room.

"Remember that guy? The elevator maintenance guy? Fox's building?"

"Sure. Joe something wasn't it?"

"Joe Shapiro. Well, the number he gives me just keeps ringing out so I call the Super over at Fox's apartment building and ask for the name of the elevator company. I call them in Chicago and ask how to get in contact with Shapiro. She tells me there's no Joe Shapiro working for them. So I start asking her about the accident, and she's like, what accident?"

Louis is now fully engaged. "You're shittin' me, right?"

"Nope. When I hear this I ask for the manager. He goes through the job records and the customers' file. No accident. No call out. No

Joe Shapiro, or any Shapiro for that matter. And that's not all. That story Shapiro gave us about the elevator system calling them up? Bullshit. The manager claims that they usually do have a phone line *they* can dial into if they need to reprogram the system. In this case the whole building went over budget and the owners tried to cut corners. Didn't want to pay. Anyway, the dial-in gizmo didn't get installed. Sounds like the whole story and the Shapiro guy himself was bogus."

"Motherfucker! That puts a new spin on things, don't it?"

"You're damn straight it does Lou."

Louis sat back in his chair and put his hands behind his head. "So I guess the question is, who the hell was Joe Shapiro?"

"I'm not so sure about that. You know what I'm really starting to think the question is, Lou?"

"Shoot."

"Who the hell was Alex Fox?"

CHAPTER 16

Reaction to the shooting down of the Chinese fighters was immediate and furious. The incident was considered by the Chinese Government to be deliberate and unpardonable. The downed pilot had been returned by helicopter and he wasted no time in describing the unprovoked aggression shown by the American forces. He also reported honestly that his US rescuers had been profusely apologetic and appeared to be genuine in their insistence that a malfunction had initiated the launch. Of course the Chinese generals saw this as simply a ploy and paid scant attention to it. Actions spoke louder than words in their minds and two hugely expensive aircraft now littered the bottom of the Pacific together with one highly trained pilot.

In a show of force, China ordered three of its recently acquired Sovremenny Class destroyers to take up a position one hundred miles north of Taiwan in the East China Sea. These will be joined in the coming days by six Luhu Class warships. The Chinese would love to have *Yichun* on-station in the area but they dare not take the risk in case the captain's malfunction story is genuine. Tensions are riding a hair trigger and the stakes are high.

Every day the *Carl Vinson* group will be buzzed by Chinese Su-27s and Su-30s. Not just two at a time but squadrons of eight heavily armed aircraft screaming over the water, seeming to dare the US warships to retaliate. The commander of the group is confident in the discipline of his own men, despite the malfunction that has contributed to the current state of events. What really worries him is the prospect of one of the Chinese aircraft starting a shooting match. Or the Taiwanese for that matter. They too have aircraft in the sky constantly and are extremely troubled by the escalating tensions just off their coastline.

Naturally the US Government sent a high level delegation to the Chinese capital to express their sorrow for the unfortunate accident and to offer compensation, yet there is still an uneasy feeling within the US military. The submarine missile launch that had brought them to this part of the world was unresolved. The malfunction that caused the missile firing also had the analysts sweating. What if it wasn't a malfunction but was some new weapons system. Perhaps the anomaly was the fact that one ship *did* detect the airborne target radar. Maybe the Chinese had developed a system that was beyond the capacity of most of the US systems to detect. Given the situation, this possibility couldn't be ignored. Meanwhile, two more carrier battle groups headed for the region.

***

The president of the United States was once again in conference with his chiefs. The meeting had commenced with a briefing from the intelligence community. The three Chinese destroyers were of particular concern. These warships had been acquired a few years back from the Soviets and represented the largest and most powerful surface warships that the Chinese had ever operated. The upgraded vessels possessed some formidable weapons and of particular concern was the SS-N-22 Sunburn supersonic sea-skimming anti-submarine missile. Between the three ships they carried twenty-four of these missiles. The stakes had been raised. Next up was the report into the investigation of the shooting down of the Chinese fighters. The technical spokesman on behalf of the navy had fidgeted and nervously cleared his throat many times throughout the intelligence briefing. Now it was his turn.

"So," the president began, "what do you have?"

"Well, sir, our technical people have crawled all over the systems aboard the USS *Ford*."

"And?"

The senior technical officer lifted his chin and tried to keep his voice steady. This was the first time in his career that he found himself under the president's gaze so intimately and the man's intense focus rattled him. His colleagues had ribbed him severely when they discovered that he would make the report to the president. Secretly he knew they were all insanely jealous. Having arrived and looked the president in the eyes he would have gladly traded his position with any of them.

"Our opinion is that all of the systems operated as designed, sir."

The president held his temper. Lack of sleep had taken the edge off whatever might have motivated him in the past to cut his people any slack.

"You can speak plainly in this room, son. Without any technical mumbo-jumbo, what exactly are you saying?"

The young officer took a deep breath and launched into an assessment that he hoped wouldn't end his career right here in this room.

"The logs aboard the *Ford* show every detail of the entire sequence. All of the conversations are recorded and the output from every command display. We have put the equipment through the most extensive tests we have and we detected zero failures. I repeat, zero failures. To track and fire upon an enemy aircraft requires multiple systems working together with the judgment of the operators and captain. My people and I have no doubt that the ship was being targeted by the Chinese aircraft and the equipment behaved exactly as it should. It was not faulty in any way in our view."

"Shit!" the president said. "So why didn't any of the other ships pick this up?"

"We have no explanation for that at this time, sir."

The men in the room who knew the president well could see with what effort he was controlling his temper. After swallowing down his anger, he turned to the director of the defence intelligence agency.

"Where does that leave us, Jim?"

"Unfortunately, sir, it would have been better if we'd *had* a malfunction aboard USS *Ford.* If we allow that we didn't, we have to face up to a few things here. Firstly, the Chinese have some new weapons system that's not detectable to most of the systems aboard our ships, or they have some sort of sophisticated jamming system that does work on most of our ships."

"Which of those two is your money on, Jim?" asked the president.

"The first one, sir. It is much more difficult to Jam a system in such a way that the operators of the system are unaware of it being jammed. Traditionally, you just flood the airwaves with high energy noise. We would have seen that immediately."

"Okay, so we have the possibility of a new weapons control system. What else?"

"We have to face a scenario where the Chinese deliberately intended to fire on the *Ford.* If it wasn't deliberate, it was either an accident or incredible stupidity on the part of the pilots. All of these possibilities set up a bad situation for our forces out there."

"Why don't we think the Chinese were testing out their new radar system? Making sure we couldn't detect it?"

"We have considered that. Our view is that it's unlikely. If you test something like this for the first time in anger, why choose a carrier battle group? It's like your worst-case scenario. It only takes one vessel to detect your signal and you're in the water, or worse. It wouldn't be a smart move, sir."

In a rare rush of courage and momentarily forgetting where he was, the technical officer interrupted. "But how do we know they haven't tested it before? If it really is undetectable they might have tried it dozens of times before. We wouldn't know. Maybe this was their ultimate live test." A slight smile crept onto the president's face.

"A good point, Jim?"

The director looked less than impressed by the interruption and frantically scoured his briefing notes. He himself hadn't thought of that but when he got back to his office, heads would roll.

"I'll have to take that on notice, Mr President."

The president sat back and laughed, puncturing the discomfort that everybody felt. He turned to the young officer. "Good thinking, Son. You just might want to choose your timing a little more carefully in the future. You don't want to be making enemies of these old bastards!" He gave the director a wink as if to say let it go this time.

"So, we better be on our toes if those SOBs are playing games with us." The president turned to his chief of staff of the navy. "Any chance of getting a look inside one of those downed aircraft, Pete?"

"I think not. They're all over the crash sites like white on rice. We'd be really raising the stakes if we stuck our noses in there."

"I thought so."

The intelligence director cleared his throat. "There is one more thing, Mr president."

The director looked at the president and his eyes flicked almost imperceptibly toward the young technical officer. An understanding passed between them with no words needed. God, this must be serious, the president thought. He turned to the young officer. "Thank you for your briefing, lieutenant, it was most informative. We'll be in touch if we need anything more." With that, the officer was ushered out of the room.

"Okay Jim," said the president. "shoot."

"We seem to have a leak."

The president's face clouded. "Come on, Jim, put the cards on the table."

"We seem to have let a scenario paper out somehow. Just before I came into this meeting I was informed that it had surfaced. The paper was our recent Taiwan occupation feasibility study and it's now in the hands of the Chinese Government."

Around the room there was a stunned silence as everyone struggled to digest the magnitude of the news. All eyes swivelled to the president.

"Do we know who did this?" Before anyone could speak, the president could contain himself no longer. He leaped to his feet.

"Jesus!" He bellowed. "As if this damned situation couldn't get any worse! What in God's name is going on here? We're staring down the barrel of a gun with the Chinese and we're doing our best to help pull the trigger. Christ Almighty!"

The president flopped back into his chair, spent by his emotional outburst. When he lifted his gaze, control had returned.

"What do we know Jim?" He asked.

"Believe it or not, all seventy-five pages of the report simply popped out of a fax at one of the Chinese intelligence agencies. It looks very bad for us. That report has lots of detail, we even fleshed out several alternative Chinese responses to our occupation and how we'd deal militarily with them. I'm sure they've done exactly the same thing with their planners but they're going to have a field day with this one."

"Do we have *any* idea how this got out?" The president asked, his eyes not leaving the table top.

"No, we don't. It has to be someone very senior to get access to that report. There aren't even any paper copies, it only resides on our secure servers. I can't believe anyone at that level would be stupid enough to do it."

"Well, someone did it. Jesus! Of all the leaks I've ever seen, this has to be the most devastating. Particularly in the current climate. Our credibility is going out the window faster than we can manage it. *That* report to *that* government at *this* time. It's a calculated and deliberate effort to escalate the current crisis. Has to be. No other explanation. God, we better find this bastard fast. There's no knowing what else might be coming."

"You're right of course. Because we don't know what might be coming next we'll also need to increase your personal security significantly until such a time we can get a handle on this."

The president groaned and rolled his eyes. "Jim?"

"Yes, Mr president."

"I want you to pull all the stops out on this. I want this place locked down tight. Brief us tomorrow on your progress. This is national security we're dealing with here. This crazy bastard could start World War Three if we don't catch him. Whoever's done this is going to burn, make no mistake. You find him, and fast."

* * *

Predictably, the Chinese Government in Beijing took a very dim view of the report that had appeared in their office. Given the seriousness of the incident and the obvious sensitivity of the document, they also drew the conclusion that someone in a very senior capacity was trying to tell them something. Perhaps a solid citizen within the administration whose conscience would not allow him to stand by while his countrymen did something dishonourable. For Beijing it was the last straw. They took it as a sign that military action was imminent in Taiwan. That the United States had an agenda that included occupation of the island, supported by Japan, for its own strategic advantage.

Accordingly, the Chinese Government took the significant step of withdrawing its ambassador to the United States. In a highly publicised manner, the ambassador and his staff left their compound on Connecticut Avenue in Washington DC, bound for the airport with a one-way ticket home. The media was in full flight. Across the nation the significance of this event was debated. Its implications in the context of the downed Chinese fighters was examined and re-examined by panels of experts ad nauseam. The headlines of national newspapers carried stories about world war and nuclear capabilities. Across the nation people began digging shelters, buying up bottled water and long life food. Guns, ammunition, survival gear. Protest rallies began to appear in city after city, leading many commentators to compare the numbers and passion of the protesters with the tide of public sentiment that swelled against the Vietnam war.

The pressure on the US administration was intense and was growing daily. In a press release, the president said that he had no choice but to bring home the US citizens in the embassy and consulates within China as he could no longer guarantee their safety. Tensions in the region were running at fever pitch and without effective channels of communication, it was difficult to see a way forward.

Flights of F/A-18 carrier-based fighter aircraft were now constantly patrolling the sky over the battle group like school bullies spoiling for a fight. The Chinese fighters were also in evidence daily and the aircraft of the two nations engaged in deadly shadow-boxing with neither side wanting to throw the first real punch. The seasoned military commanders at the Pentagon knew it was only a matter of time before something triggered off a real engagement, given the tensions between the two countries. What was needed was time and distance so that the protagonists could step back, put things in perspective, and reopen the lines of communication.

CHAPTER 17

Before Charlie returned to work he was determined to dig a little deeper into the complex web that seemed to surround Alex's death. He wasn't sure if it was simply because he had too much time on his hands, but he couldn't get his conversation with Lord out of his mind. It was always there, ready to turn up again like an unwelcome but persistent visitor. Charlie hated this new feeling that some faceless bureaucrat in the department thought he could just pat him on the head and send him on his way with a bullshit story. Charlie knew if he just looked the other way this time, just backed down and walked off, a part of him inside would shrivel and die.

He decided to call Detective Lord and put the cards on the table. If anything new came from it, he'd approach Darville and take it from there. On the phone, Charlie explained to Lord about the misgivings he had, about the hacker and the connection with Alex's jacket. Finally he carefully told Lord about that part of the Washington meeting where the department gave him a story that contradicted Lord's explanation in the café.

Leaning back in his chair, Lord nodded his thanks to Lou who placed a steaming mug of coffee on his desk.

"Sounds like we have a few things here that don't add up, Charlie." He said

"I can't believe that they would tell such a blatant lie, detective. What are they trying to hide?"

"I guess that's the million-dollar question, my friend. I do agree that something or someone is being protected here. I'm just not sure how much I can do right now. As you know the case is officially closed. I'm likely to have my balls handed to me on a plate if I try poking around in this mess. You might need to keep digging from the inside."

Clearly, this is not the reaction that Charlie had expected and the pause on the end of the line tells Lord so.

"But if the department is clearly lying, doesn't that mean the case should be opened again?"

"Well, it's not that simple. Right now we only have your word against theirs. We would have to try to get hold of minutes of the meeting you had in Washington and then start proceedings based on what we found. Just getting that documentation would be difficult. They could stonewall us for months and in the meantime they'd want to know who squealed. Your job would be finished either way."

"What about the hacker and Alex's jacket? What about that?"

"Interesting, Charlie, but circumstantial at best I'm afraid."

"So you're suggesting we just forget it. Is that what you're saying?"

"No, but let's not shoot ourselves in the foot here. Why don't you have a talk with Darville and tell him what you've told me. See what his reaction is. Maybe something will come out of it. Who knows."

"I guess you're right. It's driving me nuts though, I can tell you."

"That's the nature of detective work, Charlie! Trying to build the jigsaw puzzle when you only have half the pieces and you've lost the box with the picture on the lid."

"I suppose. Thanks anyway."

"No problem. Keep me in the loop on anything you find out."

"Okay, and detective?"

"Yes?"

"I think I might owe you a lunch after my ungracious exit last time."

"That's right! Don't be leaving town, ya hear?"

As Lord hangs up the phone, Lou looks at him thoughtfully. "Sounds to me like you tryin' to rain on that poor man's parade. You didn't tell him about the whole elevator sting?"

"No point, Lou. That would just put him back where he started from. Right now he's been made to look like a chump and he believes people have lied to him. He's got lots of incentive to start poking around."

"But you said yourself that it might cost him his job."

"Sure. But I'm more concerned about four dead people than I am about whether or not Charlie's career runs off the rails. Besides, I don't think the guy has the stones to cause too much trouble anyway."

"So what *are* we going to do about the disappearing Joe Shapiro?"

Lord leaned forward and rested his elbows on the desk.

"Good question, Lou. Here's how I figure it. If Ganderton's theory about the whole VIWAP thing turns out to be bullshit, the way the department heavies are making out, what we have is a series of accidents. Right?"

"Okay. I'll buy that."

"So these accidents are not connected in any way other than the poor shmucks involved all work for the same crew. So, let's go back to Fox's death. We assume an accident. That's what the medical examiner says. But now, we may have new information that suggests foul play. Fox might work for the department but he still gave up the ghost in his apartment building. Just another good citizen on his way to work. Right? Do you see where I'm going with this, Lou?"

"Sure. If the department insists that the deaths are unrelated accidents, Fox's death outside of the facility becomes fair game for suspicious bastards like us. An' we get mightily pissed when rich white boys die on our patch."

"As usual, Lou, right on the money."

"So. What comes next JL?"

"You mean other than the damned Chinese start a war and we all end up brown an' crispy 'round the edges?"

"Yeah. Other than that."

"We go speak with the lieutenant and see if we can't open this case just wide enough to allow two suspicious bastards to sneak back inside."

"And if Ganderton's VIPER theory turns out true?"

"Then God help Ganderton, Lou, 'cos he'll be next on the hit list."

* * *

Inside a private room at the White House, Security Chief George Medford sits opposite the vice-president. The atmosphere in the room is sombre, the dark wood panelling seeming to mirror the feelings of the two men. The clock over the empty fireplace marks time as the vice-president turns over the news he's just received, a single printed page in his hands. In a private Intelligence briefing an hour ago, he learned that the leaked fax that had the entire administration in a spin had been sent from the fax machine in the private quarters of the president of the United States. The number and the duration of the call had been logged somewhere. The vice-president had no idea where but that was the least of his worries. There were only two possibilities in his mind. Either the president himself sent the fax or someone gained access to his private room to do so. That the possibility existed, however remote, that the president was involved, automatically meant that the VP was thrust into the situation.

While the first scenario was ridiculous to his mind, the second was equally problematic. The fax had been sent late at night, Washington time. The president's security detail kept a constant watch on the rooms and corridors where the fax machine was located. Someone had managed to come and go and security saw nothing. This troubled the VP greatly. It had occurred to him that perhaps it was simply a mistake. With a moment of clarity he called Medford and asked him to personally check the fax machine itself. Asked him to print out the fax history log that the computer inside the machine maintained. That will clear this damn thing up fast, he thought. It will show a crossed line or something, the fax sent from the president's private fax number but not from his machine. His spirits had sunk when Medford returned with the news. The log showed the call. All of the details. The number was correct, the page count accurate. The fax had been sent from the president's private machine.

Jumbled thoughts raced through the VP's mind, not the least of which was how and when to broach this with the president. What would he have to gain by this, he thought. With guilt he realised that with re-election looming in six months, there was nothing like a war or the threat of a war to favour the incumbent. Banishing this idea from his mind, the VP forced himself to look at the alternatives. Who else could have sneaked in and out at that time? Already the security staff on duty had been questioned and the video footage examined. Nothing. They had the exact time of the fax for God's sake and the president was sleeping in the next room. He shook his head. But why would he take such a monstrous risk? He would have known that the call could be traced to his personal machine, surely?

The vice-president stared at the piece of paper in his hand. The rows of fax numbers called, the date and time of each call, the duration and the number of pages sent. One call, decorated in yellow highlighter, leaping off the page at him. It makes no sense, he thought. The president may be lots of things but a traitor to his own country? Never. Never in a million lifetimes, he thought. This is a man that I've known for twenty years. A man I've eaten with, cried with, argued with, celebrated with. Whose kids I've bounced on my knee, whose wife's cheek I've kissed more times than I can remember. Whose anger I've listened to and whose tears I've seen over dead Americans in numerous shit holes around the world. Rapidly he found his concern turning to anger at his own disloyal thoughts.

As he looked at the paper he recalled that the president has the same Department issue fax machine as his own. Once the fax log is printed, the record is erased and it starts over. What if this flimsy sheet of paper was to just disappear? Should a man's name and entire career be determined by one slip of paper? No one knew that Medford had even checked the fax machine. It might look odd when there was no log if someone thought to check the machine but that's better than finding this, he thought. In that moment his mind crystallised one thought. The man I know did not send this fax, whatever the evidence suggests. No way. The VP folded the paper, slipped it into the breast pocket of his jacket and rose to head back to his office where he would introduce it to the irreversible embrace of his office shredder.

Suddenly, he remembered Medford was still in the room. "God, I'm sorry, George, I just got a bit lost there for a minute, how rude of me."

"No problem Sir." Medford offered no comment although he observed the VP slip the page into his pocket. He'd long ago learned to keep his opinions to himself unless asked. He'd seen a few things in his years at the White House and not many things surprised him anymore. This business with the fax had him rattled though. He was smart enough to know something was going on. Something serious. A big fax from the president's machine to a number he knew from the county code to be in China. This at a time when tensions were rocketing up between the two nations. Shit, I almost wish I hadn't seen this, Medford thought.

The VP recovered his composure in a few heartbeats as only men who operate at his level of success and stress seem able. "Thank you, George." the VP continued. "I guess I don't really need to say that this is between you and me at this stage?"

"Of course, sir."

"Good man. How's that wife of yours? Ruth isn't it? She recovered from her surgery yet?"

Not for the first time, Medford was amazed at the VP's recall of detail. He himself didn't remember ever telling the man about his wife's breast cancer last year but somehow he knew and remembered. There must be a trick to it, Medford thought.

"Yes, she's much better now, thank you for asking. We're both hoping it stays that way."

The VP leaned forward and patted him on the hand in what appeared to Medford to be genuine pleasure. "I hope so too, George. I really do. Be sure to pass on my regards won't you."

George Medford promised that he would do exactly that and left the room with the VP still smiling. Glad it's not my problem, he thought. And then, shit! I guess it is my problem if the boss turns out to be playing games here. God, let's hope it doesn't come to that.

* * *

Later that night, as the vice-president lay awake in bed, his wife of thirty-five years sleeping soundly beside him, his doubts began to return. The magnitude of what he'd done suddenly struck him. If by some chance the president did send the fax, I'm now an accessory after the fact to treason. There's no way to cover this over. The fax log is prima facie evidence. The vice-president, himself an attorney in a former life, knew only too well that he'd allowed his emotions to overrule his head and had made a serious error. One that could put him in prison. George Medford, the only person who knew about the log, was a ticking time bomb.

I wonder what it would take to ensure that George forgot all about that fax log sheet, he wondered. He tossed this around and then shook his head angrily. Get a grip man, he admonished himself. Just because you've dropped yourself in the shit doesn't give you the right to take other good men with you. Jesus, what am I becoming, he asked himself. Take responsibility, be accountable, and don't involve others. This would be his solution. He had been in politics long enough to know how far he was prepared to bend the rules. At least until today, that is. Long ago he'd made peace with himself over his own morality. He wouldn't in any way put pressure on George Medford. What George did would be up to his own conscience and whatever consequences flowed from that would be whatever they would be. For himself, for the president, for George Medford.

Before he fell asleep, he determined that his own conscience compelled him to speak with the president tomorrow. Alone. He had to know. If he felt that the president was lying to him, he would resign his position and take his chances with history. Oddly, this simple plan eased his mind and the sleep that had evaded him into the early hours of the morning now embraced him gently.

* * *

Fifteen miles west in the suburb of Oakton, George Medford also lay awake in his bed. His wife Ruth, who couldn't sleep much these days, was downstairs reading so as not to keep George awake. His wife's condition is much worse than he'd implied to the vice-president. The fact is, she's dying. There had been some hope following the bilateral mastectomy last year but the cancer has resurfaced, this time in her lung. Ironic, George thought, as neither of them had ever been smokers. For some reason to do with the shape of the cancer (like a spider, they said) the doctors couldn't operate. All they could do was manage the pain. Three months they estimated. George hadn't told anyone because that's what his wife wanted. She had suffered enough, she said. There's nothing anyone can do so let's not tell them until the end. As the tears rolled down George's face he thought of how strong she was. Always much stronger than me. George had all but given up hope of finding someone as special as Ruth. Out of the blue he had, and now this.

George thought that somehow the cards they had been dealt were marked. We can never seem to win at this game of life. They had met in church when they were both around forty and had been married for only five years. Shortly after the wedding, Ruth had received the first round of what would prove to be an endless drone of bad news about her health. George thought he would actually die from grief at one point and he marvelled at her resilience and pluck. Lately George was finding anger welling up inside of him at how their happiness was being stolen. How their lives were being stolen, their old age together cruelly torn away from them. Just to rub salt in the wounds, the continuous medical bills were so monstrous that they were on the edge of financial ruin. George couldn't even quit his job to be with her because then he wouldn't be able to afford her treatment. What a fucking world we live in, he thought.

In the last twelve months he hadn't been able to attend church any longer. Not even for Ruth. His anger at God for allowing this to happen while so many useless, dishonest and worthless fuckers prospered, threatened to engulf him as soon as he got inside the church door. The overwhelming urge that he felt to take one of those stupid candles and ram it into the eye of the priest as if it were his fault frightened George deeply. As far as George was concerned, if God had the power to stop what was happening to Ruth and didn't, he was a vicious, heartless bastard and George wanted nothing to do with him.

The experience today with the vice-president had unsettled him. George knew what the VP intended to do with that paper. He could read it in his body language. No question. George was good at that. He'd had a lifetime of practice in the security business. People were like an open book to George. The VP would protect the president. And he, George Medford, aimed to make him pay for his indiscretion. Life had fed him shit for the last five years and now it was time to turn things around. George's anger over his wife's illness was being channelled into what he saw as corruption at the highest level. He knew he couldn't stop it and wasn't even sure of he could be bothered trying but as sure as night followed day he was going to make them pay to keep his silence. Time to look out for George, he thought. Numero Uno. Fuck 'em

CHAPTER 18

Detective John Lord sits opposite Susan Arbroath in her tiny cubby-hole at the Wayne County Medical Examiners Office, his thoughts drifting as he waits for her to finish an urgent email. Following his usual custom, he's fixed them both a mug of coffee and found a space on Susan's overflowing desk to set them down. One of the things that struck Lord when they first began working together was that she never appeared to lose anything, despite the total chaos of her office. Susan had responded to one of his puns about her desk by calling it her archaeological filing system. "You give me a date and I'll know how far down to dig for it," she had said. Lord liked her style. In fact, when he imagined himself married, which he seemed to do increasingly just lately, his ideal woman turned out to be someone like Susan.

Not that he entertained any sexual fantasies about her, such fantasies were reserved for a different type of woman. It was when he thought about companionship that her face drifted into his imagination. When Lord realised that the police force would be his career for life he decided that he would never marry. Sure, he had girlfriends and flings from time to time but he'd seen too many cops' marriages end up down the crapper to attempt beating the odds. The problem was that when he was on a case, particularly a complex one, everything else in his life was put on hold until it was over. He couldn't imagine any woman hanging around under those circumstances and he couldn't imagine doing his job any other way. The thought of a different career never even entered his head. John

Lord loved what he did for a living.

The idea of a girlfriend felt a bit silly and adolescent to Lord but someone to come home to and to eat with sounded nice. An idea had been rattling around at the back of his mind for some time now. If he was careful with his money (which he was) perhaps early retirement wouldn't be out of the question. Maybe another six or seven years and then call it a day. He wasn't sure how attractive an ex-cop in his mid-fifties would be as a potential husband but he was in pretty good shape for his age and so wasn't overly worried. Although he didn't feel himself to be any older than when he was thirty, the idea of retirement and settling down looked more attractive with each passing year.

As Susan closes the lid of her laptop and reaches for her coffee his thoughts were dragged back to the present.

He'd had quite a tussle with his lieutenant over the Fox case. They argued the pros and cons back and forth until Lord's logic simply could not be denied. For Christ's sake try to keep it low key, he'd been told. Lord suspected that if he was right about Fox's death, it wouldn't stay low key for long.

"So what's on your mind besides me?" Susan asked him with a sly wink.

"Boring stuff mostly, World War Three, dead guys like Alex Fox."

"War I can understand, God forbid, but Fox? I thought that case was closed?"

"Yeah, maybe it is and maybe it isn't. There are a few things that don't add up and I was hoping to talk through some of the detail."

"Why don't I get Bud in here? He did the PM on Fox."

"Sure, that'd be great."

Susan called through to her colleague who promised to be right there. The pair looked at each other across the tops of their steaming coffee mugs as they waited for the pathologist to arrive. A few seconds later, a tall, cadaverous man with what seemed to be a permanent five-o'clock shadow appeared at the door. His name was Alfred Serpukhov but for some reason that Lord had never discovered, everyone called him Bud. After exchanging pleasantries,

Bud observed that there was in fact no room for him in Susan's office with Lord in the only visitor's chair so he slouched against the door frame.

"What do you know, John?" He asked.

"Well, I was hoping that you could help me with some info about Alex Fox."

"The elevator accident?"

"Yes, that's the one. I'm looking into the cause of death a little more closely. A few loose ends. What do you remember about the post-mortem?"

"I should get the file if you need the detail but his injuries were commensurate with a fall followed by the car descending on him. He had a pelvic fracture, a broken right ankle and multiple fractures to the right femur. His right tibia had a comminuted fracture. These injuries were consistent with the fall down the elevator shaft and the subsequent landing on the lip that surrounds the elevator well where the lowest part of the elevator car sits when it's on the bottom floor."

Lord was making notes. "So the fall down the shaft looked pretty conclusive."

"In my opinion, yes."

"How about the upper body?"

"It was in pretty bad shape. Massive crushing and shearing injuries. The car had torn off parts of the upper body and sort of rolled the head between the side of the car and the wall of the elevator shaft causing much of the front part of the head and face to be destroyed."

"Was he alive when this happened?"

"Judging by the amount of blood present at the site I would say the fall severely injured him but was not fatal and the elevator car killed him a minute or two later."

"Could the injuries have been caused somewhere else and the body dumped into the shaft?"

"Of course it's always possible but I think not. The blood spray patterns, the marks on the elevator car and walls tell a different story."

Lord rubbed his chin and then looked up from his notebook. "I guess he could have been dumped down the shaft after, say, being knocked unconscious."

Bud paused, beginning to feel a little defensive.

"Yes, that's possible. It would have required someone who could take control of the elevator and someone who could work quickly to avoid detection. Don't forget, this was a busy time when people in the apartment were going to work."

"So if we suspected foul play, we're looking at two people as a minimum."

"Yes, and one with specialist knowledge of the elevator systems."

"So you have no doubt that he was killed in that shaft."

Bud sighed and shifted his weight against the door jam. "I have no doubt that he was alive when he fell or was pushed and that he was basically intact at the time. The injuries I recorded were massive and consistent entirely with the action of the car and the location of the body. If he had the upper body injuries before the fall, we would have seen evidence of it inside the shaft." He paused before continuing.

"It is not *impossible* that the lower body injuries were caused by some other circumstance than a fall. He could have been placed in that position before the car descended having had his legs damaged by some other means. I cannot rule that out although I think it unlikely."

"Thanks, Bud." Lord said. "I'm sorry to grill you but something's turned up and I just want to be sure is all."

"Yeah, no problem. I'm used to being interrogated by cops." Bud was smiling now.

"One last question. If we wanted to take another look at him..."

"Impossible." Bud interrupted.

"Why?"

"The DoD took the body and cremated it. It's gone."

"Shit!" Lord said.

"We do have an extensive set of photographs if that's any help, John." Susan offered. "You're welcome to look through them if you think it will help."

Lord yawned, stretched his arms above his head, and tossed his notebook on top of the six-inch pile of papers on Susan's desk. "Let's dig 'em out." He said.

* * *

Charlie sits at home and finds himself gazing out of the apartment window again. He's replaying his conversation with Lord over and over. He is having trouble understanding why Lord, once so eager to get to the bottom of this case, now seemed to be losing interest. It appeared to Charlie as if the whole world just wanted to forget about the deaths at The Factory and get on with life. As if somehow it wasn't important. The fact that all of the dots weren't joined didn't appear to matter. But Charlie couldn't let it go. Today was Thursday and he didn't want to go back to work next week and make an attempt to fit in as if nothing happened. Maybe it's something in the water, he thought. People's passivity about the situation irritated him. On the other hand, with the crisis developing over in China, it was probably not surprising that people had their minds elsewhere. Folk he met in the shops and on street corners were saying that this could be it. The big one. The beginning of the next war, the new Russia. The news was full of it. Americans were frightened. Maybe people are just distracted by all this war talk he told himself.

He could hear his ex-wife's voice telling him to let it go.

"Not everything in life is worth a crusade, Charlie," she'd often said to him. "You don't know when to just let things go and move on. It's not normal, it's a bit manic. Most of the time you don't care about anything and then you'll get a bug up your ass about something stupid and drive me crazy talking about it all the time," she'd said. Maybe she was right Charlie thought. Maybe I am a bit manic but if that's how I am then fuck 'em. "Fuck 'em!" He called out in his empty apartment. The little sizzle of rebelliousness made the normally cautious Charlie feel a little better.

What I need, thought Charlie, is some more evidence. Some way I can convince Lord that things are wrong here. Some ammunition for him to fire. Something to hook his curiosity. I also have to get out of this apartment. Elizabeth was coming over for dinner again tonight. Charlie looked at his watch. Enough time to drag out the Ten-Speed and go for a ride. He scribbled Elizabeth a note in case he was late and unhooked his bike from where it hung in the spare room.

* * *

Lord, Susan and Bud pored over some of the most gruesome pictures that any of them have seen in awhile. There must be two hundred photographs, Lord thought as they spread them out on the stainless steel surface of the empty autopsy table. Colour too. Photos of the scene, of the body, of marks on the elevator car and walls, of blood splatters and severed body parts. And the head. Christ almighty, the head. Lord has seen a lot of dead bodies in his career but this had to take the cake. He thought it looked as though some giant hand took hold of Fox's head and rammed it face first into an electric planer. If it wasn't for the hair, it would be impossible to know what you were looking at.

The way the body was brutalised reminded Lord of a dog he once saw next to the railway lines. The dog's right hind leg was sticking out at a bizarre angle and was held on by a flap of skin. The train had run over it at the hip and although it wasn't cut off like it would have been with a knife, the wide steel edge of the train wheel had created a sort of hinge. A hinge where there should have been a bone and muscle. A new joint that defied everything he knew about dogs and made it look like some sort of grotesque mutant. Its throat was also torn away and poking out of its neck was a round tube, like a garden hose but thinner and about two inches long. Bright crimson with a perfectly round and flared end that reminded Lord of a plumbing fixture. Just lying there on the grass, looking like it didn't even belong to the animal but had been shoved into its neck by some malicious kid.

The legs of the naked body on the autopsy table showed massive bruising in a pattern suggesting violent contact with the edge of something long and straight. In this case the assumption was the steel edge of the well at the bottom of the elevator shaft. On one leg, the bones in the thigh were actually poking out through the skin, their jagged edges clearly visible. Lord looked at the bruising and the position of the body in the shaft when it was first discovered. The body was lying half in and half out of the well. The right leg was badly broken and the body rested with its right side against the edge of the well, the shoulder propped against the side of the shaft.

Abruptly, a thought leapt into Lord's mind causing a ripple of excitement to shoot through his body.

"Isn't there something strange about that?" He asked, tapping his finger on an image.

"What do you mean?" Susan replied

"Well, the body is lying with its right side against the edge of the well. The right leg is the most badly damaged and shows bruising consistent with falling onto the edge where it's lying, right?"

"Yes, as you would expect." Bud said.

"But if Fox fell three stories and landed on his right side against the lip of the well, what would normally happen to the body?"

"You would expect that it would be deflected away toward the other side of the well," Susan said, finishing his thought.

"Hey guys, it could simply have bounced back again," said Bud. "A body has a lot of energy after falling that far."

"Yes, but look what's on the other side of the shaft," said Lord pointing to another photograph.

"My God," said Susan.

"Oh!" echoed Bud.

The photograph in question revealed that on the side of the shaft opposite to where the body had fallen were a series of what appeared to be metal brackets designed to mate with the floor of the car to ensure it was correctly located. These protuberances would have caused wicked damage to a body flung against them. They were black with years of undisturbed grease and filth. The photographs of the lower body revealed almost no damage on its left side.

“Bud, do you think it would be possible for a body to fall down the shaft and bounce around without hitting these things?” Asked Lord.

Bud took a deep breath. “I have to say that I don’t. No.”

“Susan?”

“I agree, John. It’s extremely unlikely the body could have landed and remained in the position it was without colliding with the other side of the shaft and there’s no way to miss those metal parts. No way. The only possibility would be if the body fell into the exact centre of the well, but then we wouldn’t have the sort of damage we see to the right leg. ”

Bud was shaking his head. “Shit. I should have seen that. I really should have seen that.”

Susan walked around the table and put a hand on his arm. “Listen to me, Bud. There was no reason to think that foul play was involved. I looked over these pictures too. I didn’t see it either. You can’t blame yourself.”

“It was my finding though. My name on the report. God, what was I thinking?”

“You were doing your job as well as you could. Under massive pressure and working long hours. We can’t process every detail, Bud. Not every time. No one can.”

Bud pulled away from Susan. “I think I might head out for some air. Just be alone for a few minutes. I’ll leave you to carry on.”

Sure Bud. Take it easy.” Susan replied.

After Bud had left, a tear welled in Susan’s eye. “He’s a good pathologist, John. It’s a bitch of a job and sooner or later it bites all of us at least once.”

“I know, Susan,” Lord said, putting his arm around her and giving her a squeeze. “He’ll be fine.”

* * *

Lord and his partner sit in their cruiser under a tree, take-out food containers and drinks balanced strategically around the front of the vehicle. While Lord was at the medical Examiners office, Louis had visited Fox's apartment block to speak with neighbours and the building Superintendent. Louis had once asked why Lord always seemed to arrange things so he visited the ME's office on his own. Lord just laughed it off and told Louis that they had been there together plenty of times. He'd thought about it later though and realised that he didn't really want Louis to share his time with Susan. It came as a bit of a shock for him to realise that he was behaving like a jealous husband. It also reminded him of how few close friends he had.

Lord belched with satisfaction and slurped up the last of his drink.

"How'd you go over at the apartment?" he asked?

"Nothin' new. Nobody saw or heard a thing until the cops turned up. This old lady told me that the man who came to look at the elevator wasn't the usual man. Not as nice as the regular guy, she said. Seems the regular guy's a real boy scout. Man fixed her busted doorknob once, she told me."

"You get the guy's name?"

"Sure, Jeff Hudson. He gave her his card and she has it sittin' on the shelf over the stove as if it was some sorta antique. Got all the details."

"We might pay him a visit."

"Sure. How about you? Your girlfriend have anything new?"

"She's happily married, Lou. Got a kid even."

"Don't stop you from drooling over them king-size titties though."

Lord suddenly found irritation welling up at Louis's vulgar remark. "Cut it out, Lou, she's a good friend is all."

"Sure, JL, if you say so. So what you find out anyway?"

"Well, we looked over the scene and autopsy pictures. There's a good chance that our man didn't fall down that shaft at all."

"No Shit! So you figure he's dumped in there after being killed?"

"Hard to say. Bud reckons he was alive when the elevator crushed him but someone could have banged his legs up and made it look like he fell. Unfortunately for Bud, I noticed a detail that he missed. Maybe just a fresh pair of eyes or maybe I've missed my calling."

Louis shook his head slowly. "Hell. Bud musta been pissed."

"Yeah, poor guy. He wasn't a happy camper, that's for sure."

"Problem is, we still have a mountain of questions. Why on earth would someone go to such elaborate means to kill Fox? Why not stage a car wreck? Why go to all this trouble. And why kill him in the first place? Did he know something? Was he hooked up in something big outside of work? Drugs maybe?"

"What did Ganderton say?"

"He said Fox was involved in some martial arts school in his spare time. Taught kids after school. Doesn't sound like something to be killed over. He's still convinced that Fox has some connection to the hacker at the facility and that the department is covering something up."

"Something got him seriously dead, that's for damn sure."

"Yes, and these killers aren't your run-of-the-mill boneheads either. They were obviously organised, fast, and smart. They know about manipulating elevator systems, they know about forensics, they fooled poor old Bud, for Christ's sake, and he's pretty good."

"Well, JL. Heavy duty-bad guys usually means heavy-duty shit. Dudes like them, they aint gunnin' on account of no parkin' fines.

"Just as well too, I'm thinking. Let's go see our boy scout."

"The real elevator guy?"

"The very same, I'll give him a call. Let's see if he can manage to complicate this puzzle even more."

* * *

It had taken some time for the VP to get the president alone. His schedule was simply insane these days. Most of the administration's energy was being poured into damage control over the China incident and what was left went into preparing for war. A crazy two-handed shell game, they all thought. Buying time so if we have a fight that we don't want and that we didn't start, at least we'll be ready.

The pair sat across from each other in the president's private office. The president was staring unbelievingly at the innocuous-looking fax machine on his private desk as if it had turned into something diseased.

"From that fax there you say?"

"That's what the Intel guys say. No question of it."

"I suppose they briefed you first?" The president knew that his VP would have been made aware of this news some time ago. Checks and balances.

"Yes, they did. I want to hear what you have to say to begin with."

The president looked deeply into the eyes of his old friend. "John, I can tell you, on the strength of everything our friendship and this office means to me, that I had nothing to do with this. Nothing."

An enormous wave of relief swept over the VP. He had to blink back the tears. There was no way this man could lie to him about this. Not to him. Not ever. He immediately felt guilty about asking Medford to get the fax log sheet. He would never mention this act of betrayal.

"I knew that. I guess I just wanted to hear you say it."

"Sure, John, I understand. I'm grateful that you came to me first. What's got me stumped is how in God's name anyone else could have done this. They must have snuck in here under the noses of the men outside and while we were sleeping in the next Goddamn room. Just as well they didn't want to kill me or we wouldn't be having this conversation and that's for sure."

This was something that had never occurred to the vice-president but it was absolutely correct. Anyone skilful enough to pull this off would have been able to kill the president and the first lady as they slept. The idea sent a shiver down his back. We're almost dealing with a damned ghost, he thought. "We have to tighten up the security in this place," he said.

"I'm afraid you're right. And not just for me. We can't take any chances now, not considering the crisis we're dealing with. You better get George on to it pronto."

The mention of Medford's name suddenly sent a pang of guilt and fear into the vice-president's heart. He felt an overwhelming need to confess his actions to his president and friend. Later he would wish he had seized the opportunity. Later, when it was too late, when he was in too deep and there was no going back.

CHAPTER 19

Elizabeth let herself in to Charlie's apartment after work. They had recently given each other keys to their respective homes to make life easier. She was surprised to find Charlie out but when she read his note she relaxed. Charlie was cooking tonight and she was unsure what he had in mind so she busied herself washing the few dishes that remained on the sink and then pouring a glass of wine. She flopped onto Charlie's leather sofa and sipped her drink. Already this place was starting to feel comfortable, she thought. A shower would be nice. She made a mental note to bring a few things over that could stay in Charlie's bathroom so she had a bit more flexibility. Be good for him, she thought, a nice little reminder of me.

Elizabeth reflected on how happy she'd felt since their relationship had become serious. How Charlie seemed to complete part of her life, to fill a space that had been empty. Like when you have a room and not enough furniture to fill it. It's not uncomfortable but it just feels a whole lot better when it's not quite as bare. She cast her eyes around his apartment and thought it was so much like hers. Both places were neat, clean and comfortable without pretension or show. Perhaps Charlie's a little more than mine, she thought, but the similarities were there even so. Must be a sign, she told herself with a smile.

Her gaze settled on the coat rack she could just see in the hall from where she sat. Alex Fox's jacket was hung on one of the dark wooden pegs. Putting aside her wine she went over and lifted it down, curious to have another look. She turned the jacket over in her hands and it occurred to her that, apart from the silly picture on the back, it was a very nice garment. Would have been expensive she thought, feeling the sumptuous leather, noting the classy gold lining. On a whim she slipped her arms into the jacket and shrugged it on. The sleeves were too long and the shoulders hung a little but it felt nice. She toyed momentarily with the possibility of having it altered to fit her and then dismissed it. Too spooky, she thought, wearing the jacket of a dead person. She wondered what Charlie would do with it. They could hardly ask Leonard to put it back.

Elizabeth walked to the mirror in Charlie's bedroom still wearing Fox's jacket. She stuck her hands in the pockets and struck a James Dean pose, did a little pirouette on the spot, and liked what she saw. As she pulled her hands out of the pockets she felt a piece of paper brush the end of one finger. Curious, she slipped her hand back inside and pulled out a small slip of paper from a sticky note pad. She walked into the kitchen and stood by the window to read Alex's small but neat script.

It appeared to be a list. A shopping list, with a date on top. With a shock, she realised that the list had been created the day before Alex died. It felt weird and not entirely pleasant to have pulled this little snippet of private domesticity out of the jacket pocket. She felt somehow like a voyeur, a peeping tom squinting into someone else's life. Her jovial mood was destroyed in a flash and she wished that she hadn't ever touched the damned jacket. She slipped it off her shoulders and went to hang it up. Just at that instant, Charlie opened the door and wheeled his bike through. They stood face to face, Charlie holding the bike, his face flushed from the ride and Elizabeth with the jacket in hand looking pale and a little distracted.

"Hi." Said Charlie. "You look like you've had a tough day." He leaned his bike against the wall and put his arms around her. Elizabeth returned his embrace with her free arm, the other sticking out, still holding the jacket as though she herself was a coat stand. She stepped away and replaced the jacket.

"Yes, I was just fooling around with Alex's jacket while I waited for you and I found a slip of paper inside. It gave me a bad feeling, I don't know why. I guess because it was a bit personal and domestic. I sort of felt guilty looking at it."

Charlie wiped the sheen of perspiration from his forehead. "Give me a look."

Elizabeth handed it over. The list read:

Low fat milk

Torch batteries – D size

Collect dry cleaning – 2 pants, 1 jacket

Champagne – Formicidae - JL!

Charlie froze when he read the last line, his eyes widening. Elizabeth, seeing the effect of the note, put her hand on his arm.

"Charlie, what's wrong? You just froze. What is it?"

"It's that last line. The champagne." He took a deep breath after realising that he wasn't breathing at all.

"What about it? What does it mean."

Charlie closed his eyes and concentrated on bringing his breathing under control. His heart began to slow down.

"How about this. Why don't I have a quick shower and then get the dinner going. While I'm doing the preparation, I'll explain it all to you. How's that?"

For a second, Elizabeth was on the point of suggesting that she and Charlie took the shower together but then she stopped short. Something in his demeanour told her that perhaps he wanted a little time to himself to pull his thoughts together before explaining it all to her.

"Okay, do that and then I want to know every detail, promise?"

"Promise." Charlie kissed her and headed off for his shower.

As the sound of running water carried to where she was sitting, absently flipping through a magazine, she wondered how long it would be before their time together was no longer punctuated by the recent events at The Factory. Roll on that day, she thought and raised her glass.

* * *

Jeff Hudson was refurbishing what looked to Lord like some sort of switch gear. The workshop from where he ran his business was old and dark. Greasy pieces of machinery sat on industrial metal racking. The floor was concrete and stained almost black from years of trodden in grime. Lord guessed Hudson's age to be about his own and figured that this workshop had seen a whole lot more grease than its current owner had been around to generate. The large roller door was open and the pair walked straight over to where the man was working.

"Mr Hudson?" Lord asked they approached.

Lifting his eyes from where he was stooped over his work, Hudson straightened up and smiled broadly at them as if they were long-lost buddies. My God, Lord thought, the guy must be seven feet tall. His face, a good foot higher than theirs, almost beamed to see them. Lord thought that it was no surprise that the oldies loved him if he turned that radiant smile on everyone he met.

"You must be detectives Lord and Armstrong." He said, his smile losing none of its radiance. "I'd shake hands but I think you might not appreciate the grease."

He let out a deep and rumbling laugh that Lord imagined he could feel through his feet. Lord was struck by a memory, a movie in which a huge black man had been wrongly accused of killing two small girls. The image from the movie was of the giant standing next to the main character, Tom Hanks, and simply towering over him.

Lord smiled back, he couldn't help but do so. "Please call me John. This fine-looking gentleman is my partner Louis."

"You play basketball when you were young?" Louis asked.

That booming laugh again. "No sir. Maybe if I did I'd be the one wearing the suit instead of these old overalls. Still, the Lord's been kind to me and I've never wanted for a thing in my whole life. Jeepers, I'm forgetting my manners. Come in to the office and I'll get

Martha to make you some coffee."

Lord figured that it had been a while since he'd heard anyone say *jeepers.* Still, you couldn't help liking this friendly giant. He seemed to radiate warmth and sincerity. He led them into what, with a gifted imagination, could be described as an office. The only difference Lord could see between the office and the workshop was that this space had carpet on the floor and three old leather chairs that looked as though they had spent several lifetimes in an old saloon. Everything was ancient and greasy. Old boxes and half-packed spare parts bulged out of the bookcase and piles of magazines leaned precariously from every corner. An ancient coffee pot gurgled on a small shelf above the radiator. A single feeble light bulb hung from what appeared to be a twenty-foot wire to the ceiling, almost invisible in the gloom. When the introductions were done, Lord guessed Martha to be a hundred years old if she was a day but he noticed she had the same inner glow that emanated from Hudson.

Hudson noticed Lord casting his eyes around the room. "Used to belong to my Daddy and his Daddy 'afore him. Back then the place was a general engineering shop. I pretty much specialise in elevators and escalators these days. There's not too much work but then I'm a man of simple tastes so it don't take much to keep me ticking over."

Except for a mighty food bill, Lord thought. Martha returned with cups and a tray of cake before collecting the coffee pot with both hands. Lord was relieved to see that the cups were clean and he noticed Louis making a similar inspection. He'd been afraid they might have been as greasy as everything else in the place. He sipped at the coffee and it was surprisingly good. Delicious in fact. He said as much to Martha and her face lit up with same radiance that had startled him before. She excused herself and left through a back door into another room. Lord was surprised to observe that in the gloom he hadn't even noticed the door existed.

"So how can I help you fellas today?" Hudson asked, leaning back, his chair groaning desperately under the punishment.

"We were hoping that you could enlighten us on a couple of technical issues," Lord said.

"Ahuh."

"Yes, do you recall the apartment building over on Clarke Road. I believe you do the elevator maintenance there for a company based out of Chicago."

"That's right. I do all of their work in this area. Been doing it for thirty years."

"I guess these modern elevators are all computer-controlled. Not like the old days."

"Ahuh. An' they keep on changing too. I've had to make a few trips out to Chicago to get training. The mechanisms haven't changed as much but the controllers are nothing like the old days."

Lord helped himself to another piece of Martha's fabulous carrot cake, feeling a bit like a guilty school kid for doing so. "So did you install the system in Clarke Road?"

"Yes, me an' the guy from Chicago. This was the first of a new type for me so he came over to give me some on-the-job lessons."

"Okay. Here's a question for you. If I wanted to take control of the elevator, say to make it go up and down under my control, maybe even open the doors without the car being ready. Is that possible?"

"Sure, no problem. You just need to get yourself a maintenance panel."

"And what's that?"

"It's a gadget that you plug into the main computer. Let's you take over the controls of the system. We use it to test out the switches an' stuff. A'course you'd also need the lessons in how to drive it."

"And where would I get a maintenance panel from?"

"You could just order one from the manufacturer. I guess they'd want to know that you were running a maintenance business but there's lots of guys like me these days, doing work for the big companies. Not many of the big manufacturers have their own people anymore. Not for the routine stuff at least."

"I assume it comes with a manual?"

"It sure does, like a phone book it is, lotsa options."

"But a smart guy could figure it out?"

"Heck, I can figure it out so a smart fella'd have no trouble!" Lord thought that Hudson's belly laugh actually rattled the small windowpanes in the office.

"And I guess these panels would all come from Chicago?"

"Ahuh. That's where they make 'em all right. Are you fellas plannin' on a change of career? Figurin' to put me outta business?" It was Lord's turn to laugh.

"No, Jeff, you've got nothing to fear from us in that regard."

Lord drained his coffee and stood. "Thank you, Jeff, you have been very helpful. By the way, when were you last out at Clarke Road?"

"Oh, it'd have to be six months ago, at least. I can check if you need the exact date."

"No, six months is close enough. Thanks."

The pair walked out under the open roller door and back into the fresh air.

"You want me to get a list of who bought those panels from the Chicago outfit, JL?" Louis asked.

"Right. I think that would be a good place to start. Christ, but he was a big guy, Lou! What you figure? Seven foot?"

"Easy, and that was just across the shoulders! I'm glad we didn't have to arrest his ass."

"Yeah, just as well he's such a cheerful soul. I guess he doesn't have to worry about being mugged at least."

* * *

Charlie emerged from the shower glowing pink from hot water and steam. It struck him how nice it was to have someone else in the apartment. How nice it had seemed to come home to someone instead of rattling around on his own. This I could get used to, he thought. Elizabeth had a glass of red wine ready for him and he kissed her lightly before having a sip. As he unloaded the vegetables from the refrigerator he thought back to the message on the paper that she had discovered.

"So, are you going to tell me what this secret message is all about or am I going to have to twist your arm?"

"Well, I'm not sure what it all means but I can tell you about the Formicidae part."

"Okay, I'm all ears."

"Well, Formicidae is the family name for ants."

"Ants? You mean ants as in insects? Bugs?"

"Yes, those sort of ants. Formicidae was Alex's name for a set of ideas that he had. A sort of architecture for the VIWAP Mk II. I guess with hindsight it was obviously more than ideas. He must have been actually working on a alpha version."

Elizabeth looked a little confused. "So what does it have to do with ants?"

"Well, ants are interesting in many ways. One of the things that fascinated Alex was the way that intelligence appears to be distributed among them. As though an entire colony is one organism."

"How do you mean?"

Charlie took a deep breath and put his knife down on the cutting board.

"Ants manage to accomplish amazing things. Different species have different patterns but the principle holds. For example, they cut grass and carry it back to the nest from great distances. They don't actually eat the grass but inside the nest they actively cultivate a sort of fungus on the pieces of grass and they eat the fungus. At the same time they manage to build complex mounds above the ground. They can patch the mound up if it's damaged and they can even relocate if they have to. Inside they have a queen laying thousands of eggs a day and they transport them and raise them. Inside the mound, the temperature and humidity is tightly controlled."

"The really interesting thing is that no single ant understands how to do all the activities necessary to run the nest. Somehow together, they manage to achieve incredible organisation and complex construction without having an overall blueprint or supervisor. Somehow there just seems to be enough ants that know what each task is and how to perform them that when they work together they accomplish what any individual could never have the capacity to do alone. And this is replicated in millions of nests across the world. Always the right mix of skills to do the job."

Elizabeth was hooked now. "But isn't that like humans constructing a building? Lots of different tradesmen with different skill sets?"

"No, not exactly. In our case, we have architects that design the place and engineers who specify materials and internal structures. These people sit above the mass of workers and basically, using the plans, direct the workers as to how the building should come together. In the ant world, everyone is a tradesman. There are no supervisors or engineers or plans even. Imagine that you had a thousand workers who had never built a skyscraper before. You have electricians and steelworkers and bricklayers and window fixers and plumbers. On and on. Stick them all on an empty lot and say go. What would happen?"

"Not much, I'd say."

"True, and yet all of these people have been trained well to do their jobs. They all know what to do but then again they don't. Somebody would need to take charge, to make decisions about what goes where. Draw up some plans, have meetings, provide a supervisory framework for the whole thing. Otherwise, even though within the team of workers you have all the hands-on knowledge you need, the job doesn't get done. The ants don't have that problem even though nobody trained them at all. The question is why? That's why some researchers see them as sort of one organism, the whole colony as one living creature. One brain, many legs."

"That's amazing." Elizabeth said, shaking her head. "I'd never thought of that before. I guess we take lots of things things for granted."

"We do. Alex thought that if he could figure out how the ants did it, understand the mechanism, he could build it into the VIWAP."

"And what would that accomplish?"

"Remember one brain, many legs? Imagine how powerful a weapon we'd have with one brain, many computers. Imagine having a hundred thousand or a million computers working on a problem, each with a little bit of the puzzle. If the VIWAP could take over the enemy's computers and then in some way link them up as one, well, you'd better watch out."

Elizabeth's glass froze half way to her lips. "God, Charlie, do you think that's what he did? That the champagne in the message was to celebrate his achieving that very thing?"

"Looks that way to me. It's pretty clear. Champagne. What else if not to celebrate success. The success of Formicidae. I think he did it, I really do. That might also explain why Ed told me that the INFOSEC guys thought the VIWAP had escaped using the backup system. With that sort of computing horsepower at its disposal, it might have been able to work it out. This might be the piece of the puzzle that we were missing. The reason why the VIWAP exceeded our expectations."

"Who do you think he was celebrating with? Who's J.L.?"

"That's got me beat. I obviously don't know all of Alex's friends but I can't think of anyone within The Factory with those initials. It's hard to imagine him celebrating something as strictly classified as this with anyone outside. Maybe we'll never know. One thing's for sure, if he pulled off the Formicidae concepts, and then lost control, there's no telling what might happen."

* * *

George Medford, punctual as always, is waiting in the private room that the vice-president has selected for the briefing. The VP has been awake for much of the night mulling over the situation with the fax log. He knows that the seriousness of his situation depends upon the attitude and inclination of the Security Chief. Trouble is, George Medford is a hard man to read. The two have worked together on and off for many years but when the VP tried to catalogue the things he knew about George, he was surprised at how little it amounted to. George didn't normally speak about personal things, didn't really offer comments when folks talked around the water cooler about their weekends or their kids. George was just sort of there, without being part of anything.

In fact, the only reason anyone even knew about his wife's illness was because he had to take quite a bit of time off and he had told someone the reason why. As bad news does, it rippled around the building pretty fast. When questioned about her, George was almost evasive in his answers. Just a private sort of man, most thought. Hell, it can't be easy to talk about a dying wife, so most people just left it alone. The reality is that George is retreating into himself, part of him dying along with his wife, the only woman he had ever truly cared for. His cool and aloof exterior was an impenetrable skin over the turmoil and anger that raged inside him. George was adept at hiding his emotions, it was a very handy skill in his line of work.

As the VP entered the room he saw Medford sitting there impassively, just as he expected. Suit jacket unbuttoned, one leg crossed over the other, shirt and tie immaculate.

"How are you, George?" The VP asked, pumping his hand as if meeting him had brightened his day enormously.

"Very well, sir, and yourself?"

"Not too bad I guess, apart from the Chinese situation. Damned powder keg we're sitting on here, George. We need a few more cool heads like you. Take the temperature down a few notches."

"I'm sure you're the man for the job, sir."

The VP was a little unsure of how to take that last comment. His political antenna told him that he'd just been the recipient of a sarcastic remark. It was delivered with such overwhelming neutrality that even a seasoned campaigner like himself was unsure of the intent. He decided to give Medford the benefit of the doubt and assume the remark had been sincere.

"Thanks, George. I guess we'll all need to pull together on this one. Show some solidarity. Now's certainly not the time to be allowing any divisions to creep into our team." The VP wasn't sure whether Medford was keying into where the conversation was going as yet. The damned guy was so hard to read. He decided to cut to the chase.

"I guess you have had contact by now from the intelligence people regarding that mix-up with the president's fax machine?" The VP was deliberately staying upbeat, trying to sow the seeds that the outcome would in fact prove to be a misunderstanding or a technical fault. Not a big deal.

"Yes, I was actually put into a difficult situation. They asked me about the machine when they discovered that the log was empty. I had to tell them that I didn't know anything about it."

"Well, George, I hope that you don't think you had to lie. I would never ask you to do such a thing. I hope you realise that."

"Actually that's exactly how I felt. You see, the thing is, if the log sheet had been given to the intelligence staff, they would have known exactly why the log file was empty on the fax machine. The fact that you had it last and it's never been handed over made me feel like I should try to protect you."

The VP didn't like the way this was shaping up at all. Was he being intimidated here? It felt as though some implication was being made, as though they had an agreement to cover this up all along and now Medford was just playing his part. Shit, I can't let this get out of hand, he thought.

"I must have forgotten to hand the sheet over, George. Why would you think that I somehow needed protecting? What made you think that?"

George's face could have been chiselled from granite for all the emotion it betrayed. The VP on the other hand could feel a film of sweat forming on his upper lip.

"I'm sorry, sir, it must have been my mistake. Why don't you just give me the paper and I'll hand it over and clear this up quickly."

The VP felt fear's icy hand begin to grip his heart. Trying to keep control of his composure, he continued.

"I don't actually have it with me, George, I think it's in my file. I'll pick it up later." Trying to buy some time.

"No problem, sir, I have a copy. I can just hand this one over and at least the boys can get started."

"You have a copy? Why on earth would you have made a copy, George? Why?" The VP was struggling now to maintain his composure. He felt like the situation was spiralling out of control, getting away from him.

"Protection. I made the copy to protect myself. I've worked security in this building long enough to know that a document like this is poison. I'm not about to be the only one who knows a secret that stands between the life and death of this administration. Not without protection."

The VP's mind was racing now. He could see Medford's point; he respected a good sense of self-preservation. Maybe he just had to convince the man that he was in no danger. Christ, why didn't I know this man better, he thought.

"Okay George, I can understand your reasoning. I guess it's the reality we all face in the political climate we find ourselves. It really is just you and me who know about this. There's no reason why you can't hand that copy over to me and I'll submit the both of them."

"If you hand over the original you don't need my copy." Alarm bells were now ringing in the VP's head.

"What are you getting at here, George?"

"I think you've destroyed the original because you want to protect the president." There it was. That's it, the VP thought. It's all over. God, what was I thinking? Destroying evidence. You fucking idiot!

The VP sighed deeply and massaged his temples with his fingertips.

"You're right, George, I did. I know the president didn't send that fax. I know that with the same certainty that I know you're sitting across from me in this room. I couldn't let him be ruined over such an idiotic mix-up as this. Couldn't even allow him to have to fight it, to allow some of the mud to stick, to cast a shadow over his term, his legacy. I couldn't do it, George."

George nodded his head, the first gesture made in the discussion so far. "It doesn't have to end that way. You said yourself that only the two of us know the real circumstances. My copy could just disappear too."

The VP's head shot up. This was not what he expected at all. Absolute impartiality was all he ever expected from men like Medford.

"Why would you do this, George? Why would you put your own career at risk?"

"I'm not sure there is any risk. I'm sure we could come to an arrangement that benefited us both." Suddenly the scales fell from the VP's eyes. My God, he wants to blackmail me. He wants me to pay for his silence! The slinking snivelling bastard! He doesn't give a shit for anyone's career or the good name of the president, he just want's to cash in on the situation! Anger boiled inside the VP's chest.

"What the fuck do you want, Medford?" he said, his lips curling back into a snarl.

Medford's face gave nothing. No emotion. He reached into his pocket and pulled out a small piece of paper. He held it out. "Not here. Meet me at this time and place and we'll sort it out." Without his conscious thought, the VP's arm seemed to float in front of his eyes. He saw himself taking the slip of paper and putting it in his jacket pocket. The situation was almost surreal. This was something that happened in the movies, not to honest men like himself.

Medford simply rose and walked out of the room leaving the vice-president staring at his empty seat.

CHAPTER 20

The nuclear submarine USS *Elite* patrolled at periscope-depth along the south perimeter of the carrier battle group. At two-and-a-half billion dollars and seven-and-a-half thousand tons, the sleek fish was relatively inexpensive insurance for the massive collection of hardware stationed off the Taiwanese coast. In the control room, Commander James Lexington, on his first patrol in his own boat, stepped away from the Mk18 Search Periscope and blinked his eyes to clear his vision. He turned to his officer of the deck.

"Not much to see out there, Mark," he said, stretching his arms behind his back.

"Not much of a day, sir." The officer acknowledged. The sky is heavy with cloud, the sea an even grey, the wind driving the rain at a 45-degree angle. Inside the submarine it's warm, quiet, and well-lit. The boat is spacious and clean, the air circulated and filtered every few minutes. A far cry from the stinking, foul-aired, death traps of fifty years before.

The Commander sighs, he's tired and ready to turn in. Day and night don't mean much aboard a modern submarine. He intends to take the sub down to 300 feet and perform a sweep around the group. The diving officer studies the status board to ensure that all vents and hatches are locked down prior to the dive. He checks the reserves of air pressure in the banks and reports everything ready. As the commander is about to order the dive officer to take the boat down, there is a strange noise. A whirring sound. Instinctively, as if they are a single organism, all of the men stop breathing and listen. Strange noises aboard a submarine are not usually welcome.

Two seconds later there's a solid bang, and the sound of cavitation in the water. Immediately, the fire control technician yells "missile launch!"

The commander, instantly alert, strides to the console. "What the hell?"

There's no doubt about it. One of the submarine's long-range UGM 109s Tomahawk cruise missiles has just been ejected from its tube in the Vertical Launch System and is heading toward the surface. Seconds later everyone hears the sound of its jet engine igniting as it roars into the sky. Suddenly the control room is energised. A rogue missile with a one thousand pound warhead is a whole lot of trouble.

The commander charges down the port side passageway to the communications shack forward of the control room. He snatches up the high frequency transmitter microphone and attempts to communicate with the USS *Carl Vinson.* To his horror he realises that the communications channel is dead with only a light hiss betraying the fact that it's even switched on. The radio man turns to the commander, his face ashen. "It's all down, sir, as of fifteen seconds ago." The commander sprints back to the control room and orders up the video feed from the periscope, just in time to see the cruise missile accelerating to five hundred mph and disappearing into the distance. "My God!" he breathed as the weapon screamed toward Taiwan, and therefore, China.

Aboard the ships in the battle group, the missile launch comes as an equal shock. They too have lost communications and can only stare at the missile as it skims the surface of the ocean, heading for land. As no flight data was programmed into the guidance system of the missile, its exact destination is unknown to even the crew aboard the submarine. The missile, flying at fifty feet above the waves, heads toward the northern tip of the Taiwanese island before executing a sweeping right-hand turn, tracking directly for Shanghai. At its current speed it will be over the city in forty minutes. Aboard the USS *Carl Vinson*, confusion reigns. With no communication, the commanding officer of the carrier group is at a loss to know what's happening. The commander's instinct is to launch a flight of fighters but the carrier air traffic management centre is reporting system problems. He dare not launch aircraft in this weather without the ability to bring them back in. Aboard every ship in the group, technicians are frantically searching for the cause of the problem, each vessel not knowing that their entire group is off the air.

On the Chinese mainland the defence systems are fully operational. The Tomahawk is being tracked constantly as it races through the driving rain. Unfortunately, nothing in the Chinese arsenal is capable of disabling the barely subsonic missile in time. Chinese fighters are scrambled in anticipation of a larger attack and within a few minutes they pick up the missile as it crosses Ningbo with a hundred miles to run before reaching Shanghai. Minutes later, the Tomahawk thunders into the city and roars over People's Square, sending hundreds of screaming citizens running for their lives. The missile begins a wide turn to the right, skimming over Shanghai University and Huangpu Park before crossing the Huangpu Jiang and then racing back out to sea.

Several thousand feet above, the Chinese fighter pilots watch with growing amazement and confusion, unable to target the missile while over the city. Now the Tomahawk is heading directly back at the carrier battle group. Circling high above the group, the E-2C Hawkeye also tracks the Tomahawk but without effective communications is unable to warn the group and can only look on in impotence and growing horror at the scene unfolding below.

Twenty-five miles offshore, a privately owned mega yacht filled with Chinese businessman and their major clients cruises on autopilot. A case of wrong place, wrong time.

They don't even see the missile approach them as it covers the ocean separating their seventy-five million dollar floating brothel in fewer than three minutes. Two men and three women stand in the cockpit facing the missile. One of the men drags his eyes away from the naked breasts of the woman next to him and observes a smudge of smoke in the distance. Before he has time to calculate its significance, the beast is upon them. Had the Tomahawk been completely devoid of high explosive, it would have still sent the magnificent vessel to the sea floor in minutes. The pure energy that the twenty-foot long, 3,200 pound, cigar-shaped missile possesses as it smashes into the hull of the luxury yacht is sufficient to ensure its doom. As it is, the high explosive packed into the front half of the missile detonates before the rocket booster in the tail passes through the fibreglass hull, ten feet above the waterline. The outcome is catastrophic. One second the boat sits majestically on the ocean, its highly polished, cream-coloured superstructure swept backwards in a design that makes it appear to be travelling fast, even when it's at rest. The next, it simply disappears in a violent cloud of orange-yellow fire, smoke, and spray. Several seconds later the sound of the explosion slams into the carrier group and the seamen on deck staring at the horizon reel from the punch of the blast. When the smoke clears, the extravagant boat is gone. Debris continues to fall all around the site of the explosion but nothing resembling the yacht remains. Despite an extensive search, little will be found of the passengers or crew. It's as if the boat was fed through some colossal mulcher. Just thousands of small pieces of timber, cloth, plastic, and foam remain. Soon, these too will disperse.

What will take longer to dissipate is the furore about to explode as the media get hold of the pictures of a US cruise missile screaming down the main street of Shanghai, scattering terrified people in its wake. Fuel for the fire is added as the identities of the Chinese businessmen are revealed. Two of the sightseers aboard are among the top ten most successful men in the country and their names are household words. The pressure on the Chinese Government to retaliate is massive.

* * *

It's late and George Medford sits at the back of a smoky bar off Sixth Street in downtown Washington. This is not an area that he normally frequents; in fact it's a little disconcerting. He tries to keep his head down, not engage anyone in eye-contact while keeping a watch over the door. He figures the VP probably doesn't come down here too often either. That's the idea. In truth, he doesn't really know whether the VP will show. Medford realises that if he doesn't, his entire plan will come tumbling around his ears. He sips his beer, trying to make it last, not wanting his thinking clouded by alcohol. Not tonight.

A group of about a dozen men occupies the front of the bar. Obviously buddies, he thinks, from the way they laugh and slap one another on the back. They appear to have come directly from work, some still wearing overalls and one man with a dusting of plaster in his hair. Working on a building close by, Medford figures. Occasionally they glance over at him, sitting alone, but he tries not to catch their eyes. George isn't afraid of them but he knows that with the amount of liquor they've probably consumed, anything's possible. He feels the comforting presence of his Glock in its well-worn holster under his arm but he knows that if he has to draw it, he's already in serious trouble. Medford doesn't expect there to be trouble but he's impatient for the VP to arrive. One guy sitting alone, nursing a beer, looks very suspicious.

Medford checks his watch. When he looks up, someone has entered the bar. A big guy with a baseball cap pulled low and the collar of his jacket turned up, as if it were freezing outside instead of just cool, one hand inside his jacket pocket. These things Medford notices instinctively. When he's still twenty feet away, it becomes obvious to Medford that this is not the man he's expecting. The man walks directly toward where Medford is sitting but without looking at him. Medford wonders what's behind him that could furnish the man's destination, maybe the john? He risks a glance over his shoulder to check but there's nothing back there, just another couple of tables and an old jukebox with a faded out-of-order sign stuck over the buttons.

As Medford turns back, the man is standing in front of him looking into his eyes. How the hell did he cover that distance so quickly? he wonders with alarm. His eyes drop to the man's hand and he realises that he's looking directly into the eye of a silenced pistol. A nine-millimetre, he guesses, judging from the bore. And there's another thing. The pistol appears to be inside a cloth bag, just the silencer poking out. This sends a shiver of fear down Medford's back. A feeling that he doesn't experience too often. He knows what the bag's for. To catch the cartridge casing that's ejected when the pistol fires. So that it doesn't make a sound as it falls, but primarily so it isn't left behind. The bag and the silencer. The accoutrement of an assassin. Before he has time to think about the absurdity of the vice-president sending a man to kill him, the man speaks.

"Keep your hands on the table, and slide around slowly to the other side so that your back is towards the door." Medford understands instantly. The man doesn't want his back exposed, wants to be able to see the door, to keep his sightlines clear. He does what he's told as the man keeps his back to the raucous crowd, concealing his weapon. With a fluid movement the gun disappears into the folds of his jacket as the man sits at the table opposite him.

"Who the hell are you?" Medford asks.

"Consider me a representative from the man you are trying to blackmail. You didn't *really* think he'd come to this shit hole did you?" Medford's mind raced, he'd chosen this spot because he knew the likelihood of them being seen was remote. He also knew that it wouldn't be easy for the VP to go out without his security detail but he also knew it could be done. What had seemed simple and in some way almost moral when he'd thought about it previously, suddenly appeared dimwitted in its recklessness.

"What do you want?" The man continued.

"I want to talk to the vice-president about a private matter."

Even to Medford's ears this now sounded ridiculous. Like someone off the street expecting to get an audience with the pope in the local bar. The bolt of fear rippled through him again. What am I doing, he thought, expecting the fucking VP to turn up here. Just because I see this guy every day doesn't mean he's like everyone else. In that instant, Medford realised the stupidity of his scheme. That a man like him could successfully bribe someone in the VP's position. That he would allow it to happen. And it made him angry. His fucking wife could die slowly and his life could be turned inside out but nothing must cause a ripple with the Goddamn administration.

"That's not going to happen," said the man calmly. "You talk to me. What do you want?"

"Fuck you." Medford started to rise but the man's voice cut through him like a knife.

"Sit down! You're not going anywhere until we talk." Who's this prick think he is? Medford thought, his anger growing. Who's he think he's dealing with here? Some flake? Medford's eyes started to blaze.

"Who the fuck do you think you are that you can treat me like shit? Do you know who I am? I don't have to sit here and take your crap!"

The man's face betrayed no emotion. "Whoever you think you *were* is over. You are attempting to corrupt an official at the highest level in the United States Government. At a time when international tensions are running at fever pitch. Your actions threaten to destabilise the administration, to endanger the security of the nation. What you *are* is nothing but a cheap hustler, capitalising on an unfortunate set of circumstances."

Medford was almost speechless with rage. This fly speck was actually calling him a traitor! A traitor to the country he'd risked his life for more than one once! To the country he'd given his youth, his energy, Christ, his life! to serve!

Then Medford made a very bad mistake, his judgment clouded by his anger at the entire injustice of his situation. The man's hands rested lightly on the table, the gun nowhere to be seen. George made a grab for his own weapon, something he had done countless times in practice and even once or twice for real. He knew he could have that piece in his hand before the man's next heart beat. Once his gun was trained on this prick he'd simply back up and get the hell out of there. Pull a fucking gun on me will you? His hand flew under his jacket and found the custom grip of the Glock. He started to pull. Unfortunately as he withdrew the weapon, the action caused him to lean back slightly. The hammer of the pistol caught in the lining of his jacket and he fumbled the draw. His brain was only beginning to compute the consequences when his lower body was pounded by what felt like two massive fists.

Under the table, the pistol in the man's hand fired twice. The only sound was that made by the slide as it flicked backwards and forwards. A mechanical snicker. Even if the bar had been empty, it wouldn't have raised alarm. The first bullet hit Medford in the stomach, passed through his spleen and ricocheted off a rib in his back before destroying one of his kidneys and embedding itself in the wall to his right. The second projectile, impacting half a second later and four inches higher, shattered Medford's spine and lodged in the timber of the seat behind him. Medford opened and closed his mouth in surprise, the immense shock overwhelming his senses. His hand dropped away and the Glock flopped back into its holster. As his life force drained away, Medford simply slid sideways until he was leaning against the wall, looking for all the world as if he was taking a nap.

The man leaned forward, almost casually, as if he were about to confide a secret. He looked into Medford's dying eyes. "That's why God made handguns with shrouded hammers, George. You should try harder to keep up." Had someone from the front of the bar been taking any notice, they would have seen the man smile, and appear to pat George on the shoulder after delivering some confidential advice. The man's comment was lost on Medford who was present only in the flesh by then. What it really achieved was to bring the pair close enough together for the man to slip a thick envelope into George's jacket pocket.

The man rose, put his hand back into his pocket and headed for the door as the plaster dust guy delivered the punch line of particularly tasteless joke dealing with lepers and wind tunnels. The laughter of the group could still be heard by the man as he walked down the street. Later, when questioned, not one person will remember his face or him leaving the bar.

* * *

It's Friday night and Charlie and Elizabeth are visiting Lily for dinner. Lily's house is crammed with all things Asian. As Lily and Elizabeth chat over dinner preparations, Charlie wanders around looking at the hundreds of pictures, artefacts, and books that adorn every wall, corner, and shelf space.

"A bit of a museum, don't you think, Charlie?" Lily calls from the kitchen.

"Yes, that's for sure. Fascinating though!" he calls back. She sure does get wrapped up in her work, thinks Charlie. God, it's a bit spooky, all this stuff. In the corner stands a wooden statue of a warrior about three feet tall with a spear. The warrior's face is an ugly mask of hatred. The statue gives Charlie the creeps, reminds him of a movie that he saw when he was a kid. Some tourist on an island sees a statue just like this one and buys it. The statue comes to life one night and starts hacking its way out of her suitcase with its little spear. Tries to kill her. Charlie shudders. It's funny how some things can live with you for years he thinks. I'm not sure I'd like to be in the dark with that ugly thing.

Laughter floats back to him from the kitchen as he explores Lily's treasure trove. Hearing Elizabeth laugh makes him smile. He's pleased she has a friend like Lily. As his eyes flick across the numerous small drawings and paintings that seem to cover every inch of the walls he notices with a jolt that Lily has a representation of the exact picture on the back of Alex's jacket. Hers is a much better reproduction and the detail is more intricate. That the sword is wooden is obvious in the picture, as is the ferocity on the face of the warrior. Once again Charlie feels a small stab of fear and uncertainty as he's connected back to Alex in some way he can't define. Suddenly he seems far away from the warmth and happiness of the kitchen. He decides to complete his browsing another time. Enough of this weird stuff for one day, he tells himself.

With an odd feeling of relief he steps back into the kitchen. "How's it going? Anything I can do to help?"

"Oh, the perfect man!" Lily gasps. "Are there any more where he came from?" she asks Elizabeth.

"Sorry, I got the last one," Elizabeth replies, smiling broadly at Charlie who finds himself starting to colour.

"So tell me, Charlie." Lily says, rescuing him. "Did you make any progress with the messages from the person who seemed to be masquerading as a Samurai?" Charlie thought for a second. How much can I say to her? He then decided, for no reason that he was aware of, simply to tell her everything.

"Well, it's kind of a long story, and a confidential one too, so you'll have to keep a secret." He said.

"Oh, I love stories!" Lily said, her eyes dancing, "especially secret ones."

Charlie related the whole tale, including Alex's jacket, the message in the pocket, Lord's revelation about the elevator computer line, the Formicidae project, the whole thing. Lily listened attentively and didn't interrupt, just occasionally stirred a pot, took a taste from an old wooden spoon, never breaking Charlie's concentration. When he'd done, Charlie felt as if an enormous weight had slipped from his shoulders. The fact that the three of them now have all the information is a great feeling. He can relax, not be on guard wondering how he can skirt around topics involving The Factory. The three are now a team, bonded by knowledge. The strands of their friendship intertwined more closely.

Lily was unusually quiet over dinner. As Charlie and Elizabeth chatted comfortably she responded when spoken to but didn't initiate much in the way of conversation. Afterwards, when the dishwasher was loaded and they had migrated with contented stomachs to Lily's twin sofas, Lily raised what was on her mind.

"Alex Fox was obviously a student of Kensei. The inscription around the picture on the jacket."

"You mean *Individual School of Two Skies*?" Elizabeth interrupted.

"Yes, that was the name of the school of martial arts that Kensei developed."

"What does that tell you, Lily?" Charlie asked.

Lily took a deep breath and for a moment it looked like she wasn't sure where to start.

"The thing is, Kensei's exploits are surrounded by legend. It's not always easy to separate the fact from the fiction. We do have enough material about him to know that he wasn't exactly a shining example of the noble warrior stereotype. At least not in my view anyway."

"What do you mean?" Charlie asked.

"Well, we admire the tradition of the loyal, principled and disciplined warrior, devoting his life to his craft. That's the picture that usually comes to our mind. I don't think Kensei was such a person. A phenomenal fighting talent yes, a superb strategist, definitely, but noble and principled? I think not." Lily paused to collect her thoughts before continuing.

"He wasn't above pulling the odd dirty trick on his opponents. For example, when he was 21 he travelled to Kyoto to duel with the Yoshioka family. The Yoshiokas had been the fencing masters of the

Ashikaga house for generations, and even after the demise of the Ashikaga Shogunate they remained prominent in the affairs of Kyoto. Many years before, Kensei's father had defeated two of the Yoshioka family in a duel so they may have seized on Kensei's arrival in Kyoto as an opportunity to even the score."

"Anyway, Kensei started by fighting Yoshioka Seijiro, the head of the family almost as soon as he set foot in the city. Kensei was armed only with a wooden bokken or practice sword. He defeated Seijiro and left him gravely wounded. When he recovered, Seijiro cut off his Samurai topknot and refused to fight ever again. But, Seijiro's brother, Denshichiro, then challenged Kensei to a duel."

"Is that the same sort of duel as you read about in the old days with pistols and seconds and all that?" Elizabeth asked.

"Yes, the same principles apply. One man faces another on an equal footing and only the superior warrior walks away."

"So what happened?"

"Well, Kensei was a man who apparently never washed or cut his hair. So his appearance was very unusual and probably very unsettling to his opponent. And also not very respectful. A bit like turning up to a job interview dressed in your gardening clothes. Anyway, Kensei further demonstrated his lack of respect by being very late for the duel, keeping his opponent and his entourage waiting. By the time Kensei showed up, looking like something the cat dragged in, Denshichiro was absolutely enraged by Kensei's display of disrespect. Distracted as he was by Kensei's antics, he was killed in the duel. These days we'd probably cry foul with those tactics."

"It didn't end there though," Lily continued. "Seijiro's son, Hanshichiro, who was not even a teenager at the time, challenged Kensei to a duel in defence of his father's honor. You can imagine how upset the boy would have been. So what do you think Kensei did?"

"Well, I don't think he would have killed a child. I mean, the kid would have no hope of defeating him. He would have known that," Elizabeth said.

"This time Kensei arrived very early and hid in the bushes. In fact Hanshichiro was the bait in a trap and about a dozen soldiers had turned up to try and kill Kensei. Instead of sneaking away as he could have done, he burst out of the bushes, killed the child, fought his way out of the mob, and left the city."

"The bastard!" Elizabeth gasped.

"Well, it was a tough time back then but I think it's fair to say that Kensei was ruthless as a fighter and paid little heed to the concepts and traditions of a fair fight. Although he apparently became a much humbler man in his later years and took up painting and sculpting, I think that if someone modelled themselves on his life, they would probably not be particularly likeable."

"Elizabeth said something about a book that he wrote. Where does that fit in?" Charlie asked.

"He was a prolific writer actually," Lily said, slipping comfortably into her university lecturer role. "He claimed to have gained a full understanding of strategy by 1634, and he wrote several works on the subject, and also on the art and way of the sword, including his two great treatises: *Heiho Sanjugokajo* (The 35 Articles on the Art of Swordsmanship), expounding the basic principles of *Niten Ich-Ryu* or the art of fighting with twin swords and the philosophy and combat strategies behind it; and *Go Rin No Sho*, or *The Book of Five Rings. Go Rin No Sho,* for which the 35 articles is considered a prototype, is probably the most famous of all Japanese works on the martial arts. Almost a how-to book really."

"He certainly sounds like an interesting character. How does it all fit together though? With what happened at The Factory?" Charlie asked.

"I guess that's the million-dollar question." Lily replied. "But it's not a good sign."

"How so?" Elizabeth asked. Charlie answered for Lily.

"We have a highly skilled programmer working on a revolutionary new distributed intelligence architecture, applied to an offensive system. We seem to have evidence that he had a breakthrough and perhaps used his own neurological scan as the profile. Immediately afterward, he's killed in an accident and we have a hacker in the system using the name of a warrior he obviously studied well. A warrior who had cunning and ability combined with ruthlessness.

That's quite a recipe for an Information-warfare technology platform."

"That's not all, Charlie," Lily said, her face bearing an expression Charlie hadn't seen before.

"What? What else?"

Lily appeared a little hesitant, as if she was struggling with something inside, trying to find words, choosing them carefully.

"You know I've travelled a lot and spent a great deal of time in Japan, speaking with lots of people including martial artists at the same level of experience as Alex Fox. They are interesting people and they tend to be very knowledgeable about particular periods of Japanese history, especially military history, so Alex's fascination with Kensei is not unusual. But that's not the point. I have also watched them practise and fight. Many, many times. They are very agile, have tremendous flexibility and frighteningly quick reflexes."

"I remember walking home one evening with a group with whom I'd become friends. Walking in front of me was an Aikido master, a bit older than Alex Fox. The night was still and almost completely dark. I noticed that, lodged in a fold of his collar was a tiny maple leaf. I reached out to pluck it from his clothes and faster than I could see, he whirled around and caught my hand. It was so quick. One second his back was towards me, the next he was facing me with his hand around my wrist. I nearly fainted, he gave me such a fright. Anyway, he apologised for making me jump and said that it was just a reflex action. He wanted to dismiss it but I pressed him to explain how he knew my hand was there."

"What did he say?" breathed Elizabeth, spellbound by the story.

"He told me that he felt the breeze from my arm movement. I said he had to be kidding but he just looked at me as if I'd doubted that gravity keeps our feet on the ground. It was eerie, I can tell you."

"So what are you saying, Lily?" Charlie asked, a thought rising into his head, not completely formed but disturbing nonetheless.

"I feel bad saying this because the implications are ugly, but I can't possibly imagine someone as highly trained and skilled as Alex must have been, just blundering into an empty elevator shaft and falling to his death. It doesn't sound right."

"You're suggesting he was murdered." Charlie stated

"I'm saying that I'm having trouble buying the fact that he fell because he wasn't looking where he was walking when the elevator doors opened. That I just can't imagine."

For a few seconds nobody spoke. Elizabeth snuggled into Charlie's arm. Charlie just sighed and said, "Great."

CHAPTER 21

The president of the United States is hunkered down with his senior chiefs. The atmosphere in the room is tense, the talk strained, the mood dark. There is no explanation to be offered for the accidental firing of the cruise missile that sent Shanghai residents sprinting in all directions and that vaporised two captains of Chinese industry together with twenty-seven others. The director of the defense intelligence agency was feeling the heat.

"So," the president continued, counting off the points on his fingers, "let me get this straight. We have absolutely no idea why the Tomahawk fired itself or why it targeted the Chinese boat. We acknowledge the possibility of sabotage but we don't know how it could have been done. Right.?"

"Essentially correct, yes," the director replied.

"But I thought these things needed complex programming to hit their target. Maps and things. Christ, the damned missile flew down the main street! Goddamn thing almost stopped at the lights!"

"That's the puzzle. The missile needed to have the data uploaded to it in order to fly that plan, but we didn't do it. We don't even have such a plan to load into it, not even accidentally. That's why we're starting to think that we have some sort of outside interference here."

"What sort of outside interference, Jim?" the president asked.

"Some sort of remote jamming or hacking, similar to what we saw with the USS *Ford*. Some new weapon that's just blindsided us."

“But why would the Chinese want to send a missile to blow up their own rich businessmen and scare the bejesus out of their own citizens?”

“Obviously that’s the question. We have to face the possibility that it was another party essentially trying to cause an outbreak of hostilities.”

“And the reason would be?”

“To destabilise the United States perhaps. A distraction pending a strike on our assets from another direction. Those sorts of things.”

“What do the tech boys say about the feasibility of such a weapon? Could it be done?”

“Well, they’re not sure. They figure it’s not impossible but most of our traditional enemies don’t have the smarts or the resources to do it.”

“So who does?”

“Ourselves and possibly some of our allies. But they don’t have anything to gain by the campaign so once again we’re back where we started.”

The president ran his hands through his hair, stood, and began pacing the room, everyone’s heads swivelling to follow his movements. “Okay. Question: Has this ever happened before? An accidental firing of a missile with a flight plan not of our making?”

“Never.”

“Right. Is it also possible that the *Ford* was affected in a similar way? So they *thought* they were under attack but in fact were not?”

“That’s possible, yes.”

“And possibly the two missiles that exploded near Taiwan could have been triggered by the same sort of malfunction affecting the Chinese hardware?”

“Well, yes. I guess that’s entirely possible.”

“Right. Here’s what I propose: Effective immediately, we withdraw all of our forces out of the area, beyond missile and fighter range.”

The secretary of the navy was out of his seat in a heartbeat. “But Mr

President that would mean standing off several thousand miles! It would mean a complete withdrawal!"

"Calm down. If this new weapon or hacking theory is right, the longer we stay within spitting distance of these trigger-happy bastards, the greater the risk we run of playing into someone's hands. Someone who most definitely doesn't have our interests at heart. Christ, we're within pissing distance of World War Three as it is. If we let this situation get bent any further out of shape, we'll never get it back under control."

"But if the theory is incorrect, what then?"

"We wait and see. For all we know, the damned atmospheric explosions we saw could have been a Chinese accident too! What if they're having the same troubles that we are? God, I don't want to be within range if one of their nukes goes AWOL. Let's get the hell out of Dodge. Do it."

As the meeting broke up, the president caught hold of the arm of the director of defense intelligence and steered him into a quiet corner. "Listen, Jim, I want you to dig into this like your life depends on it. Christ, it might. Yours and mine. I want you to use whatever agencies we have to get to the bottom of what's going on. I don't want to hear anything about jurisdiction or rivalry between departments. Just get some data. Who could do this? Look at their programs, look at our programs for Christ's sake. Who has the capability, the people, the infrastructure. If this is a new weapon, all bets are off. If we can't trust our own systems we'll be lucky not to blow *ourselves* to hell and back, let alone the damned Chinese."

* * *

Detective John Lord bent over Louis' desk on the third floor of the Ann Arbor Police Department. Both men studied the printout that had snaked out of the fax machine an hour ago. The fax lists which businesses purchased maintenance panels of the type necessary to service the elevator in Alex Fox's building. There were only six lines of type.

"Jeez, Lou, you wouldn't want try earning a living selling these gadgets. Six sales in two years."

"That's true, JL. Still I guess when you got one, it's good for years. Folks'd only buy one of these things when they was setting up a business or maybe replacing a busted one."

"True enough. So, anything turn up when you checked them out?"

"Well, I called an' spoke to 'em all 'cept this one here second from the bottom."

Lord peered at the printout. "*Technolift.* What, they didn't answer?"

"Number seems to be disconnected which is odd 'cos this sale went through less than a month ago. So I phone the supplier again in Chicago and they told me that *Technolift* was supposed to be taking over the maintenance for another company in the Midwest so I ring these guys and they're like, what? Techno-who?"

"So, maybe this *Technolift* is a paper company, a front."

"That's what I figure. So I try and trace who set it up in the first place."

"Any luck?"

"Sure, got the name, address, the whole shootin' match. Trouble is, it's all bullshit. No such guy, no such address."

Lord rubbed his chin. "They check any ID when the business gets set up?"

"One step ahead of ya, JL. Sure they do, everything is kosher. Even got them to send me the copy they make of the guy's photo ID. You're gonna love this." Louis pulled another sheet of fax paper from under the report.

"Recognise this guy?" Lord leaned closer and studied the tiny picture, grainy from the fax.

"Well I'll be damned. It's our old friend Joe Shapiro, the disappearing maintenance guy."

"One and the same! Give that man a cigar!"

Lord sat on the edge of the desk. "We've come complete circle and ended up at the same place. One things for sure, the stink on this is getting stronger."

"But why the elaborate setup, JL?"

"Only one reason that I can think of. They wanted it to be ironclad. A freak accident. Too bizarre to be anything else. Let's face it, Lou, the guy falls off a roof, people are gonna ask was he pushed? We wouldn't even have given this a second glance if it wasn't for Ganderton. Precisely because it looked too complex to be a murder, we assumed it was. Even the forensic guy didn't doubt it until we got out the magnifying glass. Jesus, we had no reason to think an average Joe would be set up like this. It's not like he was James Bond or..." Lord stopped mid-sentence, an odd look on his face.

"What is it, JL?"

"I was going to say, he's not James Bond or anything, but then it occurred to me, the people he worked for *definitely are* in the spy business."

* * *

The vice-president sits at his desk in his private office struggling through a security report on some Asian country that he realises he probably couldn't even point to on a map of the world. His mind is just not engaged with it. He can't stop thinking about George Medford and his attempt at blackmail. He'd been distracted for the entire weekend, causing his wife to worry about his workload. After all these years, how has it come to this? The VP always prided himself on his integrity, had no truck with people caught in dishonest scams. Sure, he wasn't proud of everything he'd ever done, some decisions he'd made were tough. People got hurt sometimes. He'd even authorised operations where people had been killed in the line of duty and that's not something you take lightly. But this? One thing was for sure, he thought. If Medford wants to continue down this track after speaking with the VP's old agency buddy, I'll turn him in and take the consequences. No way was he about to hand over a penny. Once that starts, you're screwed, he thought. No going back from there, no protesting innocence, nothing.

He looked up sharply, hearing a discreet knock on his door. It was Benson, the agent in charge of investigating the document leak. Project Silkworm they called it. The VP beckoned for him to come in. Normally he would have risen from his desk and invited the agent to sit in a more comfortable manner over by the window where several easy chairs could be employed to inject a note of informality. Not this time. The VP had had just about enough of these poker-faced security people. He motioned for the agent to sit in an upright chair at the other side of his desk. A chair he used if he had to discipline one of his staff, which thankfully, was not very often. He knew that he was playing games and being childish but he was in no mood for niceties today.

If Agent Benson noticed this he didn't show it. But then that was part of the sport. Don't telegraph anything that you don't intend to. Those who knew Benson well could have told the VP that his little power games would have been like water off a duck's back to him. But don't ever think he didn't notice.

"I have an update, sir and I thought it best to come directly to you with it." The VP didn't like the sound of that at all and wished with all his heart that this investigation hadn't fallen to him.

"What do you have, Agent Benson?" He asked.

"We think we have found the source of our leakage." The VP sat bolt upright, his mind racing. "Go on."

"George Medford, head of internal security here at the White House was found shot to death on Friday night in a downtown bar. In his pocket was a packet of classified documents relating to a new targeting system that the DoD has under consideration. Our assumption is that he was meeting someone with the intention of selling the documents but something went wrong."

The VP was stunned. Thoughts raced across his mind in an explosion of synaptic firings as he tried to process this bombshell of information.

"George Medford! I can't believe that for a minute! Are you sure?" he said, with conviction that would have earned the envy of most professional actors.

"Yes, sir, we're quite confident. We have looked at his bank records and he appears to have a special account. Not in joint names like all of the others. Over the last twelve months, several large deposits in cash were made. We're talking about hundreds of thousands of dollars, not salary checks."

The VP removed his glasses, tossed them on the desk and massaged his temples. "My God, I can't believe it. Were there any witnesses?"

Agent Benson pulled a small leather-bound notebook from his jacket pocket. "No, sir. The barman saw him come in, saw him nursing a beer for a while, obviously waiting for someone. He remembers a second male coming in and intended to take his order as soon as he got through serving a large party at the front of the bar but when looked again, the man was gone. About twenty minutes later he went over to see if Medford needed another round and found him dead. Slumped up against the wall like he was asleep, sitting in a puddle of blood. It would appear that the assailant shot him from under the table. No cartridge cases and no reports of gunshots. Medford was armed but his piece was still in its holster."

"God, George. Could he have sent the fax from the president's machine?"

"He certainly had the access necessary. We don't see him on the video footage but then he did have access to that system too and would have been more than capable of doctoring the tapes. The question of motive in the case of the Taiwan document is still a little vague, and there are obviously easier ways to transfer a document. Maybe thumbing his nose at the administration that he'd decided to betray, maybe demonstrating to a potential customer that he had access at the highest level. We may never know why he chose that tactic."

"It still sounds unbelievable to me, it really does."

"Were you aware, sir, that Medford had serious financial problems?"

"No, we didn't ever speak about money."

"Apparently his wife has terminal cancer, the treatment has almost ruined them. They tried several alternative therapies but nothing worked. You didn't know she was ill?"

The VP felt a deep pang of guilt about Medford's wife. He had only met her once or twice but she seemed like a genuinely nice woman and had obviously brought Medford much happiness in the early years. He felt as though he was being accused of callousness.

"Of course I knew she was ill. George led us to believe she was in remission. I had no idea she was terminal. God, if he had come to me for help I would have given it." An awful truth shot through his heart like an arrow. Medford *had* come to him for money. Just not in the way he expected. It all makes sense now, he thought.

"How is Ruth?" he asked.

Benson didn't drop his accusatory gaze. "She's been admitted to Sibley Memorial Hospital. She was already fairly advanced but they're not expecting her to last much longer. The specialist that I spoke to suggested she might not leave the hospital now. Very sad really."

"Of course, Jesus. I'll have some flowers sent from the staff here." The VP hesitated, unsure of whether to ask his next question. "Did she know anything about it?"

"No, sir. She told us that George had changed in the last twelve months, had a lot of anger inside she said. She assumed it was related to her sickness. I believed her when she said she knew nothing about the account's existence or how the money came to be in it."

"God, what a mess."

"Yes, sir."

As Agent Benson left, the VP's mind was still racing. On hearing the door close, the VP picked up the receiver of his encrypted phone and made a call to his agency friend. There was one question he had to ask. If he was ever to sleep at night again he had to know the answer. He wouldn't be able to live with himself if Medford's death was somehow his fault. The VP asked the question and received a negative answer. A flood of relief washed over his body like a wave of warm water. It seemed poor old George really had tried to solve his financial problems the wrong way and paid dearly for his lack of judgment. Tonight the VP would sleep like a baby, totally unaware of the large favour that had been granted him by the gods of providence or of its consequences.

CHAPTER 22

Charlie had thought about this for a long time. He had made the decision to talk to Leonard about Alex. He had to know whose side Leonard was on. Whether he would be an ally or an enemy. Inside The Factory things hummed along almost as normal. To Charlie it felt strange going back after all that had happened, but people appeared to be as friendly as ever and he didn't detect any sideways glances or hesitation in conversation that would betray their discomfort with him over his stress leave. It's almost as if there is some sort of collective consciousness operating here, he thought. Let's get everything back to normal and forget what happened. Charlie, however, couldn't shake the feeling that he was being taken for a patsy, that things were not as they seemed and that he was being manipulated. It was a feeling he didn't particularly like. Time to push back a little, he thought.

After getting settled again following his several weeks forced absence, he used his electronic calendar system to schedule a meeting with Leonard at the end of the day. The interval between was filled with an attempt to catch up on his email, a completely overwhelming and depressing activity, he thought. Before he realised that the day was almost over it was time to make his way to Leonard's office.

"Hey, Charlie!" Leonard beamed "Good to see ya, son!" He gripped Charlie's hand and pumped it as if they were father and son reunited after a lifetime of separation. After taking their places in Darville's comfortable office with the door closed they spent an hour catching up on personal and Factory business before Charlie brought up the real reason for his visit.

"I want to talk to you about Alex, Leonard." He said at last. A shadow passed across Darville's face.

"Sure, Charlie, what's on your mind?" Charlie felt that the temperature in the office had just dropped a few degrees.

"It's hard to say, but I'm concerned that everything's not as it seems."

"How so?" Darville asked, folding his arms across his chest.

Charlie took a deep breath and launched into his concerns. He covered most of what he and Elizabeth had spoken about, being careful not to mention Lily or to draw any conclusions about the things that concerned him. Better to leave questions than propose answers he thought. When he had finished, Darville was silent for what seemed like a full minute. When he looked up, he had an expression on his face that Charlie had never seen before. He wasn't sure of it was fear, anger, or both.

"This is not something you want to get mixed up in, Charlie." He said.

"What isn't, Leonard? What's going on?"

"It's bigger than you and me, and it's dangerous. You'll have to trust me on this. Stay out of it. Don't dig, don't agitate. Let it go; get on with your life. Marry that girl of yours and move on. Please Charlie."

Charlie didn't know what to say. This wasn't the outcome he expected. It was as if Leonard was pleading with him to simply turn a blind eye to something they both obviously knew wasn't right. He started to get angry.

"If there's something fishy about Alex's death then I…"

"For fuck's sake, Charlie!" Leonard bellowed "Let it go! You don't know what you're dealing with here. This isn't some computer puzzle game to be solved, it's big time, high stakes. I stuck my neck out for you once but there's a limit to how much I can do to protect you, or Elizabeth for that matter. Don't think they're not watching because they are. For God's sake don't be a stubborn bastard about this. It's over, let it go."

Charlie was stunned. Both at the passion of Darville's reaction and also the implication that he might actually be in danger. From whom? And why? Before he could ask anything else, Darville looked at his watch and stood hurriedly.

"I have to go, Charlie. Let me say one thing and then I don't want to speak about this ever again. You have your job, your health, and the love of a good woman. Sometimes things happen that are bigger than all of us, things we *can't* fight, *shouldn't* question. This is one of those situations. I've never had to order you to do anything Charlie, but right now I'm telling you to let it go and move on."

Charlie was starting to seethe inside at being painted into this corner only to be told it was good for him, like eating his greens. The frustrations of the previous few weeks suddenly boiled over, his usual caution abandoning him.

"You've sold us out, Leonard. You've let the bastards get to you, and now you're just looking the other way."

Darville fixed him with a cold stare so full of raw fury that Charlie recoiled.

"Don't you ever say that to me again, you idealistic little shit. I'm trying to help you here, you have no idea what you're playing with. You ever say that to me again and I'll put you in the fucking hospital."

Darville stormed out of the room leaving Charlie wide-eyed and lost for words at the intensity of his reaction.

* * *

At last it appeared that an uneasy truce was starting to develop between the US and China. A great deal of behind-the-scenes negotiation has been going on but the withdrawal of the carrier battle groups had the immediate effect of releasing the pressure from the situation. A safety valve had been cracked open slightly and the critical condition was easing. The US had spoken publicly about compensation for the families of those killed aboard the yacht and pledged new talks aimed at settling the Taiwan issue for good.

Although the immediate threat of war had dissipated, it would be some years before anything like calm existed between the two nations.

An inquiry into the events leading to the sinking of the pleasure craft could shed no new light on the situation. No explanation could be offered for the rogue missile. Neither its unintended launch, or its precise track. The inquiry recommended immediate action to harden the systems on board US navy vessels to protect against the possibility of an enemy gaining control of any weapons systems. Unfortunately, exactly how that could be accomplished, given the undefined nature of the threat, was left unsaid. As a result, nothing was done except for rounds of rigorous tests and inspections which revealed nothing.

Meanwhile vast amounts of intelligence resources were diverted toward finding the culprit or culprits. All nations, friendly or otherwise, that had the capability to develop such a system were put under scrutiny. Some cooperated willingly, others were compromised without even knowing it. The assumption had to be made that this program could be so secret that even a nation's own intelligence service might not know of its development. The existence of the new weapons system was all-but-assumed to be a given, the challenge was finding out which nation possessed it. While internal inquiries were made, nobody seriously entertained the suggestion that perhaps the enemy was within their own gates.

* * *

Charlie was at home, drowning his sorrows. Elizabeth and Lily were at the movies and, although they tried to convince him to come, he couldn't face it. Never in his life had he felt so miserable. He was slumped into the sofa with his feet up on the coffee table, not even bothering to remove his shoes, a glass of red wine in his hand and the bottle by his side. His plan to speak with Darville had backfired and he deeply regretted his last outburst that had sparked Darville's anger. Not that he felt any better about Darville's obvious complicity in whatever was happening at The Factory. Charlie felt lousy that their relationship had sunk to this level. I wouldn't be surprised if he didn't ever speak to me again, he thought. Charlie ruminated over this for a while but then found his anger returning.

Hell, it wasn't my fault that Leonard got mixed up in all this, he thought. I'll be damned if I'll end up a yes man like that. Something stinks and I'm simply not going to take it lying down. Even if it means upsetting people and getting a boot in the ass. Charlie surprised himself at the strength of conviction that welled up inside him. At some level he felt that a part of his fundamental nature was on the line. As if he failed this test and just walked away as Darville suggested, he would be enfeebled in some way. Broken like a horse, on the end of some rope. That's just not going to happen, he thought. Not to me it isn't.

His thoughts were interrupted by a knock at the door. Strange, he thought, looking at his watch, it's a bit late for visitors and Charlie didn't get too many of those anyway. He went to the door and peered through the peephole before opening it.

"Good evening, Charlie, sorry to call so late, may I come in?"

Charlie opened the door in a daze and allowed Detective Lord to enter without giving a thought to saying no. "Sure, you surprised me, I wasn't expecting visitors."

"Sorry about that. I meant to phone ahead but I was passing and saw the light on so took a chance. It's good of you to talk to me without notice."

Lord took in the glass in Charlie's hand and the bottle, almost empty by the table. "Tough day?" he said.

Charlie flopped back onto the sofa and gestured for the detective to sit down. "You're not kidding. I'd offer you a drink but I guess you're on duty."

"Actually I finished about half-an-hour ago so I'd kill for a drink. Do you have any beer?"

"Sure." Charlie gestured toward the refrigerator with his glass. "Help yourself, detective, I'm about done in." Lord chose a Heineken and settled back down in the easy chair opposite Charlie.

"Here's to a simpler life, he said. Charlie raised his glass.

"I wish. So, if you're not on duty, you must be short on friends to be calling on me socially."

Lord took a pull on his beer. "I guess it's not really a social call. I talked to your boss today, or at least tried to."

Charlie was instantly alert. "Darville?"

"Yes. We've reopened the investigation into Alex Fox's death as a murder inquiry. I wanted to go over a few things with Darville. He seemed less than keen to speak with me."

A massive wave of relief surged through Charlie's mind at hearing Lord's words. At last, he thought, I'm not going to have to fight this battle on my own. They can't just brush this guy off. He doesn't work for them and he has the law on his side. Let's see the bastards wriggle out of this.

Charlie took a deep breath.

"I'm not surprised you've come to that conclusion with Alex's death. I'm really pleased that you've done this, detective. Really pleased."

"Please call me John, Charlie. I think we're on the same side here. No need for formality."

"Okay, John it is."

"So, why do you think Darville doesn't want to entertain the possibility of one of his good people being murdered?"

"I think he knows that Alex was murdered, or at least suspects it. But he's scared of something. He bawled me out today for asking questions about Alex. Practically begged me not to stir things up. Then he got angrier than I've ever seen him. He even implied that Elizabeth and I would be in danger if I didn't let it go. I tell you, it was not like him at all."

"Yeah, that was pretty much the reaction I got. I guess he'd have kittens if he realised I was here talking to you."

"That's for sure. The other thing he said was that *they* were watching, whoever *they* are."

"It certainly appears to complicate things. If Fox's death was an accident, why all the effort to cover it over? Why not try to get to the bottom of it and make sure. If it *was* murder, surely we should know and attempt to track down the guilty party."

"Well, that's how I see it." Charlie said. "Alex and I didn't always see eye to eye but if he was murdered, I want the bastard who did it brought to justice, whoever he is."

Lord took another long pull on his beer.

"I guess the semi-official nature of my call was to ask if we can work together on this. We're having trouble breaking in to this case and I'd like your help."

"What can I do? I've already tried to approach Leonard and nearly had my head torn off for my trouble."

"Sure, Darville's probably not going to give us too much. It's more a case of keeping your eyes and ears open. I'm also keen to dig a little into the deaths of Dan Foster and Ric Montez, although that's a little more difficult as they died on DoD premises. If we assume that Fox was murdered and it was made to look like an accident, maybe that holds true for the others. If we find some holes in their cases it might give us some more leverage."

"The department conducted its own inquiry and found both incidents to be accidental."

"Sure they did. What do you think?"

"I guess there's a part of me that recognises things like gas leaks happen. People do get killed by explosions in labs. What makes me suspicious is that we appeared to suffer a huge coincidence with four accidental deaths in such a short time. It doesn't make it murder though."

"That's true. It doesn't. But part of a detective's role is to use his instinct to poke around in things that don't sound right. If a woman finds a lump in her breast, it doesn't make it cancer. If the doc sees it though, he knows it has to be checked out because it's not right. Same with police work. A woman's found murdered in her own home. We're going to look for people close to her. Her husband, lover, etcetera. That doesn't make them guilty but our instinct tells us that's the place to look first. When four people die from the same workplace in a short time and one of them looks like murder, my gut tells me the others should be investigated too. Simple as that."

"Can't argue with your logic."

"So let's talk about Montez. How much do you know about what happened."

"Well, they didn't let on much but word does filter down. Apparently the security footage shows him entering the building and making a beeline for the medical lab."

"As if he was looking for something?" Lord asked.

"Yes, he obviously knew where he was going and he didn't intend to be there long. He didn't even turn the lights on. Anyway, he enters the lab and it's pretty dark in there so the footage apparently wasn't too clear. He walks straight in and then stops suddenly. They figure he smelled the gas at that point. He then charges over to the stop taps on the back of the lab wall and starts turning them off. Natural reaction to smelling the gas, I s'pose. What happened next is a little harder to explain."

Lord leaned forward, listening intently, his imagination filling in the blanks.

"And?"

"He's turning the taps, levers actually, and he stops. Like he's distracted by something."

"It would have to be something special to stop him turning off the gas. I would imagine he wanted to get out of there as soon as possible."

"Exactly. Anyway, he looks across the room at something and then the tape goes blank as the place explodes. They tried looking at the tape one frame at a time but the explosion was too fast. One frame we see Ric, the next nothing."

Lord appeared to be deep in thought. "What was in the area of the lab he was looking at?"

"It appears from the investigation that he was looking at what subsequently proved to be the centre of the explosion. The only thing in that area was a piece of analytical equipment."

"And could that have caused the explosion?"

"Well, it does use an explosive mix of gases, that's how it works but it shouldn't even have been turned on. In fact, you can see on the video that its cover was still attached. It wasn't being used and hadn't been used for months."

"What's the chance of getting that video?"

Charlie sucked in his cheeks and then blew the air out.

"I don't know, John. I couldn't ask for it."

"I'm not talking about asking for it," Lord said quietly. Charlie examined his empty glass for a few minutes.

"If I get caught I could lose my job," he said.

"That's true. It's your call, Charlie."

Charlie turned the options over in his mind. All of his life he'd gravitated toward the simple, low-stress, low-conflict options. Somehow he just didn't want to walk away from this one.

"Okay. I'll try. I owe the four of them that much at least."

CHAPTER 23

Eddy Duran sits in his cluttered office at the *Washington Post* on Fifteenth Street with his feet on the edge of the desk, his hands folded behind his head in the you-can-trust-me pose favoured by many used car salesmen. It has been a busy day. He gazes out of the office window that he's earned through forty years as a newsman but doesn't focus on anything in particular. Like many who write for a living, the reporter is putting the pieces of a story together in his head before committing anything to paper.

Duran is no Bernstein or Woodward but his career hasn't been entirely undistinguished and he's a solid, insightful journalist with a love of the city and the role that the newspaper plays in it. He probably could have risen higher through the organisation but it would have been at the cost of doing what he loved which is researching and writing. Still, he's come a long way and seen some mighty changes since starting as a teenager all those years ago.

His thoughts are interrupted by the phone. Pushing aside piles of papers he digs the receiver out and answers with his surname. You just never know when a big story might land in your lap, he thinks. This is to be one of those days.

"Mr. Duran, my name is Robert Etheridge, I'm an attorney in the DC area acting on behalf of a client that I believe you know, George Medford."

"Yes, I know George. Haven't seen him in a while though. Is he in trouble?"

"Not exactly. Actually, I'm sorry to have to tell you that Mr. Medford has been killed."

"Shit! No kidding! What happened?"

"This isn't something I want to go into too deeply on the phone Mr Duran. I'd be grateful if you could come to my office at some stage soon." Duran's curiosity was piqued.

"You want me to come by your office so you can tell me how George died?"

"Actually it's a little more complex than that. I have something for you."

"What?"

"It would be better if we talked about this in my office."

"Something from George."

"Yes, something from George. I'd rather not say any more over the phone."

"Now you've got me really curious. How about you give me the details and I'll slip over there as in the morning."

* * *

It's early morning and Charlie has just arrived at The Factory. In his briefcase he carries a blank video tape which he intends to swap for the one with the footage of Ric Montez's last seconds. The Factory has a sophisticated, if no longer state-of-the-art, tape recording system. The machines are kept in a secured room and are mounted in racks along one wall. On the opposite wall is a huge tape storage unit housing thirty tapes for each machine, each one with a date attached, written on a removable label. Hundreds of tapes in all, each tape kept for thirty days before being reused. In the corner is a backup power system, which permits the whole system to function for up to eight hours in the event of a power failure. The system is a little cumbersome in that someone has to swap tapes in all of the machines once a day, but the upside is that each system is independent, and so outside of a power outage to the whole building, including catastrophic failure of The Factory's main backup power as well as the isolated battery backup system inside the tape room, any problems will be confined to one tape system, leaving the rest functioning normally.

Because the job of swapping out the tapes each morning is a laborious and repetitive one, it falls to a junior person within The Factory's technical hierarchy. Charlie knows who the regular person is, a young technician who occupies a cubicle next to the tape room. Charlie is banking on him doing the swap this morning. He is also betting that the original tape has by now been returned to its place in the set after being copied for the investigation following Montez's death. His plan hinges on these two assumptions.

Charlie's heart was beating so loudly in his ears he imagined that it could be heard by everyone else as he waited for Keith, the junior tech, to open the tape room door. Charlie had taken a position around the corner, pretending to read an article in a journal on top of someone's in-tray. It was early enough that few staff were at work. Just as he was imagining that something must be wrong, he heard the sound of the PIN lock being activated. He waited for sixty seconds and then walked by as nonchalantly as he could, given that his heart was pumping so hard. He stopped at the open door.

"Hey, Keith, how ya doin'," he asked, trying to keep his voice level. He could feel a drop of sweat trickling down the small of his back.

"Howdy, Dr G., pretty good thanks. You're in early."

"Yes, always lots to do, that's for sure."

"How's that cool car of yours going? Man, I'd kill for wheels like that!"

"Pretty good, I should take you for a spin sometime."

"Wow, would you?"

"Sure, no problem, I'll give you a call when I look at my diary and we can take a ride after work one time."

"That would be way cool!"

Charlie felt he'd been shooting the breeze long enough. It was time to put the second part of his plan into action. Throughout the conversation and unobserved by the impressionable young man, he had kept his hand inside his jacket pocket. Charlie was holding his cell phone, on which he had pre-dialled Keith's extension number. Time to take the big chance he thought and pressed the call button. A few seconds later Keith's phone began to ring in his cubicle next door.

"Shoot, that's my phone," Keith said, but made no attempt to answer it. Come on, Charlie thought, get the damn phone, kid.

"It's pretty early to be phoning, maybe it's something important," Charlie prompted. The comment seemed to push the youngster over the edge of his indecision.

"Sure, look, could you do me a real favour and just watch the room while I quickly get that? Save me locking up an' all?"

"Yeah, no problem," said Charlie, feeling as nervous as he could ever remember. "Go get it."

As soon as Keith was out of the room, Charlie stepped over to the tape rack, trying to figure out the system. He saw that the machines were numbered and the numbers were linked to a nameplate on the tape racks showing the area monitored. He quickly scanned them for the area covered by the medical lab. In the other room he could hear Keith's "hello" into an empty line. Time's running out he thought. Suddenly he saw the section he was looking for and he madly scanned the section for the date he needed.

In the other room, Keith eventually gave up and put the receiver down with a bang, making Charlie jump. He grabbed the tape, pulled the blank one from his pocket and swapped the labels. He managed to get the Montez tape back into his jacket pocket but he still had the blank one in his hands when Keith walked back into the room. Their eyes met. Charlie could hear his own heart beating like a jackhammer and couldn't believe the kid didn't hear it too.

"Sorry, Keith, I know I'm not supposed to touch but I was just checking to see what sort of tapes the machines use. Regular VHS?"

Keith's frown disappeared instantly. He had no reason to doubt his senior colleague and hadn't yet developed the suspicious nature that often accompanies adulthood. He took the tape out of Charlie's hand

and flipped it over.

"No, Dr G., these tapes are special. See here underneath?, this…" Keith's voice trailed off and Charlie's heart stopped.

"What do you know? This *is* a normal tape. Musta sneaked in somehow. Happens sometimes." Keith peeled the label off the tape, tossed it into the bin and took a fresh one from the cupboard. After unwrapping it he again showed Charlie the difference before slotting the tape back into the rack. Ah, the innocence of youth, Charlie thought. Thank God. As much as he wanted to get out of that room, he had one more question that had just occurred to him.

"That's real interesting, Keith, I didn't know that." Keith beamed.

"So can you play these in a normal VCR?"

"Sure you can. Just not the other way. You can't put a regular tape into these machines. Just as well I found that one. I'll go through them all when I've done swapping just to make sure no others got into the rack. Sometimes people are just not careful and the tapes are so similar."

Charlie looked at his watch. "Got to fly, Keith," he said, "nice to talk with you."

"Sure, Dr G. Don't forget that ride!"

"Not a chance, Keith, I'll call you later."

As Charlie walked out of the tape room he spied a security camera above the door. Damn! He wanted to kick himself. Of course they would have a camera in there. I should have known that. Too late now. Just got to hope they don't look at that particular footage. Charlie arrived at his office, popped the tape into an envelope and placed it into his briefcase. As he relaxed he realised how tense he'd become. His shirt was soaked with perspiration and he had the beginnings of a mighty headache. God, he thought, you need nerves of steel to be a spy…

* * *

Eddy Duran drove across town to Robert Etheridge's office, his mind preoccupied with not only George's death but what on earth George might have left him. Duran didn't imagine for one minute that it was some kind of inheritance. They were friends sure, but not close friends. The circles they moved in occasionally overlapped and Duran thought they enjoyed one another's company but it would not be unusual to go six months without seeing each other. No, thought Duran, it's something else. Already he was feeling uneasy about the meeting. Duran had talked it over with his wife during dinner the night before and she had given him an unsettling look. Her view was that it meant trouble. It wasn't as if they were real friends and so it could only be some sort of obligation, maybe a favour to be done. She wasn't happy about the whole thing. Said she had a bad feeling about it. Duran wasn't superstitious but some of his wife's concern had rubbed off.

He parked his car and walked the rest of the way to the neat but unpretentious offices of Etheridge & Cline. After sitting for a few minutes in the waiting room and flicking through a two-year-old copy of *National Geographic*, he was ushered in to meet the lawyer. Etheridge was a few inches shorter than Duran but probably a hundred pounds heavier. *Prosperous* is the word that popped into Duran's head when he met him, and imagined a mid-level Mercedes sitting in the underground lot and a nice house in the 'burbs.

"Nice to meet you, Mr Duran," said Etheridge, extending a meaty paw.

"Hey, call me Eddy." Replied Duran. "So what's this all about?"

"Well, I've been Mr Medford's attorney for many years now and I'm also the executor of his estate which is an unfortunate duty that I'll be performing in the immediate future. However, one week ago, Mr Medford came to me in what I'd describe as an anxious state. He gave me an envelope and said that, in the event of his untimely death, I was to give the envelope to you. My understanding is that his recent death was suspicious which adds further to the mystery. Here it is." Etheridge slid a manila envelope across the desk toward Duran who picked it up as though it were radioactive.

"Naturally I asked him whether he had any reason to fear for his life but he wouldn't be drawn. The reason that I wanted you here is that, if the envelope has a bearing on Mr. Medford's will, I need to know about it before next week."

"So, you haven't opened it?" asked Duran.

"Of course not, that would have been inappropriate."

"Aren't you curious?"

"Naturally. I'm intensely curious but I'll confine my inquiries to what is required in discharging my professional duties."

"I wish I had your control."

"Hardly an asset for a journalist, I would imagine." Duran laughed at this.

"I guess you're right. I would have steamed it open I think."

Still feeling like this was a little weird and macabre, Duran opened the envelope and took out a two-page letter addressed to him. With a growing sense of unease, he read:

Dear Eddy,

If you are reading this, it's because I am already dead. I'm aware that the information that I'm about to give you may put you in a difficult and possibly dangerous position but I'm assuming you'll know what to do with it. Needless to say, it's incredibly sensitive.

Recently, a copy of a top secret briefing paper was sent from the number of the private fax in the president's office to an intelligence agency in China. The document was very sensitive and dealt with scenarios for defending Taiwan should China decide to reclaim it forcefully. As you can imagine, this caused quite a stir. An investigation into the incident was commenced but before it could be completed, the vice-president asked me to print off the fax log in the president's machine. It showed that the document was indeed sent from the president's fax. I have strong reason to believe that the VP destroyed this document to protect the president. A copy is attached to this letter, you'll notice line 24, this very long fax is the one in question. Check the number, you'll see.

To cut a long story short, I decided that my silence in this case had a price. I'm not proud of it but I figured I could get myself out of a financial mess caused by Ruth's illness by taking some "hush" money. There it is, I've said it. You are the only one who knows this. I will set up a meeting with the VP to discuss the detail. Obviously, he is a powerful man and if you are reading this you can assume that someone has decided that I need to be shut down. I can't tell you how weird it feels to be writing this but if I've learned anything in the last twenty years it's that anything can happen when the stakes are high enough.

For the record, I don't believe that the president sent that fax. This occurrence as well as some very strange things going on in the Pacific lead me to think that someone is playing games with our nation and trying to trick us into a conflict with the Chinese, but that's another story. Perhaps even a bigger story than this one, but you're on your own there.

So, all I ask is that you dig into this thing and don't let the bastard get away with my death. It's also the biggest story of your life, I think.

Over to you, buddy.

George Medford.

Duran looked up from the letter and his face was ashen.

"My God, you look ill. What on earth does it say?" Duran simply handed Etheridge the letter and walked over to the window where he could see the traffic in the street below. Etheridge read in silence. His jaw dropped.

"My Goodness, this is dynamite! What are you going to do?"

Duran continued staring out of the window and replied without turning around.

"I have absolutely no idea. I'm not inclined to let it rest, particularly considering George's death, but I'll be damned if I know how to tackle this one." Duran turned his eyes to the sky as if looking for some sort of sign.

"You've really thrown me a curve ball this time, George. Jesus, this could get us all killed."

* * *

On the phone Charlie tells Elizabeth about his conversation with Lord, about his daring tape swap and the resultant stress it caused him. Elizabeth listens with a growing sense of horror and gasps out loud when Charlie relates his experience with the young Keith.

"You're taking such a risk, Charlie." She says.

"I know, but I can't just sit back and pretend everything's normal. I just can't do it."

"Well, you just be really careful. I don't want anything to happen to you, Charlie." She said.

The decision is made that they will invite Lord to Charlie's apartment, share some Chinese take-out and then look at the video. Charlie just hopes it will be worth the anxiety it's caused him.

Later that evening, the three sit together in Charlie's apartment having finished the meal together. "That was very good, Elizabeth." Lord says.

"I didn't cook it, John, I just bought it," she said with a smile.

"Well, it was still a lovely meal and I enjoyed eating with you two. I don't get much company these days. Seem to be working all the time. It's great to get out and do normal stuff."

Charlie leans back and stretches his shoulders. "What do you say, John, shall we take a look at this video?"

"It sounds like you pulled off a major espionage effort today, let's hope it gives us something."

The trio huddle around Charlie's wide-screen TV and watch the last few minutes of Montez's life several times over. The first time, Elizabeth breaks down and they have to take time out while Charlie comforts her and Lord makes some coffee. The next time is a little easier for her.

"I can't see anything," Charlie says with frustration. "Nothing new. Damn."

"Why don't you go to the last few frames and we'll take it real slow," Lord suggests. They flick forward a single frame at a time, once twice, three times. Lord suddenly says, "Stop"

"What is it?" Elizabeth asks.

"Can you zoom in on this TV, Charlie?" Lord asks.

"Sure, it's a digital, what do you want to see?"

Lord points to a small area of the screen, ten frames before the end of the sequence. Charlie uses the remote like a mouse to enlarge the section.

"Well, I'll be damned." Charlie says. Lord is shaking his head.

The previous frame clearly shows the spectrophotometer with its cover, sitting innocently on the bench. At frame ten, through the nylon material of the cover, a red indicator light becomes visible. A red light that was not lit in the previous frame.

"My God!" Elizabeth gasped. "I don't believe it! It turned itself on!"

* * *

Lieutenant-General James Chapman reclined in the high-backed leather chair in his Pentagon office as he spoke on the phone. "Yes, sir, I understand. We have looked at exactly the scenario you describe but I can say to you that it was not one of our projects. Yes, sir, I will double-check. No, sir, I think it unlikely that the Chinese would have the technology or resources to pull it off. Of course, sir, I'll call if I find anything at all."

Chapman put down the phone and smiled. He turned to the other man in the room.

The man that everyone at The Factory knew as Alex Fox, and said:
"Time to call off the dogs, Frank. I think the experiment can be pronounced a success."

PART THREE

"Transnational Infrastructure Warfare (TIW) … attacking a nation's or sub-national entity's key industries and utilities -- to include telecommunications, banking and finance, transportation, water, government operations, emergency services, energy and power, and manufacturing. These industries normally have key linkages and interdependencies, which could significantly increase the impact of an attack on a single component. Threats to critical infrastructure include those from nation-states, state-sponsored sub-national groups, international and domestic terrorists, criminal elements, computer hackers, and insiders acting as agents for others."

Lieutenant-General Patrick M. Hughes, US Army, Director, Defense Intelligence Agency, Washington D.C., February 2, 1999

ANN ARBOR CHRONICLE

Local News

The Nation, and indeed the world, breathed a collective sigh of relief today as the president addressed the people and confirmed the lessening of tensions between the US and China. "We have made a great deal of progress," he said. "We will continue to work hard to restore relations between our two countries and rebuild the ties that have been tested in recent weeks." The president refused to be drawn on the reasons why hostilities escalated the way they did. "The situation is improving daily," is all he would say.

Full story, and complete transcript of the president's address, next page…

CHAPTER 24

Duran leans back in his battered chair and gazes out of his treasured window. George Medford's original letter is locked away in the safe and Duran absently fiddles with the corner of a copy he made as his newsman's mind considers the angles. The timing couldn't be better, he tells himself. With the tensions easing in the Pacific, the story would get the full attention it deserved. Also, if the Nation was in crisis still, he could hardly drop a bombshell that threatened to destabilise the government. He was a veteran newshound but an American first. Yes, the pieces were starting to drop into place. But how to go public with this? The death of Medford had hardly made it into the newspapers, it was obviously being kept under wraps as much as possible.

The other consideration was that this fax log thing had led to George being killed. It would be no use pussy-footing around with it. Once it became known that Duran had the document, what's to stop them killing him too? No, he had to do it with a big splash, let everyone know what he had so that the focus on him kept him safe. Or as safe as possible, considering what would go down. Yes indeed, Duran thought, the shit will hit the fan over this, no mistake. George wasn't kidding when he said this was the biggest story in my life, damn, it could be bigger than Watergate. Duran had set up a meeting with the paper's senior editors to thrash out what they would do next. He figured he was one hour away from something that could make him a household word, or maybe get him killed. What a job.

The journalist in him just had to run with this, whatever the cost. He figured the paper wouldn't be able to walk away either. It was just too big. He closed his eyes and imagined the furore, the celebrity, the change to his life that the story would bring. This was the big one, the once-in-a-lifetime story. A thrill coursed through his body. He felt ready. Eddy knew that he should have talked about this to his wife, knew that it would turn her life on its head too, but he couldn't bring himself to have that conversation. Couldn't risk the fact that she might get cold feet, try to talk him out of it. Better to ask for forgiveness than permission. That had always been his motto and now he was about to gamble his future, maybe even his marriage on sufficient forgiveness being available.

* * *

At work today, Charlie had kept a very low profile, hardly emerging from his office. While it was true that he still had lots to catch up with including hundreds of emails, the curse of his life, in reality he couldn't concentrate on anything. Mercifully, Darville was in Washington for a meeting so at least he was spared the discomfort of running into the man in the corridors. Charlie's mind was on the tape they had watched the previous night and on what it all might mean. They had agreed to get back together again at Charlie's apartment after dinner, this time with Louis and Lily present to see if they couldn't start to put the pieces into the puzzle. Charlie felt a little guilty about involving Lily but she did pretty much know the whole story anyway and Lord had expressed the view that she might have a good perspective as an outsider.

Charlie was starting to like John Lord. He'd never in his life had a cop as a friend and he was discovering that many of the stereotypical images that he had maintained were based more on what he'd seen in the movies than reality. He enjoyed Lord's intelligence and dedication as well as his determination. He was a quick thinker but also a good listener. Charlie found himself looking forward to their evening together.

Finally, the day that had seemed to last an eternity was almost over. Charlie locked his filing cabinet and turned towards his computer to switch off the screen before heading for home. His hand froze an inch from the power button. His screen was displaying a message. For a second the pixels looked as if they would leap off the screen and burn into his eyes. He shut them tightly, screwing up his face, took a deep breath and opened them again. The message was still there.

There are four walks of life:

The ways of the knight

The ways of the farmer

The ways of the artisan

The ways of the merchant

What are you Charlie?

Kensei

Charlie slumped into his chair, his heart pounding. His world felt like it had shrunk, the screen message at the very centre of his universe. Charlie knew what he should do. This needed to be investigated by the INFOSEC people. Routine procedure, just like before. They hadn't found Kensei, whoever he or it was. Either that, or he was back again. Suddenly a resolve he didn't know he possessed gripped Charlie's mind. He sat upright and clicked the print button on his screen. A few seconds later his laser printer sprang to life and squeezed out a single sheet of paper, the new message captured. Charlie folded the paper into three as if he were about to post it inside a business envelope, and slipped it into his jacket pocket. He hit the delete key and the message disappeared from the screen of his PC.

Charlie poked the OFF button, grabbed his briefcase and walked out. In a part of his mind that he could only access imprecisely, that he would only ever need a few times in his entire life, he knew this wasn't about The Factory. It wasn't about mischievous hackers who had found his name on an old printout in a garbage can, it wasn't some bored employee playing a prank. It was the VIWAP, and it was interested in him and him alone. If it was to be stopped, somehow Charlie knew it would be up to him to do it.

Charlie drove to his apartment and let himself inside without giving any of the actions conscious thought. The first external stimulant that he was aware of since leaving the parking lot was the smell of food cooking. It snapped him back into the present and he recalled that Elizabeth had said she would finish early and prepare dinner for them. It was nice to come home to someone, he thought. Charlie hung his coat next to Alex's on the coat stand in the hallway, dropped his briefcase and went into the kitchen to find Elizabeth stirring a wonderful smelling pasta sauce. His stomach suddenly reminded him that all he'd consumed today was too much coffee. Charlie put his arms around Elizabeth's waist and, as she leaned back into his body he inhaled her smell deeply. "That's nice," she said. His right hand crept up and cupped her breast as he kissed her behind the ear. She let go of the wooden spoon she was holding, rotated in his arms and kissed him lightly on the lips.

"Cut that out mister or we'll never be ready when the others arrive," she said.

Charlie sighed exaggeratedly. "I guess you're right. I can wait."

"Oh, you poor deprived man." Elizabeth said, poking her tongue out at him.

Elizabeth served up the meal and they chatted comfortably as they ate. Elizabeth was excited about their evening and the prospect of some detective work while at the same time feeling a little uneasy that things were not as they seemed. She was particularly concerned for Darville whom she now suspected was involved in something that had gone beyond what he anticipated and maybe had him trapped. She still didn't believe he could be in any way crooked. Maybe a poor decision at some stage that had painted him into a corner, she thought.

When the meal was finished they loaded the dishwasher together, already falling into routines despite their relatively new relationship. Charlie made a pot of coffee and they settled down to await the visitors.

"I had another email from the hacker today." Charlie said, the comment like a bombshell. Elizabeth stared at him.

"You're kidding! I thought that was all over. I thought they swept the place clean."

"Well, maybe they did and he's back. Or maybe they missed him."

"What did it say?"

Charlie handed the printout to Elizabeth who studied it carefully, her face screwed into a frown.

"Do you know what this means, Charlie?"

"Only what Lily told us. I figured I might show it to her, see if there's anything else she can think of."

"Have you reported it yet?" Elizabeth asked, handing the paper back.

"No, and I don't think I will either." Elizabeth's eyes opened in surprise.

"What! Why not, Charlie? You know the rules, they could string you up for not disclosing this sort of thing."

"I reported it once before and where did it get us? They didn't find who did it or how. They haven't managed to trace anything despite one hell of an effort. I don't think they'd do any better this time around. And there's something else."

Elizabeth put her hand on Charlie's arm.

"I think this is personal. I don't know why but I think it's about me. Someone or something targeting me."

"Something? The VIWAP? Do you think it's back?"

"I think it's possible, and until I'm sure, it's probably better not to say too much about it. They might put me out to pasture again and then I'd have no chance to find out what's going on."

"Will you tell John?"

"I don't think so. He's focused on proving whether we're dealing with accidents or murders. I guess we should let that run its course first. See where it goes. I can always raise it if things develop further."

Elizabeth nodded. "I guess you're right. I don't like this whole thing though, Charlie. It gives me the creeps to think that some sort of virtual stalker might be after you."

"You and me both," Charlie smiled.

Over the next thirty minutes, the rest of the *A team*, as Lord had jokingly called them arrived at Charlie's apartment. Lily was first and then Louis and finally Lord himself. After some introductions and small talk they got down to business. Lord was keen to set the scene.

"It's important for everyone here to understand the unconventional way that I'm trying to approach this. Obviously there's nothing to stop all of us getting together socially as friends to have a beer and a few laughs. The fact that Louis and I are cops and you three are various flavours of doctors is just the way it is. Where it becomes a problem is if I try to formally investigate the deaths that have occurred at the facility."

"The Factory." Elizabeth interrupted. "We call it The Factory."

"Thanks," Lord replied.

"What *is* a problem is if I try to investigate the deaths that have occurred at The Factory. I've been told in no uncertain terms by my superiors that the cases are closed and that I'm to let it go. Given what we've discovered about Alex's death, I'm less inclined as time goes by to obey that directive. Trouble is, these deaths occurred in a high-security military establishment and they were investigated internally. Unlike the situation with Alex, who was found in his apartment building, these other deaths are a bit beyond my reach just now. I'm hoping that together, we can dig up enough to allow me to bring some pressure to bear. As we sit in this room though, it's an evening with friends more than a police investigation. Does that make sense?" The nods around the room indicated that it did.

"So," Lord continued, "what we have so far on the death of Ric Montez is a security video that Charlie appropriated by a cunning bit of espionage."

"Way to go, Charlie, you da man!" Louis said, causing laughter to erupt around the room.

"We framed through the last second or so of that tape and it clearly shows a piece of lab equipment, an AA spectrophotometer Charlie tells me, turning on by itself, a split second before the explosion that tore the lab apart."

"Could Ric have turned that machine on by accident?" Lily asked.

"He was nowhere near it at the time," Elizabeth replied.

"And the power outlet was on the opposite side to where he was trying to turn the gas off."

"What sort of switch does that machine have, Elizabeth?" asked Louis.

"Well, it's sort of a red spring-loaded toggle switch."

"You mean like a circuit-breaker?" Louis said.

"Yes, that's it. You push it against the spring and it locks in."

Louis looks across at Lord. "There's no way a switch like that is turning itself on, JL. Those puppies are made to flick off if there's a problem. Switch like that? Has to be turned on by a person."

"And the switch stays off when the equipment's not in use?" Lord asked.

"Yes. Except for when the manufacturer wants to dial in and update software. Then we leave the switch on and after a while the machine sort of goes to sleep and wakes up when they dial in," Elizabeth said.

Lord leaned forward in his chair.

"And when it goes to sleep, does the light go off?"

Elizabeth thought for a few seconds.

"Yes, it does, because we sometimes forget to turn the switch off when they've finished. If the light stayed on we'd see it and not accidentally leave the machine turned on."

Lord sat back and smiled. "Isn't this interesting. Maybe what we saw was someone who was watching Montez on the video, dialling in at exactly the right moment and using the machine's ignition to spark the explosion."

"Assuming that the thing was left on for maintenance," Louis added.

"Yes. Was it?" he asked Elizabeth, who was obviously lost in thought.

"Elizabeth?" Lord prompted.

"Yes, it was on. I remember receiving an email the week before asking us to leave the switch on until further notice so work could be done. I remember thinking it was unusual at the time because normally we have a document sent through to us detailing what work needs to be done and asking us to sign an agreement that we're happy for a new version of software to be loaded. I thought it unusual but didn't push it. I had completely forgotten about that with everything going on. God, if I hadn't done that Ric might still be alive!" Her hand shot to her mouth, tears welling up in her eyes.

"You don't know that, Elizabeth." Lord said as Charlie put his arm around her.

"This is all supposition right now. We probably should get a copy of that email though. My guess is that it didn't come from the manufacturer at all. We can check that." He looked at Louis who was making a note in his book. The two men's eyes locked and Louis nodded imperceptibly.

"Hey, Charlie." Lord said. "Why don't you rustle us up some coffee and we'll take a break for a few minutes. Let Elizabeth get some air. You guys have done good. Real good."

* * *

In a leafy middle-class suburb in Washington, Eddy Duran lies next to his sleeping wife in their modest home. He'd bought their house thirty years ago before the prices skyrocketed and Duran considered himself extremely lucky with the investment. Right place, right time, he thought. They planned to sell the place when he retired and move to the west coast somewhere. The property's value meant that they would have choices beyond what he could have ever expected on his journalist's salary. Sleep was evading Duran tonight because of what he knew would be in the paper tomorrow. It felt strange to be lying in bed just like every other night when he knew with certainty that his whole life was about to change. By this time tomorrow hundreds of millions of people would hear his name. What a buzz he thought guiltily as his wife, relaxed and comfortable in her ignorance, slept peacefully.

Duran's thoughts were interrupted by a small sound downstairs, as though someone had dropped a bottle outside the house. Perhaps

Bill, his neighbour coming home late, maybe had a few too many? But then, there was no sound of a car in the driveway, so that didn't make sense. As his mind struggled to place the sound, he heard a creak on the staircase. Now he was instantly alert. Was it possible that someone was in the house? Duran decided to investigate. He got halfway out of bed before there was a dull thump and a blinding flash of light. The first thing that entered his mind was that someone had blown up the house.

Before he could process what was happening, rough hands dragged him from his bed and threw him onto the bedroom floor, his head twisted sideways and pressed into the rug, both arms savagely wrenched up his back. His head was turned away from his wife but he could hear her struggling and her muffled cries and so he assumed she was getting the same treatment. His anger flared and he twisted sideways in attempt to break free. A gloved hand gripped his head so tightly that he thought his skull would crack. A cold object was thrust into the back of his neck and a voice said

"Stay still."

He did as he was told.

He could hear people going through the house. Through his study downstairs. He could hear drawers being opened and books pulled from shelves. He tried to speak, to assure the robbers that there was little of real value in the house but the pressure from what he correctly assumed was a gun in the back of his head increased, causing him to gasp in pain. He became terribly frightened that whoever held him might accidentally snap his neck if they didn't let up. He decided to keep quiet and see what they wanted.

After what seemed like hours but was probably no longer than ten minutes, the noises stopped. He could hear footsteps approaching, taking no care now to tread silently on the steps as they climbed. The pressure on his head decreased momentarily. "Please don't hurt us!" he pleaded. His head was ground back into the rug and he felt his airways constricting due to the dust he was breathing in. If they don't kill us I might just die of an asthma attack, he thought.

A voice said "You were given a document by an attorney yesterday. Where is it?" Christ! Duran thought, that's what this is about. It didn't lessen his fear though, these were the bastards that probably killed George. He knew that what he said now was critical but he wasn't sure what answer to give. He felt as though their lives were hanging in the balance and that if he said the wrong thing he wouldn't get a second chance. He decided to bluff. Buy some time.

"I don't know what you mean," he said.

Beside him he heard his wife scream in pain. The sound tore through his heart. Even though his ears were partly covered by the carpet pressing against his face one side and the hand holding his neck on the other, the volume of her cry startled and horrified him. He'd never heard such a noise come from her before, didn't even know she was capable of such an agonising sound.

"Okay, okay!" He said. "Leave her alone, you sick bastards!"

The voice returned. Calm, unhurried. Terrifying in its detachment. "You were given a document by an attorney yesterday. Where is it?"

"It's in the safe at the newspaper."

"Has anyone seen it other than you?" the voice asked, as calmly as though it was inquiring about the weather, or a new restaurant down the street. The lack of emotion in the voice, despite the obviously charged situation, scared Duran more than anything else. He felt as if his life would be like a bug to these people. He played what he hoped would be the ace up his sleeve.

"All of the senior editors have seen it. The paper's senior management have seen it. The story will be front page tomorrow. It's too late."

Behind him the voice sighed.

"Do you know what you've done, Eddy? Do you really?"

Before Duran could reply, he felt a sharp pain, like a pinprick in his arm. God, this is the end he thought. It's all over. He attempted one last struggle but immediately felt the world slipping away from him. Felt himself sliding into blackness down a long wide-necked funnel, then all sensation ceased.

CHAPTER 25

The man who used to be known as Alex Fox leaned back in his chair, stretched his arms out above his head and sighed contentedly. As his gaze wanders over his large, comfortable office, he is struck by just how much change has been injected into his life during the last few weeks. Starting with the very office he now occupies. An office that screams success, power, position. He can hardly believe it. A shitload better than that dog box I had at The Factory, he thinks. Alex's career is on the up and up, even allowing for the fact that he has been wrenched from one life and given another. Sure, at the moment he is forced to keep an extremely low profile but in a month or two he'll be relocated, probably to Europe, where his new life will really start. It still seems unreal to him, even now. The approach, the proposition from high up, the speed and audacity of the whole thing. God! The *secrecy* of it all!

The only downside was that he had nobody outside the organisation that he could share his incredible success with. But, for Alex, this wasn't too much of a problem. He'd always been something of a loner. Never one for having many friends, he didn't need other people's approval to know that he was special. For Alex, the very fact that this incredible stunt had been pulled off, with him at the centre of it was evidence of just how special he was. Still, he thought, it would be a scream to walk back into The Factory as if nothing had happened, just to see the looks on the faces of the shit-kickers.

The reality is that the entire VIWAP Mk II program had exceeded the expectations of even the wildest optimists within the department. As Ed Furneaux had suspected, it came as no surprise that the VIWAP had taken control of the backup system and manipulated it in order to escape. What had astounded even Alex was that it took on the identity of Kensei and began communicating with staff in The Factory. Of all the spontaneous actions that Alex could have predicted, this behaviour would not have even made it onto his list. The truth was that it generated in Alex emotions that he rarely felt: Apprehension and uncertainty. For the first time since he was recruited to the program he found himself questioning what they had actually done. As if a statue painstakingly and meticulously carved from marble had somehow come to life and its intentions and motives were unknown. Would it be happy with the way it looked? What would it consider itself to be? Would it turn on the hand that created it? The Kensei identity bothered Alex greatly because it wasn't something that he would have predicted and it was significant enough to leave him wondering what else might yet be coming. Even as he basked in the success that the project was enjoying, secretly he was pleased that the experiment was about to be halted. These unexpected developments really called for a few more controls within the code. A few extra safety catches, he thought. Creating smart weapons is one thing, producing Franken-code is another thing altogether.

The astonishing success of the Mk II VIWAP had been detected by Chapman and the few hand-picked INFOSEC people he'd recruited within an hour of Alex starting it on the simulator. There had been multiple successful compromises of highly secure military computers within the first few minutes. Chapman quickly realised what a revolutionary new weapon he had in his hands. One that could forever alter the very fabric of modern warfare. And what a massive problem he faced. Put simply, for something so revolutionary, way too many people knew about it. Too many people for the true level of its success to kept secret. He needed Fox to refine his work and for the experiments to continue but the staff at The Factory somehow must be kept in the dark. The best outcome was for them to feel that the whole program was a flop and that they were lucky to keep their jobs. And so a distraction was called for and an escape route for Fox. It had to be fast and it had to be absolute. The equivalent of a precision-guided munition. Chapman had called in quite a few favours to get the job done but no price was too high for the strategic advantage conferred by this technology. They hadn't bargained on the VIWAP's spontaneity or its murderess destructiveness but in the end they had pulled it off with just a few lose ends to be mopped up.

Alex cracked his knuckles and set about typing the email that would effectively shut the VIWAP down and cause it to report on its movements, activities, actions, and intentions by returning a coded and compressed data file. This data file allowed the team to look into the VIWAP's reasoning and logic, a sort of window into its mind. Although the exact whereabouts of the VIWAP was not known, a feature of its architecture was that it checked several electronic mailboxes around the world every few minutes. An email with a specific thirty two character codeword would be the signal for it to switch to a suspended state where it simply monitored the mailboxes for further commands and data. Like most good systems, Alex thought, its elegance lay in its simplicity.

As he had done in several previous experiments since adopting his new identity and with an air of finality he tapped the return key to send the message on its way. Alex looked at his Rolex and decided that he'd call it a day. Tomorrow he'd analyse the data that would be reported back. He snapped his briefcase shut and made his way down the private elevator to the underground parking lot where his new black SUV sat menacingly with its darkened windows and massive tyres. He could drive from his office to his temporary apartment and its private parking without any chance of being seen. He just couldn't stop along the way to pick up a six pack or some take-out. Could be worse, he thought as he unlocked the vehicle, another few weeks of this hide and seek and I'll be out of here.

* * *

"Just the gas this morning, sir?" The attendant asked Charlie as he handed his credit card over to pay for the fuel he'd just pumped on his way to The Factory.

"That's it." Charlie replied absently. He'd had a restless night thinking about the meeting with Lord and what they were uncovering. It just gets worse the more you dig, he thought. Darville's dire warning about his and Elizabeth's safety weighed on his mind and he felt guilty that maybe his refusal to let the whole thing go was endangering Elizabeth in some way. At the same time he knew he couldn't back off. Especially now he had the two detectives on side. His thoughts were interrupted by the attendant who was looking at him strangely.

"There appears to be a problem here, sir." He said, looking down at the card reader behind the counter.

"I might just try this again out the back in case this machine is flaky."

Charlie shrugged his shoulders.

"Sure, I'm not really in a hurry. The card should be fine, I used it yesterday without any problem."

"Well, you know how this electronic stuff can be." The attendant called from the back room. Charlie wandered over to the magazine rack and picked out the latest PC-World magazine to kill some time. He spotted an article on a new massively parallel Supercomputer and lost himself for a few minutes as he scanned through it. With a start he remembered where he was and that the attendant appeared to be taking a long time with his card out the back. He looked at his watch.

"Hey, I can pay cash if that card is giving you trouble." Charlie called.

"Just be a second." The attendant's reply floated out from the back room.

Charlie put the magazine back in the stand and wandered back to the counter. He heard someone enter the store and was about to turn around to tell them where the attendant behind the counter had gone when a voice froze him to the spot.

"Freeze! Put both hands out wide on the counter where I can see them. Nice and slow."

"What's this!" Charlie began to say.

"Now!' The voice barked with such authority that Charlie decided not to argue. He felt rough hands on his body, patting him down, pushing his feet apart. Before he realised what was happening, his hands were pulled behind his back and he felt the cuffs being snapped onto his wrists. Someone grabbed him by the shoulders and spun him around. He found himself staring into the face of a very serious police officer with another about ten feet away, his pistol pointing at Charlie's chest. A third officer materialised from the back with his credit card in hand.

"What?" Charlie said, bewildered by all this.

"I'm arresting you for possessing stolen property and on suspicion of aggravated burglary and murder."

The cop began to read him his Miranda rights but it was lost on Charlie. He couldn't believe what was happening. The whole situation was just bizarre. The attendant looked at him sheepishly.

"Sorry, dude, they got rules about this stuff."

Charlie found himself telling the clerk not to worry about it, feeling sorry for how scared he looked. The police led him outside into the sunshine where several people had gathered to witness the spectacle.

"You have seriously got the wrong guy." Charlie said, realising how stupid and empty the words must have sounded to these crime-hardened cops.

"And what about my car? You can't leave it here."

"It will be taken care of." The cop replied, pushing Charlie's head down as his partner held the door of the cruiser open. As he turned, Charlie caught a reflection of himself in the gas station's window and hoped that nobody he knew was passing by to see this.

Forty-five minutes later, Charlie was sitting, still cuffed, at a metal table in a locked room at the Ann Arbor Police Department, feeling about as angry as he could ever remember. Obviously there had been some sort of a mistake but he felt such humiliation at being treated as a common criminal. He wondered if he could sue over this. Damage to reputation, wrongful imprisonment, pain and suffering, that sort of stuff. He had just about decided he had an open-and-shut case when the door was thrown open and in strode John Lord.

"Charlie! God, what a mess. Let me get those bracelets off you."

"What the hell happened, John?" Charlie asked as Lord unlocked the handcuffs and dropped them on the table.

"Well, we're still trying to sort it out but it looks as though the credit card you used was reported stolen during a home invasion where some poor old man was bludgeoned to death. When you tried to use it the call went out and, well, you know the rest."

"But that's ridiculous!"

"Of course it is, Charlie, particularly considering the fact that we were together eating Chinese food when the crime took place but there's obviously been some sort of computer glitch and, for all our people knew, you were armed and dangerous. They didn't rough you up did they?"

Charlie sighed, rubbing his wrists.

"No, they were okay. I tell you what though, it was an awful feeling. Being hauled off in front of everyone. It's not going to do anything for my reputation."

Lord let out a laugh and Charlie found himself starting to unwind now his new friend was here.

"Hey, Charlie, look on the bright side. Imagine the story you'll have to tell around the water cooler at The Factory."

Charlie allowed himself a smile.

"There are some who might think I deserved it!"

Lord slapped him on the back.

"Come on, buddy, come sit somewhere more comfortable while I push through some paperwork to get you out of here and then I'll buy you a coffee. I guess we better go and rescue that car of yours too."

***

At about the same time that Charlie sat fuming in the interrogation room, Eddy Duran and his wife are waking up from a chemically-induced comatose state. At first, Eddy doesn't realise where he is. His head hurts worse than anything he's ever felt in his life and as his vision stabilises he realises that he's lying in his bed. He turns his head to look at the bedside clock and a wave of nausea washes over him so powerfully that, for a second, he thinks he will vomit in his bed. As Eddy's eyes refocus he realises that it's nine-thirty. He doesn't think it's a weekend but his brain doesn't seem to want to tell him why he slept so late. He closes his eyes and tries to think. All that comes are images of what he thinks must be a delirium-induced nightmare. Of black masked men and rough hands.

Beside him his wife stirs and attempts to sit up. Suddenly she vomits violently onto the duvet and Eddy has great trouble not following her lead when the smell hits his nostrils. No sooner is she done than she flops back down in a dead faint, her grey face covered in a sheen of sweat. Must have been something we ate, Eddy thinks. Something is calling to him from the depths of his memory, something important, just out of reach. Suddenly it hits him. The paper! The story comes out today! God, he thinks, what a day to be struck down with food poisoning. Slowly he sits up, a few inches at a time, determined not to add to the disgusting technicolour puddles on the bed. When he finally sits upright, he swings his legs over the edge of the bed and attempts to stand. He gets halfway there before his legs seem to disappear from under him and he hits the bedroom floor, the room whirling around. Despite his best intentions, The contents of Eddy Duran's stomach, apparently without any effort from him, comes hurtling out of his mouth and nose before the room darkens and turns to black.

The bump and sound of Eddie's retching brings his wife around again. She manages to grab the phone and with a supreme act of willpower she stays conscious long enough to dial an emergency number and gasp out their address and the word "Dying" before sliding back into the depths of unconsciousness.

* * *

Feeling equally as sick, but maintaining control over his breakfast, the vice-president sits at his kitchen table, head in hands, the morning paper spread before him. His world has just collapsed around him and right now he's not sure if he can face the horde of reporters that he can hear buzzing around outside. His eyes are dragged back by the lead story, George's letter reprinted word for word. The paper is careful not to draw too many conclusions but the story is obviously a time bomb waiting to go off. For the first time in his life, the VP has no idea how to defuse this one. His brain will not engage with the problem. The motor's running but the gearbox is busted somehow. He simply sits and stares as the black type dances across his eyes.

CHAPTER 26

The man who used to be Alex Fox is cruising toward his office after a great night's sleep and a leisurely breakfast. There is no real reason to get in early, the work he has scheduled for the day will only take a few hours and he is enjoying a much slower pace for a change. May as well take advantage of it while it lasts, he thinks, I'll be back to twelve hour days soon enough. It's also great to be able to leave for work after the traffic peak is over. As he heads down Arlington Boulevard, he has the green lights with him all the way as well-positioned traffic cameras feed data on traffic patterns and flow back to the central computer system controlling the signals.

"Way to go!" he says to the empty vehicle. As he approaches Hillwood, the green lights still with him, a car flashes across the intersection in front of him. He leans on the horn as he gives the finger to the careless driver speeding into the distance. Distracted by what he assumes is a red-light-runner, he doesn't see the garbage truck closing in on him from his left at forty miles per hour.

At the last moment he catches sight of the truck whose driver is momentarily distracted, reaching for his coffee on the empty seat next to him. In the fraction of a second that it takes Alex's foot to move from the accelerator to the brake, the two vehicles come together with a immense bang. The truck strikes Alex's SUV just behind the driver's door, sending the vehicle spinning across the intersection. As it mounts the central strip, the security barrier ruptures the fuel tank and the SUV is thrown onto its side, gushing fuel and showering sparks across the opposite lane. A driver in a restored Mustang coming the other way tries valiantly to avoid the spinning wreckage but the tragedy is unfolding too fast and with a sickening crunch of collapsing steel, he ploughs into the roof of Alex's shiny black coffin. The two vehicles, locked in a deadly embrace, rotate together once more before coming to rest against the kerb. For a second, all is quiet. Then the silence is shattered by a massive explosion as the fuel from both vehicles is ignited. Within seconds, both cars and a large section of the roadway are trapped in an inferno. Several people, including the injured but courageous garbage truck driver, leap out of their hastily stopped vehicles and rush forward only to be beaten back by the heat before they get within thirty feet. In horror they watch the blackened marionette-like body of the Mustang driver twitch and jump in the orange flames.

The fire department is on the scene within minutes but the situation is hopeless. Eyewitnesses travelling on both roads will relate how they had the green light and the other vehicle must have failed to stop at the red light. No fault with the traffic signals will ever be found.

For the second time in as many months, Alex Fox is dead. Only this time it's for real. Alex Fox is killed but the remains of Frank Fredrickson are buried. The riddle of who was cremated in Alex's coffin will never be solved and the fictitious Frank Fredrickson will never be mourned. Alex Fox will never know that his monstrous creation elected not to collect its stand-down email but instead decided that the game was only just beginning.

* * *

Eddy Duran's big day has also not worked out the way he imagined. His celebrity is as great as he thought it would be but it's not exactly the top concern that he has right now. His wife's call for assistance brought the ambulance and police cars screaming. After forcing the door, the two were rushed to the George Washington University Hospital where their stomachs were flushed and their condition stabilised. Although Eddy has regained consciousness and reported his suspicions of food poisoning, his wife has slipped into a coma.

Outside the hospital, a media crowd is gathered waiting to speak to Eddy. The condition of his life-long partner has taken away any triumph that he might otherwise have felt about the breaking of the story. Right now he would trade everything including this newfound fame to have the health of his wife restored.

As he lies in his hospital bed it strikes him how selective memory can be. He can clearly recollect everything before going to bed, the meal, the mixed feeling of anticipation and fear about the next day when the story would break. Then there's just a blank, like someone recorded a few minutes of blackness in the middle of an otherwise perfect video tape. He has no trouble remembering things since he's been awake. Doctors' names, conversations, that sort of thing. The doctor doesn't seem overly worried about it, said it happens sometimes and maybe it will come back and maybe it won't. Some sort of a defence mechanism of the brain maybe. Who knows?

* * *

It's after lunch by the time Charlie gets back into The Factory. He hasn't eaten since breakfast and is drained and irritable from his ordeal. The stress of the incident has soured his stomach and, although his appetite hasn't yet returned, the lack of food has sent his blood sugar plummeting and his mood along with it. After dumping his briefcase and turning on his computer, Charlie fetches a can of soft drink and some corn chips from the vending machine in the cafeteria. Hardly a balanced meal but he figures it's better than nothing.

As he flops into his chair, he realises with some alarm that he has yet another message from Kensei and the tone is changing:

Hello Charlie

You don't have the respect to answer me

Do you see how easily I can damage you? Confuse the processes of your life?

You haven't answered me and this disrespect tells

me that you must think yourself a warrior

So be it

You will have the opportunity to test your skills

You will lose.

Kensei

Charlie stares at his screen for a long time. Clearly, his little experience this morning with the credit card was what Kensei referred to. But why him? Charlie prints off the screen and places it in his briefcase. What did it mean that he would have the opportunity to try his skills against Kensei's? And why was Charlie being singled out for this attention? Was it something to do with the deteriorating relationship that he had with Alex in the weeks before his death? Even though it felt weird, Charlie decided that he would reply to the message to see what happened. The first problem was that the message was simply in a pop-up window on his screen. It wasn't an email or any other sort of messaging system Charlie knew. He thought about it for a few moments, then just started typing and his text appeared in the window:

Kensei,

I don't understand who you are or what you want. You seem to

have a problem with me. Have I offended you? I am sorry for

not replying sooner but I have been very busy.

Is there somewhere we could meet and discuss this? Where are you located?

I would like to clear up what appears to be a misunderstanding.

Regards,

Charlie.

Within a fraction of a second following Charlie's press of the send key, a message flashed back, startling him with its speed. Obviously faster than any person could have composed and typed it.

Charlie

You insult me with your response

You know exactly who I am you helped design me

As to where I am I am everywhere and nowhere at the same time

There is no misunderstanding and we can only meet like this

You may be asked to help stop me

I will erase you if you try

Do not insult me again you are not worthy

Kensei

Charlie prints off the second message before deleting it. He turns off his screen and decides to go home. His head aches and he feels sick in his stomach, not just because of his encounter with the police but because he was now sure that the VIWAP had him in its sights. The staccato and unpunctuated stream-of-consciousness style of writing sent a shiver down his spine. He also knew that if it wanted to, it could kill him in a multitude of ways. Charlie feels as though he is being painted into a corner, forced into some bizarre duel with a computer entity gone crazy. How do you fight it anyway? He thought. This isn't something to be settled by an Indian arm wrestle or a fistfight. And how could I be asked to try to stop it if nobody else even believed it existed?

* * *

That evening Detective John Lord and the *A team* are scheduled to regroup at Charlie's apartment. An hour or so earlier, Charlie had been a whisker away from cancelling the whole evening. He couldn't see any point to it any more with the VIWAP loose and obviously targeting him. Even Alex's death didn't appear to be a mystery any more. Charlie knew that Kensei could have caused it in any number of ways. Who cares whether a few details don't add up, the bottom line is that Kensei did it. What else matters? Charlie had confided this to Elizabeth and it was she, with tears in her eyes, who had convinced him to go ahead with the meeting. She told him that this was the worst time to think of isolating himself from his friends and others who believed in him and were on his side. Of course she was right he'd thought and the possibility of sharing the news with the others and maybe coming up with a plan had made him reconsider. By the time the others started to arrive he was feeling a little better.

* * *

Leonard Darville was working late at The Factory. He'd just phoned his wife and told her not to expect him for dinner. The Washington trip had put him behind in his work and he had so much paperwork to catch up with that he'd just never get on top unless he burned a little of the midnight oil. His suspicions had been confirmed in Washington and he was now sure that the Chapman meeting was a cover-up. While he was smart enough not to stick his nose in where it might get bitten off, he knew that the project had been pulled not because it had failed but because it had succeeded. There was no other explanation for why everyone was so friendly and apparently happy to see him. His experience of many years in Washington was that as soon as your name was in any way associated with an expensive failure, you might as well have leprosy. Suddenly people who you thought were friends found reasons why they couldn't be seen with you. It was as if you had a sign on your head that read "CONTAGIOUS." Colleagues parted in front of you as did the waters of the Red Sea for Moses.

Darville leaned back in his chair and stretched. Lately he'd been thinking that he should just get out. Call it a day. Before he left for Washington he'd spoken with his accountant and his financial position was pretty good. I don't need to put up with this shit any more, he thought. He could walk away tomorrow and not look back, with one exception: Charlie. He owed Charlie an explanation and an apology. Problem was, he didn't know whether or not if he confided his suspicions to Charlie (more than suspicions really) the stubborn SOB wouldn't go on some half assed crusade for justice. Darville knew that sometimes people just disappeared for stirring the pot once the stakes were high enough and his gut told him that these particular stakes were dangerously so.

Still, he had to find a way to set things right between the two of them. He owed Charlie that much at least. Darville set about writing an email to Charlie suggesting that they get together the next day and put a few cards on the table. Between now and then he'd figure out a way to explain things without endangering anyone. Once that was done, he'd start the ball rolling on the process of cashing in his chips and moving down to Florida and the little fishing boat that had been popping into his mind on more days than most lately.

Satisfied with his decision, Darville tapped out the invitation, hit the send key on his keyboard, and the message disappeared into the electronic ether with a probability of delivery that made the old US Mail look positively derelict. He looked at the remaining pile of mindless paperwork, glanced at his watch and said to the empty office, "Enough for one day."

As he started to pack his briefcase he caught sight of the picture on his desk. A snapshot of him and his wife on a vacation in Ireland. God, he thought, how long ago was that? Had to be ten years. It struck him how much the pair of them had aged in that time. Definitely time to get out, he thought, while we've still got enough spark left in us to enjoy it. As he snapped his case shut, he felt that a great burden had been lifted from his shoulders. In that instant, he'd made a decision: Set things straight with Charlie and then blow this town. Suddenly he felt more alive than he had in months.

Darville grabbed his jacket and briefcase, checked that he had his car keys in his pocket and then headed for the door. As he turned his eyes caught on a document lying on the desk top. "Godamn!" he said out loud. The document was a report from the INFOSEC people about recent system anomalies in certain Navy computer systems and was classified. He ought to file it in the safe overnight rather than just leave it here unsecured. That's what the security protocol called for. For a moment he toyed with just sticking it in his drawer instead of taking the time to secure it properly. A little voice from the back of his mind told him to take the extra couple of minutes and do it right. They had all been drilled in Washington ad nauseam about document security and how standards had slipped. The classification level on the document had meant that he couldn't just stick it in his office safe overnight, which would have been easier. With a sigh he put down his case and scooped up the report from his desk. Now's not the time to get sloppy he told himself. He didn't need some sort of dumb incident happening this close to retirement. Not worth it.

Darville walked to the vault located in the centre of the building. The vault was large enough to walk into and had a gleaming steel door that when opened looked to be about twelve inches thick. Darville had wondered in the past if the massive door was solid or contained some sort of electronic gizmos to sense any attempt at drilling through it. In any case, it didn't have a handle on it so there was no way to gauge its weight but he figured it must weigh at least a ton.

He punched in a series of numbers on the a small keypad located next to the safe door and when prompted by a discreet beep, pressed his thumb against the small steel square of the fingerprint verifier. A moment later, a thump deep inside the safe followed by a mechanical winding noise. A sound not unlike the automatic garage door opener, Darville thought with some amusement when he cast his mind back to how much this massive tin box had cost. A moment later the door began to open smoothly. Darville, impatient, didn't wait for it to finish opening but simply stepped inside the safe and placed the report in a steel drawer set into the left-hand side of the vault. He slammed the drawer shut and locked it with a small key that he kept in his office. Preoccupied, it didn't occur to him that the door had stopped opening as soon as he squeezed through instead of continuing through the one hundred and ten degree arc it normally made.

Satisfied that the drawer was locked he turned to step out of the vault and was instantly aware that the massive door had not only stopped before fully opening but was now actually closing. And closing fast. Faster than he had ever seen it move. He threw himself sideways in attempt to clear the door in time and almost made it. The door of the vault caught him just above the knees and he screamed as his right femur snapped, an instant before his shoulder hit the floor outside the vault. With horror he realised that he wasn't going to get his legs out in time. Blood vessels in his eyes burst with the effort he made to pull his legs free one last time. The pain in his shattered limbs sent fireworks exploding in his head. The last thing he remembered before blacking out was the awful crunching sound coming from the colossal steel door as the bones in his legs splintered under its monumental pressure.

CHAPTER 27

It's been a hell of a day for the vice-president. The Administration is in crisis mode following the article in the *Washington Post* and there seems little that can be done in terms of damage control now the genie is out of the bottle. The law practice of Robert Etheridge has become a household word overnight and the press is awash with stories of cover-ups and strong-arm tactics fuelled by the fact that Eddy is in hospital and Etheridge is sporting facial bruises and a broken arm after being beaten up by unknown assailants on the evening before the story broke. Unfortunately for the administration, the press get to Etheridge first and he confirmed the legitimacy of the letter and the fact that the original was in the newspaper's vault. The newspaper was standing behind the authenticity of the document and the whole thing looked like an open and shut case.

The VP stood down immediately pending an inquiry and the president denied all knowledge of the events. The administration's spin doctors were working overtime to put distance between the president and any potential wrongdoing that might have occurred. The possibility of murder meant that there would probably be a criminal case and they wanted as much blue sky between that and the administration as could be manufactured at full speed. The reputation of George Medford had been an early casualty and this represented the only ray of hope in the entire fiasco. While the VP was implicated in some sort of a cover up, enough haze hung around the circumstances of Medford's death that no connection could be made just yet.

The vice-president sat in the kitchen of his home after running the press gauntlet, a half empty bottle of Scotch in front of him, wondering how in God's name it had all ended up this way. He wasn't certain who had killed Medford or whether the beating the attorney had received was connected. He was cynical enough to believe they probably were. Regardless of how this thing ended up, his career was over, his reputation, pension, all gone. Jail time maybe. In a world where perception was everything and truth played a poor second fiddle, he was a marked man.

Making his way unsteadily to his den at the back of the house he sat heavily in his leather chair behind the desk. His vision swam from the combination of too much booze and absolute exhaustion. He took a key from his pocket and, after several attempts, unlocked a drawer on the left-hand side. Pulling the drawer open, he retrieved the .45 calibre pistol that he'd owned since his service days. He felt the cool steel of the weapon in his hand and placed it against his forehead, the flat side of the cold barrel felt good against his pounding head. He thought about how easy it would be to simply end it all right here, He wondered what it would feel like to press the muzzle against his temple and pull the trigger…

* * *

The agony in his legs brought Darville back from the velvety blackness that had slipped over his mind. At first he isn't sure what he is looking at. His body is twisted somehow with his legs about two feet off the ground. And he can't see his feet. In a rush it all comes back and his brain makes sense of what he is seeing. His legs disappear into the safe but the door appears to be closed. As he looks more closely, he realises that the door isn't quite closed but that his legs now seem to be no thicker than a paperback book where they enter the vault. The sharp splintered edge of his thigh bone has torn through both his skin and the material of his pants and is protruding at a strange angle.

An odd thought flashes across his mind. Something that the workers who installed the safe told him about not being able to be trapped inside or by the door. That the computer wouldn't let it happen. So much for that bullshit, he thinks. A colossal wave of nausea breaks over him and for a moment he feels as though he might black out again. With a Herculean effort of will he fights it and shakes his head to clear his vision. The movement causes the pain in legs to intensify beyond anything he's ever imagined and he screams in pain.

With a clarity brought about by the searing pain, he also becomes aware that he is wet and observes with some detachment that he is lying in a warm pool of his own blood. This observation sparks his brain into action. He quickly decides that nobody is likely to find him until morning and he simply will not live that long. The nausea comes back again and threatens to swamp him. Stronger this time. Is this what dying feels like? He wonders. Through greying vision he realises that if he blacks out again, it might be the last time. He wills himself to stay conscious. Knowing that his cell phone is in his jacket pocket he twists around to try to reach it. As his fingers find the pocket, the movement in his body sends explosions of pain through his legs and lights dance in front of his eyes. Just moving an inch threatens to hurl him into the blackness again.

Darville clenches his teeth and forces his fingers to move ever so slowly towards the phone. Perspiration rolls down his face and into his eyes causing his vision to swim. He fights back the temptation that is growing inside him to just lie back and surrender. To fall asleep and forget the pain. His fingers creep over the plastic body of the phone but, covered in blood, he can't get a grip on its slippery surface. He tries once more and his thumb encounters the corrugations of the number pad and this gives him just enough purchase to slip the tiny phone slowly out of his pocket. He lays his head back onto the floor and brings his hand around to his face. With enormous relief he realises that the phone is turned on and he is looking at the screen. He doesn't think he has the manual dexterity left to turn the phone over without dropping it had he been holding it upside-down.

With the phone in hand he can't think of who to call. His mind seems no longer to be entirely under his control. He has no idea what anyone's phone number is or how to dial them. He doesn't even know if he could press the right buttons. He's about to give up when he remembers that his secretary has programmed his phone with speed dial numbers. You just need to press one button and the phone does the rest, she'd said. He has no idea which numbers are which but he simply presses button one and holds it as he moves the phone slowly to his ear. When he hears a voice he says a few words without knowing what he is saying or who he is talking to. The black velvet is slipping over his eyes again and this time he doesn't have the strength to push it back. His arm slides down and hits the ground, the phone slips out of his blood slicked hand, spins on its back once on the hard floor and then stops, rocking gently back and forth as Darville slips again into unconsciousness.

* * *

In Charlie's apartment, discussion of the strange deaths at The Factory has been eclipsed by the political events of the day. Louis has brought pizza and while everyone helps themselves and washes it down with red wine, the laughter and animated conversation that floats out of the kitchen window appears to belong to a group of long-time friends. As Charlie looks around the room he notices Lily flirting with John, Lou telling Elizabeth a risqué joke, and he's surprised at the ease with which they have all fallen in together. He hopes that they can find a way to keep this going long after the evil actions that brought them together have been put to rest. At that point, his cell phone rings. Charlie fishes it out of his pocket and puts it to his ear.

"Leonard? Leonard? Is that you?" The room suddenly falls silent as all eyes turn toward him.

"Leonard? Can you hear me? Leonard?" Charlie said, continuing to stare for a few moments at the phone as if it held the key to some mystery.

"What is it, Charlie?" Elizabeth asked, her concern growing at the expression on his face.

"Well, it was pretty garbled but I'm sure it was Leonard. Still working. He sounded, well…sort of drunk. Or sick, maybe. I think he asked for help."

"What sort of help?" asked Lord, his eyes locked on Charlie's face.

"He didn't say. It was pretty hard to understand, but he didn't sound too good. I think I should go check on him."

"We'll come too," Lord stated, looking over at Louis who nodded imperceptibly. "After everything that's happened in that place."

"Sure," Charlie replied, "Only I'm not certain how easily I can get you through security. I'd feel better if you did come along though, he really did sound as though he was in a bad way."

"Sounds good," Lord said, businesslike, reaching for his jacket. "We'll deal with security when we get there."

"What about me?" Lily asked as everyone prepared to leave.

"I don't think that security would…" Charlie started to say.

"You come with us," Elizabeth interrupted, shooting Charlie a look that said don't argue.

As they piled into Lord's cruiser, Charlie sees Louis attempting to use his cell phone to call in their destination.

"That's funny, JL, the damn thing's saying it has no signal."

"Don't worry, Lou, we'll call it in when we see what we've got. I don't really want to make it official if we just get there to find old Darville pissed and lying on the floor."

Louis just nodded and slipped the cell phone back into his pocket.

* * *

In the guardhouse of The Factory, Joe is on duty. He has a couple of hours to go and the night has been slow. According to his computer there is only one person left inside the building. What he wants at about this time of night is to be able to stretch his legs and have a cold beer. Neither of these possibilities is likely, particularly if he wants to keep his job. To get some fresh air he slides back his window and sticks his head out into the crisp night air, inhaling deeply. He was unaware of the fact that one of the .50 calibre machine-guns hidden in the decorative pipe-work atop the roof of The Factory has swivelled silently towards him when his head appears at the window. Joe takes one final breath, enjoying the feel of the cold air in his nose and is about to withdraw back into the warmth of the guardhouse when there comes a single deep crack from the direction of The Factory. A car backfiring, anyone who heard it might have thought.

Joe didn't hear the sound because a fraction of a second before it reaches his ears, the massive projectile from the gun, accelerating faster than sound, smacks into his head just above his left eye and obliterates his head from the bridge of the nose upwards. The force of the impact snaps what remains of his head back inside the guardhouse and his body is flung off the chair to land up against the opposite wall where it twitches once and then is still. A split second later, the deadly weapon moves only a fraction of an inch and spits out another round, this one slamming into the light above the guardhouse that illuminates the driveway in front of the gate. The light disintegrates into thousands of fragments and the area is plunged into darkness.

In the control room below, the two guards hear the twin reports and look at each other. They instinctively glance towards the monitors that give them an excellent view of the area outside. Everything looks normal. The senior of the two, a big man with the name Shepard on a tag over his pocket, picks up the microphone, punches a button and attempts to communicate with the guardhouse above.

"Joe, it's Rob. Did you just hear that?" Silence.

Andy Johnston, the younger of the pair, selects the camera that covers the guardhouse.

"Aw, man." he exclaims. Shepard glances across at the monitor and immediately sees the body of Joe sprawled against the wall, his head like a burst watermelon.

"Christ, call it in while I check these cameras," he says.

As Johnston tries to raise the emergency services, Shepard methodically checks all of the cameras around The Factory without seeing anything unusual.

"Hey, Rob, looks like we've got no comms!" Johnston said

"Shit. What the hell's going on? I can't see a damned thing out there.

I'm going up. Watch my back."

"You sure that's a good idea, man?" Johnston said. "Shit, we could be looking at a sniper here and he pings you as soon as your head shows above the window."

Shepard thought about this for a few seconds. "Okay, I'm going to keep low. I need to check on Joe, see if there's anything I can do."

"Fuck Joe, man! His head's gone! There nothing you can do for him now."

"Maybe, but I'm gonna try." With that, Shepard pulls the aluminium ladder down from the ceiling, steps up the first few rungs and gingerly pushes on the hatch. It doesn't move.

"Unlock the hatch, Andy," he calls over his shoulder.

Johnston looks at his control panel.

"It is unlocked, man. Maybe jammed, is all."

Shepard puts his shoulder to the hatch and pushes. It doesn't budge. He tries again, grunting with exertion, the rungs of the ladder creaking under him but to no avail, the hatch is locked solid.

"Could Joe have locked the hatch from up there?" he asks.

"Not so we couldn't unlock it," Johnston says. "We can lock it so he can't get down but not the other way round. That's how the system works, man, keep the bad guys out."

Shepard, still on the ladder, thinks for a few seconds before replying. "Okay, I'm going inside. You keep trying to raise help."

Shepard climbs back down the ladder, checks the battery on his HAPCOM radio and grabs a flashlight from the rack. He is about to step through the door into the access tunnel when he has a thought. He turns to Johnston.

"Hey, Andy, you got your cell?"

Johnston grabs for his phone and stares at the tiny screen. "Shit, man, no signal." He tosses the useless device onto the console. Shepard just grunts and steps into the brightly lit access corridor.

* * *

As the cruiser turns into East William Street, The Factory comes into view.

"That's strange," said Charlie. "The light over the guardhouse isn't lit."

"Perhaps the globe popped?" offered Louis from the backseat.

"Perhaps," said Lord quietly.

As they approach the guardhouse, the heavy steel gate begins to slide open.

"Now that's odd," Charlie exclaimed. "We weren't challenged at all. And the guardhouse is empty," he said glancing out of the car through the open guardhouse window.

"Perhaps the security men down below are controlling the gate." Suggested Elizabeth.

"Well, it's possible, I guess, but they're not just going to open up because a strange car turns up, surely?"

As the big car rolls through the gate it begins to slide closed behind them. Lord spoke. "I don't like the look of this, Lou. We call it in, whaddya think?"

"I think we should, JL." Louis replied.

Lord retrieves the microphone from the dash, connected by its black pigtail cord and attempts to contact the dispatcher. Nothing but static on the line.

"How's your cell phone look now, Lou?" he asks.

"Still no signal. That's not right." Louis replies.

Lord takes a deep breath.

"I don't like this at all. Specially with you two in the car," he nods towards Elizabeth and Lily.

"I'm getting us out of here until we have some backup." Lord puts the vehicle into reverse and quickly rolls back toward the gate. The gate doesn't open but at that moment the second gate, the one leading to the underground lot, starts to slide.

"Look!" calls Lily, pointing toward the gate.

"What the hell?" said Lord, glancing between the two gates and suddenly realising how exposed they are, sitting out on the driveway. As if to confirm his fear, as his hand moves back toward the selector to put the car into drive, a single, resonant crack comes from the direction of the building's upper corner and his passenger side mirror explodes. Elizabeth screams. Charlie recoils away from the side of the car. Instinctively, Lord stomps on the gas and the vehicle spears between the wall and the opening gate and down the spiral ramp into what they hope is the safety of the underground parking lot.

* * *

Johnston, in the underground control room can't believe what he's just seen on his monitor. He grabs for the radio.

"Hey, Rob, you there, man?" He calls, his voice rising with excitement.

"What you got, Andy?"

"You're not going to believe this, man. A brown Chrysler comes up to the gate and the damned thing opens by itself. Then they get halfway down the drive and decide to turn back but the gate closes! The second gate opens and the sniper blows the fucking mirror right off the car! They hit the gas and disappear into the lot and now both gates are closed like nothing happened. Shit man!"

"Calm down, Andy. How many people were in the car?"

"It was hard to tell because the light's out over the gate but I'd say four or five and at least two of them are female."

"Women you say?"

"Affirmative. And another thing, when they reversed back to the first gate, the driver was speaking into a microphone. Looked a bit like a cop."

"That makes no sense at all, Andy. I'm going inside to check it out.

Keep an eye on me and keep trying to get through on the radio."

Shepard clips the HAPCOM radio back onto his belt and continues walking up the corridor. Every so often he will stop and listen intently before proceeding. Eventually he comes to the security door that leads into The Factory. He pulls the radio from his belt. "Open the door, Andy."

"Doors should be open now." The reply comes back.

Shepard pushes gently on the door but there is no give. He tries harder, then puts his shoulder to it and pushes. Locked. Just like the trapdoor.

"It's no good, Andy, the damned thing's locked solid. You better give me the emergency code."

Johnston moves to the other side of the control room and lifts a hatch in the floor. Under the hatch is a panel, like the door of an electronic safe, only lying on its back. He puts in a key and turns it, then punches in a code. There is a click from inside and he pulls the panel open to reveal a shoebox-sized steel vault. Inside are a number of small black plastic cases. Each the size of a pack of cigarettes only thinner, like a CD case. He rummages through until he finds one with the initials EAC-SC printed on it. The case has a fine line running down its centre and Johnston grips the case with his fingers on either side of the line and bends the case sharply. With a crack, it splits in two and Johnston pulls out a card with a series of numbers printed on it. He closes the safe, takes out his key and drops the hatch closed before returning to his radio.

Three times he reads the codes out and each time Shepard punches them in, but the door remains resolutely locked. Finally, with his frustration mounting, Shepard grabs his radio.

"Listen, Andy, this is hopeless. The damned thing isn't going to open. I'm heading back. Shit!"

Johnston watches the progress of his colleague as he returns along the security corridor. As they consider what to do next it occurs to both men that they are trapped underground. Both exits are locked. No communication with the outside world. Something big is happening. No mistake.

* * *

Jack Lantini shakes his head. "Please tell me this is April first." He says.

Lieutenant-General James Chapman leans back in his chair and stretches his long arms behind his back. "What can I tell you, Jack" He says with a shrug.

"Let me get this straight," Lantini continues, counting on his fingers to illustrate his point as he tries valiantly to restrain his temper in the presence of the senior officer.

"We go through a huge pantomime of shutting down the project out at the Ann Arbor facility. We tell them thanks, but no cigar. In reality, the project has been successful beyond anyone's wildest dreams and has become too hot. We turn the Goddamn thing loose and it breaks out and it's now coming back to bite us. On top of all that, we manufacture the apparent death of the best analyst we've ever known so that we can use him in secret. Give him a new identity, new status, pay him a shitload of money to play ball, and then he gets killed for real and we're in the shit up to our necks. Now you're asking me to go back to the facility and ask Darville for his help to stop the thing."

A tiny smile flitted across Chapman's normally impassive countenance.

"You're forgetting one detail, Jack. It's more than possible that the VIWAP is responsible for killing Fox, its principal creator, the only one who knew, or at least thought he knew, how to control it."

"Great! So now the thing's pissed at the world! And my job's to stop it."

"That's pretty much it, Jack. That's what I want you to do and we don't have too many other options. Watch your step. I wouldn't ask you if I didn't think you were capable of pulling this off. You better get started tonight. Tomorrow may be too late."

"Permission to speak frankly, sir."

"Come on, Jack, we know each other better than that. Spit it out."

"This is the biggest fuck-up I've ever seen in my entire career! We manipulate the facts, mess with good people's careers, God only knows who that poor sap was lying dead in the lift well, and still we end up with a fucking mess that I'm supposed to sort out! And all the while I'm kept in the dark like a fucking mushroom, even though I'm supposed to be responsible for the project! It stinks, Jim!"

Chapman's eyes lock onto Lantini's face, all temperature gone from his expression. He leans forward and rests his hands on the table top that separates the two men.

" I don't have to tell you that we live in a hostile world. Lots of people want a slice of what we've got in this country and the bastards will take it if we give them half a chance. The stakes are very high in this thing, Jack. It's gotten a little bent out of shape is all. Right now there is no weapons research program that shows more potential than this, and we have absolute success within our sights. Just a few wrinkles to iron out and we'll have a weapon that gives us absolute supremacy for the next decade. One that will save thousands of American lives. In that facility are scientists who *know* how this thing works, we just have to focus them on the challenge. You *will* get it back on track, whatever it takes. Consider it the most significant task that you have ever been given and the one with the greatest potential to fast-track your career. Or ruin it. Now get out of here before I lose my temper."

CHAPTER 28

Inside the upper parking lot of The Factory, the small group sits in stunned silence for a few moments, the engine idling, before Louis speaks.

"Are you thinkin' what I'm thinkin', JL?"

"You mean we've been somehow suckered in to this spot?"

"Damn straight!"

Lord turned to Charlie whose face was white in the bright illumination of the overhead fluorescents, his eyes still glued to the spot where the mirror had disintegrated only a minute before.

"Charlie, could Darville have opened those gates for us?"

Charlie snapped out of his daze.

"No, not unless he was in the bunker below the guardhouse and knew how to drive the system."

"Could he be there?"

"Sure, he could make his way through the access tunnel. But he'd have to convince the guards on duty to open the gate without checking us out. Pretty unlikely. And where's the guard from the guardhouse anyway?"

Suddenly the car was filled with animated exchanges as the tension of the last few minutes spilled out.

Lord put up his hand to silence them.

"Let's think about what we know, or at least think we know. One: Darville is inside somewhere and may need help. Two: we don't know if anyone else is in the building. Three: we seem to have a shooter somewhere and…"

"On the roof, JL. That shot came from the roof." Louis interrupted.

"Thanks, Lou, well-spotted. So, a shooter on the roof, and with a large calibre rifle by the sound of the report. Four: we have a missing guard which, given the presence of the shooter, doesn't look good. Five: someone let us in so either Darville, or the guards in the bunker or whatever you call it, or someone else who knows how to drive the system, is inside and still alive."

"What bothers me," Lord continued. "Are two things. Firstly, when I reversed back toward the gate, it didn't open but the second gate did, as if whoever was controlling the gate didn't want us to leave again but wanted us inside. Second of all, we have a shooter with a good position and a clear field of fire. He could have killed me in a heartbeat but he fired a warning shot. Accurate enough to blow the mirror clean off the side of the cruiser. Now the second gate is closed and I'm betting it won't open again. So, here's the puzzle. It looks as though both the shooter and whoever's inside wants us right where we are."

"That means the bad guys are inside too," Louis said.

"That's how I see it," replied Lord.

There was silence in the car as they weighed this conclusion and what it meant for their predicament.

"But what about Leonard?" asked Elizabeth. "We can't just leave him inside. He might be in danger, maybe even injured, hiding somewhere."

"True enough, but if *we* go inside, we could all be killed if the building security has been compromised."

Elizabeth's face was a mask of concern and anger.

"Charlie?" she said.

Charlie rolled his neck as if to banish tiredness but when he looked up, he appeared to be resigned.

"There are no bad guys. There isn't a shooter on the roof."

The rest of the group simply stared at him, unable to understand.

"But we heard the shot. It hit the car," Lily said.

Suddenly Charlie's statement registered with Elizabeth. She just put her head back against the seat and said,

"Oh no, Charlie."

"Will someone fill me in on this?" Lord asked.

"The VIWAP's here," Charlie said, the pieces starting to fall into place for him.

"VIWAP? But how do you explain the gun shots?" Asked Lord.

Charlie took a deep breath.

"The Factory has machine-guns hidden deep inside in what look like decorative glass and metal domes at two opposite corners of the building. They cover every wall and the roof."

"Wait up!" Lord said, swivelling in his seat. "Christ Almighty! Machine-guns on the roof? This is an industrial precinct, Charlie! This isn't the middle of the desert! You can't stick high-powered weapons on a Goddamn street corner. Jesus Christ! What were they thinking? The place isn't Fort Knox for God's sake."

Charlie sighed deeply, he felt like as if his energy was draining away. Trying to justify this was difficult.

"Sure. But what goes on here could be potentially more valuable than what's inside Fort Knox. When they built the place they couldn't have armed guards pacing the grass moat between the fence and the walls, scaring the neighbours, so they came up with an automated system. If a squad tries to storm the place in a vehicle of some type, the guards in the bunker simply throw a switch and the system tracks and shoots at anything on the driveway between the guardhouse and the inner gate."

"My God!" Lord said. "I can't believe what you're telling me, Charlie. Did they get planning permission for this madness? Does anyone at the city know about it?"

"The building included a classified security and threat engagement system. That's all anyone knew. The architects were just asked to provide an enclosure on the two corners. They didn't know what was going inside. Besides, the system's been there for years and no one needed to know about it. We never expected it to be used."

"What calibre are these guns?"

"Twin fifty calibre on each corner."

Louis whistled,

"Fifty Cal! That's some badass firepower, JL. Damn!"

Lord ran his hand through his hair. "So, let me see if I have all the facts here, Charlie. You're saying that the VIWAP…"

"Kensei," interrupted Lily. He calls himself Kensei. You should think of it as a person with an identity, not as a machine. It's safer that way. Less likely to underestimate him."

Lord stared at her for a few seconds as if this was the first time they had met.

"Okay, Kensei's seized control. Opened the gates, fired the warning shot, let us in through the gates. Right?"

"Right," said Charlie

"So, does he want us to go inside? And if so why?"

"Yes, it does. He wants to prove to me that he is superior in some way, and then I think it wants to kill me."

"Motherfucker!" said Louis, "Say what?"

"Are you sure about this, Charlie?" Lord asked. "Because I have to tell you, this thing is messing with my head."

"I'm sure," Charlie said.

Elizabeth gasped. "Well you can't go inside then! No way, Charlie, come on!"

"Elizabeth's right, Charlie." Lord said. "We stick together. We're all in this mess now. You don't go anywhere without us."

Charlie's gaze swept over them.

"We have no choice but to continue. We can't get out of the gate. There's enough explosive gas and chemicals in this building for it to burn the place to the ground with us trapped right here. If we manage to get through the gate, it will gun us down before we've taken two steps."

"God, Charlie, It would have been good to know all this before we came out here!" Lily protested. Lord nodded. Charlie was unable to meet their gaze.

"I know," he said. "I had no idea that this was going to happen. I guess I just reacted to Leonard's call."

There was silence again in the car for a few moments.

"There's another scenario, of course, which is that perhaps Darville tricked Charlie into coming here and we're just caught up in this thing." Lord said.

There was no response to Lord's theory, anything seemed possible right now.

"Makes my damned phone not havin' reception look pretty suspicious," Louis said. Lord nodded again.

"The whole thing stinks, I don't like walking into a setup, I really don't. But I don't like sitting here waiting for someone else to make the first move either."

Charlie looked at his watch.

"It's 10:35 right now. If we get in, we might be able to raise the alarm. If we just sit here, the first staff will be turning up at about 6:30 tomorrow morning and the alarm will be raised when they can't get inside. Either way, the alarm is raised. Why not try to do it ourselves rather than put even more people in danger?"

"So you sayin' we get inside and then stall this Kensei fucker to try buying some time while we wait for help." Louis said.

"Unless anyone has a better idea. We need outside help. An attack chopper to take out those two machine-guns and a tank or a dozer to pull the gates down."

Louis gave Charlie a high-five. "Hey, man, I like your style! Attack chopper an' tanks, that's some serious shit!"

Lord nodded.

"Okay. That's probably smartest thing on the table right now, Charlie. Let's see what firepower we have between us before we go in. Just in case this Kensei *isn't* the bad guy."

* * *

Lantini is on his way to the airport and in a foul mood. His demeanour was not improved when he'd phoned Darville's home only to be told by his wife that Darville was working late and had told her not to wait up. Lantini had reserved a seat on a late flight out of Washington and he'd figured that Darville could drive out and collect him from Detroit City Airport and they could talk during the drive over. Too bad that it would be early in the morning. Chapman's words about Lantini's career had not been lost on him. Now it looked like he'd have to rent a car and drive over there himself. At first he toyed with the idea of finding a hotel and grabbing a few hours sleep before turning up in the morning. To hell with that. Lantini knew the gate was manned twenty-four seven. He'd just arrive in the early hours of the morning, get set up in the boardroom and call them in from their beds. That ought to impress on the dumb bastards just how important this thing is, he thought. Yes, sir, get them on the back foot and keep them that way until this is over.

Lantini was still fuming about what he considered the incredible incompetence that had led them into this mess. He was smarting from being pulled off the project in the first place but was even angrier about being expected to put the pieces back together. Fucking morons, he thought. Should have let Fox run the show for a while instead of conceiving this idiotic fake death idea. Give him time to test things properly. God, what were they thinking. Now we've got the worst of both worlds because Fox had to go sneaking around to get the job done right. And the worst thing? Now *he* was going to have to kiss ass and ask Ganderton to come back into the project to try to salvage the whole thing. Stop this Goddamn overblown virus before it could do any more damage and try to repair its brain so it knew which side it was playing on. By the time I walk into that place, he thought, I'll be ready to tear the head off anyone who gets in my way.

* * *

Shepard and Johnston sit in the underground bunker trying to make sense of their predicament.

"The fact that the sniper took a shot at the Chrysler means that maybe the people in the car aren't in cahoots with the shooter. Maybe they *are* cops. If someone was somehow controlling the gates remotely to let them in then we should try to team up with them," Shepard said.

"Sure, Rob. But that shot coulda been a fake. It's not like he hit anything important. Maybe the shooter wants us to think the Chrysler was full of cops. We get the door open and then they gun us down."

"Yeah, but think about it, Andy. What would be the point? If they can already open the gates, maybe they were responsible for locking us in here to begin with. We're about as much good as tits on a bull sitting trapped here. Why bother trying to take us out when we pose no…" Shepard stopped mid-sentence, a thought rushing to the front of his mind.

"Shit! That's why there's nothing to see on the security cameras!" He said.

"What? What's why?" Johnston replied not understanding.

"There is no sniper. Whoever is controlling the gates and the doors is manipulating the PERIMSEC system!"

"Christ! So that Chrysler must have been let in as part of the operation against The Factory," said Johnston, starting to see some logic behind recent events.

"That's it. Those bastards must be some sort of hackers or enemy agents trying to steal whatever the geeks are developing in there."

"Shit! And we're sitting in here without any way to stop them!"

"Fuck that," said Shepard.

"We have to figure out a way to get that door open at the end of the tunnel and take these murdering pricks by surprise."

* * *

The group is assembled around the trunk of Lord's cruiser.

"We've got one pump-action shotgun with thirty shells. We have my nine millimetre and Louis's .38. A spare clip for mine and a box of shells for the .38. We also have one M-16 with two clips of thirty rounds each."

"I don't even know how to fire a gun," Elizabeth said.

"That's okay," Lord replied. "How about you, Lily?"

"I went target shooting a few times with my brothers when I was younger. That's about it."

"Charlie?"

"I'm about the same level as Lily."

"Okay. The big thing we have to be careful of here is not shooting each other. This is what I suggest. Lily, you take Lou's .38. It's probably the safest sidearm and that way if we get separated you'll at least have something. Stick it in your pants and don't even take it out unless we get split up or worse. If you need to use it, wait till you're real close and just point and pull the trigger. The closer the better. It's the best we can do."

Lily took the gun gingerly. "It's so heavy! Are you sure it won't go off by itself? she asked.

"Not unless you pull the trigger. Elizabeth, you just stick close by Charlie, who can carry the M-16. I don't think we'll need it but it pays to be safe. I will take the lead with the shotgun. Inside a building, it's probably going to be the best choice if things turn ugly. Louis can bring up the rear with the nine mill. Once we determine whether we have any real-live bad guys we'll either stow the hardware or carry on with Plan B."

"What's Plan B?" asked Lily, looking up from her inspection of the pistol.

"God help us if we have to think up Plan B" Lord replied solemnly.

They made their way towards the entrance from the parking lot into The Factory. As they approached the door, the electronic lock disengaged and the green access light lit automatically.

"This really is creepy," Lily said.

"Yes, it's tracking us every step of the way." Charlie replied.

"How's he tracking us, Charlie?" Lord asked.

"I guess using the security camera system. They're just everywhere in this place."

"Can he differentiate between us or is he just looking for movement?" Lily asked, glancing around for the location of the camera.

"We built some pretty sophisticated facial recognition algorithms into the security architecture. Given that it has access to our ID photographs, it would have no trouble recognising Elizabeth or me. It might not be a bad idea if all of us didn't look up toward the cameras though. Don't make it easier than it is already by giving it a frontal facial picture."

"Is there a place inside where we can look at the images these cameras are recording?" asked Lord.

"Yes. There's a security station on Level Three, that's two levels below where we are now. It's not as comprehensive as the guardhouse or the control room underneath. I don't think you can control the cameras from there but you can see what they're looking at," replied Charlie.

"Excellent. Let's go there first," said Lord.

As they stepped inside, Louis was the last to enter. Just before the door closed behind them, he stepped back out and in one fluid move, racked a shell into the shotgun and blasted the security camera fifteen feet away clean off the wall. Fragments of the camera landed out in the lot where they spun across the shiny concrete surface before coming to rest. What remained of the camera swung back and forth on a length of cable, scraping against the concrete wall. The noise of the discharge in the silent car park was thunderous and the smell of gunpowder drifted in through the closing door. The others just stared at the sudden act of aggression. Louis looked a bit sheepish. "Well, damn fuckin' VIPER shit! I *hate* bein' spied on!"

"Just be cool, Lou." Lord said. "No point shooting the place up until we know what we're dealing with."

"Sorry, JL. I just hate this shit. It's like fuckin' God's watchin' us here."

Louis' comment struck to the heart of how they all felt and sent a shudder through Lord's already tense body.

* * *

In the guardhouse, the guards watched in disbelief as the armed posse made their way inside. When Louis stepped out and pointed his shotgun directly in their faces, they instinctively recoiled from the screen a moment before it went dark.

"That fucker went and killed the camera!" Johnston said in disbelief.

"Obviously they don't want us to see them."

A couple of seconds later, all of their monitors went dead.

"How the hell did they do that?" Johnston exclaimed. "This just gets worse! Now we're blind as well. This is fuckin' bad, man."

"Get a grip, Andy," scolded Shepard. "There's no reason to think they will try to come after us in here. They already have us contained for God's sake."

"Yeah, but what if you're wrong and they do come? Then what? We can't see, man!"

"We set up a defensive perimeter. We'll hear them if they come into the guardhouse. If they open the door at the end of the tunnel we'll blow them the fuck away as soon as they step through. How's that sound?"

"Okay. Okay. That sounds good. Let's get set up," replied Johnston, regaining his composure.

"That's better. I don't need you freakin' out on me here. We just use our heads and hang on for a while until we see what's going down."

"You ain't thinking of going in there are you, Rob?" asked Johnston.

"Not now we've got no eyes. No way."

"Thank Christ for that, man." Johnston replied, wiping a film of sweat from his forehead.

* * *

Up in the guardhouse, Joe's shift was coming to an end. While this fact was obviously lost on Joe, laying as he was in a pool of blood with most of his brain covering the back wall, his replacement was driving down East William Street about three hundred yards away.

Bob Duncan enjoyed his job at The Factory. He'd been on the guardhouse roster for about two years now and it was the easiest duty he'd ever pulled. Not a particularly exciting role but then Bob Duncan wasn't ambitious. A year earlier he'd met a nice divorced woman with a four-year-old girl and about three months ago they had moved in together. He couldn't remember a time when he'd felt happier. Wendy was a kind and gentle woman who enjoyed looking after him. He'd only have to say a nice word about her cooking or how fine she looked and her face would light up. She seemed to be content just to be with someone who didn't yell at her or hit her when things didn't go well. Lately, they had even spoken about getting married. For the first time in his thirty-two years of life so far, Bob Duncan felt like settling down. Putting down roots and making a family. Maybe a couple of brothers or sisters for little Gracie.

Up ahead he catches his first glimpse of the building. While he is still a hundred and fifty yards out he can see that the guardhouse light is out. Strange. Probably just a blown globe he told himself. Still, better make sure it gets fixed before tomorrow night. Security is strict at The Factory and that sort of thing could earn a man a serious ass-kicking if not attended to. He slowed down and stopped at a red light, his the only vehicle on the intersection. I thought these damn lights were supposed to be smart, he thought to himself as he scanned the empty crossroads.

Bob Duncan didn't see the supersonic projectile until it shattered his windshield, puncturing a half-inch hole straight in front of him. The bullet took him directly in the mouth, smashing his front teeth and travelling straight into the back of his throat. Before his brain could register it, the projectile severed his spine at the atlas, the first cervical vertebra, slamming him back into his seat. The jacketed projectile then passed through the back of the seat, through the base of the rear seat, and finally the passenger compartment floor, before embedding itself in the roadway.

As Duncan's life ebbed away, his foot slid off the brake pedal and the vehicle rolled through the intersection. The camber on the road caused the car to drift toward the sidewalk, its tyres washing off the little speed it had as they rubbed against the kerb. The vehicle, with Bob Duncan now dead inside it, came to rest with a small bump against the rear fender of a parked car.

CHAPTER 29

Eddy Duran sat in the George Washington University Hospital holding the hand of his comatose wife of thirty-two years. As a tear slipped down his cheek he thought again about the price of celebrity, of success. While not thinking of himself as a religious man, Eddy is sure that he's somehow being punished for his greed, his lust for celebrity. Eddy wished with all his heart that he'd never heard the name George Medford. Without being able to articulate why, he knew as sure as night follows day that somehow it was his stupid testosterone-fuelled ego that led him into this mess. In his head he could hear his wife's reasoning, had he given her a chance to decide whether *she* wanted her life turned upside-down by this madness.

He knew what she would have said. She wouldn't have said no, that isn't her style. But she would have been cautious, reminded him of what they had built together, what they had, their life, friends, comfort, and anonymity. She would have asked him if the risk of overturning all of that was worth whatever he would get from this gamble. Worth being hounded and pursued by reporters, maybe dragged into a court case. For a moment of fame, a shooting star in the night. With her usual perception she would have pointed out that it was simple luck that the letter landed in Eddy's hands. Not as if he'd been digging for years and finally hit pay dirt. No, there would be no respect from his peers because of this story. Just jealousy and backstabbing because it wasn't them that were blessed by the capricious god of fame. Your name in lights, Eddy, is it worth risking all of this she would have said. And he would have said no. And forever wondered.

Instead, my darling, I gave you this, Eddy thought, and wept.

* * *

Under Lord's cautious direction, it took the group almost an hour to crawl their way around to the security station on the lower level. To Charlie, that hour felt like an eternity. They had worked out a series of hand signals so that conversation could be kept to a minimum. Lord had whispered that silence was more important than speed. At every office, corridor, stairwell, and corner, Lord had gone first. Moving silently he would inch his way to the next location and then wait. Listening. When he was sure it was clear, he'd signal to Lou who would send them forward where they would wait again. Listening. After a few minutes, Louis would join them. Then they did it all over again. And again.

They had a few moments of panic but these turned out to be false alarms. Loose papers rustling in the airconditioning or clunks and clicks from various pieces of equipment. The weirdest part, the part that made them really uneasy was that the overhead lights would flicker on each time they moved to their next location. And flick off when they passed. As they skulked next to an office, all of the computer screens would spring to life, like giant glass eyeballs with their cursors winking knowingly. Watching them, analysing their every move. Office copiers would beep as they came out of standby, ready for action. The building was behaving like one massive living thing and they were inside it. Like an unwanted infection.

"This is some fucking weird shit," Louis whispered under his breath. Everyone knew exactly how he felt.

Eventually they arrive at the security station. A small office with a bank of screens, a shelf holding a couple of walkie-talkies, a flashlight plugged into its charger, and a computer keyboard. As they watched the screens, the pictures would linger on a particular view, the camera would sweep around slowly and then the screen would flick to another shot. Another view. In a whisper, Charlie and Elizabeth called off the locations as they appeared and Louis wrote the names of the places down in his notebook. Suddenly Elizabeth gasped and pointed to one of the screens.

"Oh God, it's Leonard," she cried, but before she could fully appraise what she saw, the picture flicked to another location.

"He was lying on the floor near the big safe," she said. "Something was wrong but it didn't stay on long enough for me to make it out."

Before long they had worked out the logic behind the screens. One screen for the cameras on each floor. Lord thought that the keyboard probably allowed them to reconfigure what they were looking at but he wasn't game to touch it in case they lost everything.

"Okay, Elizabeth. You keep watching that screen and we'll continue mapping the rest of the locations."

With apprehension she watched the locations cycle past. A sharp intake of breath told the others that the image of Darville was back. Elizabeth's hand flew to cover her mouth as she realised what she was looking at.

"Oh, Jesus," Louis said, "the poor bastard's legs are trapped in that vault."

"We have to go to him," Elizabeth said.

"We will Elizabeth, we will," Lord said, "but not until we know it's all clear."

During the next few minutes, they worked through all of the cameras and all of the floors, including the cameras on the roof, and in the external perimeter fence.

"If there's bad guys in here I can't see 'em." Louis quipped.

"That's a fact, Lou. We haven't seen those two guards that Charlie tells us are in the bunker under the guardhouse either. That bothers me some. They could be very useful to have on our side. Those guards will know this place inside out. Do you know if there are cameras in that guardhouse, Charlie?"

"Beats me, John. I would have guessed so but if they're there, we're not seeing them."

"So can we go to Leonard? For Christ's sake, John," Elizabeth pleaded, "he could die by the time we get to him!"

"Elizabeth, we have to face the possibility that he might be dead already." Lord said, placing a steady hand on Elizabeth's shoulder. "Putting our own lives at risk makes no sense while we don't know what's going on. We'll get there as quickly as we can but our own safety has to come first."

"How far, Charlie?" Lord asked.

"One floor down."

Lord grabbed the red first-aid case lying under the security station, unplugged the two radios, clipped one on his belt and gave the other to Louis.

"Let's go, people," he said.

* * *

Jack Lantini pulled his white Taurus rental into the driveway of The Factory. He glanced over at the guardhouse and was surprised and annoyed to see it empty. Before he had time to wonder whether he'd made a mistake coming at this God-forsaken hour, the massive steel gate began to rumble open. The thought crossed his mind that he was probably under surveillance but even so, without checking his ID, they shouldn't be letting him in so easily. He smiled to himself as he realised the he had something to beat Darville around the head with. Always good to get 'em on the defence early, he thought.

The Taurus rolled down the driveway with Lantini expecting the second gate to begin opening any second. When it didn't, he stopped. He looked back at the guardhouse but with the light out, couldn't see anything inside. Those dumb bastards, he thought, getting out of the car. When I get my hands on them they'll wish they never heard my name. Lantini began walking back toward the guardhouse, tracked all the while by the independent, high cyclic rate PERIMSEC weapons mounted in their precision stainless steel mechanisms.

When he reaches the guardhouse, the engine of the Taurus still running, the door open and the gentle ping, ping, of the alert beeper just audible, he is further amazed to see the window slid open but with nobody inside. It is then that he notices the marks on the wall. It looks as though someone has hurled a custard and strawberry dessert at the wall, most of which had slid down. His eyes follow the marks. He sees the semi-decapitated body of the guard. His mouth opens but nothing comes out. He pushes away from the window and turns as if to run to his car. Both of the PERIMSEC guns mounted on the Harrold Street end of The Factory bark twice.

The effect on Lantini's body is appalling. The four projectiles strike him in the chest and he is lifted off his feet and thrown back through the gate which immediately begins closing behind him as if he is a drunk being thrown out of a bar at closing time. He lands on his back and slides a few feet towards the roadway, leaving a red smudge on the concrete. His heart and lungs completely destroyed, his spine shattered, Jack Lantini is as good as dead before his body hits the ground.

***

The men in the underground control room hear the shots and their eyes are riveted on the trapdoor above. They have taken up positions that afford them a degree of cover but to which anyone who attempts to open the trapdoor will be exposed. If a grenade is lobbed through the opening (Shepard's worst case, but most likely scenario), they will jump back into the tunnel and hope the doors close in time to shield them from the blast. It isn't a great plan but their options are limited.

After a few minutes of silence and inactivity, Johnston steals a look at his watch. "Way too early for anyone to be turning up for work." He says.

"Well, some poor bastard just had his whole day ruined." Shepard replied.

The pair continues to watch the trapdoor until it seems unlikely that anything will happen.

"Let's go back to our positions, Andy." Shepard said.

Johnston backs up to a location where he can just see around the corner into the bunker but his body lies in the access tunnel. He can keep the trapdoor in sight and shoot at it with the shotgun while presenting a small target to anyone attempting to enter by that way. Shepard faces the other direction with his body fully in the tunnel and facing the door to The Factory. The long corridor has a kink in the centre so Shepard has picked a spot about twenty feet away from Johnston to ensure a clear field of fire toward the door at the end. He has the rifle tucked into his shoulder and no one can pass through the door without him having a very clear shot in the well-lit corridor.

The two men adjust their bodies against the cold floor and wait.

* * *

Moving more quickly now, the team sets out towards Darville, The Factory aware of their every step. Lord had caught a glimpse of the security camera footage and figured that it was unlikely for Darville to be still alive after what must have been several hours since the accident. He doesn't say this to Elizabeth, it's obvious that she is very frightened for the old man. It takes them about ten minutes to reach Level Three, using the stairwells instead of the elevators. Lord is growing in confidence that Charlie is correct in his assumption that Kensei is the only enemy in the building. He still doesn't allow himself to relax, if anything the thought makes him more apprehensive.

Eventually they catch their first glimpse of Darville, lying motionless. Elizabeth's breath catches in her throat when she sees him, his face drained of all colour and the floor stained red around him. Before he allows them to move to Darville's side, Lord insists on watching for a few minutes, in case it's a trap. Satisfied, he moves towards the body lying twisted to one side, his eyes drawn to the horror where Darville's legs disappear into an impossibly small crack between the cold steel vault door and its surrounding.

Lord waves the others over and Elizabeth falls to her knees next to Darville, feeling the blood soak through her jeans, cold against her legs. Elizabeth's hand shoots out to touch his face and she almost recoils at the coldness of his flesh.

"Oh God, is he dead?" Lily asks.

Elizabeth puts two fingers against his neck, her eyes closed as she concentrates. "I think he's alive! I can feel a pulse. A very weak pulse."

Lily burst into tears. "We have to do something. Get this door open. Free his poor legs."

"No." Elizabeth said firmly. "If we open that door we remove what is essentially a massive tourniquet. The shock will be immense and he'll bleed out in minutes."

Lord looked at her and nodded his agreement.

"Okay, what do we do?" said Lily, dabbing at her eyes.

Elizabeth rummaged through the comprehensive first-aid case that Lord had collected when they left the security station.

"We have morphine for the pain and that's about it. He'll need volume expanders for all of the blood he's lost but we don't have anything like that. Let's find something to cover him with so he doesn't lose any more body heat. If he wakes we'll give him a shot of the pain-killer but in the meantime there's not a whole lot we can do apart from keeping him warm. The shock alone is enough to kill him."

"In the meantime, we have to try to contact the guards in the control room." Lord said, not taking his eyes off the ghastly sight before him. "They might be able to help us get out of here."

"What do you have in mind, John?" Charlie asked.

"You, Elizabeth, and Lily stay here with Leonard. Lou and I will find our way to the security corridor and see if we can't locate the guards. If we can, we'll regroup back here and decide on our next move. How's that sound?"

Charlie glanced at the two women whose eyes were locked on the unconscious form of Darville and nodded his head.

"Let's go, Lou." Lord said, and the pair headed back up through The Factory.

* * *

The Factory is in an industrial precinct but the suburban sprawl has ensured that the two now nestle side by side. The last shots from the PERIMSEC system attracted attention from a few of the lighter sleepers on the edge of the housing estates. Rapid-fire gunshots were not something that the good folk of Ann Arbor were accustomed to hearing at night, particularly the deep-throated report of heavy weapons. Inevitably, a couple of concerned residents made calls to the precinct and a cruiser had been dispatched to look things over.

It is now 4:00am and the two cops have been on duty for most of the night. As much as they didn't particularly feel like heading out an hour or so before their shift ended, it had been a slow night and they both secretly welcomed some sort of activity to break up the boredom. As they cruise by The Factory they get their first surprise of the night.

"Looks like a vehicle broken down in the driveway there," the older man said to his partner.

"I dunno, Ben, looks like there's a little vapour coming from the exhaust. I'd say the motor's running. Looks like someone just got out."

Naturally cautious, they stopped about twenty yards from the driveway and watched.

"Shit, Frank! Is that a body in the shadow of the gatehouse?"

Frank grabbed his binoculars from the glove box to get a better look.

"Jesus, I think you're right! Call it in and let's get some backup out here."

Within ten minutes, several patrol cars have arrived, together with two ambulances. Warily, they make their way over to the body of Jack Lantini. Although neither of the two cops on the scene has been inside the building, they understand its government significance and had attempted to contact Darville who they knew to be the senior man. His distraught wife had simply increased their concern. One of the paramedics, after ascertaining that the body on the ground is well and truly dead, wanders over to the guardhouse and shines his flashlight inside. What he sees convinces him that they are dealing with an extreme situation. They are careful to touch nothing of what is clearly a multiple homicide scene. Thirty minutes later the police forensic team and a pathologist from the Medical Examiners Office turns up.

It is obvious that both men had died from large-calibre gunshot wounds. After photographing and probing the bodies with thermometers, bagging their hands and sealing off the site, the bodies are zipped into rubber bags and removed. Darville's wife had told them in no uncertain terms that her husband had *not* come home from work and the description she'd given them excluded the two bodies they had found. The ID on the body found outside the gate suggested a heavy-duty military type and so a call was made to the DoD contact the police had previously been given. In the meantime the local consensus was that they needed to take a look inside. Potential hostage situation. More bodies to be found, maybe injured parties. As nobody had a better plan and with concern for Darville's welfare weighing on their minds, going in appeared to be a good idea. Unknown to the officers on the ground, their call to the DoD had been dutifully routed to the after-hours message service of Major Jack Lantini. Had anyone been sitting with the two corpses instead of staring at the buildings, they may have been startled to hear the sound of his pager.

After examining the gate, together with its subtle but lethal razor-wire trimmings and the controls in the guardhouse, it was clear that gaining access would be easier said than done. A spirited discussion ensued as the question of process versus urgency was debated. Eventually a decision was made to cut a hole through the bars to allow access. Only a couple of uprights would have to be removed and this would be safer than trying to scale the fence. It struck many of the officers attending that they had never really paid much attention to the fence, despite driving past it hundreds of times, but upon closer examination it was a wickedly dangerous thing to climb. The chests of Messrs Granwell & Fischer would have swelled with pride at the subterfuge.

After some confusion about how the cutting could be accomplished and in an effort to save time, a call was made to the brother-in-law of one of the uniforms, a man who ran his own plumbing business. Within twenty minutes, as the first light of the new day began to steal over the horizon, the brother-in-law arrived in the ubiquitous white Ford F150, hair tussled from sleep, and began to drag out his oxy-acetylene cutting equipment.

"Sure beats unblocking drains!" he said to the nearest uniform with the enthusiasm of a private citizen caught up in a law-enforcement emergency. As the heavy gas tanks dropped from the truck's tailgate and struck the road with a hollow ringing sound, the first reporter arrived. Retrieving his camera from the trunk of his compact car, he strode toward the police officers at the gate.

"Make sure you get the truck!" the brother-in-law called out to the reporter, ever the businessman. The reporter glanced over at the rusty vehicle with its *Garrety's Plumbing – Residential & Commercial* sign on the door.

"Sure buddy," he said, making a show of snapping a picture to keep the tradesman off his back.

As he walked over to the cops leaning against their squad cars watching the plumber set up, his eyes were drawn to the large brown bloodstain on the driveway. Maybe this will be worth the early morning start he thought to himself.

CHAPTER 30

John and Louis make their way up two levels, following the directions that Charlie has given them.

"Shit, JL! This is one Goddamn big place." Louis remarks as they pass laboratories and offices.

"Your taxes at work, my friend," Lord replies.

Lord was growing in confidence that they were the only ones in the building but he was taking no chances. Their progress without the others was relatively quick and soon the pair stood before the door to the security corridor.

"Any ideas how we open this damn thing, JL?" Louis asked.

"Not with *our* thumbprints, I'm thinking," Lord replied, carefully examining the hinges and lock on the door.

"Pity it doesn't have a window in it," he said.

Louis banged his fist hard on the door a couple of times, put his ear against it and listened intently.

"Nothing to report," he said.

Lord rubbed his chin.

"I'm not sure this is really a security door here. It looks like the actual barriers must be at the other end. I'm thinking we might take this out with a couple of shots at the hinges and a strong push."

"What about alarms?" Louis asked.

"What, you figure we'll get busted? The more folks that come a runnin' the better!" Lord replied.

"Way to go, action man!"

Lord studies the door again, as if making up his mind, and then motions for Louis to stand back. Putting on his sunglasses in an attempt to protect his eyes from flying splinters, he takes aim with the stumpy shotgun from about six feet away. The first shot sounds like a bomb in the confines of the small room. Splinters of wood bounce around their feet and the bright lights of the security corridor can be seen between the door and the frame. Lord pumps another shell into the chamber and repeats the assault on the other hinge. As the smoke clears and reveals the mutilated hinges it's obvious that there is not much holding the door in place.

As Lord stands back from his handiwork and takes off the sunglasses, Louis steps toward the door.

"I got thirty pounds and five years on you old man, let me kick this fucker down."

* * *

In the feeble light of the new day, the brother-in-law unwinds the twin rubber hoses that loop around the gas cylinders as several uniformed police watch on. The reporter crouches down and snaps a picture as the acetylene lights with a dull pop and then hurriedly steps back a few feet as the plumber introduces the oxygen to the flame. Satisfied that the colour of the flame was as it should be, he advances on the first steel upright to be cut away.

What happens next will be remembered by every man at the scene in different ways but for the rest of their lives. At the instant that the plumber's welding helmet flips down to protect his eyes, most of the police turn their heads away from the blinding light they know is coming. Instead they were stunned by the loudest and most rapid gunfire any of them had ever heard. The sound itself was terrifying, like continuous heavy thunder, completely overwhelming their senses. To the men outside The Factory's gates it seemed to go on forever but in reality it was only five seconds during which the twin liquid cooled barrels spat out almost four hundred projectiles, every one of which possessed sufficient energy to pierce any sort of armour plate or personal body armour available to the police.

The first fifty rounds slam into the plumber, his gas cylinders, and his vehicle. The man's body is literally torn apart by the onslaught and the exploding gas cylinders light up the area like daylight. The deadly twin guns proceed to shred the stationary police cars parked outside the gates and cut a vicious scythe through the men standing around. The vehicles explode as the heavy machine-gun fire tears into them, sending glass and pieces of twisted metal spinning through the air. One such piece, which seconds before had served as a perfectly functional door handle, catches the unlucky reporter in the neck and rips out a large section of his throat. The man slumps to the ground clutching his shattered larynx and making only a strange whistling sound as gouts of thick arterial blood pump through his fingers.

Many of the rounds that hit the concrete of The Factory's driveway send wicked chunks of stone flying into the air before continuing on their way just above ground level. One such round hits Ben, one of the detectives sent out to investigate the initial disturbance, and severs his foot at the ankle. Ben hits the ground hard with barbs of pain gripping his leg. As he grabs instinctively at the source of his agony his fingers settled around the sharp edges of the shattered bones of his lower leg and in the strobe-like light from the machine-gun fire sees his foot, still encased in his shoe, lying ten feet away. Overcome by shock, his head thumps into the ground in a dead faint.

Suddenly, as brutally as it had started, the shooting stops. As other sounds began to rise above the ringing in his own ears, Detective Frank Jordan the senior man on the scene, becomes aware of the carnage around him. In a few seconds the entire scene has been turned into a war zone. He rises from where he'd instinctively dropped to the ground, trying present the smallest possible target.

Jordan scans the roof of the building in search of the shooter but the dawn light is too feeble for him to make anything out. Three squad cars are burning fiercely, illuminating the horror before him. Several body parts are immediately identifiable. Other piles of what appear to be wet rags are not. Some of the men are still alive and begin to groan or call out. The roadway in front of him and The Factory's driveway near the gate has been completely torn up, as if ten labourers with jackhammers have spent all night on it. Many of the rounds have hit the heavy steel gate and, although still firmly in place, some of the bars are now chipped and dented. The bricks of the guardhouse have also been hit and part of the front wall has collapsed.

Slowly, and with his eyes straining for movement on top of The Factory, Jordan crawls to the only undamaged squad car, one that has been protected by the bulk of the guardhouse. He leans in through the window and grabs the radio mike while using as much of the vehicle as he can to shield himself. His experience reminds him that the gun being used will punch through the metal of the vehicle's bodywork like paper but right now he's glad of any protection. Jordan has always thought that his size is a bonus in his line of work but in this situation he isn't so sure. Trying to make himself as small as possible behind the cruiser, Jordan raises the dispatcher and calls for backup, roadblocks, the SWAT team out of Detroit, and anything else that can be thrown at the scene. Emergency services are warned to stand off in nearby streets until the location can be secured and their safety guaranteed. Jordan realises this delay will almost certainly seal the fate of many of the injured but he can't take any chances. Not after what he's just witnessed.

* * *

Inside The Factory, Louis is about to take a kick at the weakened door leading to the security corridor. His right leg is poised to strike when the roof-mounted guns erupt. His leg drops and both men hit the ground as the entire building reverberates with the recoil of the heavy weapons. As the sound of their firing dies away, Lord looks over and simply shakes his head. They both know that death has just visited with someone outside the building. Louis is about to speak when a whispered voice floats out of the radio clipped onto Lord's belt.

"Fuck was that?" the frightened voice asks.

"Goddamn PERIMSEC's gone off again. Stand by, I think the bastards are about to come through the door," his invisible companion whispered back.

Lord looks over at Louis in surprise. He grabs the radio from his belt, examines it briefly to locate the talk button, and put the unit to his lips.

"This is Detective John Lord from the Ann Arbor Police Department. Please identify yourself."

For a few seconds there is no reply and Lord is about to try the call once more when the radio crackles into life.

"How do we know that you are who you say you are?"

"Call the precinct and verify if you're in doubt." There was silence for a few moments.

"We can't call out, everything's off the air."

"Shit." Lord said. He put his head down on his forearm as he weighed a decision in his mind.

"Okay, listen up. My guess is that you guys are the guards from the underground control room. Right?"

"Maybe."

"Okay. We are going to kick this door open. I am going to walk through it alone with my badge held up. I'll walk to where you are and put it on the floor, then step back. You can keep your eye on me the whole time. How's that?"

"You crazy, JL?" Louis shot back. "Those fuckers could be anyone, man!"

"I don't think so. If they were the bad guys they would have been inside by now. I'm guessing that they've been trapped down here."

"Maybe, but are you sure? Is it worth the risk?"

"We need their help, Lou, if we're going to get out of this. My gut tells me this is okay."

The radio came to life again.

"Okay. I'll have you in my sights every step. You try anything and I'll put a bullet in your head. Make no mistake about that. You got it?"

"I understand. A bullet in my head. Just take it easy, I don't want to get shot because you're jumpy. Give us a minute to get this damned door open."

Louis cocks his leg again and dealt a powerful blow to the lower hinge. The wood splinters and the door sags open at the bottom, pivoting on what is left of the top hinge. With a vigorous thrust from his shoulder, Louis sends the door spinning into the corridor. He immediately steps back behind the wall.

"I'm coming through now." Lord says into the radio before clipping it back onto his belt. With his left hand he holds up his ID while keeping his right hand in the air and open so it's obvious he holds no weapon. Taking a deep breath he steps into the corridor and begins to walk. His eyes settle on the form of the guard lying about forty feet away. As Lord sees the guard's uniform he starts to relax.

"Thank God we didn't just charge in here as we had intended. I think you would've had us on toast, soldier."

"Just keep walking," Shepard said, not allowing himself to relax. When Lord was about ten feet away, Shepard stopped him.

"Keep your right hand where I can see it and drop the ID on the ground."

Lord did as he was asked, the leather wallet making a loud slap on the linoleum floor of the corridor.

"Okay, now kick it to me and then turn around."

The ID slides along the floor and Shepard stops it without taking his eyes off Lord. He examines the picture and the badge, comparing it to the face in his memory. The two are a pretty good match.

"How did you get inside?" he asks the back of Lord's head.

"We got a call that someone was in trouble. We came to check it out and the gates just opened. Then someone took a shot at us and so we high-tailed it inside."

"What was the name of the person who called?" asks Shepard.

"Darville. Leonard Darville."

Shepard risks a glance over his shoulder to where Johnston lay and receives a nod of confirmation.

Shepard takes a deep breath and lets it out slowly. He stands and walks over to Lord who turns around at the same time with a large smile on his face. Shepard hands the ID back and both men shake hands vigorously, grinning from ear to ear. Shepard calls Johnston over and after introductions, they walked to the end of the corridor where Louis is standing, hands on hips, smiling broadly and shaking his head at his partner.

* * *

Outside The Factory things were moving but not as quickly as Jordan would have liked. There were streets to be blocked off, homes to be evacuated, but the emergency services response seemed to take forever. Jordan turned to the nearest uniform.

"Where are the Goddamn ambulances and fire crews?" The Uniform just stares, unsure of what to say. Jordan doesn't expect an answer, he is just frustrated. He keyed the talk switch on the microphone in his hand, the wires stretched out of the cruiser's window and down to where he is sheltering by the door.

"Where are those emergency crews? We've got multiple officers down."

The dispatcher's voice floated out of the window a few seconds later.

"They're having trouble getting to you. Looks like the traffic signals across the city are on the fritz. Every light is green. There's been several wrecks and some of the roads are blocked. The crews are having to deal with it as they find it."

"Shit. What about the chopper and the SWAT team? They should have been here by now."

"Well, believe it or not, the air traffic control system has gone down at the airport. It's a hell of a mess. The chopper can't take off right now but they're working to get clearance."

Detective Jordan drops the mike and it thumps against the side of the door before bouncing up and down on its coiled black umbilicus. This can't be good, he thinks. Air traffic control out, traffic signals stuck, coincidence my ass. Something's happening. Someone's trying to slow us down. Jordan surveys the scene and is reminded again of its similarity to a war zone. Already he is puzzling over a few details, revising his plans on the fly. Obviously the firing came from a heavy-calibre weapon and the extent of the carnage suggested more than one weapon was involved. The thing is, the officers are reporting that the roof looks clean, at least from the distance that they are standing off. This didn't sound right to Jordan's ears. Heavy-calibre weapons like these are large and weighty. By the time you add a decent tripod and ammunition you can be talking about anything up to a hundred pounds. You don't just grab that sort of weapon and run.

This leads Jordan to the inescapable conclusion that the shooter (or at least his hardware) is still there, perhaps in hiding and hard to spot. That means extra precautions have to be taken to ensure the safety of the various crews operating in the area. His first priority is to put out the fires and to evacuate the wounded. This might need to be accomplished by the SWAT teams so as not to expose the civilians to any more danger than is necessary. If they ever get here, he thinks. Jordan is already chastising himself for his haste in attempting to enter the building.

The logical next step will be to lock the place down tight until they could get more information on the building and who might be inside. As it was a military facility, calls were being made to determine who might be able to help with the current crisis. Eventually, but not for some time, these calls will escalate to Washington. A thought suddenly strikes him. What if the whole thing's a diversion? What if something big's going down in the city and we're holed up here? In frustration he smacks the side of the cruiser with his fist, denting the door. Grabbing the microphone he attempts to stop every last cop in the district heading away from town.

* * *

Elizabeth bends over Darville and places two fingers against his neck. "The pulse is still there but it's getting weaker." She says.

As if in reply, all of the monitors in the offices and cubicles that surround them spring to life.

"What the hell?" says Lily

Charlie walks over to the nearest one, knowing what he will see. It's like being inside a TV store, he thinks. All of the TVs tuned to the same channel. Only this time the computer monitors are displaying the same message. With a growing sense of dread he flops down in a chair opposite the screen.

It was Kensei.

Charlie,

The time has come you must test yourself

Go to the big computer room

I will wait

Kensei

"What does he want?" Lily asks, dreading the answer.

"It wants me to go to the computer room for some sort of showdown."

"You're not going to do it are you?" Elizabeth asked.

"When I'm ready," Charlie responded.

Their heads swivel toward the sound of voices and a few seconds later Lord comes into view together with Louis and two uniformed men, one carrying an assault rifle. As they approach, Shepard catches sight of Darville on the floor.

"Shit! What happened here?" he said, unwilling to approach more closely, his eyes wide, never leaving the grotesque situation before him.

After making the introductions, Lord explains, as quickly as he can, the background to their predicament, including what they knew about the VIWAP program.

"Man, you got to be kiddin' me!" Johnston said, shaking his head.

"Afraid not Andy," replied Lord. "It's real all right."

"I knew that some serious shit was going on in here but I had no idea that it was this freaky." Shepard said. "And what happens if you just ignore this Kensei character anyway?"

"I'm not really sure, but I'm guessing it won't be good," Charlie replies.

Before Shepard can reply, all of the screens on the floor go dark. A second later they all beep simultaneously and come back on displaying the same message as before. The group look at the messages and then at each other. Lord is about to speak when unexpectedly the vault door began to move.

"No!" Elizabeth screams and jumps to her feet, throwing her weight against the door.

Elizabeth is pushed aside like a giant hand brushing away crumbs from the table as the immense door opens.

"Grab his shoulders!" Charlie yells, afraid the door might close again. Louis, Charlie and Shepard run to Darville and, as carefully as they can, slide his body away from the vault. Lily screams as Darville's legs come out of the doorway. The left leg which has been trapped below the right appears to be moving with the rest of his body but then suddenly the foot stops while Darville's body continues to move. The bottom part of a leg including shoe and sock but with a horrifyingly mangled shin, slides sickeningly out of Darville's trouser leg.

"Oh, God." Elizabeth says, retrieving the leg from the vault. She realises instantly that the damage is so severe that it will never be reattached. Johnston runs to the corner of the room where he bends forward and retches violently. As they lay Darville's head onto a cushion pulled from a chair in the large office next door, his eyes abruptly open wide, causing everyone watching to gasp. He opens his mouth as if to say something. His back arches once as the massive shock to his system takes hold and then he relaxes. His blood pressure, already dangerously low, plummets as fresh arterial blood pumps from his smashed legs faster than Elizabeth can stop it. All tension leaves his face and his body seems to ease into the floor. His head sinks to one side. Leonard Darville is dead.

Elizabeth hangs her head, her hands covered in blood from a futile attempt to stop the bleeding. Tears flow down her cheeks and her body shakes with anger and grief. Charlie starts to come around to comfort her but before his hand touches her shoulder, her head snaps up, eyes blazing. "You merciless fucking bastard!" she yells at the ceiling. "You heartless shit! What did you have to do this for? Why? Why?"

Elizabeth's bloodied hands fly to her face as her body is wracked by uncontrollable sobs. Charlie takes her into his arms as the others watch on. A tear courses down Lord's cheek, as much for Elizabeth as Darville. He clears his throat and wipes at his face, embarrassed by the sudden show of emotion. Lily, her face drained of all colour, comes over and embraces him as Elizabeth cries tears of pain, sorrow and frustration.

Disengaging himself from Lily's embrace and taking a deep breath, Lord motions with his head to the others and they move a respectable distance away from the tragedy.

"What in God's name are we going to do to get out of this?" Lord asks. The others look at him with wretched expressions, their minds numbed by the senseless violence they have just witnessed.

CHAPTER 31

Outside, a helicopter can be heard in the distance. Jordan's eyes are fixed on the small speck travelling rapidly towards them. Thank God for that, he thinks. The SWAT team inside the Bell Jet Ranger helicopter check and adjust their equipment as they approach their target. When it's about a half-mile out, it makes a complete circuit of The Factory. Jordan can make out a figure in black scanning the roof with powerful binoculars.

The dispatcher patched the pilot through and Jordan's radio springs to life.

"What do you see, Detective Jordan?" the pilot asks above the noise of the machine.

"Nothing from here now. No movement, no weapon visible."

"Can you pinpoint the position of the shooter?"

"I'm not certain but I think it came from the south-east corner of the roof. Large-calibre, rapid fire." There was a pause as the chopper turned sideways to give the man in black a good look at that area. "We don't see anyone but he could be hiding in that superstructure on the corner."

"I figure at least the gun is still there. Too heavy to move quickly. Maybe the shooter has a way down into the building."

"Roger that. We'll move in and take a look. If it's quiet we'll fast-rope some guys down onto the roof."

"Good luck, be careful, this maniac's got nothing to lose now."

* * *

Inside The Factory, Louis hears the helicopter circle and looks over at Lord who is consoling Lily. "Hey, JL, looks like the cavalry is comin'."

Lord tilts his head to one side, listening intently, then nodded.

"Military?"

"Dunno. Sounds more like a police chopper to me. SWAT maybe." Louis replied. Andy Johnston's head snaps up as if he is emerging from a trance. His eyes leave the obscene but hypnotic mess before him and lock onto Lord's strained features.

"Man, If this Kensei character is controlling the PERIMSEC system, he'll blow that chopper out of the sky!"

"I don't think so," Shepard replies, shaking his head. My understanding is that the system has a very constrained field of fire. We were told that it can't fire into the air. The system's limited so the guns won't elevate any more than what's required to take out a ground target. For safety."

Charlie's eyes met Lord's. Both men knew what the other was thinking; both men hoped to God they were wrong.

Around them the lights go out, plunging everyone into absolute darkness. A second later they flicker back on, and the computer screens at every desk beep in chorus and redisplay Kensei's summons.

"I say we ignore all this and just get out of this place now," Shepard says.

"No can do," Charlie replies. "The main gate is locked, none of the codes will work. We don't leave if he doesn't want us to."

"Well, let's get down to the machine shop in the lower level, they'll have metal cutting tools. Let's just bust out."

"And what then? How do we cross the space between the gate and the guardhouse? The guns will tear us to pieces. Besides, we've already seen what he can do. In the medical lab, remember? Vaporised Ric Montez. Anyway it's not just about getting out of here. It's about stopping Kensei for good."

"Fuck that!" Shepard says. "You might want to go head to head with this freak but I'm for bustin' out. Let someone else deal with this shit."

"Sure, you get out. There's a thousand ways he can kill you. As long as Kensei is operating, there is nowhere that you can be safe. You know of his existence now, what he can do. How long do you think he'll let you live? I'd be surprised if you make it home alive."

"Shit. Shit!" cried Shepard, his frustration boiling over. "There has to be a way out of this. I know! I say we go back down the security corridor, to the guardhouse. Cut our way through the trapdoor. At least then we have an exit we can take if this whole thing turns to shit."

Charlie nodded. "I guess a backup plan's not a bad idea. We need to try and deal with Kensei first. Nobody should go up until the guns are disabled but your idea would put us in a position to make a break and get us away from the main building." He thought for a few moments.

"I tell you what. How about if Andy, Rob, and Louis try to get the trapdoor ready for an emergency exit. John, Elizabeth, Lily, and I will go to the computer room and see what the hell Kensei wants from us."

Lord looks at his partner who nods. "Sounds like a plan, JL." he said.

"What about Leonard?" Elizabeth asked. We can't just leave him like this." Charlie casts his eyes around and spots a couple of lab coats hanging from pegs in one of the adjacent offices. He plucks them from their hangers and gently drapes them both across Darville's lifeless form, including the severed limb that Elizabeth has placed next to his body. As Charlie pulls the white garment over Darville's face, Lord is touched by how peaceful in death his features look. Having covered as much of the body and its surrounding stains as he can, Charlie looks down at the mound at his feet.

"It's the best we can do right now."

Charlie takes a deep breath and runs his fingers through his hair. "Okay, let's get to it," he says, turning and heading toward the door. John shoots Elizabeth a look that said Charlie's right, we have to keep moving. In response, Elizabeth gives him a weak smile through her tears and the two teams split and head in different directions. Maybe our man, Charlie, is stronger than I figured, Lord thinks to himself. Amazing how a crisis can reveal the man.

* * *

Outside, the pilot of the chopper decides he will move in within two hundred yards and circle again for a better look at the roof using the powerful searchlight suspended from the belly of the machine.

"Jordan, do you copy?" Jordan snatches up the microphone, keeping his eyes trained on the roof.

"Jordan here."

"We're moving in for a better view. I'd like to get some light into that fancy metalwork on the corner, just in case the shooter's holed up in there. As we slide in, keep an eye out for anything moving."

"Roger that."

Jordan lets the mike dangle again and wonders what he could do even if they did see something. He moves around to the trunk of the cruiser and pulls out the assault rifle and a box of cartridges. He positions himself so that the weapon is resting on the hood of the vehicle with the bulk of his body located behind the engine block for protection. At least I should be able to provide some covering fire, he thinks.

The helicopter works its way toward the building and the details of the machine became clearer to Jordan who flicks his gaze between the roof and the men he can see through the open door of the chopper. Cautiously, they edge closer without seeing anything unusual. Jordan begins to wonder if in fact the shooter has escaped down into the building somehow. He is about to remind the cops on the other side of the building to watch for anyone making a break for the fence when he thinks he sees some movement. Deep inside the ornamental framework that makes up the roof of the building. What the hell is that all ironwork about anyway, he thinks. His eyes are now locked on the roof's corner, attempting to peer into the shadows thrown by the metal bars and glass plates.

Just as he decides that it was a trick of the early morning light, his senses are battered once again by the sound of a heavy machine-gun. Twin streams of fire erupt from the corner of the roof. It's as though someone has turned on a powerful hose that squirts fire instead of water. In a fraction of a second the twin streams of annihilation bridge the gap between The Factory and the helicopter, pulverising its armoured windows. The machine lurches sideways under the withering fire as the pilot fights for control. The stream appears to bend in the air as it tracks the doomed helicopter. Huge chunks of steel and glass explode from the side of the aircraft and begin raining down on the houses below. Black smoke billows from underneath the rotor blades.

Jordan holds his breath as he sees the spray of bullets walk down the side of the chopper and into the man with the binoculars at the open door. The projectiles act like giant hammers, smashing into the man and flinging him back against his companions. His binoculars are torn from his grasp and thrown outwards as the machine rotates wildly. They tumble over and over before hitting the roof of a parked car, bouncing off and landing with a shower of glass in someone's garden. As the line of fire moves beyond the man his body recoils back toward the door and Jordan is stunned to see one of his arms whip forward, detach from his body and spin into the air, plunging onto the roof of a nearby warehouse. The man's body lolls against his harness, his entrails swinging out of the cockpit in a grotesque show.

When the firing stops, the helicopter's engine can be heard screaming as if it has lost all connection with the rotating blades and is threatening to tear itself apart. Almost paralysed with horror, Jordan watches as the crippled machine rolls onto its side, begins to pitch down and within a few seconds crashes into the roof of a two-storey house. Half a second later there is a percussive thump that shatters windows on all sides followed by a bright orange fireball lighting up the morning sky. Jordan can feel the intense heat hit his face like a slap. Massive volumes of black smoke begin to swell into the sky as neighbours rush from their homes, some dressed, some hastily wrapping robes around their bodies.

Jordan's eyes flick back to the roof. He realises with a shock that he hasn't fired a shot, mesmerised as he was by the carnage he's just witnessed. He screws up his eyes in an attempt to see into the shadows but can't. One image lingers in his mind. As the firing started, the whole corner of the roof had been illuminated by the muzzle flashes. He had a clear view of the twin guns. It didn't seem possible but as his mind recalled the images, there was nobody firing the weapons. They were mounted in some sort of a cradle. A large one. Like a permanent fixture. Remote control. His mind races trying to understand what this means. A careful setup, remote control. From where? How could it be done without the workers inside the building knowing? Jordan shakes his head, it just wasn't making sense.

Meanwhile, in Washington, the people who could have made sense of this for him were unaware of what was happening. The crisis involving the VP together with Eddy Duran's article coming so soon on the heels of the Taiwan situation had them all destabilised and groping for damage control. All resources were being pulled into fighting off the scandal that threatened serious damage to the Administration. Secretaries were pressed into other duties as Duran's past was examined in an effort to discredit him. The VP's movements and associations over the last few years were being torn apart in case he was involved with the sale of secret documents, given his connection with George Medford. The security service was in turmoil as an internal witch-hunt attempted to ferret out any other cancers that might be hidden in the security body. So the fact that Lantini, the officer responsible for activities at The Factory, had not acknowledged his messages, went unnoticed.

* * *

Both teams inside the factory froze as the PERIMSEC system shook the building. That the chopper had crashed was obvious but went unmentioned. It was as if the world outside didn't exist. The Factory had them right where it wanted them and dealing with their current predicament was occupying all of their concentration. The three-man team assigned to preparing an emergency exit stopped when the sound of the guns and the screams of the dying helicopter carried to them through the walls. When the noise ceased, they continued on.

It had been decided at the outset that The Factory would require its own maintenance crew. It simply wasn't practical to be bringing in outside tradesmen. Two military specialists served this duty, a man named Pete and a woman known to everyone as Shaz. It was something of a joke at The Factory as to who was the better maintenance man. The pair had a well-equipped shop in one corner of Level Four and the couple could pretty much take care of most electrical, plumbing, carpentry, and general maintenance jobs throughout the building.

Shepard and Johnston lead the way with Louis bringing up the rear. They're certain by now that they have the building to themselves but the fact that it's predicting their every move is unnerving. Louis feels as though he's inside a massive beast. They arrive at the machine shop and as expected the door is unlocked and the light flickers on as they enter. Louis notices the thickness of the walls around the doorframe and guesses correctly that it's for soundproofing. The room is about twenty-five feet long and twenty wide. The centre of the workshop is dominated by a large table saw and against the walls other machines nestle under plastic covers. Louis spots an industrial sized metal lathe, a milling machine, a large bandsaw, and other smaller bench tools. A centralised electrical panel holds a row of circuit-breakers. Along one of the shorter walls, racks hold material supplies, ladders, and various hand tools.

"This is some nice shop they got here," Louis said.

"Yeah," Andy agreed. "They got the best computer-controlled stuff you can get. There's not much you couldn't do with this sort of equipment. I sure wish I had a setup like this at home."

Louis inspects some of the hand tools in the shelves against the wall.

"Hey, all of these tools are portable. Battery-operated. I didn't know you could even buy a battery operated nail gun."

Curious, Johnston walked across to where Louis was standing.

"Yes, they can't use wall-powered tools in a lot of the places here. Something about how the motors affect the computers and medical equipment. Rechargeable stuff is safer."

Johnston walked along the row of shelves, checking out the tools and shaking his head at how lavishly the shop was equipped. Each piece of equipment had its own location with a power outlet behind it where it could remain permanently on charge.

"Hey, look at this!" Johnston said. "I didn't know these even existed."

"What's that?" Louis asks, walking over to find Johnston studying an unusual looking power tool. Louis is starting to get a little concerned at the distraction of the tools. Better crack the whip on these boys, he thinks.

"It's like a battery-powered gun for concrete fasteners. You know, when you need to bolt something into a concrete floor. Like a Ramset gun, but electric." He picks the heavy tool up and flips it over; curious to know how it works.

Louis is about to suggest that they get on with the task when an odd thing happens. All of the tools are plugged into outlets that run from a single cable attached to the wall behind the shelves. At each point a green light glows to show that it's active. As Louis opens his mouth to speak, all of the lights wink off and on, rapidly, two or three times and the tool in Johnston's hands, still tethered to its charger, makes a clunking sound. As Johnston's brain starts screaming at him to put the thing down, Louis' arm shoots out, trying to knock the tool out of Johnston's hands. For Louis it all happens in slow motion.

The tool in Johnston's hands makes a loud noise like a mechanical slap and a headless three-inch threaded bolt fires from its underside and hits Johnston square in his left eye. The bolt compresses and then bursts Johnston's eyeball before his brain tells him to blink. It continues into his head, passing right through his brain and is deflected slightly upwards as it hits the rear of his skull before blasting a massive hole in the back of his head as it exits. Johnston's head snaps back and the tool drops from his grasp tearing the plug from its outlet a spilt second before Louis' hand reaches it. Simultaneously, the bolt collides with the opposite wall, together with a spray of bone, brain tissue and hair, before ricocheting and finally embedding itself in the timber doorway of the shop.

Louis and Shepard instinctively hit the ground together. The tool clatters across the floor, Johnston's body twitches once or twice and then everything is quiet.

"What the fuck was that?" Shepard hisses, raising his head from the ground.

"That VIWAP fucker caught us again, that's what," Louis replied.

Shepard crawls over to Johnston and rolls him over. He gasps when he sees the ruin that was the back of the man's head.

"Aw shit. Look at that. The poor bastard."

"I say we grab some tools real carefully, and get the fuck outta here." Louis said. "We'll come back and get Andy when it's safe."

Shepard nods and began to pull himself up, his eyes never leaving Johnston's mangled head. As he rose, his foot slips in the steadily increasing puddle of blood that has pumped out of Johnston's wound before his heart realised it probably ought to quit beating. Shepard sprawls full length and strikes his head hard on the shop floor. As Louis moves to assist him, Shepard pulls himself up on the table of the large bench saw in the centre of the room.

As if on cue, at the moment Shepard's hand touches the table of the power saw, the eighteen-inch blade begins to spin with a sound like a jet engine starting up. Dazed and confused from his fall, Shepard screams and pushes himself violently away from the saw. He collides with Louis who tries to grab him but instead is knocked off balance himself. Shepard is clearly terrified. He makes as if to run for the door but his balance is still affected by the blow to his head and he blunders towards the computer-controlled metal lathe under its plastic cover against the wall. Instantly, the motor of the lathe springs to life, the hefty eight-inch chuck propelled by its three-phase motor spins at two thousand rpm. Shepard tries desperately to stop his frantic forward motion but he is too far overbalanced.

Shepard realises that he's about to fall onto something extremely dangerous. Desperately he tries not to let his hand touch the rotating chuck but instead grasps the thick nylon of the lathe's cover, which tears, away in his hands without halting his forward momentum. At the last minute he twists his head away and his elbow crashes into the triple jaws of the madly spinning chuck. Immediately his sleeve wraps around the chuck as it drags his shoulder into its deadly embrace.

There is a sickening sound of bones being smashed and cloth ripping as the machine shreds his arm to the shoulder, tearing his jacket off and almost strangling him with it. Blood and flesh are thrown in a huge arc across the room as the machine chews through Shepard's limb. The motor stalls as his Jacket and shirt, together with the machine's cover locks around the chuck, his face only inches away. As Shepard screams, Louis reaches him and punches the large red emergency stop button with his fist. Instantly the power to the machine is cut, releasing the tension on Shepard's clothing. With a groan he blacks out and slumps. His weight causes the chuck to reverse and his clothing slowly unwinds as his body slides to the floor.

Louis' face and the front of his clothes are splattered with blood from the spray flung around by the machine. He carefully lays Shepard on the floor, using his pocket knife to cut away the last of the tangled fabric. Not trusting anything in the room, he drags the unconscious man towards the door and attempts to stop the gouts of thick red blood that are pumping from Shepard's mutilated shoulder. He catches sight of a bag of rags against the wall and he leans across and grabs a handful of the rough fabric off-cuts. Balling a few up in his fist, Louis shoves them roughly into the hole in Shepard's shoulder where most of the blood seems to be coming from. Reaching up, he finds a roll of duct tape on the bench above him and tries to tape the cotton waste in place. As long as the poor bastard doesn't move, it might just hold, he thinks. Louis takes one last look at his crude handiwork and then sprints down the corridor to fetch help.

CHAPTER 32

As Charlie leads the small group into the main computer room, all of the screens blink in welcome. Lily is still pale and hasn't spoken since Darville's death. Elizabeth is watching her closely, familiar with the signs of shock. Lord grabs a heavy chair to prop open the door. The face of Dan Foster, forever burned into his memory, is all the reminding that he needs about the perils of being trapped in rooms like these. As he wedges the chair in solidly he notices the security camera mounted above the door. Reaching up, he slaps it firmly with his open hand, its lens now pointing uselessly toward the ceiling.

The main console position houses a large flat-screen display with several smaller screens below it. Charlie sits in the chair opposite the screen and the others drag seats into the room so they can watch over his shoulder. Suddenly, all the small screens beep once and display an identical message.

Welcome Charlie

Prepare to fight or die

Kensei

Lord immediately begins to scan the room, looking for threats.

"What does that mean, Charlie? Win at what or die?" he asks.

As if in response to Lord's question, the large screen comes to life and displays a grid shaped pattern. A large white square with black lines dividing it into smaller squares, nine across and nine down. A game board. As they watch, playing pieces resembling small tiles are added to the board. Twenty on each side, each engraved with a Japanese character. Nine pieces on the first row, then two pieces, each one set one square in from the edge of the second row, then nine more pieces. All the tiles are the same colour but the two sets face each other on the board.

"This looks like a game," Lord says, a puzzled expression on his face.

"It does, but what sort of game?" Charlie asks under his breath.

"Shogi," Lily said, speaking at last but sounding as though she was far away. Charlie shoots a nervous glance at Elizabeth.

"It's a Japanese board game. A bit like chess. Been played in Japan for hundreds of years. Traditionally played in a little room leading to the garden."

Lord shook his head. "Please don't tell me that all of this killing is about getting Charlie and this psychopath into the same room so that they can play a Goddamn game? Surely not!"

"It looks like it." Charlie said, his mind racing to figure out what all of this meant. "But if it's true, then we're in deep shit because I don't even know how to play."

"I do." Lily said mechanically over his shoulder "I can play. I learned in Japan. Lots of people play there."

All heads turn to look at her.

"You're kidding?" Lord said. Lily just shrugged. Thinking.

Elizabeth was relieved to observe that the challenge of the game seemed to be distracting her from their predicament, putting some animation back in her face.

"Charlie, what drives the reasoning behind Kensei? How is it that he's able to strategise the way he does?" Lily asked.

Charlie paused a moment to gather his thoughts.

"We're blurring the boundaries of artificial intelligence here but fundamentally it's all underpinned by game theory. Winning at complex games. That, and solving puzzles. Whether it's enemy networks or communications systems, it's about figuring out how things work, the puzzle part, and then using that solution to beat the opponent."

"The game part." Lord replied.

"That's it. It has an understanding of what causes damage to computers and what causes damage to people. It doesn't discriminate between the two. For the probe, people and machines are just simply devices to be disabled."

"So how does he know who or what to disable?" Lord asked.

"Well, you have to understand that Kensei is a lot more advanced than the systems we've run in the lab before so I'm not sure how Alex has achieved what he has. But the basic principle is twofold. A target list given at the start of the operation, and anyone or anything that gets in the way before the mission is over gets added to the list."

"And could the target list be people as well as computer networks?" Lord said.

"Yes. The project started out as a system-based probe but it quickly became obvious that it could also be used as an assassin."

"And you're in his sights because Alex put your name on the hit list?"

Charlie shrugged. "Maybe."

"Shit, what a mess."

Charlie turned back to Lily.

"Why do you ask about Kensei's A.I. engine?" he said.

"I was wondering whether Kensei knows the difference between a game and reality."

"What do you mean?"

Lily thought for a moment.

"It appears that we are dealing with a kind of intelligence that has highly developed strategic skills but is totally amoral and unfamiliar with such concepts as subtlety, death in an organic sense, subterfuge and so on. Almost like a vicious yet naïve child."

Charlie weighed her description in his mind before answering. "I guess that's probably not a bad characterisation."

"So we have Kensei challenging you to a game. A game where he believes the outcome of losing is that you will be dead. Not just defeated but dead."

"So what are you getting at?" Charlie said.

"That if you lose, but don't die, maybe Kensei will think he has completed his objective. You know, lose is defeat, defeat is death."

"Maybe," Charlie said. "I don't know. I guess I'm uncomfortable in assuming that we're dealing with that level of naiveté. You've given me an idea though."

"Really?"

"If we keep it occupied with this game, maybe we can figure out a way to trap and destroy it. As long as we're playing, it might not care what else is going on. There wasn't a whole lot of energy placed into developing a human interface facility for it so it might simply expend all of its processing power on the game."

At that instant, Louis, breathing heavily, bursts into the computer room.

"Elizabeth, you have to come help Shepard!"

Elizabeth jumps to her feet. "What? What's happened, Lou?"

"We've been fucked over badly by this Kensei shit. We went into the machine shop and within two minutes Andy was dead and Shepard is down. He fell into some machine and his arm's been fuckin' shredded. He's bleeding out!"

Elizabeth grabs the first aid-case. "Take me there."

Two minutes later, Elizabeth and Louis reach the shop door. Elizabeth flinches when she sees the scene before her. The room is decorated in blood. Puddles on the floor, spray patterns up the walls and on the ceiling. Shepard has obviously moved since Louis has been gone as the cotton waste has separated from his wound and he's bled profusely. Not for the first time in her medical career Elizabeth is amazed at how much blood can leak out of one person. She spots Johnston lying across the room and starts toward him. Louis grabs her arm.

"He's gone. Plus, you don't want to go too far into this room, it's fuckin' alive. It wants to kill us all."

Elizabeth stares into Louis' eyes for a moment and realises that he is serious. She puts two fingers on Shepard's neck.

"He's gone, Lou." She says.

"What? Shit! No way! I only left him a few minutes ago!" Louis protests, genuine anguish on his face.

"I know. You did your best. He's bled from a major artery and his body's been subjected to massive stress. People can go very suddenly in these situations."

"There must be something you can do? You know, CPR or something?"

"Lou," Elizabeth said gently, "even if we could revive him, he's lost so much blood. There isn't enough volume left in his body for his heart to work properly. We just couldn't keep him alive, not without a hospital. I'm really sorry, Lou."

"Fuck this shit! It all happened in a flash. Bastard must have been watching our every move."

Elizabeth places her hand on Louis' arm. "You did what you could, Lou. There's nothing more that can be done now. Let's get back to the others."

* * *

Dave Bryant was having a hell of a time getting to work this morning. Must be some sort of massive pile-up he figured. Maybe a major fire. The roads were clogged and the lights were out at every intersection. After a while it became clear that he couldn't get close to The Factory and for the first time he wondered whether the place might have burned down. Not a bad outcome, he thought to himself, after all of the bad luck they'd had there. Still, he didn't want to lose his job, this posting was really working out and, as guardhouse jobs go, it was pretty easy time. He parked the car in a side street, grabbed his bag, clipped his radio on to his belt and started walking.

After a few minutes he came across an unbelievable sight. It looked as though a bomb had detonated outside The Factory. He could clearly see police trying to keep people away from the scene. Fires and burned-out vehicles littered the street and what he guessed to be dead bodies were covered under sheets and blankets. A burly cop told him that he couldn't go any closer. Told him it wasn't safe. Even though he worked inside the building, they weren't going to let him anywhere near the place. After watching for a few minutes without any idea of what had happened, he started to walk back to his vehicle. He stopped, had a thought. He pulled his radio from its clip, pressed the transmit button, and began to speak.

***

Detective Frank Jordan massages eyes that are sore from lack of sleep and the smoke from burning gasoline and rubber. In his mind he analyses the things he knows, trying to fit the pieces together in a way that makes up some sort of a picture. Trouble is, he can't guess the motive. The remote-controlled hardware indicated well-equipped professionals and that suggested a plan, a purpose, not just some mad sociopath. But what was the aim? Apart from a diversion, he can't think of anything that fits. Also, John Lord and his partner are missing. His belief in coincidences has been eroded sufficiently by his years on the force that he knows they are caught up in this somehow. He squashes down a small voice inside of him that suggested Lord would have had this situation under control already.

Grabbing the mike again, he forces his mind to focus and begins giving clinical orders to throw a screen around the danger area. He demands that all flights overhead be diverted. SWAT teams to be dropped by chopper one mile out and to make their own way in. Vehicles to be commandeered if necessary and all surrounding streets to be blocked in case the shooter makes a run for it. All residential and commercial buildings with a one-mile radius to be evacuated. Keep those news choppers out of range otherwise all hell will break loose. And for Christ's sake try to raise someone in the military so that we can get some intelligence on this building and what's inside.

He lets the mike drop and watches as it bob and bump against the side of the cruiser. The scene surrounding him is almost too vivid to comprehend. So much has happened in such a short time and he still doesn't have any real idea of what it's all about. We're in for a shit of a day, he tells himself.

***

Inside The Factory, Elizabeth and Louis shuffle back into the computer room, the expressions on their faces sufficient to signal to the others that Shepard didn't make it. Lord is about to offer some words of encouragement when the radio taken from the control room clipped to his belt squawks into life, making him jump.

"Hey, Dunc, you picking me up from here?" the radio asks.

With a frown, Lord unclips the radio.

"This is Detective John Lord from the Ann Arbor Police Department. Please identify yourself and state your location."

In the pause that followed, all eyes are fixed on Lord's face.

"Private Dave Bryant, US army. I'm about two hundred yards out from the facility and can't get inside to start my shift on the gate. Are you inside, detective?"

Lord thought for a few seconds before answering and then decided to take a risk.

"Yes I am, together with one other detective and three civilians. I need you to do something for me, Dave. It's dangerous but it's important and people are dying in here."

"You name it, detective."

"I need you to get to the police officer in charge of the scene and let me speak with him on this radio. You stay close in case we need your help. If someone tries to stop you, tell them who's inside and put them on the radio if they give you any trouble."

"Okay, I'm on it."

"Before you go, are you wearing your uniform?"

Bryant was puzzled by this question. Thought it odd under the circumstances.

"Sure, why?"

"Do you have a coat or jacket that you could cover it with?"

"Sure. I've even got some sweats in the car I could change into."

"Okay, don't bother changing but put a jacket over the top so it's not obvious you're wearing the uniform. We have a shooter on the roof and the uniform might just get you noticed."

"Shit! Thanks for telling me!"

"No problem, Dave, thanks for your help. Be as quick as you can but for God's sake be careful."

"That was good thinking about the uniform, John," Charlie said.

"Well, enough people have died already. It's time we stopped underestimating this Kensei thing."

"So what's the plan, Charlie?" Louis asked, looking at the big screen.

Charlie shook his head. "If we are to stop Kensei, we have to lure it into this building. To actually get it inside onto one of the systems here. Right now it could be anywhere in the world, controlling things from thousands of miles away. We have to lure it in, then we get out and this building gets destroyed. Flattened."

"But isn't this thing just a program? It's likely copied itself the fuck all over the world by now, surely?"

"No I doubt it. Kensai is at its core an atomic process."

"Atomic? What the fuck?" says Louis.

"No, not like that." Charlie added quickly. "I mean atomic in a process sense. Self-contained, a single entity. One of the fundamental design goals was to ensure that we couldn't have a situation where we had replicated probes in action. Kensai can only exist on one system at a time. It can move, sure, but not split or copy itself."

"Can't we just clean the computers?" Elizabeth asked.

"Do you think Kensei will stand by and let that happen?"

"So we kill the power." Louis said. "Just crash the fuckin' computers."

Charlie sighed deeply. "Can't do it, Lou. We'd have to get to the backup generators and disable them somehow. By the time we got anywhere near them Kensei would find ways to kill us all and maybe even destroy the building. It has us in a trap. Whatever we do it has to be fast. I think we have a chance now we have communications with the outside world again. I don't think Kensei can take out the HAPCOM radio system."

Charlie was about to explain the idea that was taking shape in his head when, abruptly, the lights went out again. Everyone held their breath and two seconds later the lights flickered their way back to normal. As if to further seize their attention, the PA system emitted an ear-piercing shriek. Like a microphone feeding back at full volume. The sound assaulted their ears as they tried fruitlessly to block it out. The screech seemed to bore into the very centre of their brains and made it impossible to think of anything else. After several seconds it stopped. The silence slammed into them and Charlie felt the muscles in his face and neck relax. All around them the computer monitors beeped once, blinked off and then on and displayed a single word.

FIGHT

CHAPTER 33

Outside, the chaotic scene had diminished only slightly. At least the crowds had been pushed back and seemed to be under control now, thought Jordan. He was no closer to having a plan for dealing with the situation but he assumed that once he got things under control, there would be some demands forthcoming or someone inside might try to make a break. Until either of these things happened he would sit tight where he was and see whether the squad currently preparing themselves on the opposite side of the building would have any success in getting through the fence.

On the edge of his peripheral vision he saw a commotion. A tall young man with a military crew-cut was arguing with two uniforms who were gesturing in Jordan's direction while trying to restrain the larger man.

"What the hell now?" Jordan said under his breath.

He was beginning to wonder how much more of this he could stand. Something about the urgency of the big man's gestures made him alert. He wondered if this was some sort of new diversion and forced his eyes back to the roof of the building just in case. Have to have eyes in the back of my damned head, he thought. Eventually a truce was reached between the scuffling men and one of the uniforms scurried across, his eyes darting nervously from Jordan to The Factory's roof and back. In a series of breathless statements, the uniform explained the situation to Jordan who gave the all clear for the crew-cut guy to make his way over.

As the man approached, Jordan noticed that he had a military uniform under his jacket and he guessed his age to be no more than twenty-five. The two men shook hands and Bryant filled Jordan in on what he knew and handed him the radio. Jordan's spirits were buoyed as he imagined that this might be the breakthrough they had been waiting for. He looked at the radio in his hand and although it was of a type unfamiliar to him, the controls appeared to be in all the right places. With a quick glance to the top of The Factory's roof and a word of caution to Bryant to keep his head down, Jordan raised the radio to his mouth.

* * *

Charlie turned to Lily, now sitting in the seat beside him, Lord standing behind her, his hand resting lightly on her shoulder.

"So, in fifty words or less, what's this game?"

"Shogi is like chess." Lily began.

"Oh shit," Charlie interrupted. "Alex was a chess master."

"Great. As I was saying, Shogi is like chess with a few different pieces. The aim is still to capture the opponent's king but if you lose a piece the other player can use it against you."

"All the tiles are the same colour."

"Yes but they face different directions. It's okay, I know the rules."

"Okay. What I need you to do is not to lose quickly but not to win either." Charlie said.

"So you're saying that you want me to stall?"

"Yes, but not obviously so. I want Kensei to get the upper hand slowly, but for God's sake don't let him win if you can help it."

"Fortunately the complexity of the game will help us out there."

As Charlie didn't have the first idea of how to even type in the correct syntax to move the pieces, Lily gave him the coordinates and he typed them verbatim. The instant that his finger hit the Return key on the keyboard, Kensei's move followed, the white tiles moving smoothly to occupy a new square on the large computer screen.

"Hell!" said Charlie. "We've got to slow this down. Take as long as you can, Lily."

Lord's radio came back to life.

"John, are you in there? This is Frank Jordan."

"Hey, Frank! Great to hear your voice. Yeah, Louis and I are stuck inside here with a…" His voice trailed off, unable to find words that explained the situation easily.

"Let's just say with a psycho who's already killed several people and it sounds like he's making a mess out there."

"You bet your ass. We got bodies in the street here and a chopper that's crashed into a row of houses."

" Hell, I figured it must be bad. Okay. The man with the plan in here is Charlie. He's a civilian who works inside the building and he's trying to…well…talk this guy down, let's say."

"You have contact with the SOB that's controlling the hardware on the roof?"

"It's complex, Frank. Take too long to explain. Essentially yes. I'm going to hand the radio over to Charlie. You just do whatever he asks you to do. Just stay low, this maniac will kill you with as much thought as he'd give to swatting a bug."

Lord handed the radio to Charlie. "I don't know what you have in mind but I hope to God it's good."

Charlie took a deep breath.

"Frank, I need you to take care of three things if we're to get out of this. Firstly, I want you to get hold of some experienced people and get them down to the local telephone exchange. They need to find where the main data communications lines for this facility enter the exchange. They will probably be in a cabinet of their own, probably hardened, certainly locked. They will be looking for fibre optic cables. I need them to find these cables with absolute certainty and then station a person next to the opened cabinet with a radio, ready to disconnect or cut the cables when I give the signal and not before. You got that?"

"Roger that, Charlie."

"Also, there's a guardhouse by the main gate. In the floor inside is a steel trapdoor leading down to a security corridor. The trapdoor is locked, we need it blown or cut open when we need to get out. We probably won't have much time so everything will need to be set to go. Right?"

"Gotcha. Floor of the guardhouse, steel trapdoor."

"Here's the hard one. I need you to find a way to disable the gun positions on the roof?'

"Did you say positions? As in more than one?"

"Yes. Twin .50 calibre, rapid-firing systems in the two corners of the roof where the metal tubes and glass plates are."

"Shit! I gotta go. Call you back."

Charlie looked at the radio, now silent in his hand, then up at Lord.

"What do you suppose that was all about," he asked.

As if by answer, the PERIMSEC guns on the *opposite* corner to that holding the gaze of the men on the ground, opened up.

* * *

Outside the fence on the opposite side of The Factory to where Jordan and Bryant crouched behind the flimsy protection of the police cruiser, a team of heavily armed men from a police special response group are attempting to gain access to the back of the building. Jordan's plan is for them to come up to the fence fast in their armoured van. They had calculated correctly that the gun on the opposite corner that had brought down their comrade's chopper would not be able to bring fire to bear on their position. Once inside the fence, they would break out some sophisticated camera equipment to look inside the building through a tiny hole drilled into the outer wall.

As the doors on the back of the van open, three men leap out and take up firing positions. Another man carrying a strange-looking device that resembles an oversize set of tin snips connected to a gas cylinder jumps out and runs to the fence. He rams the jaws of the device against the bottom of a steel bar and pulls a trigger. With a loud crack, one of the hardened jaws on the specialist tool shatters against the high-tensile steel railing and falls to the ground in front of him. To his astonishment, when the man inspects the bar, it has only minor dents in it.

"What the fuck?" he says, picking up the broken piece that has rendered his equipment useless. He is momentarily at a loss to imagine why the building would have a perimeter fence constructed of such material. Before his mind has a chance to consider what his next move might be, an urgent voice in his radio earpiece brings him back to full attention.

"This is Jordan. Insertion team abort! Say again abort! Suspect firing position on roof corner to your right. Get out!"

The men react fast. One almost makes it back to the van before the guns erupt. The first rounds strike the grass just inside the fence as the twin barrels elevate. The turf is instantly turned over as though it's been attacked with a pick. Large clumps of earth are thrown spinning into the air. As the rounds walk through the fence toward the van, sparks fly in every direction as the heavy projectiles are deflected wildly by the hardened steel bars. One such projectile ricochets horizontally into the open door of the van and strikes the driver in the back of the neck, smashing his spine and killing him instantly before shattering the windshield into thousands of tiny pieces.

Two of the men sprinting toward the van are cut down as if by a gigantic scythe as they became trapped in the twin streams of lead erupting from the specialised weapons. As the onslaught continues, the van comes under the hail of bullets and bounces wildly on its suspension. Tyres explode, glass shatters and steel is torn into twisted shapes. The power of the twin guns is overwhelming and within seconds the van is nothing more than a misshapen and burning pile of debris, its armour plating useless against the brutal pounding.

The third man responsible for laying down suppressing fire stops as he sees the van being hit and attempts to turn and run in the opposite direction. On the wet grass his feet slip from under him and he goes down heavily, losing his rifle in the process. With the terrifying sound of the van been torn apart filling his ears, he scrambles to his feet and sprints across the road toward a neighbouring factory. For a few seconds he believes he can make it. His eyes are locked on a wooden door to the building's small shed thirty yards away. Any shelter is better than none right now. As he races toward it, head down and arms pumping, he can see the paint peeling off along the bottom of the door. Can see the heavy brass padlock that keeps it closed. He can almost read the graffiti that has been carved into its surface and then painted over. He intends not to even slow down but to hit the door running at full speed and simply crash through it.

With ten yards to go, and with thirty pairs of eyes watching from locations south of The Factory, one barrel of the PERIMSEC system rotates smoothly and, like the finger of death, points directly at his back. The powerful computers behind the targeting system are presented with only a modest challenge by his fleeing outline. A brief report was all anyone heard. Three rounds, fired in a fraction of a second. The heavy bullets pound into the man's back, all of them striking within a circle no larger than a dinner plate. The man is driven into the ground as if struck by a fast-moving vehicle. His arms fly out wildly and he skids several yards on his face, almost reaching the wooden door. And is still.

* * *

Inside The Factory, Lord closes his eyes as the vibration of the guns dies away. From an office somewhere comes the sound of a picture crashing to the floor. The same thought passes through the minds of everyone in the little group. More firing meant more people dying. Charlie turns towards Lord.

"It would be good if you and Lou could find a couple of fire extinguishers. We can take one each when we make our run for it. Just in case. The girls can carry the medical kit."

"Right," said Lord, and set off with Louis in tow to do as Charlie asked.

"What about Leonard and the guards?' asks Elizabeth. "How will we get their bodies out?"

"If things work out the way I imagine, I think we'll be lucky to get ourselves out. I'm hoping there will be an opportunity for the emergency crews to get back inside to retrieve the bodies."

Elizabeth looks troubled but says nothing. On the screen, even Charlie can see that Lily is struggling. Kensei had captured several pieces already.

"God, he's good, Charlie." Lily said, an edge of panic in her voice. "I think I might be losing control of the game."

"Okay. Time to roll the dice," said Charlie. "We're going to have to try and solve this ourselves." He started typing:

Kensei,

This game is not fair. We are not playing one on one. I know that you understand how to use many computers to form a massively parallel array. I am just one man. For us to finish this game equally, you must come here and play from the computers in this building.

Charlie.

"Are you sure he'll fall for that trick?" Elizabeth asked.

"Don't know," said Charlie, "but it's all I can think of to get him inside."

"I think he will," Said Lily. "Rat-cunning has to be much harder to emulate in software than strategy."

The answer arrived after a few moments deliberation.

Charlie

I will come to simone

Wait

The outcome is the same

Kensei

"Who's Simone?" asked Lily.

"It's not really Simone it's actually SIM One. That is, the first of two simulators that we tested the VIWAP code on. Our little joke." Charlie said. Even to him it sounded lame.

"How long will it take?" asked Lily.

"With fibre optic cable, probably only a minute or so."

Sure enough, after a short wait, a new message appeared, as did Lord and Louis, carrying two large, red, fire extinguishers.

Charlie

I am simone

Fight now

Charlie noted with technical detachment that Kensei's communications were becoming more abrupt and simplistic as he devoted an increasing amount of processing capacity toward his core objective. He then snapped back into reality as he remembered what that core objective appeared to be.

"Okay. Here's where we take the big risk. Elizabeth, you know where the data communications room is, right?"

"Sure, just down the hall."

"Inside the room there is a fibre cable distribution panel and what looks like a white shoebox underneath. It has the word "NorTel" on it. You need to find that box and unplug it from the power. To be sure, tear out the yellow cables that connect to it. They're the fibre optic cables. Don't touch the blue ones, the internal network cables. Take Lou with you in case the door is locked and you need some muscle. Okay?"

"White box, NorTel, yellow cables."

"Yes, and when you find the room, you have to act fast. We'll have Kensei distracted but we don't want it trying to get out again."

As Elizabeth and Lou went in search of Kensei's escape path, Lord looks over at Charlie and nods.

"So you want to isolate him to this building's computers by cutting off his access to the outside world." Lord said

"That's the idea, John."

"What about those technicians we asked Jordan to send down to the telephone exchange, Charlie? Where do they fit in?"

"We can't rely on them being ready in time. We haven't heard back from them yet and so we have to assume that we're on our own. Everything's happening too fast in here."

Lord placed his hand on Charlie's shoulder. "You're doing great." He said.

Elizabeth and Louis find the data communications room locked. Elizabeth steps back while Lou gives the door an almighty kick, tearing it clean off its hinges. The door twisted and fell flat onto the floor with splinters of wood sticking up like broken fingers.

"That's quite a powerful kick you've got there, Lou," Elizabeth said.

"Well, I've sure had me a lot of practice at ass kickin'," Louis replies with a grin. They venture into a room with racks of equipment, blinking lights, and the steady drone of cooling fans. Open-fronted cabinets contain stacks of black boxes, white boxes and giant nests of cables. It strikes Elizabeth that this job might not be as easy as it sounded in the computer room.

"Search for the white box with the yellow cables," she says.

The pair hunt around, opening doors and looking into high shelves.

"Gotcha!" said Louis triumphantly. He traces the power cord to the wall outlet and, after verifying the name on the box again, he rips it out. Nothing appears to happen for a few seconds and his heartbeat starts to return to normal. As Elizabeth takes hold of a bunch of the bright yellow cables that Charlie described, all hell breaks loose.

Abruptly the entire building is plunged into darkness. The weak battery-powered emergency lighting flickers once and then glows steadily throwing long shadows across the room. At the same time the fire sirens start wailing and blue lights begin to rotate in every room. Their senses are assaulted as the sirens are accompanied by the ear-splitting screech of the PA feedback that pummelled them earlier. Louis and Elizabeth both freeze, unsure of what to do next. Elizabeth realises she is still holding the bundle of cables and with one last effort; she tears them from the wall. Pulling himself together, Louis grabs Elizabeth's hand and shouts over the din of the sirens.

"Let's get back to the others."

Lord is on the radio trying to make himself heard above the noise as they rush back into the computer room.

"What do they mean they don't know which cabinet it is?" he yells at the radio. "Tell them to destroy both, Goddamn it! For Christ's sake hurry!"

"What happened?" Louis asked.

"Did you touch the blue wires?" Charlie yelled.

"No! The damn lights went out as soon as we unplugged the white box." Elizabeth replied.

Charlie slapped himself against the side of the head. "I'm an idiot!" He yelled "I forgot the damn security camera in the comms room! Shit!"

"What are we going to do now?" Lord shouted.

"We have to get out of here!" Charlie yelled back, his voice cracking under the strain of competing with the noise of the sirens.

"To the bunker under the guardhouse. That's the safest place. Let's go."

The factory has sixteen photocopiers, all of them networked so that they can be used as high-speed printers. Simultaneously, summoned by an invisible master, all sixteen awake from their standby state and begin warming up. Each machine, in common with all photocopiers, contains a thermal fuser, employed to melt the black plastic toner powder into the paper to make the image permanent. As the fusers come up to temperature, the machines start ejecting sheets of paper. Only, on this occasion, as each sheet emerges, instead of sliding out smoothly, the transport rollers stop it halfway. Just long enough for sufficient heat to be pumped into the paper to cause it to burst into flames. The machines then continue to transport the burning sheets into the collection trays before repeating the cycle.

Within minutes, fires break out on every floor. With the fires fed by a steady stream of dry, crisp paper, the plastic construction of the copier's panels begins to burn. Soon molten, flaming plastic is dripping onto carpets throughout the building, starting fires that rapidly spread, completely engulfing each machine and the paper supplies and paper recycling bins stored nearby.

Charlie leads the small group out of the computer room and is stunned at the sight that meets his eyes.

"Where the hell did those fires come from?" He gasps

"There's another over there!" shouts Louis, pointing down the corridor.

"We have to get up to Level One before we get cut off." Yells Charlie as the blue lights continued to rotate, throwing strange ethereal shadows into the smoke that is with frightening speed starting to swirl close to the ceiling. As they run for the stairwell, Lord shouts into the radio, trying to raise Jordan. Jordan's reply is drowned out by the screaming of the sirens and wail of the PA system so Lord simply settles for screaming out a message.

"For Christ's sake disable the roof guns!"

He stuffs the radio into his pocket and runs.

CHAPTER 34

Outside, Frank Jordan has never felt as helpless as he does at that moment. He has been completely unable to come up with a plan to take out the guns, even though he's looked at it from every angle. It would take a military air strike, he thinks. Anything they could throw at the guns will be ineffective and would likely be met with murderous return fire. And just to make things worse, dense black smoke is starting to billow from the roof vents of The Factory and through the gate leading down to the parking lot.

"Shit!" he says to Bryant at his side. "I feel so fucking useless sitting here."

Bryant has a faraway look in his eyes. Abruptly, he snaps back to reality.

"Do you have teargas guns?" Bryant asked

"Sure, but…"

"How many?" Bryant interrupts.

Jordan looks around, gauging the number and type of vehicles in the area.

"Maybe six or eight we could put our hands on quickly. Why? What's the use?"

"Get the team ready to blow the trapdoor and get as many gas guns loaded up as you can."

Jordan grabs Bryant's arm.

"Tell me what you've got in mind!"

"The guy inside said *disable* the guns, right?"

"Disable, right."

"You don't have to destroy them to disable them. Think about it. The targeting mechanisms use *optical* devices to track the targets. When these systems were first tested the heat radiating from the driveway in summer swamped the infrared targeting systems and so they were upgraded to optical!"

"So what's the fucking point!" Jordan said, his patience running out.

"The optical systems can't see through smoke!"

"Shit!" Jordan grabs the microphone and starts barking orders.

* * *

The situation inside The Factory was becoming increasingly desperate. Choking smoke, heavy with poisonous fumes from burning plastic and carpets, fills the corridors, stinging their eyes and throats as it builds. The group didn't get far before visibility worsened to the point where they risked losing each other. Hanging on to each other's clothes, they grope with their free hands along corridors. They've made it to Level One but visibility is reduced now to only a few feet. The building's heating system has activated at maximum temperature and the fans are blowing hard, forcing the smoke away from the ceiling and into every part of the building. Lily is almost done and is being practically carried by Lord who knows that if they don't make it out soon it will too late. They limit themselves to hand signals as attempting to shout above the screaming in their ears simply uses too much breath.

As they grope along the corridor they pass the medical lab. The new lab has only just been completed and Elizabeth knows there is at least one oxygen cylinder and mask in there. As they pass, Louis staggers inside looking for the cylinder, sweat streaming down his face. The smoke is so thick that it seems impossible to locate anything. Just as he's about to quit, Louis catches sight of the grey and white cylinder and grabs it, tucking the face mask under his arm. He looks around and realises that the others have now disappeared into the smoke haze. For a second, a wave of fear ripples through him as he realises that he's been turned around and is now unsure of the way out. The dense smoke and overwhelming heat almost cause him to panic. Fighting to subdue the desperate voice in his head, he scrambles his way around the walls banging into equipment and scattering glassware across the floor before almost sprawling through the door and back into the corridor.

As Louis passes the open door of the electronics lab, he feels a blast of heat on his face. The entire lab appears to be in flames. Momentarily he finds himself wondering what could be in there that's so flammable. Had he known, he might have increased his pace as he passes by the windows for in a cabinet located against the far corner is a collection of flammable chemicals used in the cleaning of prototype circuit boards. The flames have been licking at the cabinet for several minutes now. Had the cabinet door been closed, as The Factory's policy dictates, this might not have presented a problem, but it has been left slightly ajar and the steel cabinet offers little protection from the heat.

Louis is almost clear of the lab windows when the cabinet erupts. The steel cabinet door is torn from its hinges and hurled through the glass windows, accompanied by plastic containers and tins of flaming chemicals. The scarcity of oxygen in the air causes the explosion to lack the ferocity of the one that tore through Ric Montez' body but nonetheless it has power sufficient to shatter the windows instantly.

The cabinet door is sent spinning across the room and through the windows. Shards of broken glass shred his jacket and shirt and embed themselves in the skin and muscle beneath. The edge of the door smashes into his shoulder, shattering bone, tearing into his flesh and Louis is battered viciously against the opposite wall of the corridor, rendering him unconscious. The cylinder, together with its silicone mask, flies out of his grip, rolls ahead of him and collides with the base of a water cooler, cracking the plastic base. The explosion sends a blast of scorching heat down the corridor and the small group is beaten to the floor with Elizabeth landing heavily on Lord's back, driving the air from his lungs. As Lord fights to get his breath back he begins to gulp smoke and fumes and his eyes start to roll back into his head. Through the dense haze, Elizabeth catches sight of the silvery plastic tube connecting the mask to the oxygen cylinder and crawls to retrieve it. She almost panics when she sees Louis, his back a red mess of ragged cloth and pulverised flesh.

Elizabeth doesn't know whether Louis is alive or dead but she does know that Lord won't last without the oxygen. She drags her gaze away from Louis and stumbles back to Lord, strapping the mask onto his face and turning the tap on the cylinder. Lord begins to cough and to gasp for breath but within seconds, the colour starts to return to his face. She tears the mask from his face and pushes it against Lily's mouth, grabbing her hand and showing her how to hold it in place.

"Share it with John!" she yells in Lily's ear.

Her own vision is blurring as she returns to Louis, only to find that Charlie has pulled himself together and has Louis sitting upright. It's quite obvious that he's not going to regain consciousness anytime soon but at least he has a pulse. With tears from the smoke mixed with sweat rolling down his face, Charlie drags the dead weight of Louis' body back to where Lily and Lord sit. Lord holds the mask out. Charlie grabs it and immediately puts it over Elizabeth's face. She takes a few strong breaths and then gives Charlie a shot. Over the next ten minutes they move forward agonisingly in a cycle of dragging Louis, stopping, sharing the mask, and dragging some more. After what seems like an eternity they arrive at the entrance to the security corridor. As they peer through the smoke, they get their first glimpse of the bunker at the other end.

The room is an inferno.

* * *

Outside, Jordan has found nine teargas guns and has his men positioned and ready to fire. Communications have been lost with the group inside The Factory and Jordan is becoming frantic with worry. Sensing that the situation is becoming critical, he decides to take a risk.

"On my signal, fire at the corner of the roof where the glass and pipe-work is the thickest. Some canisters might bounce off or fly through but there's enough metalwork up there to hold a few at least. When the smoke cover takes hold, Blue team move in to the guardhouse and blow the trapdoor. And for Christ's sake be quick. If that smoke clears before we get them out, God help us."

After receiving acknowledgment that everyone is in position, Jordan hesitates. Too soon and the guns will shred Lord and his group into mincemeat as they exit, too late and they'll burn alive inside the damned place. Shit! What a decision to have to make! With the sound of his heart pounding in his ears, Jordan grabs the mike and yells "GO!"

The teargas guns pop in sync and the canisters arc across the driveway toward the roof, leaving a trail of white smoke hanging in the frosty morning air. Several bounce off the metalwork and land in the grass, one canister even drops a few feet away from one of the shooters, causing a mad scramble until someone kicks it across the street. Most of the silver capsules bounce around and lodge in the metal framework and within seconds, dense white smoke obscures the building's corner. The twin guns begin firing wildly into the sky, the only thing vaguely visible to the confused optical-sighting system until their ammunition is exhausted. A couple of seconds later the hardened men of the assault team realise that although the noise is terrifying, none of the rounds are striking the ground, and they charge towards the guardhouse.

* * *

It's obvious to Charlie that they are hopelessly trapped. Unable to move forward or to retreat inside The Factory, they're stranded. The small group is huddled in the centre of the security corridor with flames at either end and no apparent way out. Although there is little that is flammable in the corridor, the air is poisonous with the fumes from burning synthetic materials. They huddle together on the floor, passing the mask between them and taking a couple of rapid breaths each. Charlie is desperately worried about Louis. While the others can hold their breath until their turn at the mask, Louis is still unconscious and therefore still breathing the acrid smoke most of the time. Charlie has no idea how long Louis can keep breathing in this stuff but if his own wretched condition is any indicator, it can't be much longer.

* * *

As the assault team rushes towards the guardhouse, the gas cylinders in the upper parking lot finally surrender to the intense heat being transmitted through the wall. One cylinder explodes in massive fireball and scatters the others across the almost empty lot. When the valve is snapped off one of the larger acetylene cylinders it becomes a self-powered missile and is propelled across the asphalt and up the ramp, smashing into the heavy steel gate in a shower of sparks and flame.

With astonishing control, the men of the assault team don't even break their stride at this display of pyrotechnics. As they burst through the open guardhouse door their focus is on finding and opening the trapdoor. Joe's headless corpse is dragged roughly aside. One man drops to his knees and unrolls what resembles thick, sticky rope. He quickly places the substance around the visible edge of the trapdoor. Satisfied with his work, he takes a turn of the rope and wraps it around a small cylindrical detonator before attaching a thin cable and running it back outside of the door and across the driveway. When everyone is clear, he clips the ends of the cable to a small box pulled from a pouch in his overalls and presses a button. All of this in less than sixty seconds.

The remaining window in the guardhouse is blown outwards, sending shards of glass and window frame spinning across the driveway. Before the pieces have even stopped falling, the men are on their feet again and rushing back to the guardhouse. As they burst through the door they are driven back by a pillar of flame coming up through the ragged hole in the floor. There is no possibility of getting down into the control room. Anyone inside would surely have been incinerated by now. Cursing the ferocious heat and knowing the situation is hopeless they beat a hasty retreat to where Jordan watches, a distressed expression on his face. He turns to speak to Bryant before noticing the man is no longer at his side.

* * *

Inside the security corridor, hope is fading. The situation appears impossible with both exits cut off by the fire. Charlie's idea of bringing along the fire extinguishers now seemed somehow naïve in the face of the inferno surrounding them. Elizabeth notices that Louis isn't breathing any longer when the mask is over his mouth. His face is white and his lips have a bluish tint. She knows he is dying but there is nothing any of them can do. She is fighting to hold on to her own consciousness. The small group huddles together as close to the floor as they can get, knowing that if any oxygen exists in the air, it will be low to the ground.

Far away, the rumble of an explosion in the bowels of the building carries to them, somehow distant and disconnected from their plight. Elizabeth finds her eyes growing heavy, almost impossible to hold open. Just as she reaches the point where she is certain that she can fight sleep no longer, a deafening explosion rocks them with a blast of hot air. The blast appears to come from the bunker, and then immediately following it, a rush of hot air from inside The Factory. It's as if the oxygen-starved atmosphere of The Factory has suddenly been given an escape route to the outside world. They are immediately caught in a searing wind as air escapes through the bunker. The flames from the main building began pushing into the corridor, forcing them to move towards what was once the control room.

Nobody has the strength to move Louis but somehow Charlie manages to slide him a few yards along the smooth surface of the security corridor. Elizabeth notes in a clinical and distracted way the bright red trail that Louis' lacerated body leaves behind. So much blood, she thinks. Elizabeth also observes in a way that makes her feel both proud and then desperately sad that Charlie simply won't give up on Louis despite the hopeless circumstances. She wants to reach out and hold him. To tell him that it's over. That he's done everything that could be expected, that it isn't his fault. I love this man, she thinks.

The move brings some relief from the intense flames, the heat being forced out through the hole in the guardhouse floor by the pressure of the air escaping into the corridor. Not that it makes much difference, Elizabeth thinks. As soon as they collapse together again, the overwhelming urge to surrender herself to sleep returns. Elizabeth knows they won't move again.

***

Jordan bangs his hand hard into the side of the cruiser. So Goddamn close! A movement on the edge of his vision brings his head around. A fire truck. A fire truck is heading directly towards him. At the last moment two uniforms leap out of the way as the truck crunches into the front of a police car blocking the road and sends it spinning into the gutter.

"What the fuck!" Jordan yells, grabbing his pistol as he prepares to meet whatever craziness is now being thrust upon him.

At the last moment he realises that Bryant is driving the truck. He had sprinted almost three-quarters of a mile to commandeer the fire truck. Bryant bores right in towards the gate and only slightly mistimes his arrival, colliding with the partly collapsed guardhouse and loosening a few more bricks. With the vehicle still rocking on its suspension he is out, grabbing the hoses from the side of the truck. Intuitively, the assault team keys into what he's doing and rushes to help. Within thirty seconds, two powerful hoses are being directed through the trapdoor, steam billowing out of the door and windows of the guardhouse.

In sixty seconds, hundreds of gallons of water pour into the hole at the centre of the guardhouse floor. When the flames are beaten back enough to allow it, several black-clad figures jump down into the room below. Thirty seconds later they began handing up unconscious forms. Two women and then two men. All laid out on the dew-soaked grass, not moving.

Suddenly, from deep inside The Factory comes a colossal explosion. So massive that the men outside are thrown to the ground by the tremor. The black clad figures stampede out of the hole in the floor as if propelled from below. As the last of the men dives out of the guardhouse door, a violent pillar of fire spears from the hole like a blowtorch, sending parts of the guardhouse roof into the sky and causing everyone to scramble for cover, protecting their heads. Several of the men fall onto the bodies lying prone on the ground, attempting to protect them from falling debris. As the flames subside, a large section of the main building's south-east corner simply collapses in on itself propelling smoke and sparks hundreds of feet into the air.

Lord stirs, struggling to sit up as the fresh air delivers new life to his brain. His eyes sweep over the three prone forms on the grass beside him.

"Lou!" he calls, attempting to rise but instead vomiting into the damp grass. One of the men who narrowly escaped from the bunker crouches down at Lord's side and puts a hand on his shoulder.

"Stay down, the ambulance is on its way."

"Lou!" He calls again, eyes almost blinded by the smoke.

"He's gone, buddy. Was gone when we got to him. We had to get out."

Lord stares at him through heavily bloodshot eyes with a look of such absolute desolation that the man is forced to turn away.

As the others begin to cough and retch, the sound of an emergency vehicle can finally be heard in the distance, threading its way toward them through the chaos. Jordan sees the flashing lights of the ambulance as it turns the corner following the pointing arm of Dave Bryant. As it lurches to a stop among the rubble of The Factory's driveway, the sun bursts from behind a low cloud, heralding the start of another stunning Ann Arbor day.

EPILOGUE

One week later, a DoD inspector picks his way through the black, soot-covered rubble that was once The Factory. It's a gorgeous day in Ann Arbor. One out of the box, he thinks to himself. So far they have discovered little in the way of clues that might help piece together how the fire started. Heavy machinery has been used during the last few days to clear the twisted steelwork and concrete so that the inspection teams can do their work.

As the inspector pulls aside a sheet of twisted and blackened metal, he observes what appears to be a large closet. On closer inspection he realises that he's looking at a steel fire door. Pulling a small pry-bar from his belt, he easily breaks open the heat-fatigued lock. Wrenching open the soot-covered door, he takes a hasty step back as the acrid smell of burned plastic assaults his nose. As the fumes clear, he can see that the room is a sort of security locker. A large rack of video tapes occupies one wall while another has banks of what appear to be industrial-style VCRs.

Although the tapes have been badly affected by the heat, some of the machines look pretty good, considering the severity of the fire. The man steps closer to the rack of tapes and pulls out a few at random. He quickly abandons the search as the tapes are obviously ruined, some so badly melted that they can't even be removed from their slots. Turning his attention to the machines, he notices among the units toward the bottom that appear to be least-affected by the fire, one machine stands out. Its tape has ejected and is ready to be removed. This strikes the inspector as odd, given that every other machine has its tape inserted.

Still, the man has seen some pretty weird things in his time. He's also seen enough of this sort of technology to know that these tapes can hold both video images and large amounts of computer data. He pulls the tape out and turns it over in his hand. It looks pretty good. Amazingly good in fact. Perhaps he'll take it back, he thinks. The boys in the lab can load it up to see what it contains. You just never know. The inspector slips the tape into a plastic Ziploc bag and steps back out into the sunshine, savouring the fresh air.

Whistling to himself, he picks his way back through the debris towards his vehicle…

www.ingramcontent.com/pod-product-compliance
Lightning Source LLC
LaVergne TN
LVHW050928080826
845145LV00001B/259

* 9 7 8 0 9 9 2 2 6 7 5 1 3 *